# Have You Seen Sarah Baker?

# Have You Seen Sarah Baker?

T.A. Cruz

**Content warning:** This story contains scenes depicting alcoholism, miscarriage, domestic abuse, graphic violence, murder, kidnapping, predatory relationships, and imprisonment.


Tule Publishing First Printing, May 2023

The Tule Publishing, Inc.



First Publication by Tule Publishing 2023

Cover design by Croco Designs



ISBN: 978-1-959988-27-4

# PART I
## The Badge

# CHAPTER ONE

## Sarah

*One month missing*

*CREAK.*

The floorboards strained in the room above the cellar, forcing her heavy and swollen eyes open. It was him, and he was coming for her. Again.

Each step screamed as his boots adjusted to the rickety wooden staircase. The nails twisted. The foundation shuddered. He whistled; always the same tune when descending the flight. He scraped his hand along the banister like forty-grit sandpaper. The light bulb dangling from the ceiling swayed, highlighting things better left unseen, strewn across the wall. Screwdrivers for stabbing. Metal files to shave down bones. A hacksaw for the larger chunks of her—her entire torso maybe—which would then fit in a black trash bag tossed to the highway embankment. Every time he arrived …

Fresh vomit invaded her throat.

A numbness in her hands tingled up from the metal shackles over her wrists. They were tighter than yesterday, her penance for fighting harder than she should have. The chains were thick and wove through an iron loop cast inches, if not feet, into the cement wall at her back. She struggled her bare legs over the icy concrete, and gooseflesh trickled up her thigh. Closing her eyes wouldn't help. Plugging her ears wouldn't drown out the off-pitch notes. No, she'd still see the large shape of her captor in her head and hear the tune thumping rhythmically with her heart.

"Why?" she muttered, rattling the chains while sitting up. "Why are you doing this?" Her voice was hoarse, the same roughness you could expect after screaming for hours on end. Today she had given a round, if not three, and judging by his seemingly on-the-dot visits, it was only lunchtime.

The man stopped whistling when he neared. He crouched, set the brown tray in his hands to the floor, and slid it toward her. They stared at each other for a moment; through her terror she tried to maintain the same glare she'd given this man for the past thirty, maybe thirty-five days. It could've been longer, after all. She lost count between her hysterics and veering in and out of consciousness. Little sunlight breached the window obscured with curtains and junk thrown haphazardly in front of it. The subtle differences between daylight and dusk were as indistinct as his face.

The man before her, however, watched her vacantly. No empathy. No remorse. Only an empty, emotionless gaze. Despite it all, she silently begged for some sort of human interaction, even just to know that what she was dealing with was, in fact, human. He stood upright, turned to the stairs, and started whistling again.

"What do you want with me?" she screamed, yanking her

arms until the restraints threatened to fracture her wrists. Tangled auburn hair folded over her face and covered her eyes. Fresh tears flowed freely. "Let me out of here!"

The door atop the staircase slammed shut, dead bolted, and the shrill whistle faded into the house above. His footsteps shuddered about. Dust rained to the cellar floor. It would stop within minutes if her memory served correctly. He hadn't stirred for longer than that before settling in what she assumed was a room of some sort. She lowered her head between her knees, and a sharp whine emptied her throat. Cries for help to this point were closer to messages left unchecked on an answering machine.

She lifted her head and peered at the food in front of her. The tray itself wasn't much different than the ones used in the high school cafeteria. It was almost identical. For the smallest of moments, she wasn't shackled to some stranger's wall but enjoying the lunch period before the final two classes of the day. It was a dream. An incredibly vivid dream she couldn't stay in for long. Sarah choked back another cry and swallowed the stone-sized lump in her throat.

The chains clattered as she extended a hand to the tray and ripped it back with hesitation. She did this three times in total. Stomach acid pillaged up her throat, but she managed to force it down. He hadn't poisoned her food so far, at least to her knowledge. Maybe he was waiting for the right opportunity. A few pellets of rat killer in her bologna sandwich to finish off Sarah Baker once and for all.

No, he was keeping her alive for something. She assumed death by Oscar Mayer wasn't it.

She pulled the sandwich and crumbs dusted her legs.

The first bite required a second and even larger bite. The bread softened over her tongue, and the salty meat ignited each taste bud in sequence. A satisfied sigh, another bite, and Sarah sighed again. She paused for a drink of water, then, she attacked the sandwich once more.

After the main course was reduced to specks, she snatched the small applesauce cup and tore open the tinfoil lid. She rejected the formalities of a spoon and reared back the paste like a shot of alcohol. Some of the goopy mess slid down her mouth and under her chin.

It didn't matter. None of it did. No captive ever emerged in better shape than when they disappeared. Sarah had watched enough crime shows to know better. *They were all feral. Savage. Animalistic beyond repair.* How far gone was she? Would everyone back home—John, the high school faculty, the town—still look at her as they did Sarah Baker? Or would they see a shackled woman? A prisoner? Damaged goods? She hadn't the slightest clue.

She tossed the cup to the tray and focused on two oval-shaped pills in the smallest divider. Both were snowy white with indistinct words etched into the center. She knew what they were, had even meant to buy them herself until the man upstairs had other plans for her. How he knew she needed them was another matter that raised concern. Something she thoughtfully questioned whenever it came time for her daily dose.

He was keeping her alive for something, that much was certain, and Sarah Baker knew she wasn't sticking around to find out why.

# CHAPTER TWO

## Mills

*Three days before Sarah went missing*

SHERIFF JEFFREY MILLS drove through the Fulton backroads, a winding stretch just wide enough to squeeze through the narrow trees on each side. He remained remarkably still despite the terrain, focused on nothing more than the dirt trail in front of him.

The rocky and uneven surface wore on his tires, but the '94 Bronco had taken worse beatings. Not many high-speed chases in such a town, even though he was often forced to push the old girl up rugged, mountainous paths. He bit down on a toothpick and enjoyed the familiar wooden flavor of sour mash. Had he stopped at the station on his way, Mills might've brought the bottle in his office drawer along for the ride. No whiskey this morning, however. It would have to wait.

He arrived at the Landing, an open section in the woods where high school students gathered for unsupervised activities. Football game after-parties had been a tradition for as long as Mills could remember. Cursing the good Lord in the backseat of a car remained a constant even during the hottest summer nights.

But there were no remains of a party on this cold October morning, nor was there an inexperienced round of foreplay to interrupt. It was quiet. Far too quiet for a team on the heels of a homecoming victory. After the call he received, something in him doubted the Landing's celebrations would be the same for some time.

His deputy's squad car was perched on a lopsided hill, the rectangular headlights like eyes wincing at his sudden and untimely arrival. *Code 187*, she had told him when he couldn't sleep through the xylophone ringtone any longer.

He parked and wiped the dust from his broad-brimmed hat resting in the passenger seat. The gold pin on the front, though a bit crooked, reflected the sunlight somehow peeking through the vast tree line. Code 187 was something Mills never thought would happen under his watch, but just as the seasons would change, so would this sheriff's luck. He took a moment and inhaled what could have been his last clean breath.

Code 187—homicide.

Deputy Holloway leaned on the trunk of her squad car and stood a bit straighter when Mills exited the Bronco. The cigarette she lifted to her mouth ignited, and the chalky-white paper scorched until ashes were left in its place. Long black hair rested in a loosely fitted ponytail emerging from her tan, sheriff's office ball cap. Her already pale skin seemed to have lost a shade, though her nose and cheeks remained red.

"What do we have?" Sheriff Mills asked. He lowered the hat to his brow and grated his bottom lip with his teeth. "You get an ID?"

"Too soon to be certain."

A long-winded sigh. "Well, shit. You get a chance to look around? Notice anything out of place?" He removed his sunglasses and tucked them in his collar.

"I blocked off the scene and waited for you, sir." Her voice reduced to a whisper. She might've expected disappointment. For him to yell at her, scream maybe.

Mills tightened his rigid features. *Good girl*, he said to himself and nodded. Truth be told, he was as skeptical as any when Jennifer Holloway stepped into his office and requested a position with the Fulton County Sheriff's Department, tucked up here in the Pacific Northwest. Dispatch was his first thought. *No way she'd be useful elsewhere.*

He couldn't have been more wrong. Top marksman. Penal codes memorized front to back. A hunger in her eyes. Good was never enough. No, Holloway had to beat the stuffing out of any challenge Mills tossed her way. Though he never said it outright, he no doubt looked at her the way he imagined a proud father would beam at his daughter. "First person here. Next time, block off the scene and get to work. I can't trust you if you don't trust yourself. Clear?"

She lowered her sights to the ground. "Yes, sir."

Beyond the rash of stiff gravel and tree limbs, the body was sprawled, contorted almost. The flies seemed to gather in hordes, swarming every inch the maggots hadn't infested yet. An odor, foul and thick, wafted down the incline. It was death all right. Not the stuffy, ammonia stink you'd get from an open casket where the corpse was embalmed and appeared less human than before. No. This was a fresh, pungent death invading his nostrils. And as he moved farther, the reek only proved more horrid.

"Who left the tip?" Mills asked.

"Simmons took the call. Thought it was a prank. I mean, how often do we get reports of bodies?"

"Not often," he bellowed in a raspy tone. *Not at all*, he thought immediately. Instinctively, he hovered his hand over the hip holster on his belt; nestled inside was a Colt revolver with a fine oak handle, clasped into position by a single fastened button.

"Exactly. It should be him out here, but he begged me to come instead," she said through a thinned mouth. "Prick had a hangover and probably a new rash from one of those girls at Field and Streams Tavern."

Mills fought to swallow the acid sloshing to his neck. "I'm glad you did. Blake would've puked all over my crime scene."

"I never promised I wouldn't."

He crouched near the body's feet. The face was caved in at what he thought was the nose, but it was impossible to be sure. What may have been the victim's jaw at one point was now severed and protruding outward like the bloody tusk of an elephant. Teeth were missing, maybe the most important ones for chewing. And rot. The body had it, as did the blue hoodie and faded jeans slick with dew. Even the skin had begun to prune, shriveling into raisin-like flesh. He'd seen a lot during his tenure, but never something so horrifying. So … barbaric.

Mills poked a stick at the soil. "Jenn, when's the last time we had rain?"

"I think it's been a couple weeks."

Mills cocked his head to the side curiously and inspected the victim's clothes with the same prodding stick. "Means this one has been out here since then. You see the blood in the dirt? Rain would've washed that downhill. Have you called Luther yet? Is he on his way?"

"Not yet, sir. He usually spends his Sunday mornings listening to Pastor Ryan's sermons. Figured it best to assess the scene before pulling him away from the pew."

He turned his head to breathe, though it didn't help in the slightest. "All right, well, go give him a shout. Tell him Jesus can wait. We're gonna need a time of death."

"Why would someone do this?"

Without looking back at her, Mills pointed to the fist-sized rock lodged in the ground a few feet from the head. "Because someone wanted her dead, and fast."

×

THE OUTLINE OF a van came into view, winding the jagged path, and careful to avoid potholes and stiff terrain. Sunlight peered through darkened clouds and tree limbs to the stale white paint, a shade or two pastier than the cigarette Sheriff Mills clenched between his wrinkled lips. Though the pest control company's decal had been removed from the side panel, the markings remained visible. PETE'S PEST AND RODENTS. Went out of business years back, but the words and comically drawn roach were blatantly visible.

Luther Barnes eased in and parked behind Mills's Bronco, worn brakes screeching like a train whistle. The sheriff, leaning against his driver's side door, dropped the cigarette to the padded dirt and crushed it beneath the heel of his pointed leather boots.

"Let's go, Holloway," he said and waved her over. "Give Luther the tour."

"Sheriff?" Her eyes widened under the brim of her ball cap. "I've never handled a crime scene before, sir."

"Well, sink or swim. Your choice."

Her face drew strikingly serious. She straightened her shoulders and marched to the van, posture as firm as the crease in her dark brown uniform slacks. The door creaked open, and Luther's foot hit the remnants of a puddle when he stepped out. A small splash coated his black boots and spit water to his weathered jeans.

"Mornin'," he greeted Deputy Holloway, and nodded to Mills. "What's so important you had to interrupt the Lord's day?"

"Homicide," Holloway blurted out, an edge of nervousness in her voice. "We need an autopsy."

Mills tilted his hat to hide a grin, then crossed his arms.

"Shoot," Luther scoffed and scratched the back of his head. "Where?"

"Just beyond that clearing. Hope you brought your surgical mask, Doc. It's pretty gnarly."

"Don't be shy, Jenn," Mills interrupted. "Go show him."

Holloway's face flushed and a heavy gulp rattled her neck. She thumbed between the trees and sighed. "This way."

Jenn and Luther returned a few minutes later, each carrying the same greenish shade on their faces.

"What are you thinkin', Doc?" she asked, and lifted a

hand to cover her mouth and nose. "Been out here a while?"

"Smell like that? Yeah, at least a couple weeks." He coughed and plugged his nostrils. "Hell, I thought I'd seen it all."

"What do you say?" Jenn retrieved a notepad and started scribbling. "Can you bag the corpse and get us an autopsy report by tomorrow?"

The sheriff revealed an accidental half smile. *Good girl. And don't forget to have him—*

"And we'll need dental X-rays as well," she said. His smile deepened to both sides of his mouth.

"I can have the preliminaries for you by tomorrow, but the full report will take at least six weeks."

"Six weeks? No. Not good enough."

Mills shifted to the side to conceal the stiff chuckles bumping his chest. *Damn, I've raised you well.*

"Sorry, *Deputy*, but that timeframe is standard. Now if you'll excuse me, I have a passenger to load up." Luther pulled a joint from his shirt pocket, cupping his hand over the end to light it. The smoke wafted down the incline, and Holloway, with obvious hesitation, glanced at Mills and pointed to her cuffs.

"Luther?" Mills shifted to face him. "You do realize I'm the sheriff, right?"

"You ever try moving a dead body without puking, Jeff? If this isn't for medicinal purposes, I don't know what is."

Mills shrugged. "Can't argue with you there. Let's go, Holloway."

Jenn walked slowly toward him, hands at her hips, and stared at the ground, allowing the silence to linger a moment before speaking. "So—how'd I do?"

He pursed his mouth to one side. "Mediocre at best. But there's always room for improvement." This was nothing new. Her first arrest included tackling a belligerent man near three times her size. Mills complained that she should've had him on the ground sooner. Drugs being peddled at the high school; she should've caught the dealer with more product. The town's annual chili cook-off; she should've added more salt. All mediocre. But Mills hoped she knew what he really meant. Mediocre was another way of saying *I'm proud of you, kid.*

"Yes, sir. Should we go to the station and look over missing persons reports? Maybe track down who left the tip?"

"Eh." He paused and flipped the Bronco keys around his finger. "I could use a cup of coffee before we bury ourselves neck deep. You hungry?"

"Honestly, I don't think I could keep anything down."

THE WAITRESS SLID a plate in front of Holloway crammed with fluffy pancakes, sausage links, and a couple of poached eggs. Margery's was a small diner on the Fulton outskirts. Built alongside the highway, it was the final stop before I-5 led north through the mountain pass. There were autographs from traveling celebrities, trinkets, and knickknacks on various shelves in an organized clutter. The cobwebs and dust suggested a certain neglect no amount of deep cleaning would fix.

A hiss, the fry cook's symphony, drowned out the conversations around them; blue collars and churchgoers, never in short supply in Fulton, much less their constant gossip. Impossible to avoid in a town just shy of fifteen hundred. *Everyone knows everyone* was a common phrase, but in Fulton, everyone knew how many shits you had taken that day. Mills lifted the mug to his lips and reared back the steaming liquid, avoiding eye contact with the townsfolk around him.

Holloway narrowed her eyes at the plate and appeared to consider rushing to the bathroom, her face no longer green but pale enough to rival hospital sheets.

He smacked his lips. "Well? Dig in. You've gotta build a stronger stomach for this line of work."

She cut the pancake into a little chunk and chewed. Syrup drizzled down her lips, and she promptly wiped it away. "I told you I wasn't hungry."

"You'll feel better. Just shut up and eat." He took another sip and stared forward. Never did find it polite to watch someone eat. Found it a bit invasive, especially when that person was on the verge of spilling their insides.

Holloway grabbed the glass of water with a shaky hand and swished around mouthfuls. "So, what's the game plan?"

"Christ, Holloway. Do you ever think of anything besides work?"

"Not really. Especially when there's a killer—"

"Voice down," he cut her off in a stern whisper. "There're ears everywhere in this forsaken town. Best not to start a panic."

She leaned forward and spoke again, barely audible over the clanking plates and cups, not to mention the waitress boasting about her daughter making the varsity cheer squad this year. "You said it yourself, Jeff. Someone wanted that girl dead. We owe it to the public to find out what happened."

He tilted his head to the side. "Fuck these ungrateful pricks. My father was their sheriff for thirty-years. Got nothing but a pat on the back and an attaboy." Mills rubbed his hand over the Colt revolver, fingertips grazing each ridge of the handle. "We will do our job first, and that means investigating before disturbing the peace. We don't owe them shit else. Now, finish your food before it gets cold."

Holloway said nothing else at Margery's, and she did little else than nod when she climbed into her squad car after. They would drive their separate ways to the station, her a straight shot of course, and him, a scenic route consisting of Marlboros and fumbling the radio knob until something to his liking played. The victim, this dead girl, had rattled his young deputy's cage hard enough to shake something loose.

*It was the body. She can't stop seeing the body.*

# CHAPTER THREE

*Three weeks missing*

CAMERA LIGHTS FLASHED around the Fulton City Hall conference room. Sheriff Mills stood at the podium above the TV and newspaper reporters, shuffled through his statement, and adjusted the small mic clipped to his collar. Metal fold-out chairs were lined in neat rows and stopped abruptly before the back exits. Not a single seat was left empty.

Sarah Baker's picture rested on a mount to his left, a blown-up image of the missing teacher with a striking gaze that seemed to watch everyone inside the room. To his right was Deputy Holloway and newly elected Mayor Dan Richmond. His suit and tie evenly matched his fifty-dollar haircut. The sheriff didn't bother looking at his expression, for if he saw the same obnoxious grin plastered on every billboard and poster in town, he might've stomped off stage and left Holloway to the hyenas in the crowd.

Mills cleared his throat and furrowed his brow. "I'd like to thank you all for being here today. As I am sure most of you are aware, Sarah Baker, a teacher at Fulton High School, has been missing for the past three weeks, beginning Tuesday, October thirtieth." Some of the crowd nodded, and camera clicks filled the background silence.

"So far, search parties have combed a third of the woods surrounding our city, but no evidence has been found to support the investigation. Though foul play can't be confirmed, it is not ruled out completely. If anyone has information on the whereabouts of Sarah Baker, please contact the Fulton County Sheriff's Department. I would like to thank Mr. Baker for his full cooperation, as well as my department and the volunteers who have worked tirelessly to try to bring Sarah home safely. Now, I will open the floor for questions; however, I ask that the questions pertain to the facts and not any suspicions or rumors."

In an instant, every hand in the room shot straight up, and voices clamored to gain his attention. One reporter jumped from her seat and yelled above the rest.

"Sheriff Mills? Nina Castellano, Channel Five News. Where was Mrs. Baker last seen?"

He wiped a napkin over his brow before answering. "Our sources say she was last observed by a few students and faculty members walking to her car after school. We've received multiple reports, but none of which can be confirmed. Next question."

"I'm not finished." Her snarky tone cut through him. "Has Sarah's car been located?"

A hand in his pocket, he outlined his fingers over the bottle cap ridges. *ibuprofen*. He wasn't sure if he needed them more for the hangover or the sporadic lights blinding him. Possibly the latter. "No. We have yet to locate the red '98 Dodge Neon. But I assure you, every attempt has been made. Any county within a hundred-mile radius has the make and model. It's only a matter of time before we find it." He matched her glare until she yielded and returned to her seat. "Next question."

"Steve Morrison, *Fulton Gazette*. Does Sarah's disappearance raise cause for concern? With the murder a month ago—"

"I'm gonna stop you right there, Mr. Morrison," Mills snarled and smacked his dry tongue on the roof of his mouth. "As I stated before, this briefing is not for speculation but facts. I cannot comment on whether this is an isolated incident or if it has any connection to a previous event." He no longer rubbed his finger on the ibuprofen bottle but clenched it and nearly crushed the pills inside to dust. "Next question."

"Can you comment on the broken glass found in Mrs. Baker's home?" A hush fell over the room, and everyone, including him, stared at the man in the back. The stubble on his neck and cheeks highlighted the light brown complexion and firm features. His hair was jet black and clean cut, and he glared intently behind black-rimmed glasses.

Mills tilted his head to the right to catch his deputy's attention, and though she didn't acknowledge him, Holloway's face reddened. Jesse Alvarez, better known as AZ in the Morning on 106.5 KRFC. He had been a thorn in Mills's ass since he picked up a microphone. Quick to blame the sheriff's department for the recent crime spike in Fulton, which the public seemed to suckle from like infants.

"Mr. Alvarez, this meeting is for official press only. I don't believe that includes radio stations that force their listeners to eat dog food for concert tickets."

Small chuckles and snorts worked their way around the

room.

"You can insult me all you want, *Sheriff*, but don't dance around the question."

He leaned forward and craned his neck over the podium. "I have no comment."

A crooked grin revealed polished white teeth. "I expected as much."

"I'd like to thank you all for being here today." Mills paused and stood upright. "Again, if you or anyone you know has any information that could lead to the location of Sarah Baker or those involved with her disappearance, please contact the Fulton County Sheriff's Department. Mayor Richmond would now like to say a few words. Please afford him the same courtesy you have afforded me."

Mills unclipped his mic, walked off the stage toward the side exit, and Deputy Holloway shadowed his steps. The reporters continued to shout out for statements, but he refused with a stiff palm facing the unsatisfied crowd.

He pushed through the double doors to an empty hallway, and when the noise faded to the background, he whirled toward her. "Holloway, what in the flying fuck?"

"I'm sorry, Sheriff. I swear I didn't mean to say anything. It slipped." She scuffed her shiny low quarters to the tiles, declining to meet his eyes.

"And you're dating that dipshit now?"

She bit her bottom lip. "Well, no. I mean, kind of. It was just one date."

"Christ, Holloway. You can do better than that lowlife. You've heard what he's said about us."

"He's not as bad as you think."

His face twisted. "Not as bad? Hell, he's got half the town breathing down my neck. First the Landing, now this schoolteacher. I can barely drive around the block without some prick giving me the finger. And you go behind my back, offering up crime-scene information in return for what, a steak dinner? For fuck's sake." He lifted a palm to his forehead, and the corridor lights raked his weathered skin.

"I'm sorry, sir. It won't happen again."

An uneasy breath rattled his chest, and he placed his hands over her shoulders. "Look, Jenn. You're the best I've got. And I imagine no one better suited for the role of sheriff when I'm long gone." He noticed a distinct gloss in her eyes. "Now, I'm not your daddy, and it's not my place to give my two cents on who you should or shouldn't see. Just be careful. Okay?"

She nodded solemnly.

"Okay. And no more leaking information, or I'll have to pull you off the case."

"Yes, sir."

He kept his arms at her shoulders for a moment longer. He couldn't stay mad, even if he wanted to.

"Now, get to the station. Make sure Simmons isn't fucking up my paperwork."

"Sir." She walked at a steady pace down the hallway with the occasional glance over her shoulder. Once she was out of sight, Mills removed the bottle from his pocket, fumbled it open, and popped two pills to his tongue. Though his mouth was chalky, he managed to dry-swallow the tablets, and let them slide slowly down his esophagus.

Dan Richmond plowed through the double doors; his

sights set on Mills. "Well, that was something."

"You don't say," he rasped and rested against the corridor wall, hands at his hips.

Dan leaned in close, an obvious attempt at privacy in case one of the reporters crashed through the doors after him. "You were supposed to give those idiots hope, not lead them to believe parts of the investigation are being hidden from public view. Now we both look incompetent."

"All due respect, Mr. Mayor"—he pointed at the American flag tie poking out of Dan's blazer—"that thing you call a tie did that long before the meeting even started."

Mayor Richmond scowled, and Mills was certain none of the town had seen this expression before. If they had, well, he somehow doubted Dan would've won the popular vote. "Look, Sheriff. If you think I'm going to tolerate you screwing up my plans for this town, you're sorely mistaken. Find this fucking teacher. I don't give a shit if she's breathing. Find her. Or Fulton County will be campaigning for a new sheriff. Given the state of things you've managed to fuck up lately, you may as well kiss your pension good-bye."

MILLS SLAMMED THE interview room door behind him, more for intimidation than anything else. Might've been a broom closet at some point when the office was built in 1940, but now it served a different, and more often than not, vacant purpose. The walls, whitewashed and narrow, were squared evenly at each corner. Though the vents remained open, there was a stiffness in the air. A lingering congestion.

The florescent lights flickered, as if they, too, flinched at his arrival.

He tossed a manila folder on the table and papers spewed from the edges. He sat in an empty chair and propped his feet up. He needed a relaxed appearance for a relaxed conversation. The man on the other end, far too comfortable or at least pretending to be, hunched forward and interlocked his fingers. His hair, short, brown, and peppered gray, was offset by the dark stubble on his cheeks and neck. It all somehow complemented his long and almost pointed face.

"Thank you for meeting me, Mr. Baker." Mills removed his hat and placed it to the side. His glare cut across like a well-placed dagger to John's throat. "I just have a few questions to ask, then you'll be free to go about your day."

"Look, I've already told you and your deputy everything I know weeks ago. Why the hell am I here?"

"Routine for an ongoing investigation. Could be something we both missed." Mills reached in his uniform shirt pocket, retrieved the pack of Marlboros, and slid the box between them.

John fumbled the box and placed a cigarette at the corner of his mouth. "This is bullshit. You're wasting your time and mine."

Mills handed him a lighter. "I assure you that any information we can gather is vital to the case. Now, when was the last time you saw your wife?"

John scorched the tip, inhaled, and scoffed out smoke. "Again, the last time I saw Sarah was the morning before she went missing."

"Which was?"

"Tuesday, October thirtieth."

"And where was your wife?" Mills took the lighter and a cigarette for himself.

"At our house." His voice raised defensively. "She was sleeping. I had to leave early for work."

"At 1223 Shadow Ridge Way, correct?"

John nodded and took another drag.

"I see. And how is your marriage?"

"No relationship is without trouble, Sheriff. You wouldn't know that though, would you?"

Mills crossed his arms, and his glare intensified. It was a low blow. A truthful one at that. Mills had never married. Hadn't had more than a *wham bam thank ya ma'am* in a long time, actually. The job, this responsibility, called for more than a family man could give. How his father had managed to serve while parenting—albeit poorly—was still a mystery. No, this was *his* burden. A bed half-empty. Something always missing.

"Look, our marriage wasn't perfect by any means. We had our issues like every couple. But that doesn't change the fact that I loved her and want to find her, okay?"

"Of course you do," he replied and noted John's unusual use of past tense. Our marriage *wasn't* perfect. We *had* our issues. I *loved* her. Could've been an accident, but he didn't like the way John said it so nonchalantly. It sounded off. Sounded like John knew the wife he swore to find wasn't coming back.

"The night before, did she say or do anything out of character? Any reason to assume she'd leave?" Mills asked.

"No. Wine and a book. Her usual go-to. Why does this

matter?"

The sheriff revealed a confident grin. *Gotcha.* "Because we received multiple reports from patrons down at Field and Streams Tavern. You were there most of the night, were you not?"

"So I had a few drinks after work. Big fuckin' deal." John's irritation manifested first at his clenching knuckles and trickled up to his tightened shoulders. "Is that a crime?"

"How long were you at the bar?"

"I don't know. A few hours, maybe."

"Bartender said you didn't leave until well after midnight. An hour or so before last call."

John shifted in the chair, leaned back, and threw his hands behind his head. "Is there a point to any of this?"

"I've known the bartender, Mitch Collins, for quite some time. Good kid. Honest." That was a lie. The most interaction Mills had with Mitch Collins was a wave for another shot of whiskey. Truth was, Holloway did the questioning, and Mitch, an obvious infatuation with the deputy, spilled everything like a tipped trash can. "Said you didn't leave alone that night either. Tell me, who is Katie Bowman?"

John's eyes widened, and his chest lifted with a heavy breath. He tried to regain his composure, but the poor attempt failed to go unnoticed. "I'd like to call my lawyer."

"We're just having a conversation." Mills raised a brow and smirked. "Did Katie accompany you to 1223 Shadow Ridge Way, where you supposedly saw your wife drinking wine and reading a book? An early morning book club, perhaps?"

He slammed his palm to the table and a *crash* echoed off each wall. "I'd like my fucking lawyer, now!"

# CHAPTER FOUR

## Holloway

*One day before Sarah went missing*

"EASY. EASY!" SHERIFF Mills coached her, the blunt stench of whiskey on his breath.

Any slower and the stitching needle would be a new accessory for his shoulder. She pierced another layer of his skin, watching the way his blood dripped down to his abdomen like beads of water.

"I *am* going easy. Now sit back and shut up."

He paused for a moment. Didn't even flinch when she pushed the suture outward, pulling a long string of black thread between them. Mills wanted to say something, she was sure of it. Maybe it was because he wasn't accustomed to having anyone, a woman in fact, telling him to shut up. Jenn had never said that to him before, but when you're dragged out of bed at two in the morning to provide first aid, professionalism could take the backseat.

"Who was it?" she asked.

"Rick Berman."

Jenn tightened another notch of his flesh together. This time he flinched. "Christine?"

"Christine." Mills nodded.

"What'd he use?" The incision curved. It couldn't have been a knife. It was far too uneven and jagged.

Mills snarled, "Corkscrew."

"A corkscrew?"

"Bastard came at me like a bottle of wine, okay?"

This time, Jenn smirked. "He took out the town sheriff with something from the silverware drawer?"

"Ha, ha. Very funny. Finish up, will ya?"

Jenn chuckled and continued. "You know, I'm not exactly qualified to be doing this."

"I know." He took a swig from the bottle at his right. "Better you than some doc at the emergency room. Rather die than be in one of those stuffy rooms."

She finished the final stitch and cut the black thread, leaving enough room to tie the knot twice and one more time if needed. "Well, let's hope this doesn't get infected. Is he—Rick—at the station?"

Mills glared at her curiously. "Of course he is. Simmons hauled him off before I called you."

"Good."

"I'm sure Christine is thinking the same right now."

Jenn removed her blue plastic gloves, each finger coated in the sheriff's blood. "How long are you going to hold him?"

"Are you asking if I'm going to officially file a report this time?"

Holloway hung her head. She was. She just couldn't say it aloud. Not because she was talking to her superior. Not because every bit of her bearing demanded it. But because of the memories creeping to her mind.

When she glanced up, he was staring at her, his blue-almost-gray eyes fixed. "I'm sorry, kid. I am. Rick should've been sent upstate the first time. You were right. I let my personal relationship get in the way of Christine's safety. He won't hurt her again. I promise."

"Good," Jenn said again and turned toward the waste-basket. "It never just happens once, you know."

"I know. Believe me, I know better than most."

"Me, too."

There was a long silence between them. It seemed neither had the will nor the desire to say more. There they sat, both as quiet as the Fulton streets after closing time, Holloway considering if things might've been different had there not been a second or even fifth domestic dispute call from her family home as a child. If the police had taken her calls seriously, well, maybe things would have been different. She would never be certain. The only thing she knew for sure was that it wouldn't happen again under her watch.

"You were right," Mills said again and gave a lengthy yawn. His head was tilted. His arms were sprawled, even the one with a newly fashioned stitch. The long, black thread dangled like a stray hair ready for plucking. She didn't bother removing it. *He can deal with it in the morning.* The sheriff slouched further, as if a magnetic force were pulling him closer to his pillow blotched in large red dots. "You're always …"

He was laying down now. His head comfortably rested among the linens, his body seeming to beg for the covers at his feet.

"Always what, Jeff?"

Mills nestled deeper, an eye half-open while the other was shut. "You're always a step ahead …"

Holloway gathered the blankets and placed them over him. "I was trained to be, sir."

The sheriff tilted his head to the opposite side of the pillow and mumbled, "Not by me, you weren't."

She sat there for a moment, puzzled. Jenn even shook him a few times to see if any more answers would come from his partially hidden face. Nothing. No explanation. Christ, not even a snore. He was sleeping more peacefully than she imagined herself to lay at night. It didn't make sense. Who else would've trained her? Gave her the keen ability to see what others dismissed so easily? It couldn't have been the things that kept her up at night. The visions of her mother lying in a pool of her own fluids while a strange figure, one Jenn herself couldn't recognize as her own father, stood over the body.

No, that wouldn't help anyone *be a step ahead.*

# CHAPTER FIVE

## Mills

*One day before Sarah went missing*

JEFFREY THOMAS MILLS hadn't been older than nine, a scrawny blond-haired boy sitting on the living room rug cross-legged. He was watching *The Lone Ranger* on the TV a few feet from his knees. The revolver in one hand and a toothbrush in the other, he split his attention between the idiot box (as his dad called it) and cleaning the gun down to its engraved grip. His dad, the reek of Budweiser circling around him, couldn't lean back farther in his plush green recliner without damn near tipping the thing over.

There were empties scattered on the side table next to him, enough to be used in a bowling match. He was somewhat surprised his dad hadn't knocked them down in one fell swoop while reaching for the beer he was currently nursing. Momma had spent the past forty minutes in the kitchen and only entered the living room when he called for another hasty refill. She did, and each time planted a kiss on his daddy's balding head.

Jeffrey found a spare bullet in one of the six chambers he was scrubbing and marveled secretly for quite some time before he pocketed it for safe keeping. His dad hadn't noticed. If he had, Jeff might've ended up with a swift smack at the back of his head for playing with Daddy's things. He wanted to keep it. Maybe show the other kids at school. *What he don't know*, Jeffrey said to himself.

He glanced at the television after careful chamber cleanses, ensuring every hint of gunpowder and forming rust had been wiped clean. He hated the way the oil would stay on his fingers for days afterward and how the metallic stench would follow him around like a stray dog. But week after week for as long as he could remember, his Sunday night consisted of cleaning and polishing Daddy's revolver.

"Sheila. Beer," his dad had said and shook the bottle for emphasis, splashing the little bit of lager remaining.

"Just a minute, dear."

His mother was more patient than most. He couldn't remember a time she had raised her voice, in fact. And even now, while elbow deep preparing dinner for a man too drunk to taste it, her response was still as sweet as ever.

"No. Now!"

"I need to wash my hands, dear—"

"I didn't ask for a goddamn excuse!" he cut her off. At this point his father had stood—stumbled—from his recliner, effectively knocking the congregation of bottles over. Although none had broken, the barrage of hollow clangs on the wooden floor still managed to drown out the Coca-Cola commercial on the TV.

Jeffrey reared his head slowly, afraid of the monster sure to be seen behind him. His dad wasn't wearing boots but stomped his feet viciously as if he had, and heavy ones at that.

He continued to yell at her from the kitchen doorway, this time more incoherent obscenities than Jeffrey himself could understand. His fists were balled. His stature, while drunkenly slouched, was intimidating, nonetheless.

"I can get it, Dad," he said.

"Shut the hell up, Jeffrey!"

He did as he was told. His father's word was gospel in the Mills's home, and Jeffrey would sooner scorn God than Jacob Mills. One hand on the unfinished revolver, he dug his freehand in his pocket, fingers grazing the cold bullet.

"I'm trying to finish dinner, J—"

A thunderous smack echoed from the kitchen into the living room. His mother's small yelp followed. Jeffrey slammed his eyes shut the way he had so many times before.

"You will not talk back to me in my house, ya hear?"

When she didn't respond immediately, another swipe cut through the air and connected. It wasn't a yelp coming from his mother anymore but stifled cries.

"Now finish my fucking dinner before I really get—" His father's voice trailed off as a loud click erupted behind him.

"Leave her alone." Jeff practically spat the words, training the muzzle at his daddy's large back. *Always aim for the biggest target—that way, you never miss,* he had told Jeff when they would take their quarterly hunting trips in the Fulton wilderness. Now, Jeff was the hunter and his dad was the animal he had to put down. The revolver was heavy, difficult for him to keep steady with one hand, but Jeffrey did.

"I won't tell you again, Daddy."

His father turned. His mother was holding her red-tinted cheek.

"Jeff, put that down," she pleaded. "Go to your room, honey."

He stood firm. "No. You won't hurt her anymore. You hear me?" His face drew serious. The Lone Ranger never cried when he aimed his gun at a bad guy, and Jeffrey sure as hell wouldn't either.

His father smirked. "S'not loaded, you little shit. What are you gonna do? Throw it at me?"

Jeffrey cranked the chamber to the side, showcasing a single bullet, and flipped it back into place equally as fast. His mother and father both widened their eyes.

"Jacob, please don't hurt him. He doesn't know what he's doing."

"Shut up," he snapped and took two cautious steps forward, his arms raised defensively. "You gonna shoot me, boy? You think you got the stomach?"

Jeffrey rubbed his finger gently on the trigger while a thousand different thoughts punched at his gut.

"You gonna kill your own dad?"

*Yes. No. Yes.*

His daddy took two more steps and loomed over him. "That what you want?" He snatched the revolver by the barrel before Jeffrey could weigh down the trigger and struck him on the side of his face and ear.

Jeff could only hear his heartbeat thump wildly, accompanied by the awful sting of his father's knuckles on his cheek. He watched as his dad flipped open the spindle and emptied the chamber. For a moment, Jeff was certain he was going to finish the job by stomping on his ribs. Maybe take off his belt one loop at a time and lash him until he was covered head to toe in welts.

He did neither. Jacob Mills laughed.

"Look whose balls finally dropped!" he said and chuckled even louder. It lasted for what seemed like an agonizing minute. His mother's face was still pained, and Jeffrey was more dumbstruck than before. When he finally settled down, Jacob Mills hunched over and stared his son in the eyes. "You aim at somethin', boy, you better be ready to shoot. Ya hear?"

"Y-y—yessir."

Jacob set the revolver on Jeffrey's thigh. "Finish up and get ready for dinner."

"Yessir," he said again and nodded this time.

His daddy returned to his recliner. No kick to the ribs. No more smacks to his momma's cheek. No more monster. It was almost as if he had forgotten everything when he went back into the living room, and all was once again right in the Mills's family home.

✕

THE MORNING SUN stretched over his brow and rested firmly on his closed eyelids. Sheriff Mills, an arm off the bed and the other under the pillow clenching his revolver, peered at the window through a single dilated eye—always the trusty right. Condensation coated the glass pane and trickled down to the frosty corners. He coughed, a violent hack with the aftertaste of tobacco, whiskey, and a memory best forgotten.

He lifted the blanket and eased up to sit. The strain in

his back tightened. A draft caressed his worn, leather-like shirtless skin. The scar at his shoulder, mangled flesh stitched together with a sewing needle after a fifth of bourbon, served as a bloody trophy to the night before.

The station had received a call that Rick Berman was smacking around his wife again. Domestic disturbance turned drunk and disorderly, and when the sheriff intervened, it escalated to attempted murder. Whether the judge would consider a corkscrew a deadly weapon or not was still up in the air. Simmons hauled Rick to the drunk tank to sleep it off, and Holloway, despite her lack of first-aid knowledge, sutured Mills best she could. *Dammit, kid,* he cursed her silently while inspecting the wound. *This shit ain't gonna heal right.*

Mills walked to the bathroom, washed his face, and stared at himself for a moment before brushing the sour mash slippers off his teeth. Sink water spit and gurgled to the porcelain, disrupting the silence not only in the bathroom but his own head. The shower allowed a scalding hot or ice-cold temperature. He chose the latter and twisted it on with the pliers serving as a makeshift knob.

After he was clean—well, clean enough in his opinion—Mills buttoned the khaki uniform shirt from the top down. He folded his matching tie and adjusted his dark brown slacks, a hard crease in each pant leg. *Appearance is everything* repeated in his head, the voice accompanying it as rough as gravel.

Mills retrieved the revolver from under his pillow, flipped open the chamber—still fully loaded—and holstered it. There was a distinct amount of neglect from one chamber to the next, gunpowder residue and rust noticeable in each. It was the least of his worries.

×

THE '94 BRONCO glided down Fulton's main street. A bleach-white finish and faded-black fabric interior. Cigarette burns marked up the roof's upholstery near the driver's window, and a distinct crack in the windshield spread across the entire glass surface like lightning shattering the sky. Sheriff Mills sipped from the tall coffee in his free hand and clenched the other on the steering wheel at the midnight position. He waved to the people he passed, no more than a subtle flick of his wrist.

He parked at the station, a single-story building wedged between city hall and a barber shop—the same place he would go a few times a month for a trim and straight-razor shave. Though stubble trickled on his neck and chin in silver strands, the rugged reflection in the rearview grew on him.

*Another time*, he told himself, rubbing his palm to his cheek.

Deputy Simmons stood at attention when Mills walked in, uniform wrinkled and doughnut crumbs falling off his lips. "Mornin', Sheriff," he announced through a mouthful and pointed to the pink box on his desk. "Doughnut?" Combat veteran with two tours in Afghanistan under his poorly fastened belt, Blake Simmons had traded the army fatigues for a Fulton County deputy's badge. His pale features contrasted the beige, button-up shirt. Fiery red hair was meticulously combed forward, and the sides were clean shaven. His jawline was stiff and freckled, and his eyes were as brown as the chocolate doughnut he shoved in his mouth.

"As you were, Deputy." Mills saluted him while moving toward his office, and Simmons eased back to his chair. The ceiling lights glared off staples in the weathered carpeting, connecting the gaping rips and tears. Fulton's budget on law enforcement had tapped out each fiscal year faster than the check would arrive by post. The ugly tan carpets, for now, would have to stay.

Holloway popped her head up and peered over his desk as he entered the rectangular, windowless room. "Morning, Sheriff," she greeted him and revealed a wide grin.

"Holloway? What the hell are you doing?"

She slammed a stack of folders near his computer monitor. "Just cleaning up a bit. When's the last time you organized these case files?"

He leaned to one side, placed a hand at his hip, and slurped from his coffee cup. "Christ, kid. Get the hell outta my office. That shit *is* organized."

Holloway lifted a rotted banana peel from the drawer and raised her brow.

"Ah, right where I left it."

"What about this, sir?" She paused and brandished a black label bottle, hand engraved etchings at the neck. "We're not supposed to drink on duty."

"Lighten up. This job will kill ya if you take it too seriously." He snatched the whiskey from her and set it on the desk. The caramel liquid sloshed and settled. "I've been the sheriff for twenty years, and the only thing stopping me from eating my Colt is a sense of humor and a little flavor in my morning roast."

Her face tightened and her large, always curious eyes winced as he added a few shots to his coffee cup.

He pointed the bottle neck in her direction. "You take one sugar or two?"

"No thank you, Sheriff." Her stern voice wavered with offense. "Maybe Simmons will join you."

"This is my *good* shit. He can stick with decaf."

Holloway collected the files, evened them together, and placed them back in the drawer.

"Speaking of Simmons, have you asked about the call he took? Does he know where it came from?" Mills poked his head through the doorway and watched Blake, finger deep in his nostril, staring at the ceiling. "I'll take that as a no."

She sighed. "I'm on it."

"How's our friend doing in the back?"

"I wouldn't exactly call someone who tried to kill you last night a friend."

"We were ironing out the details on whose house we'd have Thanksgiving at. I'm going out on a limb, but I think I'm hosting." He winked, and she shook her head on the way to her desk.

He spent the next ten minutes shoving the papers, files, and his whiskey, of course, into their respective drawers. None of which were stacked, folded, or abstained from in a proper manner.

"What you got for me, kid?" Mills asked when he reentered the bullpen.

Holloway whipped around, ponytail swaying, and tore the page off before it finished printing. "Local number. Call was placed around two A.M."

"Now we're talking. Get me a name and address."

She eyed the ceiling tiles for a moment, a vacant contemplation, then stared back at the paper and pulled the cell phone from her front pocket. "Sheriff? We need to call Luther."

"Luther's busy with the autopsy. Leave him be."

Holloway shook her head. "No, sir. This is Luther's number. Luther placed the call."

✕

SHERIFF MILLS HAD tried Luther's cell for the past twenty minutes with no response. The endless ringing remained in his ears long after the calls ended. As the Fulton County coroner, pathologist, toxicologist, serologist, DNA analyst, and religious nutcase, it wasn't uncommon to reach his voicemail.

The tip to a murder scene was completely out of the ordinary. Normally, Mills filled him in on those details. *So, why didn't you say something at the Landing? You had to know we'd trace the number.* Mills hit redial.

*You've reached Luther Barnes of the Fulton County Coroner's Office. Please leave your name—click.* Mills slammed the corded phone to its hook on Holloway's desk.

"No luck?" She glanced up at him.

"Nothing. What time is it?"

She tilted her cell phone. "Just after ten."

He tried again, and one more time after that for good measure. *You've reached Luther*—Mills tossed the phone to her desk, and Holloway fumbled with the cord before it hit the floor. "Keep trying. I'll drive over." He took one last pull from his coffee, threw on his dark brown fleece, and pushed outside.

The Bronco stalled. Once. Twice. Then turned over.

"Atta girl, Rose," he said, and patted the dash like a dog performing a trick on command. She lived a long life on unleaded and overdue oil changes. Mills would have found it difficult to part ways. When he thought of any woman he'd ever loved (or thought so at least), Rose somehow managed to make the top of the list.

"Why *Rose*?" he'd been asked on occasion. A fair question, given there was not a single ounce of red on the thing. He'd never admit it outright, but the year he picked her up, *Titanic* played at the local theater, and he found himself particularly fond of a certain redheaded actress.

There were but a few places Luther could've been: his office a couple blocks down, the First Baptist Church across from Margery's, or his house out in the sticks. Mills hoped one of the first two, for a hike in loose gravel and wilderness this close to lunchtime was far from tempting.

He parked outside the Fulton County Coroner's Office, a narrow, almost trailer-sized building attached to the local hospital. The rusted-brown exterior had no windows, and the white blinds over the glass door allowed little daylight to enter. Ammonia and cotton, the regular odor to expect, poured out when he entered, and Mills positioned himself at the counter.

"Luther?" He clicked the bell next to the business cards scattered on the faux granite surface. The only response he received was the hiss and rattle of the ceiling vent. A hand at his revolver, Mills advanced cautiously toward the back room. The overpowering stench intensified.

"Luther?" he asked again. "Luther Barnes? It's Jeff."

A soft clanging teased his ears.

A shadow swayed, slightly visible beneath the doorway. Mills lifted the revolver to his chest and cocked back the hammer.

"Fulton County Sheriff's Department." He tilted his head and clicked the shoulder walkie. "Holloway. I've got a possible 459."

"Burglary? Do you need backup?" she asked eagerly.

"Nothing I can't handle, kid. Jus' keeping you advised."

He counted to himself for a few seconds and thrust open the door, barrel aimed and his finger tracing the trigger. "Shit," was the first word from his mouth. "Luther?" He sighed and holstered the Colt. "Learn how to answer the goddamn phone."

Luther peeled off the headphones from his oddly shaped crown and shifted in the stool near his desk. Pictures and files were splayed over the surface. "Sorry. I work best with a little Charlie Parker. And watch your damn mouth in my office."

"Well, Chuck almost got you a new hole to breathe out of." Mills gestured toward the photos. "How's it looking?"

"Nearly done with the prelim. I would've called when it's ready, ya know." Luther shrugged.

"Not here for the results. We looked into the phone number that gave the tip to our new friend. I need to know why you didn't mention knowing about the body before you scooped it up."

"Whaddya mean?"

"The call came from your cell phone, Luth. Your number. I'm not saying this is your doing, but I need to know why you were at the Landing and why you didn't come forward initially. We've known each other how long? You really think I would've thrown the book at you?"

He scratched at the balding patch near the back of his head. "I don't understand, Jeff. The first time I saw this body was when you called me. Put that on Papa's grave."

"Your father is alive, and he lives in Mobile, Alabama."

"Figure of speech. What time was the call made?"

"Around two A.M. Sunday morning."

"Hmm. Can't be right. You sure there hasn't been some sorta mix-up?"

Mills closed his eyes to conceal them rolling. "Positive. Did Deidra by chance use your phone?"

"No. No." He shook his head and scratched at the same spot. "Dee wouldn't take my phone without asking or stay awake late when we have service in the morning."

"I think I need to speak to your daughter, Luth."

"You can piss up a rope for all I care. You'll leave her outta this."

"If you didn't call, then it had to be Deidra. She's my only lead. Either we can go ask her some questions together or you're gonna get a ride to the station for interfering with an ongoing investigation." He chuckled to keep the conversation casual.

The attempt fell flat. Luther stood from his desk, lengthy brow furrowed, and loomed his impressive six-and-a-half-foot stature over Mills. "I said"—he pressed a finger to his badge—"you'll leave her out of this."

"Luther. You're puttin' me in a tough position."

His features softened unexpectedly. "She's my baby. You know that. She's all I have left."

"Then help me find the bastard who did this." Mills waved his hand to the photos of severed and bloody flesh. "So no one else's baby ends up like this."

Luther hung his large head. "Fine. I don't agree with it, Jeff. But if finding this demon will protect my Dee, the good Lord would want me to help you."

"I'm not exactly sure I'm doing God's work, Luth."

For the first time in minutes, Luther cracked the same grin Mills was accustomed to. "I'd rather side with the devil I know than the devil I don't."

# CHAPTER SIX

*Three weeks missing*

JOHN BAKER SAT across from Mills, shoulders tensed and a scowl on his lips. They waited quietly, as they had for the past fifteen minutes, only trading sideways glances between drags from their cigarettes.

*I'd like my fucking lawyer, now!* John had screamed, and even slammed his hand on the table for emphasis. Mills had expected the response. Hoped for it, actually. The man was under a microscope. Every move or emotion scrutinized by not only the town but, at this point, the entire state. *He doesn't cry enough. How many search parties has he gone on? He did it. It was him!* The husband was always the prime suspect in the court of public opinion, after all. Even the guilty ones pretended to care about their spouse's safe return. So far, John had done nothing of the sort.

The air stiffened, more from the uncomfortable husband's silence than the temperature rising with the afternoon sun. *I'll sweat it out of you*, he scolded John internally and grinned at the thought. This was the first good interrogation in years, and Mills, the arrogant bastard he was, intended to savor every moment.

The doorknob twisted, and pungent aftershave filled the room before he even crossed the threshold. Mills, boots on the table and heavy eyes still set on John, refused to stand or even acknowledge the man entering. With his face plastered on every billboard and bus stop in Fulton, it came as no surprise Harper Reed was the first name out of John's mouth. His sheer presence tightened the already cramped room. He lifted a well-manicured hand and placed a briefcase between them.

Harper stood at the table's head, arms behind his back, showcasing a crooked grin. The finely tailored suit, a soft gray-and-black pinstripe, clung to his slender figure, and his slacks were hemmed just above polished, and in Mills's opinion, ugly-ass dress shoes.

The pictures and ads had done no justice to his sleazy demeanor. It wasn't until Mills was face-to-face with him that he realized how so many crimes as of late were left unpunished. Traffic violations tossed out like leftovers. DUIs reduced to minimum charges. This rat-faced lawyer was conniving, willing to do whatever it took to win a case. Mills had to be smarter. More conniving then the two men staring back at him.

"I'd like to speak to my client alone for a moment," Harper demanded and left little room in his stern voice for rebuttal.

"He's all yours, *Harper*." Mills excused himself to the hallway and leaned against the opposing wall. Muffled sounds slipped through the door cracks, but their conversation remained too low to eavesdrop.

"Called for backup, huh?" Holloway strolled forward and offered a Styrofoam cup. "Coffee?"

He gnawed at his cheek until nickel lathered his molars

and tongue. "Fucking coward." He raised his hand, grabbed the drink, and slurped the steamy, bitter liquid.

"You think he has something to do with it? That he might have killed her?"

"Ain't no body, Holloway. For all we know, she left this miserable bastard and started a new life somewhere else. Can't say I'd blame her. I don't know who's worse, the husband or his lawyer. Both are asswipes."

Holloway chuckled and tried to hide the way she snorted. The sound was reminiscent of a pig's grunt. He fought the smile forcing itself through and faced forward. "If she is dead, hell, her body will tell us more than these clowns ever will. I have a feeling we will need warrants from here on out."

Holloway nodded. "Do you want me to get started on that?"

"Nah. Let these fuckers squirm a bit."

"I'm not sure there's much more we can get from the house anyway. We searched the place top to bottom. No blood. No forced entry. Besides the broken vase, it's clean."

"John and that slimy fuck in there don't know that. No point in letting him off the hook so easily. If this is a homicide, all signs lead back to him. For the time being, he's our only suspect with a motive to have Sarah disappear." Mills raked a hand over the stubble on his cheek and tossed back nearly half the cup in a single pull.

The door creaked open slowly, and Harper, blazer now off and slung over Mills's chair, waved him inside, as if inviting him into his own damn office. *Smug son of a bitch.* The sheriff slammed the door behind him for good measure.

He refused to sit this time and relaxed his stiff arms shoulder's width on the table across from John. "You ready now, *son*?" His question, though more condescending than he intended, seemed to tighten both of their postures.

John crossed his arms, leaned back and cocked a brow.

"Where were you the night before Sarah's disappearance between midnight and two A.M.?"

John shifted in the chair and released an easy breath. "I was with Katie Bowman."

"And are you and Katie romantically involved?"

Harper visibly shook his head within view.

John finally peered up at Mills, and a shit-eating grin slithered across his face. "No, Sheriff. We're just friends. She drove me home that night at around two A.M. I had a *few* too many, or did Mitch Collins forget to mention that part?"

Mills gritted his teeth. *Slimy fuck. You win, for now.* He pulled a photo from the folder in front of him. "Can you tell me what this is?" He displayed the Bakers' entryway with shattered glass and roses along the floors.

"We've gone over this before."

"Humor me."

"It's Sarah's flower vase. I found it like that when I came home."

Mills hunched forward. "Is there any way your cat could've knocked it over?"

"Not a chance. Our cat went missing a week or so before Sarah."

"Or so?"

John scoffed. "I don't know what day exactly. Biscuit was Sarah's pet. Not mine."

"Right, right. So, run me through the evening you came home. You walk through the door, and you find your wife's vase and—what are these for?" he asked and pointed to the roses. "Anniversary? Birthday flowers?"

"I didn't give her those. I'm not sure where she got them." John shrugged. "And yeah, that's pretty much how it happened. No Sarah, and broken glass and water all over my floor. I checked the back door. Locked. Front door, too. She was just … gone."

Mills returned the picture to the folder, closed it, and stood. "All right. Well, thank you for your time, Mr. Baker." He directed his glare to the sleazebucket. How in God's name had he passed the bar exam?

"Harper. That will be all for now." His tone said something different though. *You're next*, he thought and opened the door with a grin. "Have a good day. Oh, and if you see Ms. Bowman, please tell her I'd like to have a conversation. It's rather urgent."

John's face flushed, and neither he nor his lawyer said a word as they left.

# CHAPTER SEVEN

*One month missing*

THOUGH THE SUN remained perched in the darkening horizon, rain formed in light splotches across his cracked windshield. The gentle patters played in tune with his thumb taps over the steering wheel. He sung more so to "Don't Fear the Reaper" on the radio in his head than out loud. Never did consider his own voice appealing, even when mixed with the soothing sounds of Blue Oyster Cult.

The Bronco's tires, worn but with a fair amount of tread on each, smoothed over the slick roads. He avoided the puddles and potholes, and even crossed into oncoming traffic to do so. No one would crash head-on into the sheriff, after all. No one except John Baker, maybe.

Holloway clutched onto the roof handle, but the term *oh shit handle* might've been more accurate. "Dammit, Sheriff. At least turn on the patrol lights if you're gonna ride the center line."

*Thump, thump, thump, thump.* He bobbed in his seat, and the entire truck shook from the road reflectors. "What? I'm reading the Braille."

"Ha-ha. Get us there in one piece, please," she said with annoyance.

"Ya know"—he paused and slid his tongue to his receding gum line—"you didn't have to come with. I would've been happy to show face to the orange vests myself. Might've saved me from your constant bellyaching, too." Mills smirked and elbowed her arm.

She retaliated with a white-knuckle fist to his thigh.

"Ah, shit!" he grumbled and ripped his foot off the gas to stretch the charley horse. "You trying to cause an accident or something?"

"Slug bug."

"Huh?"

Holloway tilted her head to the side. "Slug bug. I hit you."

"You do realize you gotta see a bug to slug in turn, right? Can't just go around punching people, you fucking goober."

"What kinda bug?"

"Not an actual bug. One of them old camper vans or beetles. Volkswagen? Am I ringing any bells?"

Holloway shrugged and wiped away the fog building on the windshield. "So, how far you think the hike will be today?"

"Eh." He peered at the thickening clouds overhead. "My guess, the rains will wash out the search. No point in getting stuck up there and needing our own search party."

"A shame," she said but mostly sighed.

"You're telling me. I just polished these boots."

Her face soured, and her voice raised an octave, effectively drowning out the radio. "Your boots? Sarah Baker is out there somewhere, and you're worried about your boots? She could be hurt, or worse. Show a little compassion."

Mills, despite the overwhelming urge to say more, bit his

tongue and sank lower in the seat. Simmons would've found it funny. He didn't dare say the thought outright, not because he needed Holloway's approval, but somehow the thought of her disappointment twisted his insides. "You're right, kid. Bad joke. *Sorry.*"

Her lips thinned to a narrow, almost uneven line, and she acknowledged with a single wrist flick.

Radio squelch interrupted the silence. "Hey, uh—Sheriff?" Simmons's voice broke through the static.

"What the hell ya want, Blake?" he groaned.

"What color is that missing lady's car?"

He rolled his sunken eyes and clicked the handset. "Red. Like your fuckin' hair. Shouldn't be that hard to remember."

"You guys better get down here." There was panic in his voice. Excitement maybe. "I think I found it."

# CHAPTER EIGHT

*One day before Sarah went missing*

TO MILLS'S SURPRISE, much of Fulton High had remained the same since he, too, had wandered the halls. Four evenly spaced corridors were filled with classrooms and lockers; cement paths led to each, complete with metal awnings overhead. Wooden benches with things carved into the surface were scattered haphazardly around the quad area. Whether it was a new relationship on campus or a new victim to harass via etched words like *loser*, *nerd* or *slut*, it too would be promptly painted over by summer, leaving those memories a bitter stain the school would soon forget.

Two large buildings formed the gymnasium and cafeteria, laying on the opposite end of the classrooms. The administration office seemed to have the exact bricks from his time, though the crimson red rectangles had dulled to an unappealing shade of cracked burgundy.

Mills sucked on the toothpick between his teeth and opened the office door, motioning Luther inside first. They stood at the counter and waited for the woman typing viciously to acknowledge their presence. Her hair was neck-length and dirty blond. She homed her amber eyes, framed with horn-rimmed glasses, on the computer screen.

Mills cleared his throat. "Good morning, Janice."

She glanced upward. "Jeffrey," she said as if reading from a list of tardy students. "Looking miserable as always. What can I do for you?"

"And you have always been a peach. Not here to chit-chat. We need to speak with Deidra Barnes." He thumbed toward Luther. "It's rather urgent."

She rolled her eyes and scoffed. "Regarding?"

"Sheriff business. Above your paygrade." A sly grin forced one side of his lip to curl. "You understand."

Janice huffed a short breath and clicked the mouse a few times. "Room 105. Try not to disrupt any classes. The fire alarms still have locks because of you."

"Not here to relive the glory. Like I said, business. Good day, Ms. Walsh."

"It's *Mrs. Peterson*. Has been for thirty-five years."

Mills winked and started for the door. "You're right. Jus' never liked the way it rolled off my tongue."

They arrived at the first corridor, the numbers 100 through 110 painted in bold lettering near the top of the door. A draft, lemon-scented floor cleaner, dust, and probably mold, poured out and dried the long cut in his cheek. Before he stepped inside, something gave him pause. A brick flower bed by the entrance was practically vacant, a casualty of the fast-approaching cold, he assumed. Only one vibrant red rose remained among the dozen frayed green stems, a lone soldier ready to battle the winter onslaught ahead.

Luther, with a cue from Mills, leaned against the lockers next to room 105, and Mills peeled open the door slowly. The rows of students shifted toward him, eyes wide and jaws agape. His attempt at subtly needed work. He smiled wanly.

Another feature of his that needed work.

"Good mornin'," he greeted and waved two fingers, then glanced at the teacher behind the desk at the front. "I need to speak with Deidra Barnes."

Her emerald eyes, magnified by the glasses riding her upturned nose, shot open in an instant. She let out a shaky breath and curled a loose auburn strand behind her ear. Something about her was familiar. Like an itch you couldn't quite scratch or trying to recall a dream some days later, it bothered him to high hell. He might've seen her somewhere around town. *The gas station off Fifth Street? A traffic stop? Margery's? Al's Grocery?* Well, trying to jog the occasion wasn't worth the headache. Probably a result of his constant buzz while on duty. He instead diverted to the name written on the upper left side of the whiteboard.

"Mrs. Baker, I presume?"

"*Yes* … um, yes, sir," she blurted out and sealed her mouth shut. She was nervous, and Mills could pick that out easier than an ingrown hair on his own chest. He wasn't going crazy, and now he was certain. She recognized him too.

Mrs. Baker glanced over her students. "Deidra Barnes?"

She raised her hand hesitantly in the back, and the whispers around the room grew. The girl stood, rubbed her hands on her jeans, and took three cautious steps toward Mills.

"Will that be all … sir?" the teacher asked.

He nodded and moved the toothpick to the corner of his mouth. "Yes, ma'am. Thank you."

Mills couldn't blame Luther for his overprotective nature

even if he wanted. Though only sixteen, Deidra had blossomed into quite the lovely young woman in the years he had known the Barnes family. She was an odd girl growing up, mostly because of mismatching outfits, the same pigtails each time he had seen her, and her affinity for gore and death.

The first time they met, she had asked him if he had ever killed anyone. He obliged her interest with a shootout story he'd stolen from a newspaper clipping a town over. She was impressed, and Mills quite enjoyed playing hero no matter how gullible the young girl was. Luther obviously loved to take work home with him. Figuratively, of course, Mills had hoped.

Now she had a smooth, brown complexion, hazel eyes, and meticulously braided hair fashioned to a bun at the back of her head. It would surprise any this apple came from the same family tree, Mills most of all. He'd anticipated that growing up without a mother during the crucial teenage changes would further decline her hygiene, as Luther was nonetheless concerned with his own.

*She must've started sneaking magazines behind Luther's back.*

"Hi there, Dee." He held the door open and allowed her to pass through. "We just have a few questions for you."

"What do you mean *we*?" she asked and stopped when Luther moved forward. "Daddy. What are you doing here?"

Luther crossed his large arms. "Jeff thinks you were playing around on my phone. Made a call to the police station. Now I tried to tell him, not my baby, but he wouldn't take no for an answer."

She lowered her head and stared at the tiles. "Daddy … There's something I gotta tell you."

Luther opened his mouth to speak, Mills placed a hand to his shoulder, squeezed Luther's tightened frame, and tilted his head to the tears rolling down Deidra's cheeks.

She picked at the fuzz on her shirt and closed her eyes. "Last Saturday. You were sleepin' on the couch. I had to be able to call him. Let him know you were asleep and I was at the mailbox down the hill. So, I took it." A heavy gulp rattled her throat. "I took your phone, and he picked me up."

Luther cracked his knuckles, and a vein emerged on his neck. "You what?"

"We went to the Landing, and when I told him I wouldn't—" She wiped the tears with her sleeve. "When I said no, he pushed me outta the car and drove off. I had to walk home, and that's when I saw it." Her voice faltered. "I saw the body and called the station. I didn't know what else to do. That awful smell." Deidra's soft whimpers turned to sobs. Luther wrapped his arms around her and smoothed his large hand over her head.

There were a lot of things Mills knew he was mediocre at. Apologies. Abstaining from booze or an easy lay. Sharing emotions. One thing he prided himself on, however, was knowing sincerity where he saw it. There was no chance Dee was involved. Even now, she was fighting the horrible images from that night, he assumed. Someone with no stomach for what was done. He could count himself a suspect before her.

"It's okay, baby. I know." Luther comforted his daughter, almost as if he had forgotten Mills was there with him.

The sheriff pinched the bridge of his nose. "Why don't you two take off? You've obviously got some stuff to sort out. I'll let Janice know she's leaving early."

They both peered at him for a moment. "Am I gonna need a lawyer, Jeff?" Luther glared grimly, and for the first time in a decade of knowing him, the coroner's eyes watered like the season's first rain after a summer drought.

"Nah. I don't believe so. Dee told us everything she knows. She's no guiltier than you or me. Y'all take off. Just get me that autopsy report pronto." He patted Luther's back and hung his head on the way to the office.

⨯

NIGHT DESCENDED ON Fulton, the clouds stretching across the sky until only a few stars in the distance remained visible. Streetlights, though most were burned out, flickered on in rows of two. Mills peered through a single, dilated eye at the stop sign ahead, nearly covered by a low-hanging branch filled with festive autumn leaves.

He waved to the citizens walking along Main Street, quickly emptying like the last hint of sunlight passing over the town. A vacancy he accepted. Welcomed. It wasn't the misdemeanors or traffic violations he was after. Oh, no. There were bigger fish. Hell, if he found someone driving more intoxicated than he was himself, well, he would chalk that up to a win. Enough to pass out on his sofa and rest a bit easier this night.

Truth was, he didn't have more than a few hours' sleep each night in the past decade. A side effect they didn't mention when you pinned on the badge. He licked his bottom lip and savored the sour mash flavor. His flask was still half full. *To the brighter side of thinkin'*, he thought between swigs and even raised the container to give himself a toast absent company. If he kept on as he had the last three circles around Fulton—a steady gulp at each stop sign—the flask wouldn't last long. There wasn't a brighter side to lean on when the booze had dried up.

He pulled halfway into the station's parking lot, stalled the Bronco, turned over the engine again, and parked. The headlamps highlighted the eggshell blinds in both the windows and door. He strutted from Rose with more finesse than half a pint should've allowed, but his dragging boots and breath revealed the obvious.

Holloway, buried deep in the stack of files on her desk, shifted and met his gaze when he careened inside. She turned back to the paperwork abruptly. "Evening, Sheriff."

He winced at the fluorescents raining down. "Damn, it's bright in here. Where's Simmons?"

"Date. Asked me to cover." Her tone, less bubbly than normal, carried a certain irritated edge.

"You gotta stop letting him walk all over ya, kid." Mills raked a hand through his hair, blinked a few times for good measure, and moved forward. "Else that's all he'll ever do."

"Yes, sir."

Mills placed his palm on her shoulder. "Now I'm serious, Jenn. Look at me." Holloway slowly turned in her chair, her sights fixed on the floor. "You have nothing to prove to Simmons. To me. You are a great deputy, and I couldn't be prouder. Now, pack up your shit and get out of here. Next time you let that dipshit walk all over you, I won't hesitate to let him. Clear?"

Holloway nodded. "Won't happen again."

"Don't take shit from the sheep, got it?"

×

THE MID-MORNING SUN grated his skin through tattered curtains, a warmth rivaling the crisp October air. Blankets rested lazily over his feet, kicked off at some point in the night. The ceiling, a pale tint with water splotches from the rains leaking through this past winter, proved familiar. *Home.* He winced at the headache that seemed to visit him each morning, a pestering nuisance ibuprofen by the fistful couldn't fix.

Mills checked his phone on the nightstand. Two missed calls and a text. The name *Luther* lit up on the screen in bold letters.

*"I have an ID."*

# CHAPTER NINE

*One month missing*

"IT'S A LEFT down Madison," Holloway said from the passenger seat.

Mills cocked his brow and offered a sideways glance. "I know where I'm going, missy. Been walking all over this town before you were a seed in your daddy's sac."

"Gross."

He chuckled and sipped from the spiked mug in his shifting hand. "This is a shortcut. I promise ya." Though Mills said the words with utter confidence, he even questioned whether his internal GPS led them astray. Jerry Kent's Salvage. Nothing more than a patch of land filled with old beaters and worthless scrap. The exact place he drove his first car off the gravel lot, a '70 Ford Maverick. Where the rust hadn't gotten to was green like a pear. Cracked headlights. Missing bumper. Took a few pushes for the engine to turn over, but after a bit of work, there wasn't a drive-in movie he didn't see or the inside of a skirt his hand hadn't been up. Mills laughed again, more so at the memory of Janice Walsh.

The tires splashed over muddied water, and the wakes sloshed to the barren fields at the shoulder. Trees trickled in patches to the left, while the right was empty and overgrown with weeds and fiddleneck. The clouds overhead had parted, making way for the afternoon sun slowly lifting in the horizon. He pulled a cigarette from the pack on his dash and handed it over to Holloway.

She shook her head. "Trying to quit."

Mills placed the brown filter between his lips. A cottony texture greeted his tongue, and he lit it. "So am I."

"We've been to the salvage yard before. How'd we miss it?"

Her curiosity rarely failed to miss the mark. Natural instinct, more so than a wolf keen to its prey. One no amount of training prepared a deputy for. Something he noticed as easily as the way her eyes changed color to her moods. Her temperament was always easy to gauge, at least to Mills. "Not sure. But hell, I ain't complaining. A lead's a lead. You sure you don't wanna get some sleep, kid? Must be exhausted."

"I'm fine."

He knew better than to believe her. She was stubborn, much like himself. Cut from the same ragged cloth and dipped in kerosene. "Do you—?" He cleared his throat and tried once more. "Do you wanna talk about it?"

"Nothing to talk about, Jeff."

"Well. If you ever need to, um, talk about anything." The edge in his voice withered to some form of a sincere rasp. "You know where to find me."

She smiled, almost suppressed it, too. He knew better. *He knew her better.*

They arrived at the salvage yard, a few acres enclosed by sheet metal fencing and large wrought-iron gates at the forefront. Simmons leaned against his squad car, freckled arms crossed, and a far-too-pleased-with-himself expression plastered on his pasty face. Wasn't often Simmons had the lead on anything around town—that right was normally reserved for Holloway and her unmatched prowess. One glance said everything the deputy was probably thinking internally.

*I did it. I did it, and not her.*

Mills nearly stalled the Bronco pulling in, and Holloway jumped out before he could stop fully.

"Where was it?" she demanded more than asked.

"I think we should all take a moment to acknowledge who is obviously the linchpin of this force." A smirk crawled from one side of Simmons's mouth to the other like an earthworm.

"Simmons." Mills stepped out into the humid and moist grounds. The grass, fresh with dew, stuck to his polished boots. He cursed to himself and shook off the bright green blades. "Stop being an asshole and answer the question."

"A few miles in the back. Torn to shit. Window busted in. Dents and scrapes. Sledgehammer from the look of it. That's not all."

Holloway raised a brow, and she, too, crossed her arms. "What?"

"It's not red like the APB. Someone rattle-canned the thing black. Joseph Kent went to remove the engine and noticed the original red paint inside the hood, then called me over to take a look."

Mills winced. "Show me."

Rattle-canning was for those unfortunate enough to own a shit bucket in dire need of a paint job without the funds to do so. There were a few cars around Fulton with a spray-paint finish, and the owners had to decide between groceries or a better appearance for their A to B.

Simmons led them through an array of vehicles, some stripped to the frame and most on cinder blocks. Spare parts never took a long residency here. Whether the alternators or ignitions were purchased flat out or taken after dark, most of the vehicles couldn't manage to turn over a few days after ending up here.

Holloway, though clueless where to go, kept an even pace while Mills fell to the rear. His back twisted from the uneven ground. A stiffness built in his bones that added to his stern demeanor.

"How much farther?" Holloway asked.

"Calm your tits. I already told ya it's buried pretty deep in the yard."

Holloway slugged Simmons in the shoulder with more force than he'd give her credit, and he staggered to remain upright. "Christ. You hit like a man."

"Talk 'bout my tits again and the next one will be aimed lower."

Mills grinned and shook his head. *Atta girl. Take no shit from the sheep.* The way he saw it, no one, not Simmons nor himself, could ever question her. He had seen firsthand what the deputy was capable of. Mills would be lying if he said he didn't secretly wish the ginger dunce would keep pestering her. The young vet would end up on his ass faster than Mills could light another smoke.

The gravel beneath their feet lessened to a few pebbles in a sea of loose dirt, each step requiring firm footing and care.

The fencing outline came into view, as did the silhouette of a black car among the silver and beige. An easy spot. The headlights were a dead giveaway. Round like a bug's eyes. *How the hell did we miss it?*

"Here it is. Think we have a match?"

Holloway peered through the dust on the windshield. "I'll look up the VIN—"

"No point, kid. This is it."

She tilted her head and stared curiously. "How can you be sure?"

"I've been doing this job long enough to know that when something seems out of place, it usually is. Simmons, go talk to Joseph and see what information they have and when it was brought here."

Out of instinct, Simmons lifted his right hand to salute but stopped himself. "Yes, sir."

Mills removed the leather gloves from his back pocket, slid them on, and approached the passenger door; the window was smashed in and glass bits blanketed the gray seat. Holloway did the same but maneuvered around the driver's side. Fist-sized dents marked up the spray primer exterior, applied rapidly if he had to guess by the subtle red streaks remaining. The door squealed when he wrenched it open, and the fractured shards spilled to the dirt.

"Careful. There's glass everywhere."

Holloway nodded and inspected the pockets inside the driver's door. He anticipated the usual paperwork stowed in the dash. Registration, insurance cards, napkins from the drive-thru.

But there wasn't a single shred of paper to be found. The

space was hollow, and despite sitting for God knows how long, there wasn't a speck of dust to take a white glove to. He checked the center console next. *Zip.* Not even the sugary ring from a fountain drink cup stained the bottom of the cupholders. The car, the only evidence they had at this point, had been wiped clean.

# CHAPTER TEN

*One month missing*

"HOW LONG DO you think it's been here?" Holloway stood upright and wiped away the sweat at her brow.

Mills, still digging under the passenger seat, took an upholstery-filled breath. He leaned out and glanced at the dirt near the bumper. "No tracks. A few weeks maybe. You check the trunk?"

"Not yet."

"Well, get to it, missy. Don't wanna be out here after dark."

She nodded, lifted the latch under the dash, and moved for the rear end. The trunk's rusted hinges shrieked when she opened it, and a soft rustling passed through the backseat. Glass bits and shards overwhelmed the area Mills searched, far too many to count the pricks his hand endured. He grazed his palm under the front seat one last time for good measure. *Nothing.*

Sheriff Mills allowed the sudden gust to soothe over his neck. Invited it even. An afternoon baking in the sun, without a damn clue, nonetheless, proved taxing for a man of his years.

He hunched to his knees, boots burying in grass and dirt,

and held a hand to his chest. The once-steady—and quite possibly irregular—thump increased in his ears. Each vein in his neck joined in sporadic symphony. An ache, a throbbing pain, radiated outward. He clutched a firm grip on the khaki uniform top and focused on the gasps he heaved in. Mills's face, now on the verge of purple, pinched tightly. Saliva gathered at his lips and spilled to the underbrush beneath him.

"Hey, Sheriff? Doesn't look like much back here. Spare tire. Some jumper cables."

Mills's body constricted fully. His jaw clamped shut. His arms and legs seized. He tried to wiggle his toes, but those too seemed to stick in place. His heart rate spiked, and the loud thumping banged horrendously in his ears like a kick drum. The wind, grass rustling, Holloway sifting through the truck, the sound of his own panicked thoughts, dulled to a high-pitched ringing. He collapsed to the ground, and his bulging eyes distorted the image of Jenn rushing to him.

# CHAPTER ELEVEN

## Holloway

*One month missing*

JENN HOLLOWAY SAT in a hospital chair across from the sheriff as she had for the past three hours—her arms folded over her chest, watching him for any sign of a struggle. To breathe, to open his eyes, to even wiggle his fingers. Something to know the old bastard wouldn't find paradise lying on his back flanked by a machine with more wires than she could count. The rhythmic beeps made sleep impossible, but she didn't mind.

"Sorry to disturb you, ma'am," the nurse said the same way he had two rounds before. "Just need to check your dad's vitals."

Jenn didn't correct him. She wasn't sure if it was due to a lack of energy or because some part of her liked the way it sounded. A daughter, too, would have pounded on their father's chest, screaming for them to wake up. Luckily enough, the CPR class Jenn had taken not even a month ago repeated in her head the moment Jeff collapsed. Had she skipped the course along with Simmons, well, she might be staring at her boss in a box instead of on a bed with a tube under his nose and an IV protruding from his forearm.

Jeff looked at peace in a way, to her at least. For once, the wrinkles above his brow didn't resemble fleshy canyons like they did when he scowled. His mouth wasn't pursed to the side reserved for chewing tobacco, and finally, his eyes. Jeff wasn't peering, almost squinting at her the way he had so many times before, a hint of judgment in each blue—near silver—iris. She was never sure why he looked at her the way he did. Said the things he said. But something in her knew Sheriff Jeffrey Mills did so for a reason. He hadn't led her astray so far, minus the occasional offering of booze while on duty, of course.

After the nurse finished penning down the glowing red and blue numbers on the screen, he left as quickly as he entered, saying nothing further.

The doctor had mentioned an issue with Jeff's health but wouldn't go into specifics, even when Jenn practically displayed her badge the way a gameshow attendant might swirl their hands around a new car. "We will know the severity after a few more tests," was what he left her with. So, now all she could do was wait and watch.

"Jenn," her walkie chirped, Simmons's voice coming through the static. "Joe has the Neon loaded up and is going to take it to the station. How's the sheriff doing?"

"No change yet. Do me a favor, will ya?"

"I'm not working your night shift again. Forget it. My shoes still have puke from the party I busted the last time!"

Jenn shook her head. "No, dipshit. Have Joseph take the car to Jeff's house. If you bring Sarah's car to the station everyone in town will see it. Next thing you know there will be reporters at our doorstep. The sheriff would want to keep this quiet until we see what we can find."

"That's not up to you, Jenn. I'm simply following protocol. And, as the ranking deputy on duty, I have determined this to be the best course—"

"Simmons!" she cut him off and caught the attention of the nurses posted at the desk outside the room. "Just shut the fuck up and do it. If I'm wrong, then it'll be my ass, not yours."

The line went silent for a moment until a simple, "Okay," broke through.

*This is what he would've wanted.* Something in her knew it. After close to a hundred hours on patrol with Jeff, it was more than a suspicion—more like a telepathic thought had passed through his unconscious mind and into hers. She felt the sensation a lot as of late. As if Jenn knew exactly what the sheriff would do or say before he did. If she was wrong, well, Simmons would finally get the spotlight. The chance to outdo her after he failed to hit a single mark on the range while Jenn's target had spot-on grouping at the chest and head.

No. She wasn't wrong about this.

"Okay. His garage will do for now. Make it happen," Jenn said and wiped the loose strands away from her face.

"Yes, *Sheriff.*" His voice was sarcastic, but another thing she didn't mind because of the way it sounded. *Sheriff. Sheriff Holloway.* There was something about the five syllables she couldn't shake. Like the past had suddenly rewritten itself from orphan to town protector. She wouldn't let another person get hurt on her watch. Wouldn't let her size or strength get in the way of saving someone again. No.

Jenn Holloway would be there.

An alarm ravaged the stagnant air in the room, and on impulse, the young deputy clutched the button fastening her service pistol. Lights flashed and painted an odd red on the walls. It wasn't the fire alarm as she expected it to be. It was …

"Get back!" he yelled at her, donned with a face mask and blue gloves. It was the nurse from before, but he didn't have the same friendly expression. His widened eyes were in pure panic.

*Beep. Beep. Beep.* Before Jenn could even step outside, four more nurses rushed in, and a doctor in tow, his white lab coat only buttoned at his midsection.

"What's—?" she tried to ask above the noise.

The alarm continued. *Beep. Beep. Beep.*

"He's flatlining, Doctor."

Holloway stared at Mills, convulsing on the bed, his weathered face twisting each time he writhed. *Beep. Beep. Beep.* The pit in her stomach dropped an extra inch. "Is … is he going to be okay?" She was no longer clutching the button on her pistol, but her fabric of her uniform shirt. "Is he going to be okay?" This time she screamed, and everyone in the room took turns glancing at her.

"You need to leave," the nurse said, an arm at each of her shoulders. "You can't be in here right now."

Part of her wanted to drop the guy. A swift knee to the gut was all it would take, and then she would be there, holding Jeff's hand while they did whatever they could to revive him. If he did go, well, he'd die knowing she was there in his final moments. But no, all Jenn did was follow the nurse out and watch him close the white curtains after reentering Mills's room.

The people in the waiting area stared, each of their eyes gaping with pity. Jenn tried to ignore it, but when someone shouted, "clear," behind the white curtain, there was no stopping it. Tears rolled down her cheeks until they finally cut off at her chin. *Not yet, Jeff,* she pleaded. *I can't do this by myself.* Part of her hoped Mills heard her. Wished he did.

*Not yet.*

# CHAPTER TWELVE

## Mills

*One month missing*

HIS FIRST BREATH in, antiseptic and cheap laundry detergent, whistled into his stuffy nose. Mills opened a single eye and peered around the small room. Four walls, painted in a cream color, boxed him in. Charts, motivational posters, and more charts. The bed proved stiff, uncomfortable on his spine, and colder than the metal railings on either side.

He glanced down and expected the same khaki shirt. His brow lifted and both eyes shot open at once. The gown—navy and gray polka dots—itched his skin to high hell. Hairs ripped from his forearm from the IV catheter's tape. Nothing, though, compared to the dull throbs pounding his skull.

"There he is," Holloway said and stood from a chair in the corner. Her hair, pulled in a messy ponytail, draped to her left shoulder. Dark circles rested under her eyes, and any ounce of makeup she may have had at some point was now scrubbed clean. "Sleep all right?"

Mills opened his mouth to speak, but the words rattled his throat.

"No, no. Save your strength. You need your rest, Sheriff."

"What … what happened?" he managed to ask, his voice hoarse.

"Doc said you suffered a heart attack. Scared the shit outta me, too. One minute you're everyday-asshole Jeff, the next you're rolling in the dirt."

"That's *Sheriff asshole* to you, kid." A gentle smile stretched across his face. "How long was I out?"

She tilted her phone, and the glowing screen highlighted the red in her eyes. He assumed the late hour to be the culprit, but then again, she may have shed a few tears for this old dog. "A little over five hours," she replied, and tucked her phone away.

"Christ. And the car?"

"Joseph offered to tow it to the station, but I figured that'd start a media frenzy. It's parked in your garage for now. Just 'til we finish the search."

*Good girl.* "Not bad. Doc say how long I'm stuck here?"

Her mouth thinned to a straight line.

"Come on. Tell me." He narrowed his good eye at her.

"Said at least the next few days—"

"Fuck sakes," he huffed out, loud enough for the nurses posted at the counter to jerk their attention to his room.

"Maybe longer."

"Why didn't you just let me die?"

Her mouth curled to a smirk. "I wanted to. But Simmons screamed like an idiot and called 911. Not much I could do after that."

"Simmons isn't CPR trained. Ambulance would've taken five. Shit, maybe even ten if they knew it was me dying. So, I guess I have you to thank. Don't I?"

"I'm glad you're alright, Sheriff." Holloway turned for the door and took one last glance at him before leaving. Her eyes said everything she refused to tell him outright. She couldn't let him, all his sins included, die in the brush on some scrapyard. No. She saved him. Not for some debt owed or because it was her duty, but to save the one person she trusted. A friend. A father almost.

"Thanks, kid," he muttered, only loud enough for himself to hear. Enough to disrupt the steadily beeping machine to his left.

*You're not him, Jeffrey.*

Those final, haunting words somehow worked their way to the forefront, his mother's voice accompanying them. *Don't become him.* He shook his head to stow the thoughts back to the cage he so desperately sealed shut. Mills had always carried a general disdain for hospitals—more so after she had passed—but now all he could feel was outright disgust.

He adjusted for a few minutes until he realized a comfortable position wasn't possible. The pillow cradled his head more like a bag of sand. The thin blankets wrapped around his legs and waist did little to prevent the draft from forcing goose bumps on his dehydrated skin. He scoffed. Cursed. Fought the urge to rip off everything and stomp away from this miserable place, but his looming headache served as an advocate. The one thing handcuffing him here.

Footsteps echoed down the hall, and a silhouette stopped at his door. The clipboard in his hands came into view first, followed by a thin, lanky man in a white lab coat, black, ear-length hair combed over to one side. His eyes, a gentle brown, fixed on Mills. He smiled out of courtesy. The same grin you'd see on a restaurant server or car salesperson—anything but sincere.

"Good evening, Sheriff," he greeted, and penned Mills's vitals.

"You the doc?"

"Yes, sir. I am Dr. Thompson, the physician overseeing your treatment. How are you feeling? Scale of one to ten?" He readied his ballpoint pen and stared forward.

"If I say one, will that get me the hell outta here?"

His soft voice thickened. "Sheriff Mills, a heart attack is fairly serious. Usually, an early sign of worse things to come. I know this isn't ideal, but I would appreciate your cooperation."

"What are you sayin', Doc?" Mills, for the first time since he arrived, sat up straight.

"Your kidneys, Sheriff. Lung and liver problems as well. None are in the shape they should be at your age. To put it quite plainly, your body is shutting down like a worn-out Buick. I'm surprised you've lasted this long." Doctor Thompson paused and rested the clipboard on his knees. "This heart attack was a warning sign. A storm your body, frankly, isn't prepared to handle."

"Is there anything I can do?"

He shrugged, and the white lab coat bunched near his shoulders. "Change your diet. Lay off the bottle. Cut back on the smokes."

"There goes my Saturday night." Mills scoffed.

The doctor narrowed his eyes and interlocked his fingers.

"That may ... prolong the remaining years."

Mills stared at the ceiling lights, wishing blindness over welling up in front of the young man before him. "How much time would that buy?"

"It's near impossible to estimate with so many variables."

Mills drew a throaty inhale. "Make it possible. How long, Doc? Don't sugarcoat it."

"Five, maybe ten years."

"Well, shit." He sucked air between his teeth. "I had a good run. If I'm gonna die, it will be on my terms. Unhook me, will ya?"

"Sheriff Mills, you need to be closely monitored for at least a few days. That's protocol. You are at serious risk right now to suffer another—"

Mills waved his hand. "I decline treatment. Now undo this shit before I charge you with obstruction." A grin emerged, and he lowered his head. "I have a teacher to find."

×

TWO PILLS. A long pull from the coffee he grabbed at the cafeteria on the way out. Two more pills. He repeated this a few times. Enough to lose count after driving away from the hospital, through town, and around the bend leading to his house.

Mills parked a few feet from his porch, the same spot he allowed the Bronco a night's rest while he stirred late into the evening, lucky for even a few hours. His boots adjusted to the staircase, and he ascended a small step at a time, counting each of them off in his head.

Dust particles swayed in the sunlight passing inside. A beige couch faced the box TV on a rickety wooden stand—the kind that required an afternoon's worth of assembly and always seemed to have leftover parts. Antennas lifted from the back with an obnoxious bend. He twisted the knob until a table lamp glowed in full effect, lighting the maple nightstand beneath the TV as well as the ashtray full of loose Marlboro butts.

Mills passed into the kitchen and ignored the dishes filling his sink, nearly level with the windowpane overseeing vacant fields for miles until they reached oak coppices. He pulled a beer from the fridge—the only reason he had kept it plugged in for as of late—and bit off the cap using his back molars.

A simple thrust slammed the door shut, nearly taking his expired coupons and photos with it. One in particular stood out, at least for him. A postcard. Not one he received from a friend or relative. Never did get those sorts of greetings. Just a card he found in a gas station years ago. Three Rocks Beach in Half Moon Bay. South of San Francisco with a sight worth the would-be day or two drive. Ocean water cascaded over the milky sand and reflected a clifftop observing the Pacific. It was the one place on his bucket list, should he ever leave the hellhole he called home.

To walk barefoot on the cushiony shore, his fingers interlocked with another's, laughing as the gentle waves washed toward their knees. It could've happened if he hadn't shut off the world around him. If he had taken some of his father's advice with the same grain of salt this beach so prominently displayed. *Duty first.* Somehow duty became the only. Even still, he would glance at this postcard between rounds, wishing to enjoy the image in person at least once, alone if need be.

His office was between the kitchen and bedroom, a cold, vacant space holding a comfy leather armchair, broad mahogany desk, and half-empty bottle of whiskey in the bottom drawer. A bookshelf hugged two corners on the right, though shelf may be more accurate given the lack of literature. He plopped himself to the chair and pulled from the bottle's neck; a bitter taste rolled over his tongue and washed down his gravel-like throat.

The typewriter in front of him was army green and had a label fixed just below the space key. Property of the FCSD. When the station upgraded to computers a decade or two ago, Mills took one for memory's sake. Never did see the point in computers, not when there was gratification in every keystroke chime. "If it ain't broke," he'd say. A fresh piece of paper in the cylinder, and a long swig from his beer. He stared at the crisp white edges for a moment, then positioned his fingers over the keys.

×

MILLS OPENED THE rear door to the Dodge Neon, intent on combing through every inch of the backseat. The tire marks and thrashed dirt leading to his garage showed the struggle his deputies had getting the damned thing inside. Not to mention the slanted parking. *Simmons.* He laughed.

He smoothed a gloved hand over the gray cushion, starting first at the headrest and down to the floorboard.

Nothing. Not even a small tear in the fabric. He shaped his fingers like a knife and cut into the fold between the middle and window seat. Found a few loose coins.

It wasn't until he heard the squad car engine filling the rural landscape that he stood upright and glanced at the horizon. He knew the sound better than most. Crown Vic. Early 2000s. The same roaring pistons you'd hear in your sleep when you spent fifteen hours a day behind the wheel.

Holloway parked behind the Bronco and stepped outside. Her hair struggled to break free from her tightly fitted bun in the last of the evening drafts.

"What the hell are you doing here?"

"I should ask you the same question," she replied. "I went back to the hospital, and they said you were gone."

"Never did like bedpans. Something about the piss splashing off the metal bottom onto your ass cheeks."

She laughed and stopped at the garage. "So, you good to go?"

"Who, me? Healthy as a horse. Doc said this old ticker still has miles to spare."

"And what did the doctor really say?"

Mills buried his face in the backseat of the Neon, certain in his steady voice, but the stiff wrinkles on his brow may have been easier to read than Braille. "Jus' told you. I'm fine. Said I should take it easy for the next couple days."

She leaned against a workbench near the driver's side and scraped her boots on the cement. "Need some help?"

"With this? Nah, I can handle it. But there is something I need you to grab. It's on my office desk inside. Paperwork I need you to look over. You know my spelling ain't what it used to be."

She shrugged and set off for the house.

Mills dug his hand to the next cushiony crevice and shoved it wrist deep. He pinched his fingers between the two seats. Something caught his pinky. Small, thin, and shaped like a credit card. One wrong move and he'd have to rip apart the entire car to get to it. *Slowly*, he chanted to himself. With careful pressure, he squeezed it and slid upward. The card, too many colors to be a driver's license, stared back at him. Blue with bright yellow font.

"Jeff?" Holloway's voice drew him out. Her eyes, a small gleam in each, widened. In the deputy's hand was a piece of paper, the same paper he had typed no more than an hour ago. *I acknowledge Jennifer Holloway as my successor*, he had written. *Brilliant beyond her years. None better suited.* There were, of course, some grammar issues, but his review was nonetheless impressive for such a young officer.

Although coming to grips with his own departure was difficult, he would be certain someone he trusted could carry on the mantle. His father had ensured that his only son would carry on his legacy, no matter how broken or bottle soaked it was. Jenn was the Mills's only hope for a true sheriff to break the cycle. A decent, hardworking, honest person to bring some form of light to the position. She was it. Holloway was his redemption.

Jenn wrapped her arms around his hunched shoulders and pulled him in close.

"Easy, kid. Don't go getting soft on me."

"Thank you."

"No reason for gratitude. You've earned it." He held her

at arm's length, and she wiped her hand under each eye. "Now help me finish strong, huh? Go out with another win?"

"We'll find her, Jeff. I promise you."

"We may have someone who could give us some answers." Mills lifted the student ID between them, and they both stared at the photo. "Now why the hell would a teacher have this?"

# PART II
# The Teacher

# CHAPTER THIRTEEN

## Sarah

*Twenty days before Sarah went missing*

"Mrs. Baker?"

She said nothing at first. The paper in front of her, Jeremy Pearson's to be exact, was shaping up to be another tiptoeing the edge of passing marks. Had he not shown considerable effort with the assignment and finally learned the difference between *there*, *their*, and *they're*, she might've given him another F to tack on his fridge. But, Sarah Baker appreciated hard work the most, regardless of how flat the attempt fell. It was, after all, his best work yet. She scribbled at the top of the page in red and glanced up from the C-.

"Yes, Mr. Watkins?"

"May I use the restroom?" he asked, eyeing the bookmark labeled hall pass on the corner of her desk.

She grabbed the wrinkled bookmark, debated adding a new layer of laminate to straighten it out, and handed it to him. He said his thanks; a slight smile flexed his jawline, and he turned for the door to the hallway. It was difficult not to notice how kind the summer was to him. The way his now-broad shoulders swayed with each step like he still hadn't gotten used to carrying them. Shawn had always been tall for his age since she'd known him, but now his height rivaled that of adult men. She watched him leave the class for longer than she should have. Longer than she had before.

Sarah retreated her gaze back to the assignments at once, fearful some of the other students may have taken notice. All it took was a rapid scan to the desks in front of her to be certain. They were, thanks to her, preoccupied—too preoccupied in fact to notice a thing outside the chapters they had been assigned. She crossed her legs and adjusted the flower-print dress over her knees. An assortment of pink stargazer lilies scattered down her hips and flourished up her torso, hugging her feminine curves. It was nothing distasteful, even if all the boys in her class seemed to take notice and sit with their ears perked like dogs waiting for a treat.

She eyed each of the students between glances to the grading pile on her desk. The collection tray was overflowing and hid the tabletop she herself stained this past summer. Another assignment. Late homework. Spelling tests. The mound seemingly hit reset every five minutes, adding layer upon layer of stark white.

When Shawn returned to the class, she did little else than nod in his direction. Ten minutes later and the bell rang. The tone was shrill. Deafening might've been a better word. She brushed the loose bangs from her brow, forced a grin, and nodded to the students on their way out.

"Have a good day," Sarah announced to one after the other. She beamed once more, the same expression she'd expect a person to fake when a photographer used that awful phrase, "Say cheese." In any photo, this was—for her at least—a way to ensure somewhere between a smile and grimace. A few pictures, including her own wedding album, had the same irritated smirk.

"Have a good day, Mrs. Baker," Shawn said on the way to the door, a small hesitation in his step. Dimples emerged on his cheeks. She cursed herself for noticing those, too.

"You too, Shawn." It wouldn't be a good day though. She knew this, but she couldn't bring herself to say it aloud.

*Bzzt. Bzzt. Bzzt.* Her phone, resting at the bottom of her purse among granola bar wrappers and other miscellaneous things, vibrated against the tile floor. She watched the light glow inside the open flap, and after a few seconds the screen went dark again. The classroom door swung shut and eventually clicked into its rightful place. It would stay there until the second period flock thrusted it open, of course, disrupting the stillness of her room with dragging feet and the groans and grunts reminiscent of farm animals.

*"Gonna be stuck at work late. Won't be home for dinner."*

Her sound was somewhere between a sigh and a scoff. No apology from her husband, just the same message she received more than a dozen times now. His paychecks certainly didn't account for the extra hours of work. No, they remained the same. Barely enough to cover the bills. After all this overtime one would assume a line for promotion. That, too, was wishful thinking. He hadn't said a good thing about work in longer than she could recall.

No. It didn't add up. She knew John Baker, and deep down, her husband was hiding something.

The corridor lights, a muted yellow, glared down to the scuffed tiles. Lockers lined each side, most blue with the occasional red. Banners swayed as the double doors were ripped open, hinges squealing at the coming and going of less-than-eager students making their rounds like hospital nurses.

Four minutes until second period. Not enough time to sneak to her car for a quick smoke, but caffeine could help the hunger rumbling her insides. Morning sun caressed her cheeks when she stepped outside and marched through the teenage trenches. Conversations better left unsaid were forced upon her ears as if blared over the intercom. Sarah ignored it and continued onward.

The teacher's lounge was a small sanctuary, but she couldn't stay too long without feeling the narrow walls close in around her. The counter, a faded gray against blue backsplash, was like the ocean on an overcast day. There were no seagull squawks or tides rushing to shore though, only a sink—practically overflowing—offering the pungent stench of mildew and neglect. Could have been the dirty dishes or the scum building around the ring that made breathing through her mouth necessary at times.

She eyed the coffeepot next to the sink, and although it was turned on, the container was filled with no more than a quarter of a cup. *Of course.* It had been happening more frequently, someone not having the decency or common sense to refill it. More often than not, she'd find herself tilting the glass container for the last few drops the way she imagined a drug addict panhandled loose change. *Just a few drops, sir. Please? I can't make it through third period without my fix.*

"Hey there, Sarah."

Coach Nathan Tanner's voice was all too familiar. She had grown accustomed to his disgusting charm—if you could indeed call it that. An ego his appearance wasn't ready to cash. The little hair remaining on his head was tucked inside a blue baseball cap riding his brow line. Nathan had put on extra weight over the summer, and his now large stomach bulged from the windbreaker he wore daily.

"Hi, Coach Tanner," she replied but made it a point to not look at him directly.

"I love the dress. It looks amazing on you." He leaned against the counter within view and slurped from his travel mug. It was bright red, and much like Coach Nathan Tanner, extra-large. It became apparent he was the one siphoning off the coffee supply, leaving the other faculty members with nothing more than regular roast remnants.

*Asshole*, she wished she could say out loud. While pouring the last little bit of coffee into a paper cup, she turned her back to him. She wouldn't give him the satisfaction of a response. No. She would stand her ground and endure the stuck-up bitch stigma spread around campus if need be. Nathan Tanner wasn't in the business of friendly compliments just because. There was always a catch. One comment would lead to two, which would lead to unwanted touching, and eventually he'd have the gall to try something because *she led him on*. No. Sarah Baker wouldn't fall for it. She was too smart for that.

It wasn't until he sucked air through his teeth that she realized that she accidentally gave him the view he was hoping for. His windbreaker crunched together like autumn leaves. He might have been rubbing his stomach, but she was far too revolted to turn around. She tilted the cup to the ceiling, gulped down the small amount of brew, and rushed for the door without looking back.

"We have a game Friday night. It'd be great if you came out and showed some support." He twisted the knobs at the sink, and water spit to porcelain mugs at the bottom.

She stopped at the threshold, not to continue the conversation but because the slight hairs on the back of her neck stood at attention. His whistling, off-tune, mimicked the band's triumphant songs blared from the bleachers on Friday nights. The sound was unnerving, and not only because of the shrill pitch. It was his doing. The sensation of being watched at all times. Coach Tanner kept an eye on more at Fulton High than his team, which could've used more coaching with a record of 0-2 this season.

Sarah dismissed the noise, the constant buzzing in her head telling her *steer clear*, and she pushed outside. The October air, rich with wilting grass and fallen leaves, seeped heavily through her nose as she walked to her classroom, slowly, but intent on beating the bell.

She glanced up from her vigilant march, and his smile greeted her from outside the hallway to her classroom. He wasn't alone, though she somehow sensed he wanted to be. A girl had positioned herself in front of Shawn, her head arched, demanding his attention while speaking—more so with her hands than mouth. Straight blond hair fell over her shoulders and bounced with each word he didn't seem interested in.

"Hi, Mrs. Baker," Shawn interrupted the girl buzzing in his ear like a gnat. The sun glinted off his gentle brown complexion, highlighting his firm jawline.

Her cheeks warmed and tightened unconsciously, and she fought off the grin by biting down on her tongue until she was certain her teeth might cut it clean off. She curled her loose red strands behind her ear and continued forward. A simple nod was all she would give him. All she could give him.

"Good morning, *Mrs. Baker*," Hannah said, her tone lacking enthusiasm. She whipped her hair to the side and sized Sarah up, her glare moving from Sarah's flats, up her torso, and finally meeting her face.

"Hello, Hannah," she said, keen to spit out her name as carelessly as students spat gum on the walkway.

She passed them with her sights to the floor, though she longed for a second glance at him. *One last time* was the idea in her head. A simple, damning, inexplicably wrong idea, and with that, Sarah continued to stare at the cement.

"Have a nice day," Hannah said snidely. Sarah wasn't excused from being taunted by a stuck-up child every now and then. Sometimes they were her students, other times they were ghosts from her own playground experiences. What Hannah had truly meant in Sarah's mind was *I hope you choke.*

More obscene words passed through her head than she cared to admit. *Spoiled little bitch* among them, but she wouldn't give her the satisfaction. Sarah simply smiled and opened the doors leading into the hallway.

# CHAPTER FOURTEEN

*Two months missing*

THE STAIRS TWISTED. The boards cracked. He shifted his weight from one step to the next. Then came the whistle, sharp and always off-tune. The song was unrecognizable but no less panic-inducing. She braced herself for the inevitable, the same thing she did each time he came to the cellar. Every day expecting him to have a knife, a pipe, a rock, for Christ's sake. For her captor to finally finish what he started.

*This is it.*

His denim pant legs swiped as he descended, and water dripped to the concrete from the glass in his hand. In the other was a small, plastic medicine cup with pills clanging against the sides. Her daily dose. The cellar shadow eclipsed his face, but he visibly glared at her. The man paused and set the water glass and pills to the floor. It wasn't until he turned for the stairs that he did the one thing he seemingly swore not to. He spoke.

"For your fever." His voice was hefty, but the words came out soft, at least softer than she imagined they would be.

Tylenol. Not the pills she expected. *My fever?* An ache thumped in her chest. *My fucking fever?* The flames in her belly were strong enough to put his death at a higher priority than her own escape. *This is it.* She rushed the man and wrapped her arms around his throat. He grabbed hold of her wrists and tossed her back easily. She attacked again, a savage scream fleeing her lungs. The man responded with a vicious swipe, his stone-like hand colliding against Sarah's temple.

The already dim lighting shuddered off and on in her eyes. She collapsed and rolled against the filthy ground, her pink cheeks now adding red to the mix. Her dress lifted to her hip bones. The pink stargazer lilies evenly matched the color of cuts and scrapes on her legs. Some fresh and a few acquired during the beginning of her confinement.

He cracked his knuckles, appearing to debate another slap for good measure. Despite the noticeable longing to do so, he kneeled, narrowed his eyes, and waited for her attention. He examined her battered legs, and his lingering try-it-again scowl trickled up her thighs to her dirty face. She fumbled to sit up and fought the chains over her wrists. Each movement rattled the woven metal like a pocketful of change.

"Why are you doing this?"

He tilted his head and gnashed his teeth. An exhale flared his nostrils, but he didn't speak. Didn't move despite her expectation.

"What do you want with me?"

There was a subtle crack in his knees when he finally stood and turned toward the staircase. As his foot hit the bottom step, the whistling began once more.

She closed her eyes and prayed the tune wouldn't continue in her head long after he stopped. It didn't work. The whistle had become her companion. The devil on her shoulder cursing her at every turn. Her eyelashes stuck together as confined tears made their escape, seeping from the fleshy prison cells and down her cheeks—one more swollen now than the other. *Calm down*, she told herself, though it was difficult to hear anything besides the sharp noise he tormented her with.

The glass at her feet, clear and mostly full, tempted her dry, scratchy throat. She reached for the cup and took note of the dirt under her chipped fingernails. A reminder. A filthy trophy to each day she survived this hell. She tried not to notice how deep the debris was lodged into the delicate skin beneath them.

But she did.

Her chains rattled while lifting the glass to her lips. Small sips. That was all she allowed herself. One gulp would lead to two, and before she knew it the cup would be empty, leaving her both disappointed and thirstier than before. No. She would resist the desire to rear the drink if she could. To savor the refreshing liquid like it might be her last. For all she knew, it could be.

She took the pills without protest and another small sip from the glass. If only he would give her something to stave off the panic in her chest. The crippling anxiety of the unknown. He hadn't touched her until today, and now, she wasn't so sure he'd have trouble doing it again. One more sip, one more wave of terror seizing her limbs.

The days blended into a nameless period. There were no school bells signaling the end of her torture. No early morning alarms. Nothing. She could only wait. Wait for this man to have his way with her. Wait to be butchered alive. Wait for someone—anyone—to save her.

The shackles clanked together, reminiscent of a rabies tag on a dog's collar when bolting toward its owner or a new hand to feed from. Had she been reduced to that? A pet? Waiting patiently for her new owner to return and keep her fed? Teacher's pet, but she knew her situation called for something worse. *Pet teacher.*

Sarah pulled the glass to her lips and took small but savory mouthfuls. She sloshed the water around and repeated until there was no more than a few drops.

"Fuck!" she screamed and smashed the glass to the concrete. Fractures bounced and diminished to splinters flying across the floor. Large pieces clanked next to her, giving the cement a sharp row of grinning teeth. She picked up the biggest bit, careful not to slice her fingers, and eyed its knife-like shape.

# CHAPTER FIFTEEN

*Twenty days before Sarah went missing*

IT WASN'T UNTIL Sarah sat behind her desk that she saw it. Nestled on the ungraded stack of homework was a rose. It wasn't a vibrant red; the flower was much softer and picked prematurely. The bottom of the stem was frayed, and she assumed it was ripped from the bush before anyone could notice. A single, rapid pluck stole this rose from its family, leaving stringy green strands at the bottom beneath thorns.

At the head of a full classroom, she glanced at each student individually, almost waiting for a hand to raise, for someone, anyone to admit to giving her the sweetest rose from the bush. No such confession was apparent, at least on their unaware, or rather, uninterested faces. She opened her desk drawer, resisting the urge to inhale the scent, and placed the rose inside. She'd enjoy the aroma later.

Though the flower was common on campus, the gesture alone was no less thoughtful. She couldn't recall the last time she was given anything outside the routine anniversary and birthday gifts. Even those were beginning to lose flair, but she'd never admit it outright.

The bell erupted and a few students still standing took their seats. Taking attendance was first on the agenda, and she had counted the class as she always did. Back left first, slowly working her way to the middle, and eventually the row of chairs against the curtainless windows allowing the near afternoon sun to breach inside.

No one chose these chairs, of course, but the kids were left without another option when the other seats had filled quickly. First and third period had no issue with it—only her second class of the day. Somehow—unless it was overcast—the sun properly positioned itself in the sky and blinded the unsuspecting English students. Each day during roll call Sarah would glance upon their squinting and miserable faces. She had been meaning to drape something over the double-paned glass, but she knew John would only complain about her spending *his* money on trivial things. "The sun is good for 'em," he would say between beer-filled belches. Sarah disagreed. No one sitting along the right side of her class had a passing grade.

She placed a check mark next to each student's name on her list, pausing briefly when she made it to the first seat in the middle row. Jessie Jenkins. She scanned the rest of the room, noticing she was the only absence. "Has anyone seen Jessie Jenkins?"

Small mutters mixed with shaking heads around the room. Different variations of "no" or "nope" formed some off-tune scale until the last person gave a simple "nah," ending the symphonic reply.

"I saw her in the bathroom," Deidra said, her small voice barely rising above the shuffling papers in the back. "She was still in the stall when I left." Deidra Barnes was one of the quieter kids in Sarah's classroom. The last time she had read a passage in front of the class, Sarah was certain by the blood draining from her face the poor girl would faint at any moment, and even sat behind Deidra within arm's reach in case she did. She didn't, and Sarah had silently thanked her for regaining her composure.

"Are you sure, Deidra?"

She nodded, said, "Yes, ma'am," and nothing else.

"Everyone remain in your seats and start reading chapter thirty-seven. I'll be right back."

Sarah left and walked toward the back of the hallway, her pristine red flats clacking against the less-than-perfect tiles along the way. Identical to the front of the school, the butt ends of each wing had a long concrete path beneath slat metal awnings. The woodshop was tucked away over here as well as two separate bathrooms in case the students couldn't hold it long enough to empty their bladders or, God forbid, the other end.

It wasn't often she'd have someone show up to class in their phys ed uniform, a gray shirt with the school logo and bright blue polyester shorts. But each time they did, Sarah and the entire student body knew the reason. *Insert name here* had had an accident. The harassment, baby coos, and sometimes diapers being thrown at them—the more creative bullies—would last until the next person had unfortunately donned the dreaded PE uniform.

When she entered the bathroom, the cool hiss of the AC vents blared down from the ceiling, as did the harsh yellow lights.

"Jessie?" Sarah asked, seemingly to no one. "Are you in here?"

One of the sinks was left on absently, and a steady water

stream circled the basin drain until the pipes allowed another mouthful. Used paper towels overflowed the trash can, and some littered the floor, scattering underneath in a soggy and makeup filled mess. All of the stall doors were partially open except one on the far end hugging the wall. It was latched shut, though there were no teenage feet to be seen between where the door stopped and the floor began.

"Jessie? It's Mrs. Baker." Sarah knocked softly.

"Leave me alone." The responding voice blubbered. Suppressive cries became audible, and each time the young girl had tried to stifle them, the sound of snot overwhelming her nose was apparent.

"Jessie, what's wrong?"

"I said leave me alone! Go away. Please. Just go away."

Despite her wishes and Sarah's obvious longing to do as she asked, she continued to stand next to the stall latched shut. What exactly was unfolding on the other end besides Jessie sobbing into her palms? Would Jessie be the next victim of name-calling and diapers thrown in her face? Was there boy trouble? Sarah didn't have the slightest clue.

"You can talk to me, Jessie. It will stay between us, I promise."

"No, it won't. Everyone's gonna find out. *Just go!*"

Sarah pinched the bridge of her nose and doubled down. "You are tardy for my class, and you better have a *damn* good reason." She placed her ear on the cold stall door, listening closely as if she might hear the hesitation rattling around Jessie's head.

"Did you have an accident?"

"No!" the young girl spat, and Sarah was sure some spittle shot through the door cracks.

"Then what is it? Let me help you."

"It wasn't supposed to happen today. It never happens this early."

The sudden realization of what was indeed unfolding behind that thin, metal door hit her the same way Sarah's own monthly visitor had been a sudden gut punch for as long as she could remember. She'd been caught off guard more times than she cared to admit by Aunt Flow making her unwanted appearance. Even had to toss some of her more expensive underwear to the bathroom trash whenever the ripe bitch seemed to say, *Surprise! It's me! Hope you didn't have any plans!* She could sympathize with Jessie.

"Do you not have anything to use?"

"No. That goddamn machine is out, too."

Sarah glanced at her left to the machine near the row of sinks. There was a paper sign on it with poorly scribbled handwriting stating OUT OF ORDER. There wasn't a single pad or tampon noticeable in each of the clear plastic slots. She somehow doubted it was indeed faulty, more like the school didn't want to shell out more money on feminine hygiene products. How they could do such a thing to the girls in school going through a monumental moment in their lives was beyond her. It was their job to keep the kids safe, stocked with whatever their young bodies needed, and without diapers thrown in their faces, of course.

"What are you wearing? Did you bleed through it?"

"My cheerleading uniform," she said slowly, but what followed came out even slower. "Yes."

"Take it off and start cleaning yourself up. I'll be right

back."

Sarah returned no longer than a minute later, her own purse in hand and determination in her step. It was the last tampon she had, though desperate times had fallen on the weeping girl in the stall more than herself. There was a half-empty box at home, and she had to pray she, too, wouldn't end up where Jessie was now. She slipped the colorfully wrapped cylinder under the door and watched as Jessie reached for it. Her bright pink nails had the remnants of blood.

"Give me your uniform."

"Wh-what?"

"Give me your uniform. I won't ask again."

After the sound of a zipper being undone and some slight rustling, Jessie handed it through the bottom opening the same way Sarah had given her the tampon. Her hands shook around it, and Sarah assumed it was embarrassment coursing through her. She swallowed her disgust and grabbed it, didn't even make a sound as she took the bundled mess in her hands and walked straight to the sink. Sarah had worried the uniform would appear as though young Jessie Jenkins had been murdered in it, and knowing the cheerleading uniforms were prone to one of the school's main colors—yellow—she had feared the worst. No. There was a pool of red, but it was only at the panty-lined area, which was dark blue.

Luckily enough for Jessie, her blood hadn't soaked through any of the areas where it would stain bright enough to be seen.

Sarah turned on the sink to its coldest setting and held

the area beneath it. She watched the water mix with fresh menstrual blood, draining the color of Jessie's nails. She added soap from the dispenser and scrubbed it with her fingers until the water ran clear. The hand dryer next to the paper towels worked remarkably well despite the loud clanks and rattles it gave while powering on.

"Good as new," Sarah said and held Jessie's clean uniform through the stall opening. "The other bathroom might have some more pads if you can't make it through the day. Maybe some of the girls on your squad could help you, too."

Jessie didn't say anything while dressing, but Sarah guessed she was nodding absently, forgetting Sarah couldn't see her. When she unlatched the door and came into the open area of the bathroom, Sarah peered over every inch of the girl, making certain there wasn't a noticeable hint of red. There wasn't, and after they washed their hands, Jessie did something unexpected.

She hugged her.

"What … What will I say? What will I tell them if they ask?" Jessie asked when they were back in front of Room 105.

"Whatever I say, just go with it. Nod your head and look like you were in trouble. Okay?"

Jessie's sullen face tightened. "Yes, Mrs. Baker."

"Okay. Here we go." Sarah thrust open the door and waved Jessie in. She waited until the girl was halfway to her desk, then she screamed at her back, shaking the entire room. "And don't ever let me catch you smoking on campus again! Am I clear?" Some students gasped. Some snickered.

"Yes, Mrs. Baker," Jessie managed and sat at her desk a

bit straighter than she had on other days. She stared at Sarah intently until she had taken her rightful position behind the mahogany desk at the front. Jessie Jenkins, a bit more comfortable in the cheerleading uniform she had accidentally soiled before the start of second period, smiled. A beaming smile in her direction. *Thank you*, she mouthed.

Sarah wouldn't grin back. No. She had to keep up the façade of the infuriated teacher ready to dish out punishment to anyone else who dared cross her. She simply scowled at the room until they all diverted their attention. When no one else but Jessie was looking, she winked. *You're welcome.*

IT WAS, MUCH to her surprise, a faster day than she could've hoped for. Lunch, the same garden salad she prepared every week, complemented her free period more than the assignments she busied herself grading. Each bell seemed to chime at a faster pace, and when the final tone blared around campus, she packed her things and was out the door before the students could lift the English books from their desks. The comfort of her couch beckoned her like an old friend wishing to catch up over coffee, or in Sarah's case, a glass of wine. Two? Maybe more.

She unlocked her car, a faded red vehicle with sunspots dabbed over the hood, sitting alone at the back of the gravel lot. The teachers' parking area. It may have been for the best to segregate the student and faculty cars, especially when entitled brats drove brand-new ones from the dealership worth more than some of the properties in town.

Sarah, however, had to teeter into the driver's seat of her '98 Dodge Neon and take in the constant dust coating the interior. She couldn't have imagined herself commuting in such a worthless heap years ago. Never would have guessed the vehicle she slouched in day after day would survive on little to no maintenance. John would get to it when he could, but she didn't imagine that'd be any time soon.

She adjusted her dress and let it flow to the seat beneath her. The dimming sun glittered at her from the rearview mirror, still high enough to be seen over the tree lines encompassing the higher peaks in town. The engine sputtered at first, then sparked to life in a triumphant, motor chamber rumble.

She flipped on the high beams any time dusk approached. This was nothing new. Hadn't been for a while. The driver's side headlight would shine in full effect while the passenger side would remain dark as if the bug-eyed car had been holding a wink for miles. John had come up with—in his mind—a brilliant, cost-effective, and laborless fix. *Use the brights so you don't get a ticket*, he had told her. *I'll take care of it this weekend.* Only he hadn't.

Six weekends later, and she still had to blind the drivers on the opposite end of the road. She somehow doubted the Neon's defective headlight would be fixed in the coming months, and with the winter season around the corner, there was no way he'd step outside into the blistering cold willingly.

Fulton hadn't changed in the years she called it home. Decayed streets ran rampant like violent tree roots. Bumpy. Jagged. Uneven at every turn. Caution cones were set absently in front of worn or ravaged concrete. None were the new vibrant orange as they should've been but a bleak, distressed yellow from the rain, heavy snow, and summer sun capable of inducing a statewide drought.

Blue collars were in large supply. Dominated the population, in fact. It wasn't often she came across men in town without sawdust sprinkled on their shirts and grease from heavy machinery smeared across their foreheads and cheeks. Some were bearded, others clean shaven, and there was of course the in-between. Most were the typical—tip their hats, and if they weren't wearing one, nod to you and say *ma'am*, type—country bumpkins. Class wasn't something she noticed often after all, and by class she had thought a clean shirt and somewhat suitable form of table manners was the minimal requirement.

What the gruff, working men lacked in conversation, their wives usually made up for in spades. Sarah couldn't recall a time she was able to complete a grocery list without being stopped by a housewife, usually a woman with two or three chicks in tow, asking various questions about the school or her least favorite subject, her marriage. Sarah would smile and answer their inquisitive and sometimes invasive questions as painlessly as she could, constantly glancing between the scribbled paper in her hand and their always exhausted faces.

It made her wonder if her inability to conceive thus far had been more a blessing than curse. When the young children grew tired of the casual grown-up talk, whining to leave would morph into an all-out screaming match in the produce section. *BLESSING* flashed like an OPEN sign each time they said their good-byes.

Streetlights in sequence flickered brightly to the roads ahead, like the series of fireworks exploding over Fulton this past July.

Passing cars flashed their high beams at her.

It was blinding. Annoyingly blinding.

She wanted to be mad. Curse at them. Yell out her open window, but she knew it wasn't unprovoked. She was, after all, blinding them just as equally. Not intentionally, of course, but they didn't know that. Maybe some had done it out of sheer courtesy, but for the most part, Sarah imagined they were all screaming at her, *Turn off your brights, idiot!* She didn't, though.

Her driveway—a quarter mile or so through lined trees—curved until the streetlight poles were hidden from view. Gravel and loose dirt shifted under the car's weight. She half expected the tires to flatten to flimsy and useless rubber whenever she drove the Neon into its rightful place.

As she eased outside, the hair behind her ears rustled free, lifted by the updraft making its sudden appearance. It wasn't something she could time as she had done with lightning as a kid. *One, two, three, four, five—five miles away.* No, these drafts were periodic and oftentimes wildly unpredictable. Her dresses were the usual casualty, swaying and exposing her thighs. Her hair was almost always a close second.

A humid warmth caressed her pallid skin, clung to her.

This was the last hint of summer before the autumn breeze took over in full effect. Summer heat was only enticing at the beginning and end. Everything in between made afternoon trips from the house a hellish endeavor. Fall would pass by like the opposing cars on the road flashing their brights. Quickly. Fast enough only to make out the brief colors and shifting winds. Winter would be worse. Worse by far.

Watching her own breath expel in thick white clouds was the first step into the unbearable season. Soon she would be bundled head to toe in two, if not three, separate layers. Moving around would be a difficult task. Driving in a car without the luxury of a heater—nearly impossible.

She slammed the car door shut and carefully straightened the dress down her thighs. The porch light extended for the tree lines, dimming just before the first oak trunk in sight. It shined over the glossy cobblestone path leading up the stained wooden steps. In the areas it didn't reach there was a void. A black, indistinguishable nothing.

Someone or something could have taken to the shadows with ease. A monster with an incredible row of jagged teeth waiting patiently to sink them into her flesh. She would scream into the wilderness, of course, but no one would come to her rescue, at least not in time to save her throat from being the main course. The next house over had to be as far as the FHS football field, give or take a dozen yards or two. No, there she would lie in her own unmistakable fluids waiting for the final treacherous strike.

*Nothing. There's nothing.*

The house itself, single story and perched on an incline, held the lightest brown shade, a color she despised but couldn't quite argue when her salary barely covered the utilities. Sarah ascended the staircase to the front door, and each step shrieked at her. If she listened close enough, the squeals sounded almost like voices. *His home.* Creak. *Not yours.* Creak. *Get out!* Creak.

Her cat, an orange tabby mix, awaited her arrival each day at the windowsill, but the darkened glass overlooking their property showed no hint of Mr. Biscuit waiting for her this night. Sarah could only see her own disgruntled glare.

She twisted the doorknob, expecting the dead bolt to catch halfway. It didn't. The doorknob twisted fully without protest. *A child. I am married to a child who can't lock a door.* Her internal curses drowned under the squealing hinges.

The door swung open with ease, inviting her and whatever the hell else wanted inside throughout the day to plop down on her couch and stab Sarah to death with the kitchen knives on the counter. The largest one would've taken one to two well-placed stabs. The steak knives might've called for multiple stabbings—her being conscious throughout them all. Hopefully, if there were a killer lurking in some vacant black corner, they at least had the common sense to do the job quick before she could scream. Before she would gargle on the blood filling her punctured lungs. It wasn't the best thought. Not something anyone would want to consider, of course. But she did, all because her husband, *her John*, couldn't manage a simple fucking task like locking the goddamn door.

She secured the handle of her purse to the hook on the wall and tossed her keys to the end table. The house was still, but the faint hum of the fridge remained steady. She paused for a moment and listened. There was no movement. No knife blades glinting off the subtle light shining in the corners. No ominous shadow looming over her. Not even the small, padded feet of her cat coming to greet her. She could be thankful there wasn't some psychopath planning to make a Sarah Baker shish kabob. Her missing cat, however, was somehow a greater concern.

Once in the kitchen, she flipped on the lights and scanned the linoleum floors. A small, blue dish sat near the rectangle dining room table by the bay window. Mr. Biscuit's bowl was practically overflowing with the same food she had left him that morning. He never did eat it all in one sitting like most fat and happy cats did. Mr. Biscuit would only eat tiny portions periodically, and Sarah would return home from school every day to a half-empty dish and half-satisfied Mr. Biscuit. He would then meow at her for more, maybe for something off the house cat menu, and eventually finish his food before curling into himself between her legs on the bed.

Something was different though. The bowl hadn't been touched.

A draft slipped through the back door and raised the blinds covering the glass window until they slapped back into place. The door was cracked open, and the kitchen light peered into the unknown darkness of the backyard. A pit in her stomach unraveled a knot at a time, like a balloon animal being carefully deconstructed. Muscles from her chest down to her toes stiffened. Her legs straightened impulsively, and her hands remained fixed to her sides. *Someone's in here*, she managed to think through her statuesque figure taking hold. Every instinct begged her to run, but she couldn't find the strength nor the momentum to do so. This, her newfound confinement, kept her in place. Stopped her from speaking. Seized her breath.

Something crashed violently behind her.

# CHAPTER SIXTEEN

*Two months missing*

SARAH PRESSED THE glass point to the bottom hem of her dress and sliced clean through. Strands frayed like harp strings. Gripping each torn side, she ripped until the slit extended up her leg. Then, she stabbed again. Butchered the outfit until a loose piece fell to the cement in front of her.

The lily print cloth seemed to stare back, pleading to be returned to its rightful place. No, she had a better use for it. The dress scrap would, in theory, provide some comfort against the sharp ends of the glass. A makeshift handle of sorts. Sarah pulled the fabric from the ground and wrapped it over the hilt of her improvised weapon, careful not to leave a single edge uncovered.

A quick slice through the air promised a swift and bloody end for the man upstairs. It whipped tremendously in the cellar, swishing like a freshly sharpened kitchen knife. This was no longer a fractured piece of glass. This was her ticket home. He wouldn't expect it, she hoped. She was, after all, the damsel in distress waiting for a big, strong man to come save her. He didn't know she wasn't some fairy-tale damsel. Sarah Baker was simply waiting for the right opportunity to strike.

He would die quickly; she would be sure of that. And the

vacant concrete in front of her would serve as his eternal resting place. The shackles were another issue. If he didn't have the key with him, there would be no way to break free from the wall. She could almost imagine the putrid stench of his weeks old decaying flesh mingling with her own drying urine.

It wouldn't take long for the maggots to infest his body, like ants swarming a forgotten wad of gum on the high school hallway. The idea tugged at her insides. Saliva lathered over her dry tongue. Vomit heaved up her throat and forced its way through her tightened lips. *Splash.* The liquid, chunky and yellow, splattered to the concrete. She spat the excess bile and wiped her wrist against her mouth.

Her underwear moistened, at first a warm trickle, followed by a stream running down her thighs to the paved floor. The odor was sour and overwhelmed the stuffy air. She had considered moving to the dry slab, her cellar bathroom, but decided against it. The urine might fend off his touch should the man decide to violate her. Another question bubbled like insulation in her scratchy throat. Besides the backhand, he hadn't tried to touch her during the imprisonment. Not that she was complaining. Just a simple, curious thought.

Small glimpses of his shape pieced together to a thick build, six to six-and-a-half feet tall, dark brown skin and broad shoulders. His face was squared and defined. His eyes, deep and callous. There was something familiar about him, though she couldn't recall what.

The chains had kept her in place, but the endless thoughts had roughed over more than her skin. *John is out there trying to find me*, she wished. She pleaded. Yet something in Sarah knew she was wrong. Sure, he may have organized a search party or two. Gotten a few of the village idiots to follow along in the crusade. This would be a trick. A magic trick from the great and powerful John. He wouldn't try to find her any more than he did the TV remote under his own ass.

He had a reputation to uphold, after all. The diligent, utterly broken husband searching under every stone. It would be a sham. One at her expense. She would be the TV remote, sandwiched between two misshapen cushions, and John would do no more than lift his arms in the air, saying, *Oh, well. We gave it our best shot.*

The door handle twisted.

The hinges shrieked.

Dust slipped through the floorboard cracks and caked over the dark yellow puddle between her legs.

His boots hit the staircase, and the familiar whistle sent a shiver down to her toes. She reached behind her back and grabbed the glass by the fabric-wrapped handle. She would be ready for whatever he had in store. Die fighting if she had to.

Footsteps swayed down each step, and his whistling bumped further off-pitch as he descended. His silhouette, stalky and wide, emerged into the light, and the rifle slung over his shoulder became visible. A hunting rifle. He was coming toward her like a soldier in a firing squad, and she was the prisoner welcoming death.

Goose bumps worked their way up her forearms. *This is it.* She readied herself, knife against the small of her back, hoping the idea of an end, whether his or hers, would be soothing. It wasn't. Panic flashed red in her eyes. *This is it.* A tear rolled down her cheek. *This is how I die.*

Struggling to breathe through the knot in her chest, Sarah released the glass knife slowly and looked at what else he was carrying. Clothes.

He tossed them to her side and aimed the rifle not for her face like she anticipated but at her stomach. Digging his free hand in his pocket, he fished out an old-fashioned key. The man kneeled, set the key to the floor, and kicked it toward her. She gaped at it for a moment and argued against the voice in her head demanding an outright vicious attack. Clean clothes would be a godsend after so much time without, and the idea of removing the shackles, even for a second, was comforting.

She snatched the key and worked on the left wrist first, followed quickly by the right. The chains rattled and thumped on the cement. Freedom dangled in her face like a pendulum until she remembered the rifle aimed at her gut. Her legs wobbled as she stood. Her knees ached, and the numbness in her backside tingled, similar to being bitten by a thousand fire ants at once. She lifted the dress over her hips, and the man turned to the side.

*Why?* She paused. It made no sense to her. A farmer would want to take inventory of their livestock. A vintner would want to taste the wine they spent an entire season harvesting. Why was this man shying away from a naked woman exposing herself in his basement? Why didn't he feel the need for a peek at the woman he was keeping all to himself?

His courtesy was surprising.

Foolish.

Stupid.

And she intended to exploit it in any way she could.

*This is it*, she told herself, regaining her confidence. She stole a second glance at his side profile before he noticed. He was blissfully unaware his life was about to end. That the last thing he'd see was Sarah standing over his corpse. *This is it. This is how you die.*

She lifted the dress over her torso and stalled at her neckline, careful to save her hair from the urine soaking through the fabric. With her face no longer covered, she looked at him again. His eyes, or what she believed them to be, were barely visible under the dim light cascading over dusty boxes and cobwebs.

He remained still. Calm. Unaware of what was coming. The blood rushed from her face, leaving no hint of rose on her cheeks. Sarah tried to swallow the dry patch building in her throat. Preparing herself to stab layers of flesh was another matter she could hardly stomach. She kneeled and grabbed the clothes delicately, fearful any sudden movements would result in a swift shot to the belly.

Still hunched over, Sarah slipped on the blue T-shirt. It was a few sizes too large but still better than a piss-stained dress. She then settled into the black sweatpants, tightening the long drawstring to conform to her waist.

Comfortable could describe her fresh apparel but maneuverable suited it best. Running would be no issue, nothing restricting like a pair of jeans or tight blouse. Her arms and legs would be allowed to move freely. All that remained was the rifle trained on her. She reached behind her heels, slowly of course, and snatched the glass knife without hesitation. Barely a scrape grated the cement.

The gun clicked.

Sarah's body stiffened.

Her lungs seized.

She clenched her eyes shut, fearful that the last thing she'd see was an orange and yellow muzzle flash.

Seconds passed. Sarah wrenched her eyes open. The stillness and silence of the cellar had returned, and she concealed the blade under her moist dress. The man adjusted his arms to the weight of the rifle, allowing another small *click* to escape. His gaze, which she expected to meet as she turned, was directed on the tiny notches in the wall, as if committing each one to memory.

The pads of her feet were as rough as sandpaper, and she didn't particularly enjoy the way they scraped against the cement. He didn't move despite her shadow looming over him. Didn't even bother to check on her. No. The man continued to skim over each mark. Undistracted by her small steps forward.

With little more than a few feet between them, she paused and narrowed her eyes on him. *You made me do this.* She drew a lengthy breath. *You made me do this.* In one smooth motion, she tossed the piss-filled dress over his face. Then Sarah rushed him.

A single shot fired.

The explosion rattled dust from the ceiling. A shell casing chimed off the cement. She gouged at his chest. Three ferocious stabs, each deeper than the previous. Blood coated the transparent blade down to the fabric handle, soaking her fingertips red. He somehow managed to chamber a round through the struggle and shot again.

He missed.

Small lines of smoke billowed between them, and the musty scent of the cellar laced with raw gunpowder. He staggered back and toppled over the boxes in the corner, head still concealed behind the blood-splotched lily print. She eyed him for a moment and directed her glare to his hands and rifle. His once firm grip had loosened.

He didn't move, and Sarah—in turn—remained frozen as well. His chest raised unevenly and stopped. Halted as if mid-thought. One final groan fled his throat. Though this man was dying, or dead, the idea to take his rifle tugged at her anyway. *One bullet. One easy shot*, she challenged herself, hesitation wrapping over her tighter than chains ever could.

His head cocked to the side, and he let go of the rifle completely. She sighed and inched closer. One step. Two. Her heartbeat thumped rhythmically, pounding in her ears. Three. He still didn't move. Didn't grab at her though she was only a foot from him.

Sarah reached for the weapon. *Just a little closer.* The wooden stock was inches from her outstretched hand. *Just a little*—she snatched it from him in one swift motion and aimed it for what she believed to be his face. It was warm. Parts of it hot even. It was heavier than she'd imagined it to be. Difficult to shoulder but she managed just fine. Her finger to the trigger, she waited. Whether to control her own breathing or to make sure he wasn't, she couldn't be sure in that moment.

*Finish it.* She traced her index over the small crescent-moon shape. *Finish it.*

*Click.*

She fiddled with the bolt, pulling it back and closing it.

*Click.*

"No. No, no, no." Sarah tried the bolt again. This time when she opened it, there was something missing. A bullet.

A sharp groan resonated in the cellar. Before Sarah could move, the weight of the rifle tripled. It wasn't exhaustion. It was the meaty hand of the man pulling it toward him by the barrel.

Sarah tried to pull back to no avail. He was winning and bringing her closer to him by the second. Terror seized her limbs. A helplessness that wasn't there the moment she stabbed him suddenly returned tenfold. Something else did as well.

Survival.

She screamed and slammed the gun into him with every ounce of force she had. She didn't wait for movement this time. She hobbled up the rickety wooden steps without looking back.

Her legs, weak and ill-prepared, ignited as each fiber stretched like worn rubber bands. She wrapped her calloused fingers over the door handle, twisted it, and shoulder charge inward. Darkness invaded the motionless house above her prison. If not for the small light above the kitchen sink, the windows peering outside would've blended into her surroundings. Beyond the sheet-covered couches in the next room, she spotted a doorframe. *This is it!* She had more hope in her head than ever.

"Somebody help me!" she screamed while leaping down the porch steps. Her cries echoed off each tree and into the dense wilderness. An eerie silence greeted her back as she limped and staggered forward. The damp mud squished between her toes, and the scent of rain loomed from the clouds overhead. Something above her own ragged breath became audible, loud enough to suspend her in place. It was soft. Gentle, even. Almost like wind passing through branches behind her, though not quite. Pinpricks teased every inch of her skin as the sound became perfectly clear.

*A whistle.*

Sarah forced herself forward despite the terror piercing through her. The whistle followed. He was outside, and he was coming for her.

"Please! Somebody help!"

The whistle responded to her plea. Closer than before.

She twisted and turned in a race through the trees. The awful tune remained constant. Screeching in her ears.

"Someone he—" A tremendous crunch rattled and shook the ground beneath her. The heavy *chomp* was fast, and agony ripped through her in an instant, first at her clamped foot and eventually to the spot below her knee. Sarah fell over, clutching her mangled leg. Blood spat from the fresh wound, some of it striking her cheeks. She could see the bear trap through her tear-filled eyes, and a row of sharpened metal teeth smiled up at her. Her ears ringing at a deafening pitch, the horrifying sound of footsteps closing in became clear.

# CHAPTER SEVENTEEN

*Twenty days before Sarah went missing*

THE HAIR ON her neck raised. Her stomach twisted. The noise, a large crash, replayed in her head. *Someone is here.* The fear of being grabbed at any moment struck her in place with her arms at her sides. Courage could be found in most situations—this, however, wasn't one of them.

Sarah trembled. Refused to breathe regardless of her lungs pleading for another hit. *Someone is here.* The legs she had perfectly balanced on her entire life somehow began to buckle. Her toes curled inside her flats. *Help*, she thought but couldn't say, let alone scream. She closed her eyes and inhaled a long, shaky breath.

"H—hello?"

No one answered. It was as quiet as before.

"Hello?" She didn't dare glance in the living room, and her reflection in the kitchen window revealed a panicked and paler than normal face. The lights flickered. The blinds slapped the open back door at a faster rhythm.

*Turn around. Turn around. Turn around.* She continued the chant until she willed power over her own frozen limbs. First her fingers, then her arms, and finally her neck. She turned slowly, although making a beeline for the backyard still seemed a better option. In the darkness of the living room, a small yellow gaze met hers.

"Mr. Biscuit." She sighed. "Where the hell were you?"

The cat announced himself with nothing more than an acknowledging meow. He rubbed his damp and prickly fur against her calves. The picture frame he'd knocked over, broken glass chunks scattered across the ground, sat face-up near muddy paw prints. Her wedding portrait. Sarah nestled in John's arms, with a smile that was anything but forced. The last time she could remember not having to force a simple grin.

She leaned over, scooped the cat up in her arms, and ran her fingers over his ears. Those were wet, too. His stomach shuddered and twitched when she rolled her hand over his spine. A soft purr escaped him. He had been on some sort of adventure, and at Sarah's expense, scared the ever-loving shit out of her.

"Come on. Let's get you cleaned up."

Sarah rinsed him off in the sink and fought Biscuit's evasiveness through a firm yet tender grip. She lowered the cat to the floor after a kitchen towel pat down, and he scampered away, leaving her to clean his muddy mess. She swept the glass shards with ease, and once the kitchen was clean enough to her liking, Sarah closed the back door and locked it tight.

She poured herself a glass of wine and sipped while walking, the smooth taste sliding gently down her throat and warming her stomach. Had she forgone the customary sips from the kitchen to the living room, the crimson liquid might've sloshed to the floor, giving her yet another thing to clean before John arrived home. Whenever that would be.

The couch in the living room was charcoal gray and placed perfectly in front of the fireplace. It invited Sarah to explore its cushions, and she could do nothing else but oblige. After three consistent buzzes from her cell phone, she knew it wasn't a simple text. Someone was calling her. Maybe John was on his way home. Maybe he would pick up dinner and they could eat together for once. The glowing screen flashed, and a name appeared.

It wasn't John. It was his mother, Barbara.

Barbara would continue to pester until Sarah answered, or she'd follow up the ignored calls with a patronizing text. *Guess you're too busy to answer. Let me know when you're finally able to talk.* Sarah had had the pleasure of responding to a few of these before realizing how less painful a twenty-minute conversation was compared to a string of snide remarks relayed through John. "My mom's been trying to get a hold of you," he had said on more than a couple occasions. He had the same condescending tone Sarah despised.

"Hi, Barbara," she said with as much enthusiasm as she could muster.

"Sarah, did I catch you at a bad time?"

"No, no. I just got home a little bit ago. How are you?"

"We are doing great. Phillip threw out his back again working on the yard, but I'm sure you know how that goes. Just as stubborn as Johnny. Can't leave a project unfinished."

Sarah closed her eyes to avoid rolling them. *No, I don't.* She couldn't imagine having any projects around her own home taken care of. *When I have the time* was the biggest excuse, followed by *next weekend.* She lost count of the promised fixtures after a handful of excuses led to her being the nagging, unsupportive, bitchy wife. His words, not hers. It was at that point she'd decided that reminding John of his promises, no matter how calm or gently she approached him, wasn't worth the trouble.

"I'm sure you've had a long day, so I am sorry to bother you, dear. But we wanted to invite you both out to the lodge this weekend. Our friends had to cancel last minute. Damn flakes. That's the third time this month. But that leaves another room, and we figured who better to come than our son and favorite daughter-in-law."

*Only daughter-in-law.* John didn't have siblings, and while neither did Sarah, it surprised her how anyone, even an only child, could grow up so self-centered. Everyone revolved around *his* daily schedule. John's wants or needs. His laundry to be washed and folded promptly. His work button-ups to be ironed until the collar was flat. Dinner, on the days he decided to come home, expected to be finished when he pulled in the driveway. If poor, innocent, momma's boy Johnny was taken care of, all was right in the world.

She brushed away her renewed annoyance with a quick swipe of her brow and swirled the glass in her palm. Gentle whirlpools disturbed the red liquid.

"So, what do you think?" Barbara asked, her tone, while sweet, was more demanding of Sarah's agreeance. *No* was not an answer she took lightly. Another trait the apple clutched while falling from the tree.

A sigh slipped from Sarah's mouth, but she caught it before it cut over the line. "I don't know, Barb. John's been busy with work lately. I'm not sure we'll have the time." *We won't have the time.* She silently praised herself. This could, in theory, save her from an awkward weekend playing perfect housewife and daughter-in-law. Listening to stories about how great his parents' marriage was after forty-plus years. Barbara's quarterly gossip on the peers John graduated with. Phillip's need to describe every doctor's visit he'd had since they saw him last in painfully vivid detail. *We won't have the time*, she said again in her head and began working through excuses for them both.

"It's one weekend! You both can spare a few days."

Sarah expected this response. First, her mother-in-law would ask. Then beg. Lastly, all-out complain. Was this how Sarah sounded to John, her words a reminiscent squawk of his own vulture-like mother? It had to be close in her mind. Barbara, unlike Sarah, wouldn't quit. The pestering would turn into a full-blown guilt trip. *You really should've come with us. We had such an a-m-a-z-i-n-g time.* It was an uphill battle Sarah was ill-prepared to fight after a long, and increasingly sober, day. "I'll talk to John about it when he gets home." Another deflection. A simple, easy, blame-pushing deflection.

*"What?"*

Sarah yanked the phone from her ear to avoid Barbara's screeching.

"It's almost six. Where the hell is he?"

"Ask your son, Barbara. He said he was working late." The phone clicked. No *I'll call you back*. No *hold on*. Just a click and silence. She smiled at the earful John was about to receive, wherever the hell he was, and pulled another sip from her glass.

Hours passed with no sign of her husband. No truck careening into the driveway, no text, not even a smoke signal. It was apparent her night would be met with the same silence most evenings shared, and while she may have been upset months ago, now it was somehow relieving. She finished the remnants of her second glass and set it in the kitchen sink. The bitter taste in her mouth could have been from the wine or how she shared her bed with a stranger each night. Both seemed likely.

She turned off the lights in the living room and retreated down the hallway, Mr. Biscuit hot on her heels. Sarah eased into bed, as she did most nights, with only the company of her tabby cat padding between her legs until the spot was comfortable enough.

The engine from his pickup drowned out the gentle creaks of the home setting, humming in tune with the scattered rocks and broken branches under each wheel. Headlights shined through the bedroom curtains and painted the fabric's burgundy to the ceiling.

*He's home.*

Over the years, she learned what to expect when he walked through the front door simply by the noises outside. Slamming the truck door and stomping boots up the porch—angry John. Creeping quietly inside, no grunts or curses—nice, calm John. Sitting outside and smoking a pack of Lucky Strikes while on the phone with his mom or boss—sober but soon to be plastered and intolerable John.

She rolled to her side and perked her ear, eager to know which would be climbing in bed with her. The truck door slammed, and a barrage of curses echoed into the surrounding wilderness. *Great.*

He stomped up the steps. The front door, solid oak and anything but light, hurled open and smashed into the wall. She closed her eyes and tried to ignore her unease. No matter the cause, it would somehow be her fault. Her. She was the burden. Sarah would be the reason he missed closing time with his coworkers. Why his mother gave him an earful. All her fault.

Footsteps maneuvered down the hall and keys rattled on the end table. Mr. Biscuit, still curled between her legs, jolted out of the covers, and his fuzzy ears rose to attention. The cat gave one last *you're on your own* glance and scurried underneath the bed before the door ripped open.

The stench of whiskey hit her before he managed to speak. *Drunk John.*

"I got a call from my mother," he said. "She wants to know why I wasn't home with my wife. Since you love complaining to my mom, next time, be sure to tell her how I'm having to bust my ass so I'm not on the chopping block this quarter." He slammed or possibly punched the bedroom door shut.

She didn't move. She didn't speak. *Go sleep on the couch.* Sarah ground her teeth together. He'd sooner force her to the couch than give up the mattress they were still making payments on. The one to help with his always-sore back from carrying this family financially. She, too, out of spite, would be just as immovable.

He unlaced his boots, and a pants zipper sliding down masked his breathing. She kept her body shifted to the wall when he slid into bed next to her. *I'm asleep. Leave me the hell alone.* The thought to play dead also enticed her. She doubted he'd show any remorse if that were the case. The drunken odor lingered and seeped through the covers. He rolled his arm over her shoulder, and she twitched at his unwanted touch. His fingers, rough and firm, worked down her waist to her hip bone. Out of impulse, she swatted at his hand and pulled the blankets to her neck.

He closed in on her, chest to her back, and pressed himself against her.

"Get off me, John," she mumbled.

"Oh, come on," he whispered in her ear. "I've had a long day." He rubbed his hand on her bare stomach and inched his fingers downward.

"I mean it, John. Stop."

"Don't be like that," he said and tugged at her underwear. "You know you want it."

Two words throbbed in her head like a migraine. Two syllables to be exact. *Stop it.* John didn't. No matter how stiff Sarah remained, he continued his insistent groping, feeling all over her. *Stop it.* Sarah reviled the touch. *Stop it.* She couldn't keep it down any longer.

"Stop it!" she shrieked, and even the small noises in the house seemed to listen.

He pulled his hand from her quickly, the way one might rear their fingers from the jaws of a Rottweiler.

"Fucking bitch!" he shouted and staggered down the hallway, taking the sour mash stink with him.

She curled into herself the way Mr. Biscuit did every night, cradling her knees to her chest. Her body trembled. Cramped. Twisted with the horrible thoughts of what her life had become. When she was sure John was out of earshot, and her eyes couldn't hold back the tears any longer, Sarah Baker cried into the early morning hours.

# CHAPTER EIGHTEEN

*Sixty-two days missing*

IT WASN'T THE rustling upstairs or the dried urine clinging to the cement that woke her. Not the chains clasped firmly on her wrists or the inward breaths filled with a moist, almost moldy taste. It was pain. Searing agony. Sarah missed the days when paper cuts were the worst she had to endure. Now, there was something much deeper to draw her concern.

The wound pulsated, and while the basement was cold, the gentle chill did nothing but burn the teeth-like incisions around her calf. Gauze was wrapped expertly around her leg, but although it appeared to be applied recently, the bandage displayed a bright currant red seeping through, as if drops of merlot were spilled carelessly to a sock.

She screamed. A raw squelch tickled and climbed its way from her throat. Snot seeped from her nostrils. *Help me. Someone—help me.* She screamed once more and writhed against the chains holding her in place. Sarah's hoarse voice harmonized with the clanging restraints and the obvious storm looming overhead. Thunder erupted in a single clap, applause for her song, mocking the three-inch punctures hidden beneath tan surgical dressing.

She inspected the wound with a hesitant hand, ready to

rear back at the first sign of discomfort. Her leg remained immovable for the most part, void of the natural sensation one would recognize while wiggling their toes. She, however, wanted to know the full extent of her injury and dabbed a finger on the lesion.

It was a poor decision.

A yelp fled her lungs, and her entire body constricted, the torment more immense than she'd anticipated. After a few seconds and large, savory breaths, she felt the pain began to subside. She gnashed her teeth and touched it again. No cry this time, but a wrathful grunt and a picket line of tears building behind her swollen eyes.

She slammed her fist to the cement and glared at the shifting ceiling, his footsteps heavy and unmistakable. "Let me out of here, you sick fuck!"

The creaking boards held still. For a moment the only noise parting the silence was generous raindrops tapping off the roof. *I hope he heard me* was her braver, less Sarah Baker thought. Her natural reaction was to cower anytime the door atop the stairs slammed open.

His pacing resumed shortly after, showering dust over her hair and shoulders. *How? How the hell can he still be walking around?* Sarah had lost count of the times she'd stabbed him, sure to have damaged one, if not, two organs. His blood had splashed against her like a paint-filled balloon popping. What frightened her the most was that he could not only stand but carry her back to the cellar.

She shifted her body and rested her back against the wall. Her leg refused to help in the slightest. Glancing down at the black T-shirt and gray shorts covering her mid-thigh, she ran her fingers over the seams. *When did he dress me in this?* This man—*this monster*—not only endured multiple stabbings, chased her through the woods, carried her lifeless body, but also opted to change her out of muddy clothes.

*Why? What the hell do you want with me?*

Something scraped against the floorboards upstairs. A wretched, trombone sound shook the cabin. The wall at her back vibrated from something being pushed across the floor above. The screeching finally stopped, and as if on cue, his whistling began. Sharp notes pierced the air and resonated in the cellar.

Sarah raised herself from the slouched position and eyed the staircase. *He's coming.* Her relaxed breathing hastened. Her gentle heartbeat thumped rapidly. While she couldn't be certain, she assumed another wave of blood was soaking through the gauze.

The man opened the door and peered downward. She thought most of his torso would be wrapped like her leg, but there were only two bandages—no larger than cocktail napkins—absent blood.

"How's the chest?" she spat.

He narrowed his eyes and descended the flight with a small metal stool in his hand. No limp. Not even a stagger. He walked in front of her, placed the seat a few feet away, and sat with his hands on his knees.

His whistle softened, and he cut it off mid-tune. Silence stuck to the walls like a greasy film, and the rain sifting through the trees and brush outside dampened to no more than a whisper. He scanned her face, as if counting each freckle sprinkled around her nose.

"What do you want now?" she asked snidely.

He opened his mouth and grazed his tongue against his teeth. "How far along are you?"

Sarah considered the question for a moment. She didn't know what he wanted with her, whether six weeks or six months into the pregnancy. To lie would be simple, and with no signs of a baby bump showing, effective. Would she be easier to kill if in the early stages? Did he have some sick limit where he wouldn't bother when the fetus had toes? There was no way of knowing.

"How *far* along are you?" he asked again, irritation in his voice.

She hawked the phlegm coating her throat and spit. The chunky, lime-green mess landed on his white tank top and oozed toward his abdomen. His jawline flexed, and he patted at the dribble with his unbuttoned plaid shirt. Sarah smirked at him.

"This is the last time. How far along—?"

"I'm not telling you shit!" she snapped, a scowl replacing her smile. "Let me go!"

He took a breath, shifted his weight forward, and stood. The ceiling light stretched his stalky and thick shadow across the room until it loomed over her. His face blurred under the eclipse, though she imagined the same disgruntled stare. She pressed her back to the wall, molding her body to the ridges and cracks. *Go upstairs. Leave me the hell alone.*

Her wishes remained that. Simple, unequivocally wrong wishes. He pushed his boot to the shackle on her left wrist, damning her arm to the scratched cement. She writhed and struggled. It was useless. Before Sarah could claw at his torso, he snatched her right hand and squeezed until her fingers combined to make a long, painful flipper. Each bone an inch away from cracking out of place.

"How far along are you?"

Sarah thrashed side to side, trying to squirm from his grip. It was pointless. "Let. Me. Go!" she shouted.

"Last chance." It came out firm. Unwavering.

Had she saved some of the gunk she'd spat at him, Sarah now would've readied herself for another loogie, this time aimed at his face. "You can't make this hell any worse!"

For the second time in less than a minute, she was wrong. The man lifted his hand to hers. *He's going to cut off my fingers.* She fought back again and again to no avail. He pressed not only her shackled hand with his boot, but her collapsed palm tighter. Heavy throbs raced through her veins.

"No! Please!"

A sharp sting pierced her skin. Not at the knuckle as she expected, but under her fingernail and into the untouched flesh beneath. The ceiling light revealed a toothpick clasped between his index and thumb. He dug it forward.

The noise that crawled from her throat was unlike any she had heard or produced. A blood-curdling squelch bounced off each wall. The punctures in her leg were like a scraped knee in comparison. This wasn't pain. This was true agony.

"How far along?" he shouted above her.

She couldn't answer, only scream at a higher pitch. The hoarseness in her voice stumbled upon a newfound limit. Screeching gravel.

The man forced the blunt wood farther.

Another wave pounded through her. Agony turned to sheer torment. While she couldn't sense a trickle of blood dancing down her wrist, she was sure by now her entire hand was covered to her forearm. Sarah shrieked again, still absent the only words to make him stop.

"How far?"

"Ten weeks!" she finally managed. "Ten fucking weeks."

He slid the toothpick out. Relief was the first sensation. The lingering ache was what she was unprepared for. Constantly rubbing another finger over the wound proved useless. Nothing appeased the suffering he caused, not even him taking a slow step backward. They glared at each other. Sarah was awaiting more unfathomable torture. He, she assumed, was searching for another lie in case the next nail needed the same treatment.

He walked past her without another word. Dust plumed off each step from his boots. She sighed and hunched forward, expecting the familiar squeal of the door latching shut.

He didn't lock it though. Didn't even close it all the way.

The thought tickled her neck hairs straight. A whistle, hollow and nerve-pinching, echoed through the cabin. Miserable and off-pitch enough to unsettle any stomach. He returned to the staircase, bringing a syringe with him.

Sarah inched back and shook her head. The chains strangled her swollen wrists, but she still fought. Writhed. As he descended, one rickety step at a time, he paused at each stair long enough to make the proceeding *thud* like a jab to her rib cage.

"No. No! I told you the truth, okay? Please, just leave me the hell alone."

*Thud.*

"I swear it's the truth. Put that thing away."

*Thud.*

"What the fuck do you want from me?"

*Thud.*

Tears filled her eyes and rolled over her freckled cheeks.

He stopped a few steps from the bottom, and Sarah reluctantly peered up. The man in front of her only stared. A vacant, emotionless stare.

"I just want to go home ..." Her cries morphed to all-out sobs, and she pleaded with both arms held outward. "Please. Let me go home."

He wrapped his free hand around her throat and pressed her against the wall with ease. Her panicked breath withered to a shallow gasp. She became light-headed and teetered in and out of consciousness. The last thing Sarah Baker saw was the man stabbing a needle to her neck and thumbing down the plunger in one fell swoop.

# CHAPTER NINETEEN

*Nineteen days before Sarah went missing*

"FIRE CROTCH. FIRE crotch. Fire crotch!" The group had closed in around her and began clapping their hands to the beat of their ridicule. The other playground noises—a basketball bouncing on the pavement, jump ropes whipping viciously, the screams and hollers from a round of tag—faded into the background, and all Sarah could hear in that moment were two simple words. *Fire. Crotch.* By themselves, insignificant. Together, a wound for Sarah Grant that would never heal.

Those collaborative voices. How spittle flew from each of their mouths. Her, shoved to the ground and cradling into herself as tightly as she could, fearing the next step in this heinous act would be to kick and spit at her.

It didn't stop when she stood up. Kept on as she cupped her hands over her ears. And even though Sarah closed her eyes, she knew it was still happening despite her two senses being taken out of commission.

Rachel Nevis had started it today, as she did most of the damage to Sarah's weakened self-confidence. A wad of Big Red chewing gum in her hair—that required her lengthy red locks to be butchered in half. The permanent marker notes Rachel made on the bathroom stall doors. *SARAH G. IS AN*

*UGLY SKANK. FIRE CROTCH WUZ HERE.* Those never wiped clean completely, and once the boys in school caught wind of her less-than-favorable nickname, the words FIRE and CROTCH magically appeared on her locker in bright red lettering.

And now, here was Rachel, yelling another horrible thing at Sarah alongside her other—equally as disgusting—peers.

"Stop it," Sarah pleaded.

They didn't. It seemed like the taunting grew louder. When Sarah opened her eyes, Rachel was directly in front of her, a menacing snarl on her lips. "Stop it."

Rachel shoved her, and Sarah nearly fell over but caught her balance.

"Stop it."

She shoved her again, and this time Sarah knew the girl who put gum in her hair, wrote nasty things in the bathroom, and now was yelling fire crotch in her face, wouldn't stop until Sarah was back where she belonged. On the ground beneath her.

"Stop it."

Another shove with more force behind it.

"Stop it!"

Rachel grinned and pushed again.

Sarah couldn't take it anymore. The sneers. The sea of merciless faces. Rachel, and how she smirked every time she pushed her again and again. Tears filled Sarah's eyes. She was falling into a fog. The playground around her was now a daze. Basketballs bounced silently. Jump ropes swung absent of the familiar *whoosh*. The other students yelled something inaudible. As Rachel readied herself for another shove, Sarah balled her fists and did the only thing she could.

She swung.

The blow landed square on Rachel's nose, and the noise of the world returned with a tremendous *crack*. Blood spat from her face and gushed down each nostril like a leaky water fountain. The other kids each took a tentative step back, fearing they'd be next for a right hook. Rachel stood with disbelief at first, and when the pain and realization seemed to take over, she cried and ran away, flailing her arms.

There wouldn't be a suspension. No, Rachel would never admit to being bested by the school punching bag. By Sarah Grant. The girl with thrift store clothes. The girl whose daddy ran out on her. The girl who never quite belonged.

×

THE MORNING SUN sifted through the curtains, over the black comforter, and nestled securely on her brow. She lifted her head and peered through a half-open eye. Nothing. No movement. No noise. Most of all, none of the drunken snoring most sunrises shared. Only silence greeted her.

Thin and icy air lingered above her, desperate to invade the stiff blankets and sheets. This morning, like most others this time of year, the scent of dew-coated grass slipped through the windowpanes, a gentle reminder her favorite dresses would collect dust until spring. It was unfortunate, at least to her. Sarah's winter clothes were still packed away in a large gray container lazily thrown to the top of her closet. John's doing. Quite possibly the whiskey's doing. It was difficult to distinguish the blame as of late.

She patted the other side of the bed without turning over, expecting John had crawled in at some point during the night, but her hand moved freely to the edge. *Good*, was her only thought. Her toes, icy and numb, cracked with every step down the hallway and carried on into the kitchen. While each morning mirrored the previous day, she welcomed the monotony. French-pressed coffee, reviewing status updates on social media, then she would stare down the clock until it was time to get ready.

Sarah slid onto the cushion, careful to keep each drop of hazelnut inside the ceramic mug, and took small pulls. Mr. Biscuit stretched near her feet and sat patiently with his cat ears perked.

"Come on." She patted her bare thigh.

His orange fur crinkled as he tilted his head, and his feline gaze fixated on hers. The bright red collar around his neck, complete with vaccination tags dangling just below his throat, rang like Christmas bells when he sprang upward. He circled the spot between her legs for a moment and curled into himself.

*"Where are you?"* she texted John. Somehow, Sarah would've been happier not to receive a response.

*"I had to leave early for work. Sorry about last night."*

She hovered her thumb over the screen. *Sorry? For what? Trying to rape me?* She typed the words screaming inside her, then held the delete button until the message was left blank. *We need to talk. This isn't working out. Maybe we should consider our options,* she said to herself, though all she could manage to type was *"Okay."* Another pull from her mug, but this time a big, scalding gulp.

"You wanna get out of here, Mr. Biscuit?" she whispered, and rubbed along his back.

He opened his eyes, purred a reply, and tucked his head deeper.

"Some help you are."

×

SHE DROVE ON the wet asphalt, showing little regard for the sharp turns and crooked streets. Though only October, the air was rich, a frosty cold winter normally displayed. A sign that snow would soon arrive. *Shit.* Another thing she was utterly unprepared for.

The once-empty streets now overflowed with teenagers, each sharing the same frown or dazed look. There wasn't a whole lot to be happy about at seven in the morning. Could she blame them? No. She, too, wanted to mirror their sour expressions but instead settled for a forced grin.

Shawn was facing away from her when she stepped onto campus. Easy to pick out in a crowd when he stood at least a foot above his peers. But they weren't really peers, were they? Shawn was somehow different. Never loud or obnoxious. Always early to each period with the same calm and attentive demeanor. Didn't raise his hand often, but Sarah knew if called on, he would answer any question with ease. No. He wasn't like them. Not one bit.

She passed Shawn and the students on her way to the hall and caught how his gaze shot between her and the ground.

"Mrs. Baker?" Principal Randolph interrupted her listless march. He was making his rounds through the school as he did every morning and apparently started with D-wing—the closest one to the staff parking lot. He stood at the patio area near the benches. "Can we speak for a moment?"

"How are you today, James?" she asked, both her smile and voice a convincing façade.

He wasn't much taller than Sarah, though nearly double in width. A plain white button-up offset his black slacks. His hair, or the little remaining, splayed outward from the sides while the top was as shiny as the tile floors in D-wing. "Fine, fine. I'd like to have a word with you about something that may have happened yesterday. Go ahead and have a seat outside my office. I need to speak with Coach Tanner for a second, and I'll be right there."

She nodded and followed the metal awnings to the brick office building, all the while replaying yesterday's events through her head. Janice Peterson, the nasty and sometimes spiteful school secretary, was fast at work typing in the students' names she was certain to be tardy if not absent into the computer logs. Sarah thought it best to avoid her at all costs. Luckily enough, the tapping keys continued without pause, and Sarah strutted onward to the hall where Principal Randolph's office was tucked away.

Two chairs were on either side of the door, usually to separate students. Whether a schoolyard scrap or a simple disagreement, this provided an invisible line no one dared to cross unless they wanted a far greater punishment. Sarah was familiar, at least in passing, with how a Saturday at school could quickly turn into a three-day suspension should the threshold be mistreated. Now, in some way, she was less of a staff member and more of a student being forced to endure Janice's incessant smoker's cough. One chair was empty; a girl sat patiently in the other. Blond hair rolled down her back from a tightly fitted ponytail, and her arms were crossed over her chest.

"Good morning, *Mrs. Baker*," Hannah greeted her, and a grin slowly formed on her face, widening to her ears.

"Hannah? Is something wrong?" Sarah intentionally added a curious, nurturing hint to her voice. The attempt fell short.

"Don't act like you don't know. I heard what you said," she responded through a pouty mouth.

*What did I say?* She immediately corrected herself. *What did I say out loud?* Sarah set her purse on the empty chair. "What do you mean, Hannah?"

"Yesterday, when I was talking to my boyfriend, Shawn. I told you to have a nice day and then you called me a spoiled little bitch."

Even Sarah was unsure in that moment if she had said it or not. But no, she knew without a doubt she would never resort to verbally abusing a student, regardless of how much they deserved it. "Hannah, I wouldn't say something like that to you—to any of the students."

"I heard you, and it really hurt my feelings." Her eyes welled on cue, a glistening blue badge of proficiency. Hannah had used this tactic before, maybe with her parents or other, less intelligent, teachers who didn't minor in psychology. They all ate out of her hand, enticing the young sociopath to do whatever necessary to get what she wanted.

It finally dawned on Sarah what was happening, but she couldn't be sure why. Was it the way Shawn smiled at her? *Revenge of the Jealous Teenage Girlfriend—coming this fall to a theater near you.* She couldn't be certain, but one thing was remarkably clear. Hannah was trying to set her up. For a suspension, maybe even termination. What parent would want their child taught by a teacher running around calling them spoiled little bitches? Surely not Dan Richmond. No, he would lead an angry mob at the next PTA meeting, demanding Sarah's head on a platter while clad in some five-hundred-dollar suit and ridiculous tie.

The thought, regardless of how uneasy it made her, also invoked something else. Something stronger. Anger.

"I would never say such a horrible thing, sweetie. Especially to a *remarkable* student."

Hannah uncrossed her arms and scratched at her slim, black leggings.

"Why, I was telling my husband this morning how it's been a treat teaching such a bright individual like Hannah Richmond."

Her blond hair waved as she shifted in the chair and raised her brow. "Are you sure? Daddy says your husband spends every night drowning himself at the Tavern. You must've said it to someone else. Maybe someone sober perhaps?"

The low blow landed exactly where intended: her dignity. If anyone would know where her husband spent his time, it would be the man he worked for—Hannah's father. He owned the town and insisted on rubbing it in everyone's face with his newest ambition. Campaigning for city mayor.

Rumor was that he had been petitioning to change the town's name, but it didn't take a genius to know what it would change to. Richmond. A town of new beginnings. The same slogan he tossed at the committee during every town hall meeting for the past six months. She had met him a handful of times at Christmas parties and company picnics. Never did care enough to hold a conversation with him or his trophy wife, however.

She sucked air through her teeth and dug her knee-high boots into the floor tile. Sarah opened her mouth to speak but decided against it as footsteps lingered down the hallway.

"Sorry to keep you ladies waiting," Principal Randolph said, files clutched under his arm and a coffee in his hand. "Come on in and have a seat." He opened the door and waved each of them inside.

Hannah's eyes lightened a shade, and her potential to burst into tears at any moment was evident. She offered Sarah one last sneer before standing, quick to enter the room first.

"Okay," he said, while relaxing into the plump leather chair. The hinges settled under his weight, and he rested his arms over the desk, fingers interlocked. "What seems to be the issue?"

Two seats were separated a few feet apart on the other end of the desk. One of which seemed to sit directly in front of him, and the other was a bit off-center. Before Sarah could move from the doorway, Hannah positioned herself within his line of sight, ensuring no tear or sniffle went unnoticed.

"Principal Randolph," Sarah began, and cleared her throat. "Hannah was under the impression I said something yesterday, but I believe that we cleared up any confusion." She eyed him while taking a seat, keen to smile after each word left her lips.

"She's lying! I know what I heard. She called me a spoiled little bitch!" Hannah blurted out and immediately covered her face in her palms. She bumped up and down as if in the middle of a hysterical fit, and for a moment, even Sarah believed her.

"I-uh. Ahem. L-let's refrain from using that language, please," he said, and adjusted his tie. "Hannah. That is a very serious accusation. Are you sure that's what you heard? Did anyone else hear it, too?"

Sarah buried her nails into the chair armrests, scratching thick lines until wood shavings wedged between her cuticles. Her body warmed and stiffened, and the boot fabric rubbed against her toes as she wiggled them nervously. There was only one other person around to corroborate her story. *She wouldn't. He wouldn't.*

"Shawn Watkins."

She gnawed on her cheeks, a desperate attempt to hide any concern. *Why would she pull him into this? To lie for her.* A second and even more unnerving thought crossed her mind. *Will he lie for her?* Auburn strands fell over her brow and tickled her eyelid, but she resisted the urge to brush it away. She did nothing but stare forward, fearing any sudden movement may hint at a guilty appearance.

"I see," he said, and reached for the corded phone near his coffee. "Hi, Janice. Can you page Shawn Watkins to my office, please? Alright. Thank you." He licked his lips and returned his hands to the desk.

A fuzzy squelch blared over the school intercoms a few seconds later. "Shawn Watkins to the office. Shawn Watkins to the office." A final click ended the announcement. The silence drew on for a moment, teasing Sarah's insides. Hannah's hands remained clasped to her face, and her bright pink nails reflected off the ceiling lights. Principal Randolph didn't hide the few glances at Sarah, holding an obvious hesitation to speak.

"Mrs. Baker?" he finally said. "Why would Hannah be under the impression you said this?"

"I didn't."

"Yes, you did!" Hannah ripped away the hands shielding her face and hunched forward. Her eyes widened and pale cheeks glowed bright red. She turned to Sarah and demanded her attention. "Wait 'til my father hears about this."

There it was. The moment Sarah had been waiting for. *Wait 'til my father hears about this.* She knew Hannah was apt to bring this threat to the table at some point. *Daddy, Daddy, the teacher said something mean to me!* She was good. Beyond her years in the art of manipulation, and unfortunately for Sarah, it seemed she rarely lost.

"Ms. Richmond, I need you to calm down," Principal Randolph intervened loud enough to startle them both. "Screaming isn't going to solve anything."

Hannah crossed her arms and pouted her lips once more. This time, real tears trickled down her face and rolled off her chin. If she hadn't been holding her designer shoes to Sarah's throat, Sarah might've applauded this outstanding performance. An Oscar-worthy one, in fact. No one would doubt Hannah was telling the truth. And if Shawn agreed with his girlfriend, well, Sarah wouldn't have to wait for a school board meeting. No, she'd be out of Fulton High faster than the extracurriculars during budget cuts.

Footsteps echoed down the hall, and each of them took turns to face the doorway. Shawn stopped at the threshold, sighed, and lifted his gaze from the ground. It wasn't Hannah or Principal Randolph he glanced at, but Sarah, and with the uncertainty in his eyes, she knew she was done for.

# CHAPTER TWENTY

*Sixty-three days missing*

THE BUZZING DRILL forced her to wake. She adjusted to the sunlight, a small crack shining between two brown curtains slung over the window. A soggy-scented draft filled her nostrils. The chains over her wrists were icy and stiff. The bed she was positioned on, a thin mattress on a rickety metal frame, faced the front door. She imagined a giant green exit sign, the same kind drivers saw on a freeway, pointing at it. Taunting her and the impossibility of escape.

He hovered over her, drill in his hand and metal screws clenched between his teeth. The chains rattled as he drove another screw into the wall behind her. She avoided sudden movements should he decide her palms would look nice against the floral pattern wallpaper, and peered up at the man slowly. It crossed her mind to elbow his crotch and flee before he finished securing her chains. If it hadn't been for her leg, that was. Her throbbing, aching, immovable, and useless leg. She couldn't walk much less run out the door. Crawling was out of the question. Now, all she could do was curse at herself for missing her only opportunity.

He fastened another screw and gave the chains a firm tug. They clanked together and remain fixed. Anchored. Another pull, this time with more weight and force behind it. Nothing. A hint of satisfaction spread into a smile on his face, and he walked toward the kitchen, unaware that Sarah was even conscious.

She lifted the solid green blanket and inspected her leg. There were thin wooden posts pressing into each side from her knee to her shin, tied together by a frayed beige cloth. New bandages were tightly wrapped around her ankle to lower thigh, displaying more white than pinkish red. The wound itself, tender to the touch and swollen, ached with the slightest twist. She bit her bottom lip and attempted to hoist her foot in the air.

"*Fuck*," she blurted out, and dropped her leg back to the mattress.

"I wouldn't try to move around too much if I were you," he said, and turned on the faucet. Water spit over his hands and panged the stainless-steel bottom. He raised his voice above the noise. "The bear trap fractured your tibia. Inhumane device, if you ask me."

A small, unintended chuckle slipped from her throat. "Inhumane? You have a pregnant woman chained to your wall. What do you know about humane?"

He turned off the sink and dried his hands with the dish towel from the oven handle. "I have spent a fair amount of time in these woods. Make the hike each spring." He paused, entered the living room, and sat on an old recliner across from her. "Are you familiar with the brown bear? Beautiful animal. A fine predator, but there's one that's worse. Do you know what that might be?"

She couldn't be bothered to answer such an impossible question in her current state. Sarah simply shook her head.

"Human. Every year dozens of men flood up here with their traps, snare some unsuspecting bear, and shoot the poor animal. No tracking. Hell, they don't even bother looking for prints. The cry. That's what they listen for. A trapped and frightened cry. So, every year I wander the trails and remove them. Almost stepped in a few myself." The man chuckled and glanced at her leg. "I do what it takes to level the playing field, if you catch my drift. Give these bears a fighting chance."

"Why are you telling me this?"

He licked his lip and stared for a moment. "You see, predators come in all shapes and sizes. Some have claws, others have"—he hunched forward—"different animalistic tendencies. I take it upon myself to even the odds. So, you see, I'm not as inhumane as one might think. I'm sure you have questions. Anyone would. Ask and I will answer to the best of my ability."

"What did you inject me with?" She kept her voice stern, the same tone she had used with her own students from time to time to deter dishonesty.

"A sedative. Needed the right amount to not kill you and to make sure there was no struggle getting you up here."

*A sedative?* While she couldn't recall much from the first time she woke up in this cabin, the flash of memories seemed to stretch longer than a day, maybe even two. *What kind of sedative could do that?* "What the hell do you want with me?" was all she could muster.

"Simple. I want to see you come to term in the safety of this cabin, and then you'll be free to go. Think of yourself like a bird with a broken wing. I'm here to set the bone, and once you're healed, I'll let you fly away."

"You're gonna let me go?" she sneered. "I don't believe for one second that, after everything, you will just let me go. I've seen your face. The sick basement where you keep your victims. Why on earth would you let me go?"

"If I wanted you dead, I would've done so by now, don't you think? I'm not a fan of ... killing." His voice lowered. He continued to focus on her, but his thoughts seemed elsewhere. "Anyone who takes the life of a human being is to be put to death. Leviticus 24:17."

"Please ... let me go now. I swear, I won't say anything. Just let me go."

He stood and the recliner teetered behind him. "Dinner will be ready in an hour or so." He walked toward the kitchen, and his weathered boots stamped against the floor. The whistling began when he reached the sink, echoing in symphony with the chains rattling on her wrists.

"Oh, and Sarah?" he interrupted himself. "I wouldn't bother screaming. No one's hiked this far in years."

×

SHE SAT AT the table in the kitchen, wrists no longer shackled, but the weight from each chain remained. Heavy, as were the breaths she took eyeing his back near the sink. The crutch he had given her to move about was set against the corner of the table. She wouldn't get far while limping with her body weight on it, and the man knew it. Sarah was doubtful she could even make it off the porch steps.

"I hope you like lamb chops," he said, head slightly tilted.

The frying pan sizzled, and white traces of smoke danced for the wood slat ceiling. He flipped both cuts of meat. Another sizzle. The smell was intoxicating, given the white bread and bologna she'd been fed for months. This would be the first time in her confinement the food was referred to as a meal. Not something prepackaged and crammed full of preservatives.

He returned to the sink to tend to the potatoes lying unpeeled in the strainer. The swiftness in every stroke, sheering the brown to starch white, was enough to unsettle her already tightened stomach.

"It's been a while since I've had the time to cook. Forgot how much I enjoy it."

"What do you do when you're not kidnapping people?" The edge in her voice was clear.

"Saving," he said and turned to meet her glare. "Saving people. Not kidnapping."

"I didn't ask to be saved. You have no right to keep me here."

He tightened his hand over the peeler and started to whistle, softly at first, then at a louder and faster pace. The song, the same one she endured even in the most uncomfortable silence, carried off-tune.

A water-filled pot on a burner adjacent to the skillet sloshed and spilled as he lowered the diced potatoes inside. He flipped on the switch, and blue fire engulfed the stainless-steel bottom. The sizzling dampened, as did his shrill whistle, and he delivered large, meaty chunks to each ceramic plate on the counter. Though the aroma was delightful, she refused to give him the satisfaction.

"The potatoes will be a minute. Why don't you tell me more about yourself while we wait? I've answered some of your questions. Your turn. How did you and the father of your child meet?"

She pulled herself out from the hunger trance and crossed her arms, saying nothing.

"Now, there's no reason for that. Least you could do. I am bustin' my hump over here, after all."

*Why would I tell you anything?* She remained silent, complete with a firm posture and narrowed eyes.

"If you're going to be poor company, I could always put you back in the cellar."

"No!" she blurted out. *Maybe he will see me as a person and he really will let me go.* A lengthy sigh, and the image of John's face returned in small, almost unrecognizable puzzle pieces. The memory of their meeting found a place in her head and, before she could stop herself, found her voice as well.

"We met when I was in college. He was a bartender near the university campus. Three Little Pigs was the name. A local dive one block from the library." Maybe it was the idea of a better time in her life, and given the current situation, a chance to escape mentally. Either way, the story seemed to flow freely from her. "I would go there Sunday afternoons for a daiquiri and to catch up on my reading. I thought he was kinda cute, but I would have never admitted it to him. Something old-fashioned was what appealed to me. Like the stories you hear grandparents tell. To be courted. Wanted."

The man set a pill bottle on the table next to her along

with a glass of water. He sat across the way with a slight wrinkle on his brow and a curious gaze.

Sarah lifted one tablet to her mouth, tilted her head, and sipped from the glass. Prenatal capsules. Off-brand, but she didn't care to make a fuss of it. "He was fit then, hair well taken care of, dressed nicely, and his eyes had … an honesty to them. I found it surprising that each time I'd see him, he'd say some cheap pickup line boys use when they don't know how to approach a woman. *Did it hurt?* or *I lost my phone number, can I have yours?* I wasn't impressed. That was not the meeting I was hoping for. The one I needed. It had to be special."

Another sip from the glass, and she stared blankly for a moment. Then, as a sudden rush of images passed through her head like an opening floodgate, a subtle smile emerged. Her first in quite possibly the last few months.

"One Sunday, late spring I believe, I was there in the evening finishing up another book to mark off my list. Oddly, the bartender hadn't said more than a few words to me that night. Well, back then I secretly called him Johnny because John sounded stiff, respectable, and nothing like the man-child playing games. Johnny suited him well. 'Strawberry daiquiri?' he asked and delivered the drink with nothing more than a stern nod. It was unusual. A piece of me appreciated the sudden professionalism, though I kind of wished for the attention I had grown to loathe.

"I thought, *why isn't he saying anything?* It had to be some sort of ploy. *Do I not look pretty enough today?* So, I leaned over the bar with my empty glass and asked him flat out. *What? Am I not pretty enough for one of those God-awful pickup lines today?* He smiled, of course, the same cheeky grin that prominently displayed the fang on the left side of his mouth like a canine incisor. Johnny the wolf, always on the hunt, and me, always his prey. Except that night, the wolf had wised up."

The man leaned forward and interlocked his fingers. "Go on."

"I wouldn't allow myself to be conquered so easily. To be a notch on anyone's belt. I refused to crawl into bed with a random guy. What I didn't expect was to fall so hard for the man-child. The wolf of Three Little Pigs. I hovered over the bar for a few seconds, awaiting his response, but he didn't say a word. He stepped closer to me and lifted his palm, revealing a quarter. A plain, somewhat filthy quarter. I can still remember the way it glinted off those horribly dim ceiling lights. Then he closed his fist and waved his free hand over it. Slowly, Johnny opened his hand. The coin was gone.

"I glared at him, annoyed, and a bit confused. *Big deal*, I thought. *You made a coin vanish.* He smiled again and closed his fist. I expected the same, dirty quarter to reappear, but when he raised his fingers, there was a slip of paper in its place. A note. A treasure for me. I unfolded the crease and read the poorly scribbled words aloud. *You are, and always will be the most beautiful girl I have ever seen.* This was what I was waiting for. Something that would make my friends groan with jealousy. Something I could cherish. I finally had the story I always wanted, and he finally had me." Her smile faded, a dimming sunlight, and now she spoke before her mind had a chance to think better of it.

"We were married a year later, and it's taken another five

to realize what he did. The magic trick was just that. A trick. He tricked me into believing he was the person I was waiting for. Not Johnny. Not the man-child. Not the wolf of Three Little Pigs. It was all an elaborate trap, and I fell right into it."

The man across the table stared at her. "While I do appreciate the story of how you and your *husband* met, he isn't the person I was asking about."

# CHAPTER TWENTY-ONE

*Nineteen days before Sarah went missing*

"Mr. Watkins," Principal Randolph said, and motioned him inside. "I was hoping you could clarify what happened in the hall yesterday. You were with Ms. Richmond, correct?"

Shawn took a few steps forward and looked at the floor. He grated his bottom lip with his teeth and slowly raised his eyes to Principal Randolph.

"Yes, sir."

Sarah's chest tightened. Each breath shriveled until only a wisp of air remained. The blood rushed from her cheeks. Sweat formed on her brow. Her cheekbones, already high on her face, perched an extra inch when her lips thinned to a straight, almost narrow line.

"Did you hear Mrs. Baker say anything inappropriate to Ms. Richmond?"

He drew a heavy breath, and his shoulders went stiff. "I'm not sure I understand, sir."

"Did you hear Mrs. Baker say anything offens—"

"Shawn!" Hannah snatched him by the hand. "Tell Principal Randolph what she said yesterday. You were right next to me. I know you heard it, too."

Sarah shifted uncomfortably in her seat. Her insides

screamed, obscenities more than anything else, and the bitter taste of anxiety rolled off her tongue and onto her teeth.

"That's enough, Ms. Richmond!" Randolph paused, removed a pen from his pocket, and clicked it. He was prepared to jot down whatever statement Shawn made. "Now, Shawn. I need you to be honest with me. Did Mrs. Baker say something offensive to Hannah?"

This was it. He was going to do Hannah's bidding and send Sarah home—to John's home—unemployed. She wouldn't be able to teach a few towns over—hell, maybe not in the entire state again. Sarah didn't know if her credentials would be pulled or not, but they might as well be. Her name would be smeared from county to county.

*Baker? You mean the teacher that attacked Richmond's daughter? Called her a spoiled bitch and slapped her?* She knew the rumors would embellish with each ear they passed, and eventually, Sarah would be known as the teacher who threatened to kill her own student.

Shawn untied his interlocked fingers from Hannah's desperate grip and straightened himself. "No, sir."

It took a moment for Sarah to realize what he said. To process two simple words. *No. Sir. No. Sir. He said no. He told the principal no. He told Hannah … no.* Sarah, her stomach still rolling in on itself, almost gasped. Thankfully, she was able to control herself.

"Are you sure about this?" Principal Randolph continued.

"I was standing next to Hannah when Mrs. Baker walked by. If she said anything inappropriate, I would've heard it."

Hannah smacked him in the arm not once but twice and

scoffed. She shifted to Principal Randolph. Her eyes, like blue marbles splashing into a puddle, moistened until tears streamed down her face. "He's lying for her! I know what I heard."

Principal Randolph furrowed his brow and pursed his lips to the side. "Shawn. Mrs. Baker. I'm sorry to have wasted your time. You may return to first period. Oh, and Sarah? You are slotted for detention this afternoon. Please let me know if you have any issues."

Sarah lifted herself from the hot seat, and both she and Shawn nodded at Mr. Randolph before leaving. Hannah attempted to stand too but was immediately interrupted.

"Ms. Richmond, I'd like to speak to you alone for a minute."

With a small grin, Sarah followed Shawn into the hall. He had saved her, in more ways than one. Hannah's father carried a power only money could buy. Hell, even John's job could have been at stake. Now, whether Dan Richmond agreed with his manipulative daughter or not, there was no proof, no witnesses to back up the story.

Principal Randolph and Hannah continued to argue, and their voices echoed down the hall and into the front office. Shawn made it a point to hold the door for her on the way out. A simple gesture but considerate.

"Thank you, Shawn," she said, hinting at a few different things to be grateful for, and continued forward.

"Mrs. Baker?"

"Yes?"

"I'm sorry. About Hannah. I'll try to talk to her."

She lowered her voice to a whisper and inched forward.

"I wouldn't waste my time if I were you. I grew up with girls like Hannah Richmond. I won't be the first or last person she lies about."

He paused and retraced her words before speaking. "What do you think I should do?"

*Run. Run as fast as you can.* Sarah couldn't say it, though, no matter how much she wanted to. No teacher in their right mind would give a student relationship advice, and Sarah, despite the longing to do just that, pretended to look at her watch and walked away abruptly. "You better get to class. I hear your English teacher has detention this afternoon. Wouldn't want to be tardy." She thrust open the door leading to her classroom and nodded in his direction.

Shawn smirked. "That doesn't sound like much of a punishment."

✕

THE REMAINDER OF first period passed by as expected—her nestled quietly behind her desk while the students, mostly Shawn, peered at her in intervals. After the bell tolled and the last few students fled, she dismissed herself for whatever coffee was left in the staff lounge. Sarah returned to the hallway minutes later and took notice of the rectangular poster slung over the wooden announcements wall. HOMECOMING DANCE was displayed in bright pink cursive, poorly drawn balloons scattered down each side, and near the bottom in bold letters was SATURDAY @ 7:00 P.M.

It wasn't until she skimmed over the time that Sarah recalled her conversation with Barbara. The lodge. She imagined the thick trees, wooded scent, and arguments sure to be had on the trip. Then she pictured a weekend at home alone. No John. No cabin toilets or showers. No Barbara or Phillip. No new doctor visits she had to pretend to be interested in. A smile slithered across her face. *They'll need chaperones. Homecoming it is.*

She reentered the classroom, a newfound vigor of excitement carrying her, and stopped near her desk. A single rose was left on a stack of assignments waiting to be graded. Vibrant red petals laid over the smooth white surface, rivaling the same shade of her lips and skin. The stem was frayed, a twin to the others she kept, and morning dew slid from the delicate blossom creating tiny droplets on a few pages if not the entire stack. Thorns staggered up each side to a single leaf. The sepals, a yellowish green, splayed outward like a hand, as if to display the beauty they held. She grabbed the rose, careful to avoid pricking her fingers, and inhaled the scent.

# CHAPTER TWENTY-TWO

*Sixty-three days missing*

HE DIDN'T MOVE. Did not speak. His fixed scowl clung to her uneasy face. He scanned her from forehead to chin, paused at her eyes, and repeated this process. Sarah knew the hesitation. Knew why the man allowed such a long break after his question. Her psychology course in university had taught her how to search for the subtle changes in expression when someone told a lie. A glance to the right. Tightened lips. Blushed cheeks. Even a smile. She excelled when it came to reading people, reading their lies rather, and knew exactly what he was desperately waiting on. The truth. An answer she wasn't ready to produce or explain.

"I don't understand what you mean." She straightened her features, revealing not a single nervous tick.

He scanned again and narrowed in on her mouth. "I think you do. How did you meet the father of your child?"

She returned his stare and counted the seconds in her head before allowing herself to blink. Another tell she declined to share. "My husband is the father."

The man smashed his closed fist to the table like a gavel, and the wooden legs threatened to drop from the impact. Both ceramic plates chimed, the same tone of a poorly rung bell, and settled on the wobbly surface. "You will not lie to me in my house!"

Sarah recoiled and tried to hide it.

"The Lord detests lying lips, but he delights in people who are trustworthy. Proverbs 12:22," he said with more edge in his thick voice. "Now, I'll ask you again. How did you meet the father of your child?"

She counted to ten and steadied her breath. "My husband is the—"

He swiped his large arm over the table and hurled the plates and cups to the floor. Glass shattered. Chunks of lamb bounced off the linoleum and rolled in different directions. He lifted himself from the chair and craned his head downward. The near six-and-a-half-foot giant loomed over her, and she realized just how small she was. "If you lie one more time, I will drag you to the cellar by your hair and shove a toothpick under all ten nails. Tell me the truth!"

She took note of the veins above his brow. The red scratchy lines around his pupils. The flaring nostrils. Most importantly, the way he still wouldn't lay a hand on her in his tantrum. She leaned back and rubbed a palm over her stomach. A sly grin tugged at the corner of her mouth. "No. You won't." Her smile deepened, as did his glower.

He yelled a deep, throaty howl and flipped the table to the side. The foundation shuddered and kitchen lights flickered. Boiling water spat from the pot and sizzled on the blue fires below. His chest heaved, a snarling pant leaving both his nose and mouth simultaneously. The man stomped away from the kitchen, through the living room, and slammed the front door on his way out.

Sarah lowered herself to the ground and carefully slid

across the floor. She grabbed the first piece of meat within reach, blew off the dust and debris, and popped it in her mouth. The lamb sliced delicately between her teeth. She found another chunk, picked off a stray black hair, and nearly swallowed it whole. Not the ideal way to eat, but she'd rather dine with the cold ground than the man pacing outside.

After picking the lamb chunks like ripe Granny Smiths from a tree, she crawled into the living room, mouth full and a few leftover pieces in her hand. A snack for the show she was sure to enjoy. It took a few minutes to climb into her makeshift bed. No easy task on a fractured leg, but she managed to do so without much discomfort. Head propped on a pillow, Sarah faced the window peering outside. A shadow swayed back and forth, highlighted by the stars shining through the oak clearing.

"She's still lying." His voice was dampened by the sheet-rock between them yet still audible. "Tell me what to do and I'll do it. I promise you."

A cramp twisted above her bladder.

"Are you sure this is what you want? That this is what you want for the child?"

She stopped chewing, afraid the sound of her incisors cutting into the meat might dampen his conversation.

"Okay … okay. She won't be harmed."

*He has a phone. And somehow out here, he's getting reception.* She tossed the thought back and forth, but one question lingered at the forefront. *Who is he talking to? John? Did John hire him to kill me after the baby is born?*

The door opened, and the man reentered. He glanced at

Sarah nestled on the fold-out couch, hands covering her stomach. Her shield. The only protection she seemed to have in this place.

"Glad to see you're still able to move around," he said, but the words were more sarcastic than sincere. He inched toward her, gently grabbed each wrist, and shackled them to the wall. The thick iron cuffs grazed her raw skin, adding a hint of cold to her burning flesh. He saw the lamb chunks in her palm and sighed. "I apologize for losing my temper. It won't happen again."

She gave him a simple, acknowledging nod. It was a tranquil demeanor Sarah decided to tap into. Now would have been the worst time to spit lamb chunks at the man suffering the first of, if she had her way, many mental breakdowns in her presence. *Keep him calm.*

"Who were you talking to?"

"No one."

"They will find me, you know. My husband probably has the whole county searching these woods." The lie smothered a sour taste on her tongue, more than the floor meat she managed to swallow. He was the last person she'd expect to come to her rescue. Maybe he had taken the opportunity to play house with the woman he had become fond of as of late. *No more Sarah to get in his way. No wife to yell at him. No one to stop him.*

"Somehow, I doubt he will. You and I know that, don't we?"

She closed her eyes and huffed a breath. A better alternative than the whimper aching to be spilled. Another nod was all she allowed herself.

After the cuffs had been fixed tightly, he gave the chain a firm tug and sat on the chair a few feet away. He interlocked his fingers and stared at her. Waiting for a sniffle, a choked back tear, something. She gave him none of the three. She, too, matched his gaze. "How long have you known?" The question rattled its way from his throat.

"Known what?"

"We both know you're too smart to play stupid, Sarah. You don't seem distraught at what I said about your husband not coming. You haven't bothered to defend him. I'd hope you know more about him or what he'd be doing with his recent free time than I do." The man eased his neck to the back of the recliner. "Spouses normally fight tooth and nail for their partner's honor. You haven't. Why is that?"

"John's a big boy. He doesn't need me to defend him."

"Maybe not," he said. "Then again, maybe you simply choose not to. So, how long have you known?"

"Are you married, Mr.—?" she deflected his question with one of her own. Insight, at times, could benefit the situation; she knew this all too well. First, she would dig for distraction, someone to be used against the man staring back. Second, a name. A formality to turn interrogation into casual conversation. The less she felt imprisoned, the less captive she acted, and soon his view of a hostage would become increasingly vague. She was willing to wager on this strategy. A smirk slithered across her mouth before she retrieved another bite of lamb for reassurance.

He let out an easy breath, not so much a scoff or sigh but somewhere in between. "Once."

She latched her claws to the opening like a vulture to a

freshly bloodied meal. "Once? What happened?"

"Jus' wasn't meant to be."

"Any kids with Mrs.—?"

The man rubbed his thick palm forehead downward. "No. I don't have any kids."

She made it a point to caress her stomach long enough for him to notice even in the darkened room. "I see. Well, I am sorry to hear that. I've always wanted to be a mother. To love and be loved unconditionally." Though partially true, she hoped this confession sparked some form of humanity within him.

"Even if the child is the product of a broken marriage?"

Sarah contemplated by tilting one side of her shriveled face. "After I have what I want, what's to say I won't just leave? Discard John as he has discarded me all these years?"

"You know," he said, and leaned forward, "there's a spider that showcases this behavior. A *Latrodectus*. Body darker than the pits of hell itself. Red hourglass on its abdomen, a warning to its prey, for their time is short once caught in her web. After mating, and like you she has what she wants, the female then eats the male. The black widow. Fitting, I'd say."

How could she have been so stupid? This was John's doing. Why else would he be defending him? He hired this man to drag her up here. Hired him to keep her out of the way. Johnny was pulling the strings. Making it appear as though he was the hopeful husband on a mission to find his loving wife. All the while she was being injected with sedatives and fed meat from the floor. Rage settled in her gut. Rage and the promise of acidic burps from the lamb digesting.

"I have never hurt my husband."

*"Physically."*

"Well, I sure as hell wouldn't kill him."

He arched a brow. "Have you thought about it?"

"Have you thought about killing me?"

"Yes."

His blunt response caught her off guard. Had she expected this honest of an answer, her question may have gone unasked.

"I spent the first few days considering it. You were, of course, much more difficult then. Aggressive. It was to be expected though. Every animal, even humans, rely on fight or flight. You wouldn't have known, of course, if that gives you any satisfaction. I would have made it painless. No. Like I said before, I don't enjoy killing. Saving is what I was brought here to do. The plan must be followed accordingly. A crime of passion is simply that. A crime."

"What plan? Kidnap and drug me?" She slapped her mended leg for emphasis and avoided a painful recoil to prove a point. "Snare me like some wild animal?"

"Your injury was your own doing. As long as you remain here, you will not be harmed."

A tear-filled chuckle, moments from her own hysterical fit. "Right. I'm supposed to believe a word you say? How many others *haven't been harmed* in these woods, huh? How many women have you shackled to your fucking wall?"

He narrowed his eyes, but a spec of curiosity lingered in each. "None. You are the only one. This I can assure you. I don't take honesty lightly, and if there is one thing you believe during your time here, trust in that."

She stared at the ceiling to force back tears. "I can't trust someone I don't know."

"My name is Michael. It is nice to meet you, Sarah Baker."

# CHAPTER TWENTY-THREE

*Nineteen days before Sarah went missing*

THE LAST BELL blared over the intercom on campus. It was, as always, a wavering tone. Sarah closed her eyes and braced herself for the inevitable headache. The three P.M. migraine she called it. Her usual, like she ordered it from a coffee shop and was promptly smacked in the head with a rock.

Backpacks zipped. Lockers slammed. Sneakers scuffed and squealed. *Another hour.* She nibbled on the pen in her hand, scraping freshly applied lipstick to the plain black cap. *Then a weekend alone. No John. No eggshells to walk over. A relaxing weekend.*

The class slowly emptied, and the squealing door hinges added to the already noisy room. Some students smiled in her direction on the way out. Sarah did the same, though less authentic and more mechanical. A shallow grin. One which, after many years of exercise, no longer strained her cheeks.

"Have a nice weekend," she said to the flock. The door swayed shut and closed her inside. She hoped the detention board somehow mixed her classroom number with another but knew at any moment her small classroom would be invaded. *Three, two, one,* and she ended the countdown by pointing at the threshold. Her timing was a bit off, but impressive, nonetheless.

A shaking handle. An obnoxious sigh. Lastly, footsteps. Not the *skipping toward a weekend of freedom* footsteps. No, these were sluggish stomps inward. Jared Stevens fixed his disgruntled gaze to the tile floors, moved for the back row, and dropped into his identical second period desk.

She had the urge to tell him to take a seat at the front, but the opening door halted her. Alexandria Hayward. Fourth period honors English. Shoulder-length hair dyed jet black. Clothes as dark as the wretched teen angst she poured into her diary during class. She took a seat near the back of the room as well, blew the strands from her displeased face, and placed her notebook on the desk, eagerly awaiting the opportunity to jot down whatever was forming in her head.

Colin Hodges was next to enter. A regular to her afternoon of punishment. She knew he would spend the remainder of the hour smacking his gum, his feet propped on the desk. It was what she had come to expect, like he could expect handcuffs when the *he's a kid* excuse ran out.

Another rattle of the door handle. Her breath caught, and a stiffness radiated down her spine. A warm, almost hot flash passed from cheek to cheek. Instinctively, she lifted the glasses from her nose to her crown. Maybe for a better look. Maybe for her to look better. He didn't drag his feet through the threshold. No. He walked straight inside with purpose.

Shawn.

"Good afternoon, Mrs. Baker." A grin stretched his jawline. The backpack added to his firm posture. He sat in the front row a few chairs over from the center. She stared at him. What could he have possibly done to end up in detention? *Her* detention. Sarah couldn't recall a time he had ever been in attendance. No, Shawn never seemed to cause trouble.

"I am sure you are all here for a reason," she addressed the small group and made it a point not to look at Shawn directly. "So, I would like a one-page essay on why you are here and how you can correct this behavior in the future."

A low groan emanated from the back. Had there been more students, she would have expected a similar sound in stereo. Not that she cared. There was no salvation to be had this day, not for the other three at least. This assignment was not for them, however. This was for her. An answer to the question nagging at her. The reason for her inadvertent lip gnawing. A way to ease her burning forehead and flushed cheeks. She needed to know.

The minutes seemed to slow, and every time she scanned the room, Shawn's focus quickly returned to the paper in front of him.

*Three forty-five. Close enough.* "After you are finished, you may bring the essays forward and enjoy the remainder of your weekend." The group scrambled for their backpacks, all except him. He continued to scribble on the paper in front of him, head now craned over his desk. Colin was the first, followed closely by Alexandria and Jared. They took turns handing over the assignment and bolted out of the door without looking back. She had no intention of reading them anyway. Well, not all of them.

Another few minutes passed, and Shawn remained firmly planted in his seat. He might need more time. Maybe explaining something out of character for him was difficult.

The overwhelming urge to know pulled her from the mahogany blockade she'd never dared cross before. Her boots tapped against the tiles as she took small, determined steps forward. He paused briefly as she stood over him, then returned his pencil to the page. The sharpened number two scraping in fine, precise movements parted the silence. There were no words written down. No explanation to comfort her. Only a drawing partially hidden by his broad shoulders.

"Shawn? What have you been doing this entire time?"

He tilted his head and met her gaze, a slight curl at the corner of his lips.

She ripped the notebook from him. "What has gotten into you? You were supposed to write about why you are he—"

It wasn't his grin that stopped her. It wasn't the sudden appearance of his dimples or the way his eyes glinted off the ceiling lights. She looked at the page in her hand. It was a sketch. A portrait of her. He captured everything. Every freckle. Her high cheekbones. The way a stray strand or two fell over her brow. Even the tiny mole on her neck normally covered when her hair was down. Slowly, a smile formed on her face, too.

She alternated glances between him and the notebook in her hand. The picture must be how the rest of the world saw her. How Shawn saw her. He had somehow managed to capture the beauty her own husband took for granted. It was nice not to go unnoticed for once. For someone to care. For someone to truly see Sarah Baker.

"Shawn," she said fondly. "I didn't know you could draw." A lie. She, of course, knew about the advanced arts course he had taken since his freshman year.

"It's easy when you have something worth sketching."

"It's lovely. Thank you." She sat on the desk to his left. "Do you plan on going to an art school after you graduate?"

"I want to." He left it at that.

She stood and placed an arm on each end of the table, leaning forward. "Have you started looking at colleges?"

"A bit here and there. I don't know. It's difficult for artists to make a good living." He shrugged and stared anywhere but her chest. It didn't seem to be modesty but more so respect.

"I went to a university with plenty of artists," she lied again.

He tilted his head, matched her gaze, and the firm posture of his lips loosened. She found it surprising. Not that he believed her, but how a hormone-driven teenager would refuse himself the chance to take a quick peek at a teacher's skin. Adult men wouldn't think twice. He *was* different.

"Most of them are fairly successful now. You shouldn't do what makes you money. You should do what makes you happy."

"Dad says I should choose something more practical." His smile faded, taking a piece of her with it.

"What does your mother say?"

He slumped his shoulders, and his grin disappeared.

"I'm sorry. It's not my place to get involved."

"It's fine, Mrs. Baker. I just haven't spoken to my mom in months."

A pause. An inward breath. Reddened cheeks and a slight glisten in each eye. These were now the things that the boy sitting far too close to her didn't notice. "Shawn. I'm so sorry. I ... I didn't know." Lie number three. It was no secret that the woman who claimed herself a mother abandoned her only son for another shot at a family. Ran halfway across the country with nothing more than a suitcase and a newfound affection for a different man. Sarah cupped a hand over his, and the warmth lifted the small hairs on her forearms. A pulse started at her chest and worked its way lower. Her stomach caught the steady thump like a well-placed net below a high wire. "If you ever want someone to talk to, I'm always here."

His smile returned, as did the softness in his near thick voice. "Thank you."

The moment lingered on, her hand over his, their gazes evenly fixed. Who would retreat from this mildly inappropriate game of chicken they were playing first? She was the teacher, after all, and couldn't be caught fondling a student's hand. She needed to let go. But something in her couldn't.

Shawn made the decision for them both and stood from his desk. He dropped his hand to his side, parted their touch, and reached for the notebook. It was a difficult thing to give back; the gift of being noticed. She did so hesitantly but ate the word *no* until it buried deep in her sternum.

A careful rip along the seam was all it took for the page to flow freely. She held her breath, making a superstitious plea to keep the portrait intact. Shawn, now the one staring down, offered Sarah the paper.

"I'm not taking your artwork," she said, "until you sign it."

His cheeks reddened, a slight hint of pink against light

brown. He nodded and scribbled his signature on the lower-right corner. *Shawn Watkins.* She scanned the name, the same one she couldn't seem to stop saying in her head. A slight tilt of her chin, and she smiled upward, a bit wider than she should have.

"Thank you, Shawn," she said, and accidentally grazed her fingers against his while taking the picture.

A half grin emerged. He leaned in. She didn't look away. She didn't blink. Her once-steady heartbeat pulsed at an erratic pace. *What is he doing?* Sarah asked over and over as he came closer. *What am I doing?*

"Shawn …" she whispered and placed a hand at his chest to hold him still. A strained sigh was the next sound to pass. "I can't."

He shook his head. "I'm sorry. I shouldn't have."

Sarah returned to her desk and slid the portrait in the top drawer. A companion for the rose cast to its crevices. "There's nothing to apologize for." She stood a bit straighter and ignored the buckle in her knees. "But I am your teacher. And we mustn't confuse the boundaries of this relationship." Each word buried the knife handle deeper to her abdomen. A sharpness radiated. Intensified. Threatened to burn her eyes.

"You're right. I'm sorry." He packed his bag and slid it over his shoulders. "It won't happen again."

"Good."

×

A PICKUP WAS the first thing she saw after passing the low-hanging branches and a beaten gravel path. John's truck. It resembled something foreign under the evening glare—not so much the truck itself but seeing it at this time of day. A navy-blue sheen reflected the dimming horizon and mountainous landscape surrounding Fulton. She wasn't sure why he was home. She wasn't sure of a lot when it came to her husband. A victim of quarterly layoffs was the first thought, but if that were the case, John would promptly drown himself in whiskey for the remainder of the night on a barstool. There had to be a reason.

Sarah nearly forgot to place the car in park before stepping out, nor did she grab her burlap sack purse from the front seat. An intruder had entered her home, and she was determined to get answers. This was the same person she hadn't seen before midnight for weeks, let alone someone actually sober enough to drive. Mr. Biscuit leaned against the window overlooking the porch, orange and brown fur pressed against the glass, an obvious yearning to escape whatever hell John was creating inside. She gave the window a gentle tap, and he wedged himself deeper between the window and curtain.

The front door's eerie creak threatened to unhinge her, and the noise from the kitchen only amplified her pitted stomach. Drawers opened and slammed. Silverware clanged together like a wind chime. He was looking for something.

"John?"

More rustling and no answer.

"John, I'm home."

She took a few cautious steps forward, then stopped. A heavy, near stomping sound shuddered into the hallway. Her face, from high cheekbones to chin, went slack, and she attempted to swallow the chalky taste building in her throat. Her stammering heartbeat rose and swelled into a dull throb at the back of her skull. The silhouette paused, no more than a pace or two ahead, and the knife in his palm glinted in the poorly lit room.

# CHAPTER TWENTY-FOUR

*Sixty-four days missing*

SHE HAD SPENT most of the evening alone on her bed, recalling their conversation, more so the way he introduced himself so bluntly. *My name is Michael. I am pleased to meet you, Sarah Baker.*

Michael. Even if she had met him at some point or another, the name Michael gave her nothing. Far too common to tell her who this man was and why he had taken her. The most important question of all: what he was really going to do with her after she gave birth?

After many hours of careful tossing and turning, daybreak parted the moth-eaten curtains and eased inside like a frightened stray. The room carried a different tone almost, a home the simple edge of night refused to reveal.

Sarah rubbed her stomach, concerned. It wasn't the size that bothered her, but the lack of movement. A twitch. Tickle. A jolt. Anything would've calmed her. Stress could lead to miscarriages. Sarah couldn't seem to think of a more stressful situation if she tried. Her soft rubbing led to a pat, and eventually a firm poke. Nothing. Only the rumble of her malnourished stomach replied. She wished she could tell the baby not to give up. How she would get out of here. How she would get *them* out of here.

"Michael?" she shouted down the crooked hall. "We're hungry." If he wanted a prisoner, Sarah would give him one. One he had to wait on hand and foot. "Michael? Are you in there?"

Sarah knew he was. It would be near impossible a man his size could pass by her undetected. Another minute went by without response, and she began losing patience. "Michael! I can't exactly get up and feed myself chained to your wall!"

A rustling, followed by two heavy thuds against the wood floors. His shadow appeared from the hallway, and he took small, sluggish steps forward. Daylight caught the aged skin of his face, accenting the crow's feet and slight wrinkles above his brow.

"Morning. How'd you sleep?"

"Shackled and flat on my back."

He rubbed each tired eye and moved closer. "If I could trust you not to run, those chains would be unnecessary."

"Trust is earned." She narrowed her mouth to a scowl.

"My thoughts exactly. I'm making eggs. Hope that's okay."

Sarah despised the thought. Eggs just wouldn't do. "I want pancakes. The baby is craving them. Extra butter too."

A less-than-enthused expression tightened his lips. "Any other requests?"

"Coffee with milk and sugar."

"No caffeine for you, Sarah. I'm sorry. Not good for the lil one."

He left no room for a retort and went to the kitchen. After fifteen minutes, give or take, Michael returned and shoved a plate in her lap. The eggs were scrambled and runny. Less cooked than she would've preferred. She eyed the yellow clump, then glared at him.

"Pancakes, extra butter. Oh, and I almost forgot. Here's your coffee." He handed her a glass of water and a prenatal tablet. "With milk and sugar."

Sarah clenched her jaw and debated jamming the fork in his thigh. She may not have pancakes, but at least she could eat with a smile. Michael moved away before she got the chance and sat in the armchair, his own plate resting on his knees. She took a bite and recoiled. The eggs were near tasteless, slimy, and in dire need of salt. He did the same, but his expression was quite the opposite. He even started humming the tune he normally whistled, happily plucking along at a new piece of egg to shove in his mouth.

"What do you do exactly, *Michael*?" She practically spat his name along with the tiny eggshell surprises she found in her breakfast. "What sort of job gives you the free time to entertain a woman you've abducted?"

He swallowed and remained fixed on his plate. "I'm a doctor. Before that, a physician for the 81st Airborne Division."

"A veteran doctor? You have got to be kidding me. Don't they do psyche tests in the military? How in the fuck did *you* pass one?"

"Language, Mrs. Baker." The thick lines above his brow deepened, as did the harshness in his eyes.

She drew a breath. Sarah needed to dig. Pry information she could use. "How long were you in the military?"

"Long enough. You wouldn't want to hear me spout off

war stories like the rest of the retirees at the VFW." Michael took another bite, and though his head was shaved, she noticed the area where his peppered hairs began to retreat from his forehead.

"Try me."

"Okay." He wiped his mouth. "I served ten years in the army. Around five were in Afghanistan. Too much death on my table to make it the full twenty. One deployment in particular, we were pinned in the Lashkagar province. Hell, I didn't think any of us would make it out alive. Most of my unit didn't." The hard edge of his face loosened. "Insurgents came in from every direction. The black rags covering their faces were all we could see in the haze. We fought for days. Weeks, it seemed like. Lost a lot of brothers and sisters. It's funny, blood is heavier than you'd expect. Thicker. You don't consider the weight until it's on your own hands."

"So, you left the army, took up a residency in the Pacific Northwest, and added abducting to your résumé? Part of your five-year plan?"

"I didn't choose for this to happen, Sarah. The decision was made for me."

Surely, no one had held a gun to his head and demanded he kidnap a teacher. A pregnant, insignificant teacher. "By whom?"

Michael interlocked his fingers and pointed to the ceiling.

"God?" she scoffed. "God told you to kidnap me?"

He returned to his plate and lifted a forkful to his mouth. "But when you ask, you must believe and not doubt, because the one who doubts is like a wave of the sea, blown and tossed by the wind. James 1:6. You wouldn't understand," he replied with his mouthful of eggs.

"Enlighten me, Dr. Michael. What prophecy has your lord graced you with?"

He rested his head back on the fabric cushion and stared blankly. "Again. That simple statement shows how little you know about me or my faith."

Sarah slipped the prenatal pill to her tongue and gulped it down with water. It was from the faucet in the kitchen but still satisfying. "Have you ever killed anyone?"

"More than I'd care to admit. What they don't tell you in the recruiter's office is how the people you kill follow you long after they're left twitching on the sands." His neck jerked. He was either choking back tears or trying to dry-swallow his latest bite.

She took note of the residing pain in his dark brown eyes, a softness she intended to exploit to her benefit. PTSD. It was covered in her course. Even while nursing a week-long hangover during those lessons, she'd committed enough to memory to use at her disposal. This disorder was usually accompanied by a trigger. Loud noises. Fireworks. Gunshots. Something that provided haunting flashbacks. Something to aid in her escape.

"Are you finished?" he asked after a long pause.

"No. Not yet."

Michael stood and dragged his boots to the kitchen. Sarah lifted the clumpy egg to her face, at first inspecting for shells until she noticed the bent metal fork prongs seemingly staring back. Each one tilted slightly in a different direction. Thin. Tiny enough to fit into—

*A lock.*

She shifted to the lock binding her chains. The size of the hole was remarkably close. Maybe a perfect fit. She scraped off the eggs and bent a single prong back and forth. It still wouldn't give after numerous wiggles.

"Hey, Sarah?" Footsteps moved for the living room.

*Shit. Shit. Shit.* The prong still refused to break. She forced the fork in her mouth at once, pretending to be mid-bite when he poked his head in and met her gaze.

"I'll need to change your bandage at some point today. Sound good to you?"

"Mm-hmm," she replied and nodded with the fork handle against her lips.

"All right." He retreated to the sink. When the water turned on, Sarah resumed shifting the prong back and forth.

Her insides screamed. He could come back at any second, and if he caught her, who knew what he'd do. She certainly had no desire to find out. She had almost given up when the metal finally snapped. There was a subtle crack, loud enough for her to hear, but she doubted Michael could over the sink water. The broken prong dropped into her palm, and she clutched it tightly. She nearly yelped with excitement but opted to raise her arms in the air triumphantly instead. The chains clattered but no more than usual. She could have been adjusting. Scratching. Anything. To the man in the kitchen, she was no sooner to escaping than before.

Sarah pushed the prong into the lock. It slid in, a bit rough at first, but then fit the way her own house keys did. Much better than she anticipated. The biggest issue would be maneuvering it around the inner cylinders to crack it open. She couldn't practice picking the lock while Michael was awake. No, he never left her alone for long. She had to wait for him to pass out for the night. Uninterrupted hours of practice was the only option. Learn how to unlock and lock it until she could do it in a matter of seconds. And when her leg was healed, nothing was going to stop her from getting home.

She tucked the sliver in her pillowcase and dug the fork into the biggest glob of egg, hoping he wouldn't give it a second glance. "Michael? I'm finished."

He stood in front of her and reached for the plate. "How were they?"

"Could've used some salt, but not bad."

"I'll take that as a compliment," he said and returned to the sink once more.

Home. The four simple letters filled her with hope. Sarah had taken the first step out of this cabin, and unbeknownst to Michael, would be home in time to give birth. Her baby wouldn't be born on some pullout couch at the hands of this man playing doctor. She grinned and patted the pillow holding her makeshift key to escape.

Water sloshed over the plate and abruptly hit the sink bottom. "Sarah?"

Terror seized her legs and goose bumps traveled up her arms. "Yes?" She tried to keep her voice steady but noticed the way panic made her hiss the S like the rattlesnakes John warned her about in their backyard. He saw the missing prong. He knew she broke it off. Home was now replaced by a different one-syllable word.

Trapped.

"Is there something you want to tell me?"

"What?" was all she could muster.

His boots shifted and squeaked on the kitchen floor. She didn't know what to do. What to say. Should she hide it in her sock? Feign ignorance? She had no idea, but as he wandered closer to the wall she was chained to, sheer dread ripped through her.

"You didn't think I'd notice?" His voice grew louder.

She wanted to scream. To yell for help. It didn't matter. No one would come. *No one has hiked this far in years*, Sarah remembered him saying. She imagined another toothpick wedged under her fingernail. The numbness from the cement floor in the basement. Worst of all, she recalled his violent outburst at dinner, and how he had thought about killing her. This was it. This was how Sarah Baker was going to die.

Michael stared at her for a moment and finally spoke. "You just pushed these eggs around and barely ate at all. Are you still hungry?"

She released the breath she didn't know she was clutching onto. "Morning sickness," she lied and prayed he'd buy into it. "I felt nauseous after the second bite."

He shrugged and ambled past the threshold. "Suit yourself."

# CHAPTER TWENTY-FIVE

*Nineteen days before Sarah went missing*

"YOU'RE HOME LATE," John said, his lengthy brow furrowed.

Sarah released an uneasy breath. "Detention. I'm surprised you're home at all." The beginnings of an argument lingered, much like the sour taste she tried to dry-swallow.

It was apparent he had the impulse to say more, but John choked back whatever resentment he was harboring and departed the hall for the lighted kitchen. "Dinner's ready."

*Dinner?* The idea of a meal she herself hadn't prepared was almost as surprising as the lack of whiskey stench she expected to radiate off him. Home after work, sober, and he made dinner? Surely, there would be a catch before she could even fork one bite of whatever aroma had seeped to the living room. *A new job perhaps? A promotion? Moving back with his mother and filing for divorce?* She passed each thought and examined the likelihood, which made her question John's motives even more.

The purse she'd left in the car had papers in need of grading, but also a rose and portrait from Shawn. She didn't want to explain should John do some digging. He hadn't before, or at least, she had never caught him before. It wasn't worth the trouble, so she simply followed him into the kitchen.

The table surface was hidden beneath an ivory-white cloth. An assortment of candles stood proud at the middle, each one dimming by the second. Glasses rested on both sides of the uncorked wine bottle. In front of the adjacent chairs were two plates. They weren't paper plates. No. John had certainly outdone himself. They were ceramic. Little decorative flowers seemingly danced along the edges. A wedding gift his parents brought back from Holland. She remembered the one of many fake smiles she produced that day, none quite as large as when she opened the neatly wrapped package from Barbara and Phillip.

"The food's a bit cold now," he said, facing the stovetop. "I can heat it up if you'd like."

"That's okay. I'm sure it's fine."

She sat at the spot closest to the wine and adjusted the dress to her knees. John spooned noodles to her plate, and the once-creamy sauce was on the verge of solidifying. Chicken Alfredo. One of three things he'd ever made. The other entrees required microwave instructions. She was shocked. Grateful even. It had been a while. Longer than a while, in fact. It would be easier to recall the last time they had a conversation absent yells or curses than a time he did something romantic for her.

*What's the catch?* Sarah forked a couple of noodles, took a bite, and scolded herself for enjoying it. Even cold, the pasta cut easily between her teeth. The flavor made her forget the rising questions, and she allowed a second and even larger helping, this time adding chicken cutlets to the mix.

John focused his gaze at the table and moved his food

around the plate, hiding the flowers at the edges. "I wanted to talk to you about last night."

She was tempted to spit out the Alfredo. *Johnny always gets what he wants.* All an elaborate second attempt, this time would be less forceful and more pleading. She gnawed the inside of her cheek and filled the glass until the red sloshing liquid settled near the brim. "Mm-hmm?"

"It was wrong. I was wrong. I'm sorry. You didn't deserve that."

*Sorry?* A long pull coated a bitter taste across her tongue. "Okay," she said, and sipped again.

"I just don't feel like we're trying anymore. You barely talk to me. Shit, you can't even stand to be in the same room as me. I want to fix this. I want us to go back to the way things were."

Sarah drew a breath and sighed at the possibilities. A divorce, while liberating, made her consider how the ends would meet without him. A teacher's salary did not provide much on its own, nor would she reduce herself to taking a part-time job at the only grocery store in town like the single faculty members at Fulton High. She would have to sell the house and move into the apartment complex off Fifth or a double-wide at Sunny Acres. Could she even afford a double-wide? Single trailer. A fixer upper at best.

Her car, on its last leg as it was, would break down in a matter of months, and John wouldn't be there to put it off until the weekend. But there was a worst aspect: embarrassment.

Regardless of what door she walked through in this godforsaken town, whispers would break the silence. *Have you heard about Sarah Baker? Have you seen her?* Voices that echoed shame. *Baker? She still goes by John's last name and not…*

Grant. It had been a long time since she had been reminded of the name her father gifted before his cliché *going out for a pack of smokes* exit. The same name she wrote on countless tests and college applications. She gulped the remaining wine and pointed the glass handle to the ceiling. Should she revert to the maiden name of a man who ran out on her? Could she?

Her marriage, all things considered, came with a bonus. A new name. A fresh start. One past she wouldn't be forced to relive any time she scribbled it on a dry-erase board. A skeleton her closet couldn't manage to fit.

"Sarah?"

She set down the glass and stared across the table, candlelight now wisps among scalding, liquefied wax.

"Talk to me. What are you thinking?"

"Maybe we should take some time apart. Figure things out." Her voice deepened and wavered.

John clenched his jaw, and the cheekbones hidden by years of neglect made a sudden reappearance. His brows knitted together. His knuckles cracked with pressure. "Apart how?"

"Go on the trip to the Elk Lodge this weekend. I have to chaperone the dance tomorrow night anyway. A weekend apart could be good for us. Give us both a chance to figure out what we want. And if we're still unsure, you can stay with a friend from work or your parents until we know the next appropriate step."

His ragged, inward breaths quickened. *Angry John.*

He slammed his open palm to the table surface, and his plate flipped over the side, shattering on the floor. Mr. Biscuit's scampering footsteps could be heard fleeing to the bedroom. "I know what I want. I don't need time. I don't need to think about shit! You are my wife." He pointed his finger in her face for emphasis. "Mine. And you will always be."

Sarah leaned back and crossed her arms over her chest. The urge to grin was concealed behind a mirroring scowl. "You sure about that?"

John jumped from his seat, and the chair scraped and tumbled behind him. His balled fists shook, and the gruff olive skin of his face pulsed red.

Sarah wanted him to do it. Wished he would. One strike was all it would take, and this stranger would be removed from her life in handcuffs. No shame around town, only pity, and that was something she could live with.

"Ah!" he screamed, and stomped to the living room, knocking over anything in his path. The front door slammed shut, and seconds later, his truck tires slid on the shifty gravel near the porch. She couldn't hide the smirk any longer, and her lips stretched until her teeth shined in the dimming room. Sarah tilted the bottle for another glass, stopping once again at the brim.

×

ONLY AFTER STUMBLING around the kitchen and cleaning John's mess did Sarah drop to the couch. The fourth glass of wine in her hand swayed and crimson droplets spilled to the polished hardwood floors. She checked her phone, but he still had yet to respond to the snide message she sent after his tantrum.

*"The Alfredo's delicious."* A clever jab she hoped made him seethe further. *You are mine.* She replayed his words through her head, unsure if the slur was him or her own drunken impression. *You always will be.* She giggled to herself and pulled from her glass once more.

Careful padded footsteps entered the living room and Mr. Biscuit stopped at the couch. He craned his furry neck, glanced at Sarah, and offered a single *meow*.

"Oh. Well, look who it is. Thanks for leaving me alone with the asshole, ya think-for-yourselfer!"

His gentle purr was the rebuttal.

"No, B. That isn't going to work this time."

His small cat eyes widened, and his tail flicked left and right like a metronome.

"Fine." She patted her thigh, and he jumped to the couch without hesitation. A few circles between her legs, and Mr. Biscuit settled into himself, orange and brown fur against her pale freckled skin. "I don't need to think about shit!" She laughed again. "Okay, Johnny. Thinking was never your strong suit anyway." She finished the glass and stood, easy not to disturb Mr. Biscuit's comfortable position.

The icy sink water flushed whatever wine remnants clung to the bottom of her glass and spun around the drain like a bloody whirlpool. A sigh wafted the red strands from her face. She was home alone, yet again.

The grasshoppers sang with her. Creaking tree limbs

added to the symphony. No matter the noise, it all muffled behind her house seemingly made of glass. "This is great," John had said, checking each window for a different view. The Realtor said the property wouldn't be on the market long, and John was certain it was *the one*.

Sarah's opinion was less enthusiastic, but for him, she would've done just about anything. "We won't have to deal with passing cars or nosy neighbors getting in our business. It's like we're isolated. No one can hear you scream out here!" He smiled until the fang showed in full effect, then winked. Little did she know how needed the privacy was. How the screams from their house in the coming years would drown out before the street.

"This will be the nursery, and we can hand paint some castles and princess shit all over the walls." John was convinced of their first child's gender off the bat. A girl. He had no desire for a son to play catch with. No. He wanted a sweet, innocent girl to spoil. To cherish. "She will barely fit in her bed because of all the stuffed animals. Rocking chair in this corner, yeah?" he asked and pointed to the empty area near the window overlooking the untouched landscape stretching for miles. Sarah had nodded back, a grin at their family's happy beginnings.

A family she could never quite deliver.

She closed her eyes and shook the thought. It hadn't happened all at once. No, this barrier, this animosity they had for each other took time. Festering for years until the mere sight of one another left them both with regrets. Sarah grabbed the wine bottle and downed the last bit of liquid at the bottom. It was John's fault. Surely, she couldn't be responsible. Well, she wasn't always patient with him, but that didn't mean she was to blame. Just like she wasn't to blame when they couldn't conceive. When she couldn't give him the little girl he desperately wanted. Tears filled Sarah's eyes. The baby they both wanted.

×

SARAH DROVE DOWN the Fulton main roads slow enough that cars continued to honk their horns, flash their high beams, and eventually pass on the two-lane street. She stared forward through dilated pupils. Her torso swayed like the curls of a sandy beach's tide. *I don't need time to think*, she practiced to herself. *I just want us.* For the first time since she could remember, the idea of John brought a smile to her face. A longing for the relationship they once had.

Headlights pierced from behind and illuminated her dash. The SUV followed her, swerved toward the sidewalk, and corrected to the middle of the road. She lifted her hand to cover her eyes from the blinding assault, and finally caught sight of a sign reading FIELD AND STREAMS TAVERN with an arrow pointing onward. Abrupt red and blue beams flashed from the rear. Her stomach plummeted.

"Shit! No, no, no," she cursed, and lightened her foot from the gas. "This isn't happening." Sarah checked her breath. "Fuck!" It was over. She wasn't going to save her relationship but ruin her own life in the process. She slowed the car, parked, and attempted to calm her spiking heart rate.

A door peeled open, and she checked her rearview. The man, early fifties and a wrinkled face hidden beneath a broad-brimmed felt hat, staggered toward the driver's side window. His uniform shirt was ironed enough to notice, and a stern crease ran down each pant leg to his well-polished boots. He knocked on the window, and she cranked it down one notch at a time by the handle.

"Evenin', ma'am," he said, mouth pursed to the side holding his tobacco. The flashlight in his hand cut the blanketing shadows across her face. "Do you know why I stopped you?"

She tightened her lips and caged her panicked breath. *Smile. Let him do the talking.* Sarah shook her head and adjusted the glasses up the bridge of her nose. The light burned in her wincing eyes, and a lingering buzz added to her already quivering hands on the steering wheel clutching the ten and two positions.

"The limit on this road is twenty-five. Do you know how fast you were going?"

She deepened her smile and shook her head once more. *Keep your mouth shut.* She wasn't sure whether to be more concerned of her breath or what intoxicated nonsense might spill out.

The man scoffed, and the obnoxious fumes of sour mash fled his own shriveled mouth. Sarah knew the scent all too well. She also knew why he remained in a firm, wide stance. *To keep from falling over.* She grinned something authentic. Something the man outside her window wasn't privy to. *You're more drunk than I am.*

"No, Officer. But I don't believe I was speeding." Her words escaped holding hands with the bitter wine left on her tongue. A leap of faith. A gamble that this man may have been too sloshed to notice.

"Sheriff, ma'am. I'm the sheriff. And no, you weren't speedin'. Quite the opposite. You were traveling at fifteen miles per hour. That's why the last three cars passed you. Not safe for a road with a double yellow."

"I'm so sorry, Sheriff. My eyesight is terrible and driving at night only makes it worse." A lie, but a strong one, nonetheless. If he did by chance peel his attention away from her neckline to her dilated pupils, her response would have given reason to the deep black circles a bottle produced.

"What did you say your name was?"

"Is. What did you say your name is?" It was a force of habit. Correcting students' grammar was her daily routine. Even now she couldn't help herself when an adult said something incorrectly. An adult with handcuffs no less. "Sarah—sir. Sarah Baker."

"Sarah, I'm gonna ask you to step out of the car."

The blood drained from her face. Her hands trembled. The sheriff opened the door and gestured for her to follow. Her smile lost slack and her mouth thinned. "Is this really necessary, Sheriff"—she moved her head until she caught the shiny chrome nametag near his badge—"Mills? I'm kind of in a hurry."

"This'll only take a minute, Ms. Baker."

"Mrs." *Stop correcting him!* her insides screamed. She wiped the sweat building on her brow, smoothed the dress over her thighs, and lifted one leg to the concrete. Sarah endured the light-headed rush enveloping her; she couldn't be sure if it was the alcohol or how fast she got up from the driver's seat. His stature was intimidating, and she tilted her head to get a closer look. Gray-and-black stubble coated his neck and chin like salt and pepper. His eyes, blue to the point of silver, pierced through the night. A finely built torso, not one sculpted in a gym but by cutting his own wood or working with his hands. Rough and rugged. Worn as the boots he evened his weight to.

"This way, please." He motioned her to the front of her car, and she hesitantly followed, keen to make each step as precise and steady as possible.

Sheriff Mills stopped near the headlights and crossed his arms. When Sarah neared, he nodded to the car. "See that?"

She glanced at the front. "No, sir."

This time he pointed to the passenger lamp. "One of your lights is out, Sarah."

Relief washed over her. She had forgotten to turn on the high beams to make it appear as though both worked. "Oh! Yes, Sheriff. My husband has been meaning to fix it."

Mills spit toward the sidewalk. "Now, I don't enjoy writing tickets. The paperwork's a pain in the ass. So, tell Mr. Baker that I said this needs to be fixed pronto or he'll be hearing from me." A lopsided grin leveled the uneven wrinkles on his cheeks. "Sound good to you?"

"Yes, sir. That sounds great."

"Well, then," he said, and tipped his hat. "You have a nice evening. And if you need to drive slow for your eyes, I'd suggest pulling over the next time you get an impatient asshole behind ya. This town's full of them." He staggered around her and toward his vehicle. After he sat inside, the flashing red and blue lights on the roof flickered off. He drove away, offering one last wave before his car vanished among the darkened streets.

Her first breath in was deep. The need to collapse was somehow deeper. Vomit rose to her throat, and before the acidic tang spilled from her lips, she promptly swallowed it back down. Pinpricks combed her neck and arms. "Holy shit," she cursed between each pant. "That was way too close."

Sarah composed herself and returned to the driver's seat. She checked the rearview and brushed at the red strands sticking to her damp forehead, pulling them into a secure bun at her crown. The Neon stuttered but started without any further protest. She needed to go home. Had to go home. She even said it aloud.

"Go home. That was too close. John will probably be there after he's had a few beers to cool off. Just. Go. Home."

She didn't. Sarah continued down the road toward Field and Streams, fighting the thoughts begging her to reconsider.

His truck was parked crooked and filling two spaces. The partially opened driver's window suggested he had chain-smoked the entire way. Sarah slowed and took a spot in the back of the lot, less concrete and more flattened gravel. Her shoes crunched against the rocky surface. She paused and bit her bottom lip. *You can do this. Tell him. Tell him everything.*

The music intensified as she neared, heightening the throbbing in her chest. Lights accented the nervous smile creeping across her face. She glanced inside to spot him before wandering around aimlessly and noticed John, sitting on a stool with his elbow slung over the bar. The fang-showing grin was enough to know he was no longer upset. Sarah had hope for a moment when she realized he wasn't angry.

But he also wasn't alone.

She watched on the other side of the windowpane. A story was unfolding that was supposed to be hers and hers alone. John, stifling laughter with his fist, and the bartender, straight brunette hair and a complexion to envy, who couldn't manage to glance away from him. The girl smirked at his every word and ignored the other patrons fighting for her attention. Her gaze, lustful in Sarah's opinion, remained fixed. Her longing was evident. Johnny, too, shared this very blatant expression.

Sarah continued to watch like an animal at the zoo, forced to observe from the confines of a cage while the rest of the world carried on without her. A blurry haze burned her eyes and moistened her lashes, but she refused to wipe away the sudden pain. He was only talking. It probably didn't mean anything.

Then a silver glint shined in his fingertips. A single brow lifted on his face, and his toothy grin followed suit. Sarah narrowed in on the quarter, spilling tears down her cheeks. *No. Please.* He closed his fist and waved his second hand over it. The bartender pursed her lips, hiding a smirk.

*Don't do this, John.*

He opened his fingers to an empty palm.

*Please, John.*

The girl gave the awestruck expression he was searching for. John closed his hand again. Sarah struggled not to strike the glass full force, pounding it in rhythm with her ragged heartbeats.

*John ... I love you.*

A slip of paper was revealed, but she didn't need to see the rest. She knew what it said. She had lived this very moment decades ago it felt.

Sarah stumbled away from the music, her sobs now the only song in the parking lot. She dropped to the driver's seat of the Neon and lowered her head to the steering wheel. Her voice cracked. The wretched sound swirled around the interior. Her cheeks held slick like the roads taking to the season's first rain. She slammed her fist to the dash. Once. Twice.

"Fuck."

She searched in her purse for a cigarette. Something to take the edge. Something to ease the ache in her chest. There was a sharp prick, and she ripped her hand back on impulse. Through her tears, she glanced inside and reached again. The soft petals shared the same deep red of her bloody fingertip. She lifted the rose to her face, and tears bounced off the flower to her dress ruffling under the steering wheel.

Sarah Baker cried that night, harder than she had cried in a long time.

# PART III
## *The Hunt*

# CHAPTER TWENTY-SIX

## Mills

*The day Sarah went missing*

MILLS HAD TRIED Luther's cell enough times to lose count. While brushing his teeth—*You've reached Luther Barnes of th*—click. After buttoning his uniform top—*You've reached Luther Barnes*—click. Even when he settled into the Bronco—*You've reached Lu*—click.

He attempted to call a few more times before pulling into the parking lot outside his office and received the same results. The voice he had chosen for his answering machine, at this point, annoyed the sheriff to high hell. It wasn't uncommon for Luther to go days if not longer without responding to a call or text. The timing, however, promised Mills a new ulcer to fight off. If he did indeed have an ID on the body they found at the Landing, this wouldn't be something to put off 'til lunch. Mills glanced at the time on his cassette player. Nine twenty-three A.M.

*Where the hell are you, Luther?*

He butt-thrusted himself inside the waiting room, intent on making as much noise as possible. The door slammed to a close behind him. He rang the bell on the counter not once but multiple times, expecting different results following the same irritating *ding*.

"Luther?" Mills shouted down the hall. "Luther Barnes? It's Jeff."

"Hold yer damn horses!" He marched from the back room, and his oblong shadow swayed in the darkened hallway.

Mills relaxed and moved his hand away from his holster. "Fuckin' hell, Luth. You ever answer your phone?"

Luther finally appeared. His regularly ironed lab coat was wrinkled and thrown lazily over the flannel shirt tucked in his jeans. His hair, the little remaining, had always been an unkempt mess with stray silver strands protruding from the sides. His eyes, however, were what the sheriff took notice of. Large red roots overpowered the whites like crimson lightning. His pupils were darker than the hallway he emerged from, and as wide as dinner plates. Thick bags protruded under his bottom lashes, giving his once-intimidating grimace a sunken, almost droopy expression. "You ever hear of voicemail?"

"Yeah, I left you three of 'em!" Mills scoffed.

Luther scratched his crown. "Must've dozed off. Took quite some time finishing her up."

"Not questioning your practice, Luth, but are you certain you have a positive ID and didn't just dream it?"

"Come with me." Luther waved him to the back room and they both eased down the hallway toward the hazy glass door reading LUTHER BARNES in bold, black letters.

The lights in the room were dim, and a sudden chill worked up Mills's exposed arms and underneath his uniformed sleeves. The stench, while dampened, still clung to the stagnant air surrounding the corpse laid flat on one of three metal tables. He debated covering his mouth and nose but decided against it when Luther moved freely without worry. He grabbed an overflowing file from his chair and slid it across the table near the body's motionless feet. Mills found it odd, disgusting even, to place it near decaying flesh. Proper practice wasn't Luther's forte.

"Her name's Jessie Jenkins. Sixteen. I sent a copy of her postmortem radiography to Dr. Eiler to look through, hopin' they'd match it with someone in town. I know I shoulda called an odontologist and filed a court order, but Eiler owed me a favor. The right channels woulda taken weeks. He faxed her patient records this morning. Hundred percent match."

Mills flipped through the X-rays of her teeth to the bloody and gruesome crime-scene photos at the Landing. "Sixteen? Christ."

"Easy now. My savior has nothing to do with the monstrosity done to this poor girl. You were on the money, Jeff. Blunt force trauma. She was beaten to death with this." Luther lifted an evidence bag, and in it, a fist-sized boulder with jagged, uneven edges. It was painted arterial red on one end, and bloody flakes stuck to the clear plastic. "That's not even the best part. Her neck was broken before whoever did it decided to bash in her skull."

"Her neck was broken? From what?"

Luther shook his head. "Not clear on that yet. To me, looks like a whiplash injury, but she was alive after, at least for a little while."

"Christ," Mills said again on impulse. Her face was still

as unreadable as before. Misshapen. The hair that hadn't been affected from having her head caved in was bleach blond down to the subtle blue highlights at the ends. She was someone's daughter. The planet they revolved around. The sheriff glanced at the ceiling tiles and fought through the sudden blur taking over his eyes.

"Anything else?"

"Toxicology will take a while to get back. Thought it best to let you know anything as soon as I did."

Mills set the files back near the young girl's feet and faltered. "No, Luth. You did good. Damn good. I just don't know—"

"How you can tell someone their baby was murdered?"

Mills nodded. "Yes." He resisted the brick wall choking his throat. Smaller inhales saved him from sobbing outright.

"Have you ever? A kid, I mean?" Luther asked and sat in the rotating chair near an empty metal table.

Another glance at the ceiling tiles. "Once. It was an accident though. Nothing like this. Don't imagine the parents will react much differently though."

"Think it'll be easier this time? Telling their folks?" Luther, chin perched on his interlocked hands, visibly chewed on his cheek.

"No. Not a chance."

⨯

MILLS, ALONG WITH Holloway, drove through the less populated roads and toward the small trailer park near the highway. Simmons had given them the address in between bites of his Philly cheesesteak from Margery's. One fifty-two Greer Lane. There was only one Greer Lane in town, and after many dealing busts and domestic disputes on the block, Mills was familiar with Sunny Acres.

*Perfect.* A mom with nothing was about to lose everything. Holloway was somehow less eager to join him than usual, maybe due to the horrible news they'd have to break. He couldn't blame her. After all, if he weren't the sheriff, he would've passed this burden on to someone with a fewer stripes.

But he couldn't pawn this one off on Holloway or Simmons. His town. His burden.

"Did Luther's daughter know her?" she asked.

Mills sucked on the toothpick nestled in his inner cheek. "Not sure. Luth didn't tell Deidra. Kinda glad he didn't. Last thing we need are texts floating around the school, getting back to Mrs. Jenkins before we can."

"Sixteen … fuck." Holloway shook her head and lit a Marlboro, offering one Mills's way. He waved his wrist to decline. "Why would some sick son of a bitch wanna kill her?"

"Wish I knew, kid. Wrong place, wrong time? A score to settle? Who knows?"

"Was she—?" She cut off the question and Mills could understand why. What had happened to her was already horrendous—anything beyond that would've been unspeakable.

"No. No. Luth checked. No signs. No struggle even. Let us hope she didn't feel any pain." He paused and flicked the toothpick to the other side of his mouth. "Let us pray she will be the only one."

He veered the Bronco down the one-way entrance. A faded sign invited them inside. SUNNY ACRES TRAILER PARK. Small dandelions were hand painted on each side of the shoddy lettering, and stick figures of all shapes and colors were holding hands in a semicircle. A combination of grass and weeds were overgrown on either side of the street leading up to the singles, and every now and then, double-wides. Distinct neglect was noticeable on each, whether rotted wood, broken staircases, or rundown cars resting on cinder blocks in the front yards. Rough was the only word to describe it.

This little community had been on the chopping block for many years, but the residents somehow won every appeal thrown at the courts. They couldn't fight back forever though, especially with the looming victory of mayor-to-be Dan Richmond and the millions he had behind him. Money lining the pockets of council members would eviscerate any argument. The appeals would be tossed out faster than the eviction notices being stapled to their front doors. Uprooting their lives and creating a new housing development was first on the expected mayor's proposals. Mills wished for a better alternative, but he was best suited to staying in his own lane.

"You—" Holloway paused briefly. "You want me to handle it?"

Mills only glared forward, mumbling the practiced apologies in his head. "No, kid. I can handle it. My department. My city. My watch. Ultimately, my fault."

"There was nothing you could've done, Jeff."

He glanced at her in both a sympathetic yet *Don't call me*

*Jeff* way. He knew she was only trying to console him. He secretly needed it. His deputy, however, was to remain professional at even the darkest of times. Better than him in every aspect. "No matter how many times you tell yourself you did all you could, there will always be a voice telling you *bullshit*. Remember that."

"Yes, sir."

They stopped in front of a trailer near the middle of the park. Faded blue, almost gray paint coated the exterior. One window overlooking the street had tin foil slung behind the ripped screen. Mills eased up the deck, and Holloway followed behind closely. The screams of what he could only assume was an infant were stifled but constant. He drew a lengthy inhale at the door and held his closed fist to it for a moment.

"Sheriff?" Holloway said. "You okay?"

He ignored her and gave two loud, sorrowful knocks. The baby's screaming intensified. "Sheriff's department." Mills remained stiff, and his voice was noticeably hoarse. "Mrs. Jenkins. I am Sheriff Mills. Just like to have a word with ya."

A shuffle of feet pounded the unstable floors and moved toward the porch. The door, after an array of many locks were undone, creaked open until she peered a single eye through the crack. "Whaddya want?" she demanded more than asked. The screaming in the background passed outside in full effect.

"Need to have a word with ya, ma'am. It's important."

"I don't know where Nate is. Told the asshole to leave the last time you pricks came around months ago. Somethin' about warrants. Didn't want no part of that."

Mills leaned against the frame and removed his broad-brimmed hat. "Not here about Nate, ma'am. It's about your daughter, Jessie."

The woman rolled her eyes and slammed open the door. Blond, raggedy hair was cut at her shoulders, and her bangs were butchered to the point of dangling in strands over her eyebrows. She held a half-smoked cigarette in her left hand, and each time she lifted for another puff, track marks visibly railroaded up her pale skin and underneath her shirt sleeves. "Christ, that girl is trouble. What'd she do now?"

"She, um … hasn't done anything wrong, Mrs. Jenkins."

"Miss," she corrected him and took another drag. A toddler wobbled up to her side dressed in only a diaper with overgrown frizzy hair and leftover food around his mouth. "And if she's not in trouble, then what the hell do ya want?"

Mills drew another breath. "Your daughter. Jessie. She was involved in some sort of altercation." He closed his eyes and outlined his fingers on his hat's felt. "We found her up at the Landing."

"Girl's always running her mouth, I swear. She here with you? Tell you who dun it?"

"Ms. Jenkins. I regret to inform you that Jessie is no longer with us." Mills lowered his head. "Your daughter has been murdered."

"No. No, no, no. She's been staying with Hannah. Told me they were practicin' cheers." Her eyes welled first and she hunched over, nearly poking the curious toddler with her lit cigarette. "No. She jus' texted me yesterday. You're wrong. She's at Hannah's. Go talk to Hannah! She'll tell you."

Mills forced back the tears he hadn't shed in decades. Maybe longer. "We have her body at the coroner's. Her dental records matched. I'm sorry, Ms. Jenkins. I'm very sorry for your loss."

The wind lost all gust. The air remained still. She produced the only horrible sound to be heard for miles it seemed, screaming on her hands and knees until her lungs should have given out. The toddler too joined in, and they both screeched as Mills and Holloway hung their heads and did nothing more than endure it.

# CHAPTER TWENTY-SEVEN

*One month missing*

"WATKINS. W-A-T—"

"I know how to spell, Jeffrey," she snapped with a dismissive wave. "He has been absent for some time. There's transfer paperwork, but it doesn't appear to be finalized yet."

Mills grazed his thumb across his dry bottom lip. "Transfer to where?"

"East. To live with his mother, I'd guess."

"Well, shit."

"Keep the foul language off campus."

"Interesting comin' from you, Janice. I seem to recall you screaming obscenities under the bleachers after homecoming."

She blushed enough for Mills to notice, a victory he gladly accepted. He tipped his hat. "Thank you for your time, Ms. Walsh."

"*Mrs. Peterson.*" She wasn't amused with his tone nor his trip down memory lane.

"Believe me. I know." He smiled his way to the door and pushed through.

Mountains outlined the horizon, perched just beneath midday sun and pillowed white clouds. His Bronco, parked along the red painted curb out front, awaited his return.

"Anything?" Holloway asked from the passenger seat.

"Kid's gone. Hasn't been to school in weeks. Might've gone to live with his mother."

"What about the dad?"

"Will you let me sheriff a bit before you cart me off to a retirement home? Until you wear this hat"—Mills paused and swiped the brim—"I call the shots, kid."

"Yes, sir." Her response was simple. Seemingly cut short from all the words she wished to exchange. She would, whether asked or not, follow him through the pits of hell and back without a single complaint. This didn't have anything to do with her succession if Mills had his way. No. This was nothing out of the ordinary for the young, talented Holloway. She always looked to him for advice, and while he found it difficult to offer when she was decades more mature than himself, he never stopped putting in his own two cents. Despite their sheriff and deputy relationship, she was and always would be the closest thing to a daughter he could ever imagine.

He evened his weight to the driver's side and ground the gears shifting to first. "His dad works at the clinic near Main Street. Think we oughta see what's going on?"

"If you say so, Sheriff." She didn't admit it outright, but she was excited—her smirk gave that away.

Mills drove around town as he always had; long cut stuffed in his lower lip and sour mash well within reach in the glovebox. After her many gripes, he chose to wait on the sauce until Holloway wasn't looking or until she annoyed him enough, whichever came first. She wanted him healthy, alert, and while it went against the direction his moral compass normally led, he couldn't hate her for it. She'd saved him after all. The only one to do more for Sheriff Jeffrey Thomas Mills than the bottle ever could. If not for Jenn, Kent's Salvage would've been his resting place, surrounded by oil-soaked dirt, rusty beaters, and tangled weeds.

He'd never pictured that sort of death for himself. Mills imagined a brilliant shootout to cause his demise. A warrior's death. Now, he'd give a kidney to meet the reaper in a warm, comfy bed, a smoke in his left hand and a whiskey glass in the right.

"Why do you think his ID was in there? A new suspect?"

"Well, our only other suspect is the husband, and even if he is a piece of shit, John Baker has an alibi tighter than the floozy's body he's taken a liking to. This kid, Shawn, may be able to tell us something we don't already know."

"John was cheating. You think she might've found her own action on the side?"

"With a student? Doubt it. She was … well, *is* a pretty lady. Any miserable bastard in this town would line up around the corner for a crack at her."

Holloway lifted the plastic evidence bag housing Shawn's ID. "I don't know, Sheriff. If I were a few years younger …"

"You are a few years younger. So was … is Sarah. But I'd bet money she had more sense than to fool around the playground."

They parked at the near-empty lot outside the Fulton Animal Clinic, a rectangular building crooked enough to offset the entire Main Street block. Flyers with Sarah's face were tacked on the light poles leading there but stopped curtly. He assumed a shortage of flyers, given that the rest of the damned street was covered with them. The town wouldn't soon forget the slightly freckled features of Sarah Baker whether she was dead or still breathing.

"Coming or staying?" he asked Holloway the same way his own mother asked him to either endure grocery shopping or feign boredom in the station wagon, picking at the seats. Before she passed, this was a regular Saturday trip. After she was gone, groceries consisted of Salisbury steak TV dinners and a six-pack.

"Can I ask the questions? Might be good practice." Holloway's eagerness didn't surprise him. In fact, he had hoped for it.

"Don't make us look stupid."

"Yes, sir."

Mills knew she couldn't if she tried. Hell, even in a clown outfit, Holloway would ask all the right things before honking her red puff-ball nose and slamming a comical pie in the suspect's face. Nevertheless, he refused to show how much confidence he had in the girl, for a badge with an ego was a dangerous thing.

Holloway exited the Bronco first, and Mills seized opportunity to sneak a few swigs from his glove box stash. The burn lasted from the parking lot to the door, and he made it a point to exhale slowly so the deputy a few paces ahead wouldn't get a whiff.

"Sheriff," she said and held the door on her back.

"You've already got my vote, for Christ's sake. Stop kissing my ass and get inside."

Animal piss was the first odor he noticed stepping into

the waiting room, like the anxious pets normally filling this area knew just what horrors went on behind the bright red doors leading back.

"Good morning," the receptionist greeted behind the counter. "I'll be right with you."

"No rush, darlin'," Mills replied with a toothy grin.

"Darlin', huh?" Holloway whispered. "Surprised you didn't tip your hat and pull roses out of your ass, too."

"Nothing wrong with being a gentleman, kid. Appearance is everything."

"What happens when they learn the truth?"

"Grown-up stuff, Jenn. You'll learn when you're older." He winked, and her face pinched tight.

"How can I help you officers this morning?"

"Deputy Sheriff, ma'am," Holloway interjected and her normally soft voice boomed with authority. "We need to speak with Mr. Watkins."

"He no longer works here, I'm afraid. Resigned two weeks ago."

Jenn leaned forward and blocked Mills from reading the nametag tacked on the girl's chest. "And why is that?"

"Moved to Ohio to be close to his son."

Holloway tilted her head, and Mills had a sneaky suspicion she was cursing internally. "Do you have a number to get in contact with him?"

"Unfortunately, no. We tried calling him last week to mail his final pay stub, but the number is no longer in service. We had to leave it at his house on Third Street."

"Do the new owners of his property know how to get in contact?"

"Oh, no. He didn't sell it. Mr. Watkins said he was going to come back after his son graduates next year. Might be renting it out, but I'm not sure. Dr. Geyser has his email, I believe. Please, have a seat. It should only take a minute."

Mills trudged first to the padded benches against the wall, and Holloway soon followed suit. Loose and short hair was stuck to the beige cushion, almost molded into the paint itself. Had he forgone the drinks this afternoon, he might've had a better mind to brush a hand over it and save his khaki pants from becoming fur magnets.

"Well," she scoffed and sat down. "This makes things difficult."

"Just a bit. So, what else can we do to find Shawn? Use that big noodle. And don't say drive to Ohio or I might take your badge."

"Family. Friends. Acquaintances. We could ask the other students around the school. Maybe they have Shawn's email. Social media account."

"Not bad. What else?"

"Call the mother?"

Mills shook his head. "No. Hell no. Haven't you learned anything from me? Both the father and son are in the wind, right?"

"Yeah, so?"

Mills showed the same toothy grin he displayed not even minutes ago. "No one's home."

"You don't mean …" Jenn's face twisted. "Sheriff. I look the other way more than I should. I have stood by you through all of your bullshit. But breaking into someone's home? I will not stoop to that level."

Mills shook his sunken head. "Oh, save me the self-righteous prude routine."

"No. You save it, *Jeffrey*." Holloway lifted herself from the bench. "You may have forgotten what the badge pinned to your chest means, but I sure as hell haven't."

Shocked might've been one of the ways he felt. Embarrassed was definitely one of them. Even though he wanted to raise his voice as loud as Jenn had, maybe even scream at her and give the receptionist a show, he couldn't bring himself to. After all, she was right. Twenty years ago, he would've never tossed the idea to trespass for evidence. He was reaching a breaking point Holloway continued to save him from. She seemed to save him a lot as of late. *You're right, kid.* He didn't say it out loud.

A small man entered the waiting area, paused, and shoved his hands in his white lab coat pockets. Jenn, still visibly angered, righted herself and approached him.

"Deputy Sheriff Holloway, sir. I apologize for the disruption."

"Dr. Geyser—erm, Aaron."

Mills would sit this conversation out, maybe to avoid her wrath or the young doctor's squirming. In any event, he'd promised her this one, and while a drunk, he was still a man of his word.

The two talked back and forth, Holloway asking what Mills assumed were all the right questions. Then she exited the clinic without even a signal for him to follow. He finally stood and caught the receptionist's eye mid-phone call. "Thank you for your time." She nodded and continued her busy work.

Jenn wasn't in the passenger seat of the Bronco but on the driver's side. "No. No. *No, no, no.* Get on your side."

She chucked his empty metal flask out the window, and it rattled on the black pavement. "Get in the truck and stop fucking whining." She didn't smile. Didn't hint at a joke. No. She was pissed.

"Are you shittin' me?"

She settled farther into the seat, grabbed the keys from the visor, and turned on the ignition.

"For fuck's sake. Kid's got bigger balls than Simmons." He sat down and felt an immediate discomfort, like wearing a shirt that had gotten too small. He could've protested. Thrown a fit. Maybe even kicked her out, but he sat there silent while Holloway put the Bronco in reverse and veered onto the main road.

It wasn't until they passed the station that he grew curious. "Where the hell are you taking me?"

"Home. Then I'm going to look through the Baker case files."

"I'll come with," he muttered, pride lumping his throat.

"No thanks."

"*Dammit.* I mean it, kid." He looked her in the eye. "No more bullshit. From now on, when I wear the badge, it'll be the straight and narrow. No sidetracks. I promise."

She considered it for a moment and said, "Fine. But if I hear any bitchin', I'll have to pull you off the case." At this, Jenn smiled widely and even snorted.

Mills chuckled. "Fair enough."

Something hit the windshield on that overcast afternoon. It wasn't a bug like Mills had guessed it to be. It was a snowflake. The first of the season. Winter had always started off slow, but he knew it was only a matter of time until the heavens opened and relentless downpours were the daily forecast. Before long, Fulton County would be covered from the streets to the mountaintops, leaving any trace of Sarah Baker hidden beneath layers of fresh powder. The search parties would stop, and the case would go as cold as the newfound temperature.

Another snowflake flittered down to the windshield. And another. And another.

# CHAPTER TWENTY-EIGHT

*The day Sarah went missing*

THE THREE SAT at the fold-out plastic table Mills assumed was her makeshift dining room set. The toddler, however, continued to run back and forth to his room carrying various toys for a show-and-tell session with Holloway. Jenn gave the same awestruck expression each time the shirtless kid grabbed whatever he could to shove in her face. "Wow! Is that your bear? Is that your horse? Wow. Look at that bunny! I used to have one just like that!" she had said. Holloway was good. Damn good. When there was nothing left for the baby to proudly show her and the small sniffles began, she scooped him up on her lap and started a round of peek-a-boo. Keeping the young one preoccupied was what Mills would've asked her to do, and he silently thanked her for always being one step ahead.

Had he not wanted to insult the already broken woman clasping her face to her palms, Mills might've asked for a window, at least two, to be cracked open. The stench of stale cigarettes lingered around the small, messy room. The white trash can in the kitchen, splotched in what one could only assume was spaghetti sauce, was overflowing, and even the rotted filth on top was beginning to mold. Shit was the most overpowering odor. Baby shit. There had to be a pile of used diapers in each of the three bedrooms, some now leaking through onto the tatty brown carpet. Had he known beforehand, he would've taken some Neutrolene from Luther's coroner stash and swiped it under each nostril.

He continued to breathe through his mouth in small gulps. Ms. Jenkins lit a cigarette between hysterical breaks, and Mills, too, grabbed the pack from his shirt pocket and joined her.

"You said she had texted you. How often?"

"Every morning almost. Jus' a" *Hey, Mom, I'm at school. Staying over at Hannah's again.* "Didn't really think much of it. She's always hanging around that Richmond girl."

The name Dan Richmond popped in his head like the backfire from a worn exhaust. Weren't any other Richmonds in town. She had to have some relation to the same man forcing Jessie and her family onto the streets. "She and this Hannah girl were close?"

She blew out smoke and her undercut bangs swayed in the cloud. "Very. She's hardly—*was* hardly ever home," Ms. Jenkins corrected herself. "She stayed with them the first two or three weeks of summer. Why I didn't think much of it when she texted that she was staying there again."

The sheriff leaned forward and took another drag. "Think Hannah might've hurt Jessie or be connected in any way?"

"No. She was always kind to Jessie. Met her a few times when they came into Margery's during my shift. Stuck-up maybe. Not capable of doing something like this to my Jessie though."

Mills grazed his teeth against his lips. Richmond wanted

them gone. All the park residents. Why would Hannah be spending time with someone from Sunny Acres? Surely, her father would have an opinion on the matter. "Can you give us your daughter's number so maybe we can track it? Find out who has her phone?"

"Yes, sir. I can do that. I do need to know something, Sheriff."

He pasted on the only smile he could, a half-crooked one, and answered, "Ma'am?"

She snuffed out the brown filter on the ashtray between them, and newly formed tears seeped from her reddened eyes. "Why her? Why'd it have to be my baby?"

He tapped his cigarette among the ashes. Faint lines of smoke danced in front of him. "I'm not sure. But I promise you, I will find out."

⨯

WITH HANNAH RICHMOND as their only hope for a lead, if not a suspect, Mills and Holloway drove to the high school hoping she would speak to them before calling Daddy first. If she was Jessie's friend, she would want to help in any way. That was Mills's best guess at least. Despite Ms. Jenkins defending the trust-fund brat, he still had a sneaky suspicion that maybe there was more going on behind the curtains.

It seemed too coincidental. Too obvious. Gain the trust of a trailer park townie and get information on the illegal activities at Sunny Acres for her father's campaign? Leverage to use against the city council? And if Jessie had found out what the Richmonds were using her for; getting her, her mom, and her little brother kicked out of their home and onto the streets, that might've been reason enough to dispose of the poor girl.

"Richmond," he said to the office secretary, who seemed to have a permanent scowl.

"Bet you can't even spell that," Janice spat.

Mills relaxed against the counter and grinned. "B-I-T-C—"

Janice cut him off and blared her nasally voice into the phone next to the computer and out of the intercom speakers. "Hannah Richmond to the office. Hannah Richmond to the office." An overpowering click echoed down the hallways outside.

"Thank you. Always a pleasure, Janice."

She responded by sucking air through her tar-filled teeth and resumed clacking on the keyboard.

Mills and Holloway both stood underneath the metal awnings in the utterly deserted hallway leading to each of the four separate wings. Holloway relaxed herself against the windows peering inside the office, while Mills took to an evened stance and crossed his arms.

"Think she'll talk?"

"She'll either cry for her friend or Daddy's attorney. Best to take notice of how she reacts to the news that her little minion won't be there to worship the ground she walks on."

Holloway tilted her head and watched a colony of ants maneuver around her shoe. "How will we know if she's lying?"

"Trust your gut, kid. You're a smart cookie." Mills recoiled. He hadn't meant to give her such a compliment, at least so casually. Yes, she was a shit-hot deputy, but to be better than him, she needed a constant drive. Motivation. A voice in her head saying that her best wasn't good enough.

While the boozing and severe lack of social skills could be blamed on his upbringing, Mills knew he had to accept some responsibility. He was not his father, despite the certain likeness they shared any time he glanced in his own cracked mirror, but there were few differences between them. Holloway would be nothing of the sort. He would be sure of one thing before he passed on: she wouldn't be him.

"Did it really taste that bad saying it out loud?" She smirked.

"Stand up straight. Are we on a case or here to relax and shoot the shit?"

Holloway righted herself and shared his same shoulder's width posture.

A girl approached them from the closest wing. Her bleach-blond hair whipped back and forth while strutting forward, waving like dandelions adjusting to a mountainous breeze. She gave them each a curious glare and paused a few feet from the office door.

"Hannah Richmond?"

She shifted all her weight to one side. "Am I in some sort of trouble?" Her tone was only outdone by the sour expression on her face. It was apparent her only interaction with law enforcement was to report a car accident or maybe someone she deemed beneath her invading the same public space. This girl had no respect for authority, whether a parent, a teacher, or city elected official. She would treat Mills no different than the other students at the school, and he was certain they all hated her.

"No, Hannah. We're actually here to talk to you about your friend. Jessie Jenkins." Mills unfolded his arms and placed his hands at his hips. "There was … an incident."

"Is this about her ditching school?"

He leaned forward. "No, no. We were wondering if you have had any contact with her in the past two weeks."

"Every day almost. A few texts why she was missing cheer practice. Why she wasn't at school. Something about her needing to stay home to watch her brother while her mom was working at that disgusting little diner."

"When was the last time you saw her?"

Hannah rolled her eyes and visibly contemplated. "Homecoming maybe?"

"Which was?"

"October 13, I think. What is all this about? Did she run away or something?"

"No, Hannah. I'm very sorry to tell you this, but we found your friend Jessie at the Landing. She was involved in some sort of altercation. She is no longer with us…" *Here we go*, he thought and glared deeply, hoping to spot any form of guilt.

Her eyes twitched and glossed over. Sudden disbelief encompassed her face. Her eyebrows rose and sunk a few times before they settled on a sunken position. She swallowed three heavy gulps and nearly doubled over. All could be associated with the very same reaction Ms. Jenkins had given them an hour ago. He knew, without a doubt, she was as dumbfounded as the girl's mother was, and in turn, just as innocent to the murder of Jessie Jenkins.

"I know this may come as a shock," Mills attempted to comfort her.

"A shock?" she shrieked. "A fucking shock? You pull me out of my class to let me know my best friend is dead and that's all you can say?" Hannah cupped her face in her palms once the tears started rolling and shook her head. "No. You're wrong! She's at home. She's watching her brother. You are fucking wrong!"

Mills drew a breath. "I wish I was, Hannah. We just came from Sunny Acres. I am truly sorry. We want to find who's responsible, but we will need your help."

Hannah's devastated demeanor shifted as quickly as she changed stances. Though her blue eyes still gave way to the streams running down her cheeks, she appeared to be on the offensive. A darkened glare. Balled fists. Trembling forearms. The young girl charged toward the sheriff without warning, stomping her pink Chuck Taylors viciously.

Holloway began to step forward, but Mills waved her off with a simple wrist flick. Holloway eased back like his thoughts were blaring over the intercom. Hannah might swing. Maybe a few times. Pain or heartache could definitely cause the unexpected.

All hundred pounds of her moved closer. Mills knew his weathered chin would hold up should she use it for a therapeutic punching bag. Hell, it had been through much worse. He wouldn't bother readying for the inevitable. A small breath was all he would take in.

"Ms. Richmond?" he asked.

She raised her arms, noticeably shaking each. Her knuckles flushed to a pigment whiter than her hair. A small moment, maybe hesitation, held her in place.

"Hannah?" he asked once more.

She slung her arms around his shoulders and sank to his chest. Her violent cries passed through them both. Mills wasn't sure if it would comfort her to rub his rough palm on her back, but he did so anyway. The sandpaper grain of his hand caught a few times on her cotton shirt. Just how long he should console her before letting go?

"It's okay. Everything's gonna be okay." It wouldn't. He knew the lie he spoon-fed her wouldn't provide any relief. It did, however, seem to be the right thing to say at the time. Some semblance of hope to keep her moving forward. "Deputy Holloway is going to take you inside to talk to Janice—uh, Mrs. Peterson. I think it'd be best for you to get out of here. Take some time for yourself."

Hannah nodded and slowly released him. The skin around her eyes had already begun to swell, and Mills knew that the puffiness would only worsen by evening. She pasted on a brave face when she met his eyes, but her quivering mouth screamed the opposite. Jessie was her friend. A true friend. One she would spend the rest of her life wishing she could have helped. She could have saved. The last thing she said to Jessie, whatever that may have been, would be seared into her memory.

Holloway escorted Hannah inside and held the windowed door against her back. Mills had hoped to give a parting word for comfort. Something for her to hold onto. Unfortunately, he couldn't find such a condolence, none at least that would foot the bill. He had heard every form of "sorry for your loss" after his father passed. For months, there was a new card placed in his mailbox from a different Fulton resident apologizing for his old man's death. *My deepest sympathies. He was a great man. He would be proud of you.*

Mills couldn't bring himself to recycle one of those cliché sayings. Not for her. Not for what she would go through. It had to be something sincere, and yet, nothing truly sincere came to mind.

It was the footsteps he noticed first, followed by her sudden appearance. A woman, a teacher in fact, strutted by the sheriff and farther down the hallway. There was a stack of papers in her hands, and some splayed in every direction like she forgot to stack them properly against her desk. Her auburn hair reflected the sunlight away from her pale, freckled skin, and her flower print dress wafted from each step. She didn't glance at him, not even once, and continued to walk without even the smallest nod or gesture. She was Deidra's teacher. Barker. No, that wasn't right. Baker. Mrs. Baker.

The phone in his khaki pocket began to buzz, and he shifted away to answer it. "Mills," he said and cleared his throat.

"I got the records for the vic's phone."

"Simmons, you better have something good for me or you're pulling a double this weekend."

He puffed out a breath on the other end. "Do I ever let you down, Sheriff?"

"Yes. Yes, you do."

"Not this time, sir. The last text sent from this phone was a few hours ago."

"Fantastic. She's still keeping up-to-date with her Twitter from Luther's cold storage." He checked both ends of the hallway for the teacher and even glanced into the quad area. There were empty tattered benches and birds picking at the unwanted food left absently on tables, but no Mrs. Baker. "How does that help me at all, Simmons?"

"Because I pinged the location of where these texts were sent from."

Mills widened his eyes. He was both impressed at Simmons's resourcefulness and dumbfounded the deputy could do such a thing. "Where? Where is it coming from?"

The arrogance in Simmons's voice was apparent. "You sure you're ready for this? Give me a drumroll."

"Stop fuckin' around and tell me. Now!"

"Geesh. It's coming from the high school. Isn't that something?"

Mills frantically glared in every direction, unsure of which door to kick in and search first. Jessie's phone was at the school and finding it could lead to who murdered her. *I'm not sure. But I promise you, I will find out.* His reassurance to Ms. Jenkins to bring whomever responsible for her daughter's death repeated each time he reared his head.

*But I promise you, I will find out.* Mills swallowed harshly. *I will find out.*

"Can you tell me where the phone is now?"

"Hang on." Keystrokes tapped in the background. "Looks like it's still there. Lemme see if I can zoom in on the property."

Find the phone, find the girl's killer. *I promise you, I will find out.* Although multiple images of a bloodied and beaten

Jessie Jenkins flashed through his head, only one idea remained. *Find out.* "Can you go any faster?"

"I think I got it. Not exactly sure what I'm looking at. It's a top-down picture, and it's a bit blurry. Looks like there's a bunch of tables and bushes."

The quad. Had he not been glancing at it in that moment, he might've been as confused as Simmons. There was shrubbery placed around the tables and benches. They formed an odd star of some sort. "Is that where the phone is?"

"No. The location dot is over a building. A rectangular-shaped one."

The four wings right next to Mills each had a rectangle shape, as well as some other structures across the quad. "Help me narrow this down. Is the phone east or west of that open area with tables and bushes?"

"East. First one east. It's bigger than the rest. Looks kinda like a—"

"A gym." Mills stared at the cement outline of a building reaching for the pasty-white clouds on the horizon. "Her phone is somewhere in the gym."

He could wait for Holloway, but it was better to let her help Hannah leave the property than perform a search. His deputy would complain. Argue. Do whatever she could to go through proper procedure, maybe get the principal involved. Mills, however, couldn't care less. A victim's phone was a hundred yards away, and he wasn't about to let that slip. He hung up on Simmons.

The blue doors to the gymnasium were in dire need of a fresh coat, and the tiger mural above the entrance peered to the patio cement with a savage, green gaze. Intimidation to be used against opposing sports teams. He wouldn't be swayed. The monster he was chasing was far worse. A true nightmare descending on *his* town. Mills ripped the door wide open and entered the tiger's den.

A meticulously polished basketball court extended across the large room, and rows of bleachers—collapsed against the wall—lined each side. His boots squeaked and echoed with each step, ruffling the otherwise silent gym. The banners loosely slung from the rafters seemed to vary from GO TEAM to FIGHT, TIGERS, FIGHT. Two doors were positioned at opposing sides in the back, each with their own male and female stick figures.

Which locker room might the phone be hidden in?

Mills dialed Jessie's number to narrow his search. Despite his own quietly drawn breaths reverberating throughout, not a tone nor vibration took its place. He moved closer to the locker rooms, taking each step as if maneuvering around glass. *Where did he put it? Where would I put it?*

It was becoming more apparent by the second that the phone he was searching for was in one of two locker rooms. "Your call has been forwarded to an automatic voice messaging system—Jessie—is not available. To leave a call back number, press one for more options—"

"Fuck's sake," he scoffed and hit redial. Before he was outcast as the town pervert, Mills would be certain—a 120 percent certain—her phone wasn't in the girls' room. He pressed his ear to the door and focused on the noise coming from within. A leaky pipe. The air conditioner blasting from the ceiling vents. There weren't any vibrations though, at least none compared to the long trills erupting from the phone in his hand.

"Your call has been forwarded to an automatic messaging syst—"

"What's behind door number two?" A simple click on his phone fast-dialed her number, and he readied himself this time on the boy's locker room door.

*Bzzt. Bzzt. Bzzt.*

Mills hung up. Nothing. The air conditioner and leaky pipe clamor returned to the forefront. One click and his phone cycled through the number again.

*Bzzt. Bzzt. Bzzt.*

"Sheriff's office," he announced himself and pushed inside. The sweat-stained stench hit him first like an eighteen-wheeler, followed by the apparent attempt to cover up whatever odor these teenagers couldn't manage behind layers of body spray. *Christ.* He held a hand to his nose. How the dirty diaper stink of the Jenkins's trailer was more appealing than where he trudged now was beyond him. "Sheriff's office," he repeated and pressed his nose tighter. "Make yourself known."

A constant *bzzt* was the only response. He followed the hum through row after row until stopping in front of the closet-sized cage near the center. The computer was left on with a tiger screensaver bouncing in all directions. Papers were overflowing from the filing cabinet to the clutter of clipboards and empty soda cans on the desk. *Bzzt.* It wasn't just the vibrations but the buzzing metal that drew him inside.

He started with the desk drawers. More papers, a few

extra PE shirts, a measuring tape, and what seemed to be a value pack of whistles. *Bzzt.* There was no phone. No such answer to the unanswered call. Mills shifted the ruffled pages on the countertop and searched underneath each stack.

*Bzzt. Bzzt. Bzzt.* It did, albeit slowly, become apparent that the rustling wasn't coming from the desk, but behind him. *Bzzt. Bzzt. Bzzt.* He pulled open the top cabinet drawer and peered inside. Files were arranged alphabetically, but whomever had done it somehow misplaced Hannah Richmond's report to the front of the row. He thrusted the folders to the back and even rubbed his splayed palm against the bottom. *Nothing.*

The second was bare besides the leftover sandwich partially wrapped and leaking mayonnaise to the rusted metal. Disgusting but otherwise empty. Mills clicked the lock on the third and reared the handle. A screen flashed until the line trilled to voicemail, leaving a picture of Jessie and Hannah illuminated on the device. In the next instant, a blackened, lifeless display took its place. Once gloved, he reached a hesitant hand for the phone and paused as the silver hairs on his neck stood straight.

"Can I help you with something, Officer?"

Mills turned to a man near twice his size looming over him. A blue and yellow hat was secured at his brow, and his windbreaker swished as he stepped forward.

# CHAPTER TWENTY-NINE

*Seven months missing*

THE WINTER SEASON in Fulton had been particularly nasty. Four highway shutdowns. Nine snow days for the elementary and high school; Mills assumed the parents didn't want their little ones trudging through blizzards to learn their times tables, after all. Snowplow drivers on constant overtime and city markers blocking off the streets they couldn't quite get to that day. Even when the sun shone over the valley, promising an end to the town's ice age, another storm reared its ugly face and picked up right where it left off.

It lasted four intolerably cold months. Then, one warm April morning, when the clouds parted and sun returned proudly to the sky, it was gone. No one knew if it'd come back. If this was simply a small break and the *pièce de résistance* was around the corner. They all expected it. Stocked up at Al's Market for it. Kept their fireplaces burning into the early morning hours even. But more snow never came. And two months after that, it had melted, leaving only green and brown landscapes for miles. Summer was here.

Although the Fulton County Sheriff's Department remained vigilant during this unprecedented winter, Sarah

Baker's disappearance was as Mills expected. A cold case. The fifteen emails Mills had sent to Mr. Watkins—courtesy of Dr. Geyser—were still unanswered. None of the students or teachers could describe Shawn in any other fashion than "quiet" or "respectful," and John Baker hadn't been seen outside his home since the first snowflake fell.

He had no excuses now, however. Two search parties absent John spoke volumes. To the citizens of Fulton. To the reporters. To the sheriff most of all. When Mills caught wind that husband-of-the-year Jonathan Phillip Baker would grace the next organized search with his presence, it was too good an opportunity to pass up.

Parley's Canyon wasn't the tallest of mountains surrounding Fulton but overlooked the entire city down to the diner a few miles from the center. Ditching a body up here would be difficult, especially with the dozens of blue-collar factory workers coming and going at all hours of the day. He wouldn't take Sarah here. Mills would bet his pension on it. His best guess would've been the ridge glaring at their backs as they hiked up the dirt path to join the orange vests forming a somewhat oblong circle among dirt and brush.

A man raised his voice above the subtle conversations, and Mills recognized it instantly. *John Baker.*

"Thank you all for coming. We're going to start in a northwest direction and split off in two separate groups covering both east and west. We will circle back and rendezvous here before sunset. Again, I can't thank you enough for all your support. Let's bring Sarah home."

John smiled at everyone individually, a grin too wide for someone whose life should be in shambles. An older woman stood behind him, hand on his shoulder, closing her eyes. She was either displaying how distraught she was at the situation or trying to telepathically pass the right things to say. She was a few years younger than Mills, and her short, plain black hair was permed in a style the sheriff hadn't seen for decades.

A momma's boy. He knew there was something off about John.

She whispered something in his ear, and the man—if you could indeed call him that—nodded absently. Mrs. Baker eventually departed his side and joined the other ladies moving northwest, leaving John alone to greet the volunteers carefully pushing forward.

Holloway veered away from Mills and took up a conversation with a few helpers following Mrs. Baker. Mills, however, was preoccupied trying to note each expression or gesture. It was when John glanced at him that his face went slack, and he turned quickly to start the climb himself.

Mills followed closely. "Nice speech."

"Didn't have anything better to do, Sheriff?" John did not bother checking his six. He had, after all, spent more time with Mills than his side piece. Long hours at the station and being a local celebrity left little room for social visits. John was the man whose wife disappeared. His face, along with Sarah's, were the most recognizable three counties over. Every news station for a hundred miles played her story on repeat.

Mills knew he was miserable, and not for the fact his wife was missing. No. That was the only upside. It was the spotlight he hated, the same way a cockroach would flee under the fridge to stay hidden. His secrets, whatever they may be, wouldn't stay that way for long.

"Heard you had a heart attack. Too bad it didn't stick."

Mills snarled at his back and debated shoving him into the brush. There were too many witnesses. "Nah, I ain't done here yet. At least one more piece of shit to put away before I meet the reaper. Getting close, too. *Real* close."

John stopped abruptly and exhaled. "I didn't do whatever it is you think I did, Sheriff. I would never hurt Sarah."

"Careful, John. Lawyer's not here to shove his hand up your ass and put on a puppet show."

John grumbled and stomped forward, intent on putting distance between them.

A soft breeze sifted between oak branches stretching for miles overhead. The leafy canopy blocked most of the midafternoon sun and obscured their surroundings to a darkened and eerie trail. As the groups split, Mills found himself alone with John's team. He didn't mind, even if he did feel more out of place than an atheist in a Sunday morning pew. Mills wanted answers. Answers he was sure John could give.

He took note of every detail. The banter this husband, and quite possibly, this murderer had among the orange-vested idiots tailing him. The unusual absence of sullen and underfed features. John hadn't missed a meal like most of the innocents he came across who couldn't stomach the thought of a loved one's death. A mourning period hit everyone differently, but it appeared to have skipped over John Baker. Lastly, how he carried himself. No frantic leave-no-rock-unturned demeanor. No grasping at straws or insisting any footprint must've been hers. He was on a stroll. Sightseeing. Buying time. All part of the concerned husband façade.

Mills wouldn't fall for it. He knew the stench of guilt.

"Sheriff? Sheriff Mills?" She tapped on his shoulder.

"Hi, Ethel," he said and internally rolled his eyes. She was a sweet woman, but Mills made the mistake of offering his private number when her husband bought a one-way ticket to the promised land. *If you ever need anything, don't hesitate to call.* What resulted was him becoming a handyman for the grieving widow. He even unclogged her toilet a time or two before deciding to change his damn number. His pity never again crossed the crime-scene tape after doing chores for Ethel Swanson.

"Have there been any bear sightings in this area lately?"

"Not this ridge. No need to worry if there were." Mills patted the hip holster housing his father's revolver. "I got you covered, dear."

Her gaze widened. "Do you think a bear might've taken her?"

"What's with all this bear talk?"

"There's tracks," she said, and pointed her boney finger at the tree behind them.

Mills decided to humor her and marched to the area of interest. Tree roots splayed around the muddy patch, and at the center of the squishy soil laid a fresh paw print. He kneeled and inspected the impression further, comparing his hand to the size. "This isn't a bear's paw, Ethel. It's a—"

The ground a few yards ahead shifted. Fallen leaves and branches rustled. Light footsteps were barely audible over his own stern breath. He peered forward at an overgrown bush, taking in the way the shrubbery shook like a distressed fish.

Something was staring back at him equally as hard. Large, piercing eyes glowed at him. The snout protruded from the bushes it hid behind. Teeth, while not all white, appeared from under its scrunching nose. A monstrous growl passed through the distance between them.

Mills retrieved his revolver calmly, thumbed back the hammer, and trained the barrel on the shifting foliage in front of him. Between the green shrubbery, a pair of yellow eyes stared back at him beneath layers of matted black fur. He held his arm in front of Ethel, and even nudged her backward in case the beast decided her to be the easier of the two. They glared at one another; neither moved nor shifted. Then the animal's protruded snout broke free from the bush, and its quivering lips revealed a row of sharpened, savage teeth. The soft growling increased to an all-out snarl.

"Back, Ethel. Get back!"

The elderly woman stumbled and nearly fell over. She muttered what Mills could only imagine were prayers into the trees above. He gave her little attention. No. He was focused on the monster stalking him. The wolf-like shape began to take form as the creature revealed itself fully. A sunken, underfed belly. Ribs practically hidden beneath a darkened coat. Fur raised from its back to its tail. Both ears were perked, and one was missing a sizable chunk from the tip. This mangy mutt had seen better days, and a .45 caliber bullet just might end its misery in his mind.

Mills had glared just as unevenly at the large dog as it had with him, but now, his own glower became less intense and more sympathetic. The canine steadied itself on one foot while the other was missing altogether. A bloodied, ragged nub still months from healing was in the place of its paw, intertwined with dead leaves and mud. He lowered his revolver and begged for the pitiful dog to simply drop dead of natural causes. One shot. He'd be doing it a favor. It wouldn't survive out here. Mills lifted his arm once more, and the animal hobbled forward, still refusing to yield.

"Jeff! No!" She thrusted herself between them, equally startling him and the black pooch. "She's hurt and scared. Can't you see that?"

Mills eased his finger off the trigger and his thumb away from the hammer. "Fuck, kid. Running in front of a loaded gun? That's a good way to get a bullet in the sternum!"

Holloway knelt mere feet from the animal and gradually held out her palm toward it. "You're not hurting her. Stand down."

It wasn't a question, a statement, or a request. This was a demand, and Mills could do nothing more than holster his weapon and comply. He may have thought a few curses at her but didn't dare say them aloud.

"It's okay, girl," she said, and inched closer to the baring teeth. "I won't hurt you. I promise." Another foot closer. "I want to help you." She extended her arm farther. "Let me help you."

"You're batshit, kid. That dog is about to rip your hand to shreds."

"Shut up for once," she said, and turned back toward the dog. "It's okay, girl. It's okay."

Slowly, the scowl began to close, and its perked ears lowered backward. Stretching her neck, the pup started sniffing the air near Holloway's hand. The raised fur on its back, though knotted, lowered and conformed to its spine.

"That's it. I won't hurt you." The dog brought its nose to Holloway's palm, and though apprehensive, licked her fingers. She gently rubbed the top of its head. "There. See. No one is gonna hurt you. You're okay now." She continued to rub the feral animal, and much to Mills's surprise, the dog even allowed a few scratches behind the ears.

"Great. You have yourself a pet. Now … what the hell are you gonna do with it?"

Holloway kept swiping her open palm against the dog's neck and back, lightly of course. "You're going to fetch me some water. She's severely dehydrated."

Mills shifted to one side. "I'm gonna wha—?"

"I'm not asking twice," she cut him off and returned her attention to the dog warming up to her. She didn't touch the injured leg directly but inspected it while petting its malnourished body.

*I'm not asking twice*, he mocked her internally and turned to Ethel. She shrugged and lifted her empty hands. *Thanks for nothing, Ethel.*

It had taken some time before he could track down an orange vest who had enough sense to hike with a water bottle in tow, and politely commandeered it without any rationalization. "Sheriff business," he had said and gave a crooked grin.

"There. Water," Mills scoffed and handed it to Holloway. "Anything else your new friend might need? Fluffed pillow? Maybe the finest steak in town?"

Holloway didn't grab for the bottle. Hell, she didn't even

bother scowling at Mills. She simply snatched it and returned her attention to the shepherd closing its yellow eyes each time she rubbed her hand down its spine. A small quip or snide remark was expected, but his young deputy refused him the satisfaction. She poured the water into her cupped palms and offered the dog a drink. Slowly, the forgotten animal sniffed her and lapped up gulp after gulp until its tongue met her skin. "There. I knew you had to be thirsty." She re-poured another handful and presented it.

"Kid? What're you planning on doing with this thing?"

She wiped her wet palm on her pants. "She's coming with us. Aaron can help her."

Dr. Geyser. He doubted the vet would be able to do much else than a quick shot and a few final ear scratches. The chances for rescue, to Mills at least, seemed slim. He had been around death for far too long not to recognize when someone had one foot in the grave. Should the dog indeed die, he imagined part of his deputy would go with it. "Not to be a thorn, but what if he can't help her? What happens then?"

Holloway stood, and the dog at her side sat with its wounded leg hovering above the dirt. "Then she will die comfortably. I will be there to show her that she isn't unloved or alone in her last moments."

*I meant with you, kid.* "Okay. Fine. Let's go." Mills took a careful step forward, and the shepherd began to snarl. "Easy now. You bite me and I'll let you roll down this hill." He reached his hand out hesitantly. "It's all right, girl. I'm a friend."

After a few rounds of coaxing and gentle pats and

scratches, he lifted the wounded dog into his arms and cradled her like an infant. Despite her frail appearance, she was still quite large and somewhat difficult to hold steady while descending the steep incline—the dog, unsure of what he had planned for it, and Mills, confident he'd need a rabies shot soon. He marched forward, however, carrying the very animal he had debated ending moments ago. For now, he would help in any way he could. Whether or not Geyser would close the final curtain was still unclear.

"Calling it a day, Sheriff?" John Baker's condescending voice carried downward and reached a tone steeper than the hill itself. "Don't you think my *wife* is a little more important than some stray?"

*Your wife might be, but you aren't.* "I'm leaving you all in the capable hands of my deputy. She has my full confidence," he announced and turned toward Holloway.

She met him with a curious, brown gaze. "Jeff, let me take her. This is your town. They are your citizens. What do you think they will say?"

"Kid, I stopped caring about what these idjits thought about me a long time ago. Plus, this isn't my town anymore." He winked at her and continued along the path. "I'll take care of this one jus' as you would. I promise. You make face with your citizens. That's an order."

×

IT HAD ONLY taken a matter of minutes for Mills to regret taking the damned dog to the clinic himself. Once inside his Bronco, a sharp whine ranging across multiple octaves fled the canine's widening jaw. She glared at him from the backseat in the rearview mirror, bobbing left and right depending on how close he cut each turn.

He tried to ignore the horrendous scratching of overgrown nails on his upholstery. It didn't work. Nothing did, in fact. Even with the radio near max volume, behind him he knew the fabric and foam cushions were being ripped to shreds. Hopefully, the Kents would have a replacement, but his Rose was far too rare to be tossed out to a salvage yard unstripped. It would be a special order, and he expected Holloway to foot the bill. He glanced at the yellow, almost glowstick-like gaze staring back at him. The shepherd pawed, its one front paw of course, at the passenger door and whined louder.

"Easy now, ya little shit," he said. "Almost there."

She barked a rebuttal he couldn't understand. Hunger was what he expected. Maybe thirst. Could've been the fact he ripped the stray from its home in the woods. She was, judging from her wild appearance, free for most of her short life. Now, she would be treated as nothing more than a simple pet. Holloway's pet. *Not his.*

Mills veered into the clinic's parking lot and stalled the Bronco driving up the paved and uneven entrance. "Fuck's sake," he said, and his only companion for the time being appeared to share his frustration, giving a stern huff. He tried a few turnovers from the center of the lot. Nothing. "Don't do this to me, girl." The starter finally ignited on the fifth attempt. Like the sheriff, his truck still had miles to spare, and he intended to drive until the engine went kaput.

He exited first, hacked a combination of green, throaty

gunk and long cut to the sidewalk, and moved for the back doors. "I swear to Christ if you bite me ..." Mills waved the shepherd out. "Let's go. Come."

She stared at him, head tilted, nose crinkled.

"Come on. I'm not picking you up again. You'll have to walk like the rest of us."

Another stern huff, this time wafting hot, putrid breath to his face. She dangled her injured and red-soaked leg above the seat and shifted her head to the other side. Her brow was no longer fixed into a slanted position but relaxed. Her once-intimidating glare was now eased enough to notice the whites in her eyes. She pointed her nose to the seat and stared up at him.

"No, no, no. Don't try and get cute with me. Out of the truck. Out!"

She only settled farther into the cushion. Her tail, bushy and near the length of her, began to swipe back and forth.

*Holloway's pet. Not mine.* He scoffed and reached inside. Once he was close enough to graze her ratty fur, Mills grabbed carefully, lifted her up, and cradled the dog as he had hiking down the incline. "Don't get used to this." She didn't wiggle from his grasp or try to break free, only extended her snout backward and let her large tongue hang sideways.

"Hi, Sheriff," the young receptionist said upon their entry. "Bringing your dog in for a checkup?"

"No, it's—I mean, she's not mine. Found her up in the woods. Roughed up pretty bad. Figured Geezer could take a look."

"*Geyser.* Not sure he will have time to see her today, sir."

She continued typing and clicked the mouse a few times. "How does next Tuesday sound? Does that work?"

Mills lifted the bloody leg absent a paw to the counter space, leaving bits of black fur and red splotches on the granite. "Does this look like it can wait?"

The girl's eyes widened, and her mouth was left agape. "Oh shit—hold on just a second." She fled to the backroom and thrust the swinging doors hard enough that they opened and closed a few times before shutting altogether.

"See what you did?"

The shepherd glanced up at him and back to the treat bowl on the counter filled to the brim. Finger-sized and dog-bone shaped, what they lacked in volume was clearly accounted for in a raw and foul odor. Mills snuck her one, and when she looked at him again, a second and third helping. She didn't chomp at his hand but simply nibbled at the corner until she could pull it in her mouth. Crusty bits fell to the wayside and even dusted his arms and pants. A hard swallow, smacking lips, and another gaze at him.

"No. Be happy with what you got," he told her and patted along her spine.

Dr. Geyser rushed into the waiting area, and his grin lost slack when he came face-to-face with Mills. "Oh, um. Sorry, I thought Deputy Sheriff Holloway had brought the animal in."

Mills rolled his eyes. "Didn't mean to disappoint."

He walked around the desk and inspected the dog from a safe distance. "What seems to be the problem here?"

"Found her in the woods. Must've gotten her leg stuck in a bear trap up there. Could probably use some water and a good night's rest."

Dr. Geyser held the mangled nub in his hand, and his stare intensified. "Probably had to chew off her own paw to get free. Poor girl. You really should do something about the hunters and those damn traps."

"Yeah, yeah." Mills sucked air through his teeth. "I'll get right on that. What can we do about her?"

The doctor rubbed his palm along her protruded ribs and more hair fell to the tile floor. "Won't be sure until I get some X-rays. Need to see how extensive the damage is."

"Can't you just bandage the leg, and I can send her on her merry way?"

He cocked his brow and twisted his face. "No. Absolutely not. I may have to amputate what's left. She's severely malnourished, has a considerable amount of mange, and in dire need of a flea and tick bath."

"Those, uh, fleas and ticks don't happen to like car upholstery, do they?"

The doctor drew a lengthy inhale and started to remove the shepherd from Mills. "I will need to keep her here overnight. Run tests to find out what we're dealing with. I must warn you though, Sheriff. This isn't a shelter, and the cost to help her, whether she survives or not, will be extensive."

"How much?"

"Could be hundreds, could be thousands. I won't know for sure until I have a firm grasp of her overall health."

A single needle easily would put the whole situation to bed, but he made that promise to Holloway. *I'll take care of this one jus' as you would.* "Do it. Do whatever you need to do. I'll foot the bill. Just get her back to me—erm, back to good health. Understand?"

The doctor nodded and started to walk away.

"Hang on, Doc." Mills took another treat from the jar. "She likes these." He gave her one last dog bone and ran his fingers between her perked ears. "You're gonna be okay. He'll take good care of you. I'll see you tomorrow, all right?"

When they headed for the silence of the backroom, she propped her head over Geyser's arm and stared at Mills the entire way.

# CHAPTER THIRTY

*The day Sarah went missing*

"SHERIFF," MILLS RESPONDED snidely, and held the device between them in his gloved hand.

The large man chuckled and extended his palm out. A simple, seemingly normal gesture one would expect from an innocent, or at least one appearing to be. He was a bit overweight to lecture the town's youth on the importance of physical fitness, and his windbreaker was covered with what could only be described as potato chip dust. "Didn't mean to offend. I'm Coach Tanner. You can call me Nathan."

Mills reluctantly shook his hand and stood upright. "Pleasure, Coach."

"You mind, uh, telling me what you're doing snooping around my office? Don't you need a warrant or something?" Tanner laughed casually and relaxed the hat above his brow to his receding hairline.

"Anything on school grounds is subject to search, *Coach*. Students' bags, faculty cars in the parking lot … offices. I'm shocked you haven't seen the signs posted next to the gym." Mills stretched the forming ache in his back and neck. "Jus' following up on something."

"Mind if I ask what?" It wasn't only the way he had asked, but the tone of his voice and a sudden pale complexion that made his once-confident appearance dwindle. His rosy plump cheeks rivaled the whitewashed walls in the locker room, and he couldn't quite figure out where to place his hands. On his hips. Arms crossed. Back to his hips.

A bell rang over the intercoms both outside and over the speaker near the door. Boisterous shouting echoed down the hallway. A barrage of teenage boys began slamming open lockers, slapping deodorant to their armpits, and throwing on the wrinkled ball of school clothes they had tossed to the cement floors. The stench intensified, and the teenagers' combined body odor wafted into the coach's office.

"Might not be a conversation for your students to hear. How about we go down to the station, and I'll get you up-to-date."

Coach Tanner peered through the open grates of his office windows, and once he noticed the boys were none the wiser, whispered, "That a request or an order?"

Mills closed the gap between them. "Ever wear handcuffs?"

He widened his eyes and took in a lengthy breath. "Gotcha. Happy to help, Sheriff. I just need to—um—take care of this next class, then I'll have a free period. Should be enough time to head to the station and answer any questions you might have. That work?" He continued to fidget about, at times tugging the windbreaker collar.

"Nah, ain't gonna work," Mills said. "Pretty important stuff."

Tanner furrowed his unkempt brow. "I can't exactly leave in the middle of the day, Sheriff. Let me at least gather my things."

"My deputy's at the office right now. She'll let Janice know we need you for information on a case. I'll escort ya to your car."

He closed his eyes and nodded. "Okay. Okay. No sweat. Will this take long?"

Mills waved him out of the small, cubicle-sized area, and patted his back. "Depends on the conversation, Coach."

Through the quad, the hallways, and into the staff parking lot, Coach Tanner made it a point to hunch his large shoulders forward while he tapped incessantly on his phone. The sheriff wouldn't give him the satisfaction of trying to sneak a glance. He knew exactly what the nervous man keeping a pace or two in front was doing. *Delete. Delete. Delete.* Mills even counted in his head every time the man swiped across the screen with vigor. Self-preservation was the only thing on his mind, and unbeknown to him, this behavior was expected.

"I'll meet you at the station. I trust you know the way?" Mills asked when Tanner evened his heavy weight to the multicolored pickup. "When you go inside, a young man named Simmons will take care of you."

Nathan nodded not once but multiple times.

Mills was about to turn but stopped and grabbed the driver's side door. "Oh, and don't worry about all that stuff you erased from your phone." He winked at him. "That's what cell records are for."

Nathan's face went slack. Any ounce of blood in his thick skull flushed to his feet hidden by plain white sneakers. A few shaky key turns and the truck surprisingly roared to life. He drove away, at times looking back at the sheriff.

Mills found it amusing to wave him off.

"Kid," he announced into his shoulder walkie.

A fuzzy squelch broke the silence. "Go for Simmons."

Mills glared at the afternoon sky, and fluffy white clouds billowed in small jet streams toward the encompassing mountain ranges. "Christ's sake, Simmons. When I say, 'Hey, Halfwit,' then I'm speaking to you directly."

Static accompanied the passing breeze. "… Yes, sir."

"Holloway? Deputy Jennifer Elizabeth Holloway?" Mills had used her full name only a handful of times, and if there was one way to irritate her to all hell, this was it. *It's Jenn*, she had scolded him, somehow politely of course, and asked that he never mention her full name again, let alone on frequency.

"Kiss my ass, Jeff," she mumbled over the scratchy feedback.

Mills chuckled and traversed the long stretch of hallway. "Oh, good. You're still in the office with Janice. I hope she didn't hear you cursing. Good Christian woman like that might just pray for ya."

"Not the best time, Sheriff."

He imagined Mrs. Peterson was, at that moment, snarling at Jenn for everything coming in over her walkie and grinned until his smile reached his ears. "Well, tell that old bat to find someone to cover for Coach Tanner for the remainder of the day. He's needed for information vital to our case. She can fuss all she wants, but this is official business. Oh, and if she gives you any lip, tell her the sheriff isn't asking."

"Yes, sir." Holloway sighed, and before she cut the line, a

tirade of callous yelling from behind her broke through the other end.

×

"YOU GONNA TELL me what you found?" Holloway asked from the passenger seat as they drove down the vacant main roads toward the station.

Mills retrieved a plastic bag with phone and held it between them. "Something he didn't want me to find."

"Is that—?"

"Yup. Jessie's phone," he said and displayed a toothy grin.

She snatched it from him and gloved her hands before removing it. "Where was it?"

The sheriff shrugged his shoulders. "His office. Beauty of public schools. No warrant needed. Prick didn't even bother trying to hide the damn thing. It's locked with a passcode, but I'm sure Simmons will be able to crack the code—"

"Done," she announced and started swiping through the many different screens. "Four digits. 6-9-0-4. Her birthday. My next guess was all zeros, but I think this generation might've caught on to parents trying that combo first."

Mills wasn't sure which impressed him more, how she was able to hack into the device with ease or how she had reviewed the young girl's file so intimately that she could recall her birthday. Either way, despite refusing to acknowledge her technical prowess outright, he still applauded her internally. "Don't get cocky. We still need something more circumstantial before we can hold him in the eight-by-eight."

"Yes, sir."

Traffic had slowed significantly in Fulton over the past few months, given the number of mom-and-pops shutting their doors and the going-out-of-business sales ending. With the lumber mill, the town's bloodline, reducing their workforce and the county's economy down the tubes, it wouldn't be long before a severe financial crisis affected everyone, including the sheriff's department barely scraping by. He didn't wish to pass off a lemon to his deputy, but unless Mayor Callahan did something, and quick, the town Mills swore to protect wouldn't survive this death sentence.

Although he half expected Coach Tanner to be racing for the border by now, much to his surprise, the teacher's jalopy truck was parked next to Simmons's squad car at the far end of the lot. He must've had enough sense to know his vehicle wouldn't last a chase up the monstrous hills leading in and out of the city. What he didn't know was that Mills wasn't sure Rose could make the climb either. Holloway jumped out first, followed closely by Mills after a pinch of the long cut was placed in his lower lip.

Once in the bullpen, Coach Tanner stood from the chair outside Mills's office like nails were spiking up his backside. The redness of his cheeks had spread across his entire face, and it appeared as though the apple-sized lump in his throat was too large to swallow. Simmons was preoccupied with different web searches at his desk and alternated his mouse hand between rapid clicks and pulls from the Styrofoam cup on his right.

Mills turned away from Tanner to Holloway and whispered, "Reach out to Judge Matthews. Get us a warrant for his truck and his home. I'll need her phone as well. He'll have a hard time explaining it."

She nodded, handed him the plastic bag discreetly, and withdrew to her desk.

"Simmons," he announced, and noticed just how many windows the freckled vet closed on the computer before shifting to him. "Did you ask our guest if he was hungry or thirsty?"

"I—uh—actually ate the last apple fritter, Sheriff. But I did offer him water or coffee."

"That true, Mr. Tanner?"

"Yes," he blurted out, and rubbed his sweaty palms against his sides. "Yes, sir."

"Excellent," Mills responded, a snide smirk stretching his cheeks. "You'll make a fine secretary one day, Simmons. Keep up the good work."

The pasty redhead glanced at Holloway, raised his brow, and crossed his arms. He continued to gloat until she snickered at him and repeated *secretary*, then the sudden realization hit him harder than the kick of a military-issued M-4. He sank in his seat, slowly spun around, and reared the rest of his coffee.

"Coach. You ready to talk?"

The man reluctantly nodded a few times and, with the plumpness of his face, was the spitting image of a bobblehead jiggling on a car dashboard. He didn't say a word while Mills escorted him to the backroom for questioning, nor did he give any reason to doubt he was guilty of one thing or another. The windbreaker swished in his cautious stride, and he made it a habit to adjust his hat every few steps as if the position he settled on didn't suit him. They sat across from each other, Mills offered him a smoke—to which he refused—and stared for a moment longer than either had anticipated.

"Sheriff? Why am I here?"

Mills lit his cigarette, exhaled toward the ceiling, and hunched forward. "How long have you been working at the school, Mr. Tanner?"

"Nathan, sir. You can call me Nathan. Around three years. Started by coaching the team—the, um, football team—and when a position opened up for phys ed, I applied."

He took another drag. "You enjoy it?"

Tanner leaned into the table and interlocked his fingers. "Some days more than others. It's a lot different than when we went to school."

The sheriff chuckled. "I'm sure my day was far different than yours. Do these students like you? Respect you?"

"Again, some more than others. Why do you ask?"

"Making conversation is all." Mills reached in his pocket and placed the bagged phone at the center of the table. "Found this in your file cabinet. Wanted to know why you might have it."

Coach Tanner glared at the device and back to Mills. "It's not mine if there's something on there that shouldn't be."

Mills waved his hand dismissively. "I know it ain't yours. I was wondering why it was in your possession. Care to enlighten me?"

A puzzled expression twitched from his brow to his mouth. "I catch the students playing on their phones all the time during my periods. Every now and then I have to take them. Shoot, I confiscate at least three or four a week."

After adding a glove to his hand, Mills lifted the device from the bag, set it on the table, and pressed the home button. An image of Jessie with Hannah replaced the blank screen. "It's Jessie Jenkins's phone. When was the last time she attended one of your classes?"

"That … That doesn't make sense. Jessie's been absent from my class for the past two weeks. I wouldn't have had a chance to take it." He reached for the phone, but Mills snatched it before he could.

Mills took another drag and placed the phone in his shirt pocket. "When was the last time you saw Ms. Jenkins?"

Coach Tanner shifted his gaze to the left, the right, and then the ceiling, visibly contemplating or searching for a proper alibi. The sheriff wasn't sure which.

"I haven't seen her for a while, sir, honest. Maybe homecoming? She was with Hannah, Hannah Richmond. She could probably tell you more about Jessie than I can."

"I've already spoken with Ms. Richmond. I'm more interested in why Jessie's phone was found in your office, *Nathan*."

He gave a curious, almost angry wince, squeezing his eyelids near the point of closing. "I'm not sure what Hannah told you or why you were snooping around my office in the first place, but whatever it is you think I've done, I haven't. I'm not some petty criminal. Where's Jessie? Have you talked to her? Does she think I stole her phone or something?"

"Jessie Jenkins was found a few days ago in the woods. She was beaten to death. Once we had a positive ID, her phone was pinged. I'll ask one more time, Mr. Tanner. Why did you have Jessie Jenkins's phone in your office?"

"Dead? Jessie is …?" Nathan Tanner noticeably choked back the large lump fixed in his throat for the past thirty minutes and swallowed. He held his palms over the table, for stability Mills assumed, and sank his now-panicked gaze to the floor. "I don't—I don't know why it was there. I don't know why any of this is happening."

Mills tilted back, plopped his boots to the table, and drew another inhale until the scorched end burned bright orange. "You care to tell me anything you *do* know?"

Three heavy knocks on the door and they both shifted their attention. Holloway entered slowly, as she had been instructed to do during questioning, and handed Mills a stack of pages clasped by a single paperclip in the top left corner. Ink lines from the fax were visible on the side margins, and a distinct signature filled the blank box at the bottom.

"Good to go?" Mills asked her.

She nodded and stood at parade rest.

"Outstanding," he said, returned the front legs of his chair to the floor and tossed the papers toward Coach Tanner.

He flinched when they hit his hand and splayed out. "What's … what's this?"

"Warrant, Nathan. T's are crossed and I's are dotted. If you would be so kind as to hand Deputy Holloway the keys to that fine vehicle in our lot, we can get started and get out of your hair."

Tanner lowered his shaky hand to his pocket and paused. "Don't I get a lawyer? A court-appointed one or something?"

"See the signature at the bottom? Thomas Matthews? You might not know him. Anyway, Mr. Matthews has determined we have enough evidence to search not only your personal effects but your vehicle and home, too. Great guy. Even better judge. Lawyer or not, I have full authority to rip apart everything you own."

His pale features somehow became a shade lighter than the papers he sifted through. There was nothing he could do, save for going into cardiac arrest and getting an ambulance ride handcuffed to the gurney. He finally, after a few more frightened glances at the bold, black letters laid out before him, retrieved the keys from his pocket and gave them to Holloway.

"We appreciate your cooperation," Mills said, and grinned. "Get started, will ya?"

She acknowledged him with a single nod and fled the room as quietly as she arrived.

"Won't be long. She's quick but thorough."

Coach Tanner clenched his fists and slammed them on the table. "What do you want, huh? What exactly do you think I did?"

"I never said you did anything, Coach. I'm jus' trying to get to the bottom of this. Jessie was your student, right? Don't you wanna make sure *whoever* did this gets justice?"

The complexion in his face had changed from blanched white to a rose in full bloom. His knuckles, however, remained flushed and under near-cracking pressure. "I barely knew the kid! She was an average student in a class of thirty teenagers! Why in the hell would I want to kill her? What could I possibly want with her?"

Mills pulled Jessie's phone from his pocket and began typing. "It's amazing how far we've come with technology, isn't it? Shit, back in my day we were passing notes when the teacher's back was turned. Now, those little checkboxes for *Do you like me, yes or no* seem a little silly, don't they?"

"What in the fuck does this have to do with anything?"

"Hang on just a second. I'm still learning how to work these damn things," Mills said and swiped a few times. "Now. I wanna show you a trick. Think of it as a magic trick. Will you place your phone on the table? It can be face down. I don't have to see it."

Coach Tanner scowled at him, even muttered something unintelligible, but did what was asked.

"This one's gonna be fun, just wait. Where the hell is the—ah, there it is." Mills clicked on the contacts, scrolled down, and tapped once more. "You said that you barely knew Jessie, right?"

Coach huffed an irritated breath in his direction but responded by nodding.

"Yeah, I knew I wasn't hearing things. All right, you ready?" Mills tapped one more time. "Abra ..."

A muffled dial tone passed through Jessie's phone followed by a sequence of numbers.

*Bzzt. Bzzt. Bzzt.*

Thick vibrations shuddered the phone facedown at the other end of the table.

*Bzzt. Bzzt. Bzzt.*

Mills took the last drag of his smoke and snuffed out the filter in the ashtray. He stared at Coach Tanner and enjoyed how each rattling tremor took a shade of color from his wide face. The sheriff revealed a crooked grin and sucked air between his teeth.

"Cadabra."

# CHAPTER THIRTY-ONE

*Seven months missing*

"SIMMONS?" MILLS ASKED into his walkie, fighting the feedback squelch while veering up the stiff terrain back toward the search site. Ash from the cigarette in his hand danced down his shoulder as he clicked the button a few more times to create a Morse code beep on channel four. "Hey, dipshit?"

It wasn't surprising that the receiver kicked on after such a disparaging nickname, and even less surprising that he picked up mid-chew. "What's up, Sheriff?" he said, slurping whatever takeout he had delivered to the station.

"You hear from Jenn?"

"Nah. Radio silence the past two hours. Want me to check it out?" Another lip smack before the line cut and static replaced the noise.

"I'm almost there. Might've lost signal during the climb. I'll keep ya posted."

The narrow trail he maneuvered left little room for the Bronco without occasionally driving up the embankments. A bigger vehicle or a less seasoned backwoods driver might've taken to the cliff's edge, unaware how shifty and loose the soil on these beaten paths became after the winter months. Mills would sooner take an oak to his front bumper than roll down the hill to an early grave.

He still questioned why the search had been set on such an incline while the less inhabited areas were at his back. Sure, he was far beyond the point of the regular lumber-worker traffic. The lumberyard was at least four quarter mile turns in the opposite direction. It was the path though that stuck out. The way a single road coiled into itself like a cottonmouth ready to strike. Any vehicle making the climb would be visible for miles.

When he arrived at the clearing, Mills noticed the majority of orange-vested volunteers had decided to call it quits. Most of them stood in a circle making small talk while others remained in their cars. Although his mother appeared to be having casual conversations with the crowd, John Baker was mysteriously absent. Given his thirst to appear as the innocent and grief-stricken husband ready to shed a tear for the public eye, this stuck out as odd to Mills but not worrisome. What concerned him most was that Jenn couldn't be counted among them either.

Mills exited the Bronco, broad-brimmed hat nestled on his brow, and started marching up the perch, taking heavy, planted stomps for secured footing. It was taxing on his knees, brutal even, but he wouldn't give the townsfolk who had seen him as an unfit sheriff the satisfaction of being right. He'd make the climb. Search all of Parley's Canyon if need be. This, for the time being, was his home, his responsibility, and he wasn't sure if it was arrogance or stubbornness that drove him forward, but he ignored the building aches in each limb and continued.

"Jenn?" he shouted into the surrounding wilderness.

Small bird chirps and twigs snapping beneath his boots provided the only response. "Jenn?" He continued upward—she would search for a high-point and peer down at the landscape for anything out of place. It's what he would do after all. She was a chip off the old beaten block.

Though sunlight traveled through the branches twisting overhead, the expected warmth had somehow become more difficult to find than his deputy. The search had ceased, that much was certain. Why Holloway was still gallivanting about with the department's prime suspect was something he couldn't quite pinpoint.

"Jenn?" Mills shouted once more, and now his breath was clouding before him in full effect. "Jenn Holloway?" It wasn't the stillness in his scan that he hated but the vacancy of his other senses. If they were close, he was sure even the slightest conversation could be heard. Noises and especially voices had thousands of trees to bounce off before reducing to whispers. There were no such whispers, however, only the squish of the dirt and impending darkness taking over by the minute. He counted his steps in his head and tried again.

"Hollow—"

An illuminated beam grazed the pink and white horizon and redirected to the ground above him. A flashlight. *Her flashlight.*

Mills pushed himself up the hill and toward the glowing area, ignoring the ache in his legs and other extremities. His boots, caked with mud, had lost all grip. But he had no intention of leaving her alone with a potential murderer.

In the distance he noticed two distinct figures. One was small and hunched in front of a tree. The second was bigger and closing the gap between them. Then he heard her voice. It wasn't casual. It wasn't excitement. No. Holloway was yelling, and Mills could only make out two words.

*Stay back.*

Mills rushed forward, forgetting each painful sensation thumping down his arms and eventually, numbing his toes. He reached his shaky hand for his holster and unfastened the top button.

"I mean it, John. Stay the hell—"

"I think the lady told you to stay back, Johnny," Mills announced while brandishing his Colt at the man's forehead and lining up the sights.

John lifted his arms apprehensively, but his eyes widened faster than a finger snap. "Uh, Jenn, what in the fuck is going on?"

"I'd like to know the same damn—" Mills paused and glanced at Holloway, who was hunched in front of a tree, digging her gloved hands into the dirt. "Thing."

"Jeff? What in the hell are you doing?" Holloway tilted her head and scowled at him. "Put the gun away."

Mills shifted his gaze between them curiously, lowered the revolver, and holstered it. "Kid? What are you doing on the ground? And why were you yelling like he was attacking you?"

"I was yelling to keep him away from the evidence." Holloway raised her hand and revealed a spray can with thick black paint running down the valve and sides. "Someone tried to bury it here along with four others."

John dropped his hands to his side and nearly doubled over. "Jesus Christ. You can't just go around waving guns at people! What's wrong with you?"

He felt the same numbness taking over his limbs before returning in tremendous fashion. "Oh. Well, uh. Good work, Deputy. Carry on."

"Yeah, another fine job from the sheriff's department," John said, passing Mills and careening down the incline. "Mayor Richmond will hear about this first thing."

"There's a complaint box at the department office if you'd rather use that," Mills called over his shoulder. "It's in a stall next to the urinal."

Holloway stood and retrieved two plastic evidence bags from the back of her belt. "Have you lost your goddamn mind?"

"Eh, no more than usual."

The scowl in her face returned. "You honestly think I'd let that tool overpower me?"

"You honestly think I'd let him try?"

She tried to conceal the smirk forcing itself through her thinned lips, and even turned to avoid him noticing. He did. Wasn't a difficult task when he could pick out her smile in a lineup of hundreds. The look of disappointment, one he had become increasingly familiar with as of late, was another he'd have no trouble recalling. While he was entirely unsure how she'd remember him, there was a hope that mediocre would outweigh the downright deplorable.

"Paint look like a match?"

She blew the stray hair dangling over her face and grinned. "I've been doing this job long enough to know when something seems out of place—"

*It usually is.* He kneeled beside her. His knees cracked

more times than he cared to admit. "Need help combing the area?"

"Already did. Boot prints are over there. Size thirteens. Looks like the suspect buried these cans here and hiked down alone. None of the volunteers had a shoe near that length, and John's feet were the biggest of the bunch."

"What about Johnny boy? What is he working with?"

She zipped the bag with three canisters and began filling the other. "Tens."

Mills cocked his brow and winced. "Guessing shoe sizes some hidden talent you failed to mention on your résumé?"

"He told me. All it took was an impressed gasp and a wow, your feet are *so* big! I bet they're twelves! Didn't even need to bat my lashes for him to spill it."

"So, this would explain—"

"Why I was up here alone with that prick in the first place?" she cut him off. "Did you really assume I was going on some romantic stroll through the woods with the husband of a missing person? The only missing persons case in the last thirty years? You really have lost your mind."

Mills was impressed. Holloway had taken John's weakness for young, pretty girls and used it as a tactic to pry out information he'd regularly withhold behind the shield of his greaseball attorney. She played him. Made him out to be the sap Mills knew he was. Desperate for the attention of the opposite sex even if they had a badge pinned to their chest. "Did he say anything else worth mentioning?" he finally asked.

Holloway shrugged her narrow shoulders. "He talked about himself a lot. His recent promotion and how much time he had been spending in the gym lately. There was something else though. Something odd whenever he mentioned Sarah. He never just said *find her*. He said *find them*."

Mills debated internally. "Meaning that—"

She cut him off once more. "That our missing teacher was expecting, and he didn't bother telling us."

×

THEY RETURNED TO the clearing, which was now empty besides the sheriff's Bronco, and began driving down the path toward town. The last remaining hint of sunlight peeked behind Cedar Pass straight ahead while a black nothingness filled the rear view. Had the lights at the lumberyard not been shining in full effect, maneuvering down might've become increasingly difficult. The spray-paint cans rattled in the evidence bags in the backseat, as did the seat belt Mills refused to fasten while descending.

"You did drop her off at the clinic, right?" Holloway asked, held her forearm out the open passenger window, and rode her hand against the waves of the evening draft. More than a few strands rustled free from her loosely fitted bun and wafted over her face until she corrected them.

"Course I did." He wondered if her hair would be more easily managed behind the broad-brimmed hat on his dash. If she could not only wear it but own it as well. If this deputy had it in her to incite authority over the town and its citizens. If they'd respect her or simply whistle or yell obscenities at her. No. She'd slam them on the pavement before they could degrade her.

He recalled his trek up the mountainside and how the landscape had nearly claimed him. Didn't seem like more than a few years ago he would've jogged up that hill with a lit cigarette at the corner of his mouth. Now he could barely crawl up without needing a grave prepared *just in case*. It was a bitter pill to swallow, but Mills did.

"Aaron say anything?" She continued to stare out the window aimlessly.

Mills gave her a lopsided grin. "How about we go check for ourselves?"

She turned to face him, a puzzled expression tensing her features. "It's past nine. I doubt they'd let us in."

"Nah. I'd bet money they will make an exception," he said, grabbed the broad-brimmed hat from the dash, and placed it on her knee. "For Fulton's new sheriff."

Holloway nervously rubbed her fingers down the top and brim, then lifted it to gaze at the pinned emblem. She tightened her pursed lips. Her large eyes somehow doubled in size and glossed over.

"Now don't go getting all soft on me. It ain't set in stone. You still need to be officially elected. From now on though, you will be the department's acting sheriff. Can't adjust your salary either, so it'll be twice the work on a deputy's pay."

"Yes, sir," was all she could manage.

"We find this pregnant teacher, you're a shoo-in. You don't? Shit, you might jus' be answering to Simmons. Imagine that. Sheriff Simmons."

She closed her eyes, giggled, and small tears traveled down her cheeks. "I'll find her. I promise I will. Thank you, sir."

"Now don't think you'll have free rein either. I'm remaining on duty to oversee the case until the town declares it official. I'll throw my hat in your corner, but these idjits will have the final say."

"Wouldn't have it any other way, Sheri—Mills … Mr. Mills?"

He veered onto the overpass leading to town and drove through the Fulton main roads. "Jeff." In many ways it sounded foreign. Different. Like a good memory long forgotten. He wouldn't be Sheriff Mills. The sheriff. Jacob's boy, some of the older residents called him. "From now on, call me Jeff."

# CHAPTER THIRTY-TWO

*The day Sarah went missing*

COACH TANNER SLOWLY reached over the table and silenced it. His pale face now teetered on the verge of green. While Mills wasn't certain, the notion did cross his mind that Tanner would puke, and Simmons would add mopping the floor to his list of daily duties.

"A little odd, isn't it? Jessie having your number. Right, Coach?"

His nostrils flared, and his thick throat rattled. "I can explain that."

"Can you also explain why her phone was in your office? And how texts were sent out weeks after her death?"

"That wasn't me!" he shouted and slammed his fists to the table. "I didn't kill her, Sheriff. I swear on everything. I wouldn't hurt her."

"Why did she have your number?" Mills leaned forward and held Jessie's phone between them for emphasis.

"I gave her my number once. Said if she ever needed someone to talk to ..." Coach Tanner glared at the table's imperfect wood grain and seemingly traced his gaze along the etchings. "Her home life wasn't the greatest. I noticed bruises a few times. Stuff you'd only see in afterschool specials. I didn't know what else to do. If I reported it, she would have been known around town as the stereotypical trailer trash with the abusive stepfather. I only wanted to help her. Let her make that call."

Mills winced. "So, you did nothing? You knew her mother or one of her boyfriends was hurting a sixteen-year-old girl, and you let it slide?"

"I couldn't report something without concrete proof, Sheriff. She wouldn't tell me what was happening at home. All I had were a few bruises that could've easily come from cheerleading practice. I tried talking to Hannah, but she called me *Coach Pervert* for asking about her friend."

Sheriff Mills relaxed in the stiff metal chair, leaned back, and lit another smoke. "When did you first notice the bruising?"

He glanced up and knit his brow together. "What do you mean?"

"At what point did you notice Jessie Jenkins, your student, was coming to gym class with bruises? Should I write it? Maybe sign it?" Mills gestured his hands in the few sign language letters he did in fact know.

Coach Tanner shook his head and removed his cap. Small strands of hair lifted with it and floated to the table. "Not sure exactly. Beginning of the year. Maybe a few weeks after."

"And that's when you gave her your number? Not an email, but your personal cell?"

"Yes, sir."

Mills took a drag. "Did she ever contact you?"

A noticeable twitch tugged at his cheek. "Once or twice. To tell me she'd miss a class. Ask what time the buses would leave for an away game. Nothing really worth mentioning."

"I see," Mills said and swiped through Jessie's phone. "Tuesday, October 4, 5:04 P.M. Her: *Where r u.*

"You: *In my office. Stuck grading fitness evals. You only did 9 push-ups? Might get a D. Lol.*"

Mills smirked, but it really was disgust twisting his face.

"Her: *Stfu. I suck at push-ups ...*

"You: *Yah, you do suck apparently,* winky face.

"Her: *Sometimes.* Smiley face. *Any1 else there?*

"You: *Nope. Wat you doin?*

"Her: *Waitin in the parking lot.*

"You: *Wanna help me finish? hehe*

"Her: *Omw,* and another fucking smiley face."

Mills slammed the phone on the table and grazed his tongue to his top row of teeth. "I don't know about you, but Christ, I don't need a decoder ring to understand where the fuck that was going."

Coach Tanner sank lower not only in posture, but in confidence. "I ... didn't ... nothing happened. Nothing ever happened between us."

The sheriff snatched the phone and continued reading despite his stomach pleading him not to. "Friday, October 12, 10:30 P.M.

"Her: *Good game, Coach. You really kicked Eastmont's ass!*

"You: *The team did good. I just called the shots. Lol. I thought for sure we'd score one more time. Kinda bummed we didn't.*

"Her: *That all you care about? Scoring...* winky face.

"You: *After a big game like that? Lol maybe.*

"Her: *Still on campus?*

"You: *Parking lot.*

"Her: *Omw.*"

Mills paused and pushed the phone away from him. Nicotine wasn't the only flavor lathering his tongue. "What does o-m-w mean, Coach? Care to answer that one truthfully?"

Coach Tanner muttered something inaudible.

"Come again?"

"On. My. Way."

"Interesting. So, your student, whom you were worried was dealing with domestic abuse, was on her way to your fine vehicle to do what? Talk about the game? Maybe go over the class schedule? Or did you two just take a field trip? Did her mom sign the permission form as well?"

The air in the small room tightened like a knob had been shifted to induce suffocation. Neither spoke; the across-the-table stare intensified. Coach Tanner tightened his mouth, and Mills, regardless of the urge to blatantly laugh at unraveling such a knot of disgusting lies, awaited a rebuttal.

Three heavy knocks on the door disturbed them both.

"Sheriff," Holloway announced and waved him outside.

Mills stood, snuffed out his cigarette, and pocketed the bag with Jessie's phone. "Mr. Tanner, I'll just be a moment. Give you some time to"—he tapped his thumb on the table—"collect your thoughts."

The coach placed his face in his palms while Mills exited the stuffy room and leaned against a wall in the corridor. He held his hands firmly on his hips—just above the belt and holster—and stared at Holloway for some answer to her intrusion.

"Thought you might want to see this," she said and lifted a wrinkled ball of fabric. White, yellow, and blue colors were prominently displayed, and when Holloway held the collar and let the cloth dangle freely, a Fulton High School cheerleading uniform hung between them both.

"Is that—?"

"Yes, sir," she interrupted. "Name is in permanent marker on the tag."

Mills grabbed one sleeve and raised it slowly. "Where was it?"

"Behind the bench seat. Well, the only seat. You can tilt the bench forward, and this was stuffed in a makeshift cubby."

He took the uniform from her and pinched it with two fingers. Gave it another glance and an even longer look at the skirt he was sure Coach Tanner's grubby hands had been up. "Anything else back there?"

"Nothing pertaining to the case. The real find was up front."

Mills set his tongue in the spot where the long cut usually rested. "Which was?"

"It had been cleaned pretty thoroughly, but I believe I have a DNA sample." Holloway reached into her pocket and pulled out a plastic bag with an evidence swab inside.

"What? Nathan's jerk-off juice?" He grinned at his new favorite phrase. "Hope you wore gloves."

"Not semen, asshole. Blood. It didn't show up under the UV until I sprayed some luminol. It's either his blood or hers. Luckily, he wasn't smart enough to use an oxy cleaner on his seats to wipe it out completely."

"Yeah, he ain't the brightest person I've ever had a conversation with. I'll take that as an early Christmas gift. Get Luther on the line and drive the swab over to his office. He can let us know within the hour if it's a match. If it is Jessie's blood, no DA three counties over would have a problem indicting him."

"Hey, uh, Sheriff Mills?" Simmons interrupted. "I have a John Baker on the line asking to speak to you. Says it's rather urgent, sir."

"Take a message, dipshit. I'm kinda in the middle of something if you haven't noticed," Mills said and waved him away. "Let's not waste time on this one, kid. Go."

"Yes, Sheriff. You want me to bag up the ...?" She pointed at the cheerleading uniform in his hands. "Put it with the evidence?"

Mills gave her a crooked, toothy grin. "Nah. I'm gonna have some fun with it."

Holloway turned for the bullpen and sat next to Simmons, quick to pick up her landline and begin dialing.

*Atta kid.* He somewhat admired her keen work ethic. Mills would be lying if he didn't say, at least inwardly, that the station had never run smoother. It wasn't his doing. Sure as hell wasn't Simmons. It was Holloway. It was always Holloway.

Mills strutted inside the interrogation room and tossed the uniform in front of Tanner. "Found your uniform, Coach. I think you've outgrown it a tad."

He raked his fingers through the little hair remaining on his head. "I know how this looks, sir."

The sheriff shrugged. "Looks pretty bad for you, Nathan.

My deputy found a rather large amount of DNA on your bench seat. Having it tested as we speak." This was a bluff. An intentional, intimidating bluff Mills was sure to raise the already heightened blood pressure of the man across the table. "A girl has been murdered. Beaten savagely and left for dead in my woods. We find not only lewd texts between the two of you but her cheerleading uniform in the back of your truck and DNA evidence as well. How am I supposed to look at this? Come on, Nathan. Help me out here. Help me understand."

"I—I swear I didn't."

"Were you and Ms. Jenkins romantically involved or not?"

Coach Tanner fiddled with his hat and grazed his fingers along the FHS stitching. "I didn't mean for it to happen. It was ... a moment of weakness."

Mills placed both hands on the table and hunched over it. "Didn't mean for what to happen? Having relations with her? Killing her? What, Nathan?"

He closed his eyes. "Relations."

"Sex. You had sex with Jessie, correct?"

Coach Tanner nodded, and the fluorescents created a sheen over his balding head.

"How. Many. Times?" Mills raised his voice after each syllable.

"Once. Just once. I ... I was her first."

"Did you engage in any other sexual encounters with Jessie Jenkins?"

He ground his teeth, and judging from the noise, nearly cracked them to pieces. "Yes, sir."

"Were you with her the night of October 13?" Mills was no longer asking but shouting.

"Ya, I guess so. I was chaperoning the homecoming dance. She was there. So were a lot of other students."

"Were you ever alone with her that night?" Mills dragged his nails over the table and clenched his fists until each knuckle was practically transparent. "Did you take her somewhere to be alone?"

"No. No, sir. I went straight home after the dance. Friday, the twelfth. That was the last time I saw her outside of school. The last time we—I swear it. Friday, the twelfth. Check the texts."

Mills beat his fist on the table like a hammer. A loud *crash* echoed off each wall. "Why did you kill Jessie Jenkins? Did she threaten you? Threaten to turn you in? Why did you kill her, Nathan? Tell me!"

Coach Tanner cupped his ears in his hands, and tears pooled at the corner of his frightened eyes. "I didn't. I didn't kill her. I would never hurt her."

"Bullshit! I want the goddamn truth!"

More tears erupted from the large man dwindling in his seat. "I swear … I didn't do it. I swear on everything."

Mills drew a ragged, hoarse breath and calmly said, "Stand up."

"What? Why?" Coach Tanner mumbled.

"Stand up!" Another hammer fist to the table.

Tanner, while trembling, did as Mills demanded. The skin under his eyes was puffier than a boxer's face after a prize fight. "Please, Sheriff. I didn't do it. I promise."

"Turn around." He cut the words short and almost

blended them together.

"Why?"

"I'm not asking again. Turn around!"

Coach Tanner's hefty body began to shudder, and he faced the wall behind him.

"Nathan Tanner," Mills said and retrieved his cuffs, "you are under arrest for the statutory rape of Jessie Jenkins." He secured the cuffs around his meaty wrists. "Anything you say can or will be used against you in the court of law. You have the right to an attorney. We both know you can't afford one, so one will be appointed for you." Mills dragged him to the door, opened it, and shoved him into the hallway. "Do you understand the rights I have just read to you?"

His subtle tears had morphed into a hysterical fit, complete with a snotty nose and slick cheeks. He didn't respond, only channeled his shame toward the opposing wall.

"Hey." Mills kicked his leg with the toe of his boot. "Do you understand the rights I have just read to you? This is where you say *Yes, sir,* and be on your merry fucking way down the rabbit hole."

"Yes … sir," he said between sniffles and harsh swallows.

Mills's grin stretched for his ears. "Well, all right then, Nathan. Let's get you booked." He put two fingers against his tongue and whistled loud enough to shake Simmons from his seat. "Hey! Make yourself useful and book our new guest."

Simmons rushed toward them, nearly knocking the files and coffee off his desk.

"Oh, and Coach?" Mills whispered. "If that blood in your truck does come back as Jessie's, expect a few more charges. I hope the football team can manage the rest of the season without you."

×

MILLS HAD REMAINED in his office for the past thirty minutes loading each round of coffee with a sour mash chaser. It was, after all, the first solved murder case the town had seen in decades. If this wasn't cause enough to celebrate, the sheriff would be hard pressed to find another reason. Radio on, blaring classic rock of course, he toasted each drink to Jessie's memory, and promptly gulped down the Styrofoam cup within seconds.

"Sheriff?" Holloway said from the doorway, nearly drowned out by music.

"Kid! Just in time." Mills filled an extra cup and extended it to her. "Saved you some of the hors d'oeuvres. Come in. Let's toast."

Holloway lowered the radio volume and dropped a stack of files on his desk. "I'm not thirsty. Thank you."

"All right. All right. I won't pressure ya. What'd Luther find?" He rubbed his rough palms together and sat in his large leather chair.

"Blood was a hundred percent match. It's Jenkins's blood."

"Excellent!" Mills lifted his cup and downed the remaining caramel liquid. "Now have a drink to celebrate. We caught the bastard. Simmons is booking him right now. Relax. We jus' did this town a service."

Holloway shook her head. "Not quite sure we did, sir.

Yeah, Tanner is a scumbag, but do you really think we have our guy? He was responsible?"

"Kid. We have texts. A confession to relations with her. Fuck, blood on his goddamn seat cushion! Open-and-shut." Mills tipped his cup to her.

"Doesn't it seem like an odd place for blood though? Why in the middle of his bench seat?"

He scoffed and took a swig from the bottle on his desk. "Who cares? Maybe he bashed her head in, had blood on his hands and wiped it off on the seat. Open-and-shut case, Jenn. We got him. *We. Got. Him.*"

"Tanner's all booked, Sheriff," Simmons said, poking only his thin head inside. "Got him locked up in the back."

"Simmons! I know you're *deputy enough* to celebrate with me. Get your ass in here."

He shifted his mouth to one side of his pasty, freckled face. "Wish I could. John just called again. Fourth time so far."

Mills glanced at Holloway and back to Simmons. "John? Who the hell is John?" He chuckled.

"John Baker. I tried to tell you earlier, sir. He said his wife is missing."

# PART IV
## The Dance

# CHAPTER THIRTY-THREE

## Sarah

*Eighteen days before Sarah went missing*

THE AUDITORIUM GLOWED. Streamers glinted like July fireworks exploding in the ever-shifting lights of the room. Students flooded the basketball court, scattering in various groups and cliques. Some braved the dance floor while others remained wallflowers, adding a collage of dresses and slacks to the backdrop. The overpowering music dampened conversations, and Sarah somehow found herself among the chaos.

"Hands up higher, Mr. Dobbins," she yelled into the boy's ear. He rolled his eyes and raised his palms to the girl's waist. *Thank you*, Sarah mouthed.

She wasn't shocked to see Coach Tanner as the other chaperone, only taken off guard each time she caught him snapping a lustful gaze between her and the mildly underdressed Jessie Jenkins. His thinning hair was split down the center, and a wrinkled navy long-sleeve—missing a button or two—clung to his stomach. She'd managed to avoid him but it wouldn't be long before he corralled her into a corner.

The slow tune ended, and students erupted in cheers when a popular hip-hop song blared. Once facing their dates, the girls flipped around in unison and began grinding their backsides against the males' fronts.

*Utter. Fucking. Chaos.*

"Arm's length!" Sarah screamed and pushed her way through the crowd. Most pretended not to hear her. "Arm's length—" She froze, and a shallow breath passed through her lips. Shawn stiffened, stood upright, and met her glare while Hannah Richmond continued to push herself against him. He loosened his square jaw, and his dark brown gaze practically said the apology for him. They stared at one another, a sudden pause that silenced the music with it. Hannah, clueless as she was, didn't realize Shawn had removed his hands from her hips and let them drop to his sides.

Sarah's weakened resolve crumbled, and before he caught his voice, she glanced at the ceiling and moved deeper into the crowd. She ignored the dancing students, taking bumps and elbows along the way, and stopped at a table near the bleachers. A large glass bowl at the center was filled with a watery blue liquid. *Tiger's blood*, they called the concoction. Paper plates unfolded in a messy row with yellow frosted cookies, bites missing from some.

"Got it from my mom's cabinet." She noticed the voice first, then peered through the stands at a group gathered beneath.

"Give me some." Another voice chimed in.

Sarah walked around and ducked to maneuver inside. Three classmates were huddled together, and each took turns passing something around.

"Don't take it all—" Jared cut himself off when Sarah came closer, eyes gaping, and mouth thinned to a small line.

He slipped the bottle behind him and tensed to a rigid state. "Mrs. Baker. How's … how's it going?" The other boys fled to the other end, and the shadows made it impossible to identify their faces.

"Drinking on school grounds? Are you really that stupid?"

He lowered his head to the filthy and neglected floors.

"Hand it over."

Jared lifted his hand hesitantly, and the vodka swam in the half-empty, pocket-sized bottle.

She snatched it from him and deepened her scowl. "If I see you doing anything else, Principal Randolph will see you first thing Monday morning. Am I clear?"

He didn't dare glance up. "Yes, ma'am."

Sarah pointed to the path leading out. "Stay. Out. Of. Trouble."

The frightened boy bolted from under the bleachers, nearly tripping over the metal fixtures along the way. She twisted off the cap and brought the lip to her nose. The obnoxious fumes cleared her nasal cavity and watered her eyes. She coughed through a sour face and shrugged.

×

"YOUR DRESS IS lovely!" Sarah grabbed a girl by the shoulders and shook her. "Keep your hands away from her ass, Connor. I'm watching you!" She motioned two fingers from her eyes to his for emphasis.

The lights cut from student to student, though she found it increasingly difficult to tell them apart. A numbness soothed over her. An invincible, emotionless sensation she willed to last until John no longer filled her thoughts. His smile. The coin in his hands. How he didn't come home last night or in the early morning hours. Despite it all, everything washed away as easy as the vodka slid down her throat. For once, Sarah was in control.

"Stand up straight, Hannah." She pushed between them, and Shawn took a tentative step back. "I love your tie, by the way." She grabbed it from the knot downward, the silk smooth against her fingertips, and flung it over his shoulder.

Shawn adjusted the tie to its neat, previous form and stared at the ground, a wide grin complementing the dimples on his cheeks. Hannah tightened the arch in her back but couldn't seem to shut her low-hanging mouth.

Sarah leaned into her and whispered, "I catch you dancing inna—inappropriately again, and you'll have to call *Daddy* to pick you up. Wouldn't want that, would you?" Sarah pretended to help her with her dress and whispered again. "Don't worry. I'm sure plenty of the girls here would love to keep Shawn company."

The near-blinding yellow lights revealed Hannah's deep glare. Tears filled her eyes and she wiped them away promptly. She looked like she wanted to say something, scream at Sarah even, but she didn't. Hannah only scowled.

"You guys have a good time." Sarah smiled and rubbed her hand over Shawn's back for longer than she should have. Then, she strutted with a pleased grin to the refreshment table to observe the crowd.

"Long night, huh?" Coach Tanner's voice hovered around her like flies gathering over garbage in the summer sun. "These kids never seem to run out of gas."

Sarah nodded and pulled the phone from her bra.

"Great hiding spot. That's where I keep mine, too." He chuckled and moved closer until his breath caught her bare neck.

She didn't bother hiding her disgust and started swiping the air for invisible gnats, or at least, one large one. If his presence was this off-putting for her, she couldn't imagine how the students tolerated it. Was he this blatantly disgusting with all the females on campus, and if so, how had he not been reported in the few years he taught and coached at the school? Maybe Principal Randolph was covering for him. Tanner had, after all, taken the Tigers to an all-state championship for the first time in a decade. Did that give him some sort of sick immunity?

Her second, and most blistering, thought was a way to get rid of him.

"I need to take this," she said and glanced down at the voicemail notification on the screen.

"Oh, yeah. Sure. I'll hold down the fort." He swayed to the rhythm of the music, and she was certain he had fixed his filthy gaze on her backside as she exited the room.

She held the phone to one ear and plugged her finger to the other. "Hey, Sarah." Barbara. She probably wanted to gloat about their trip. "John said you wouldn't be able to join us. No biggie. Love to have you though. I was wondering if you have spoken to John? We were supposed to leave this morning, but he never showed up. You guys are only a few hours away. Not sure what is keeping him. He won't answer his phone either. I'm a bit worried. Well … call me when you get this. Love you both. I'll pray—"

She thumbed the delete button and walked at a fast pace to her classroom. The campus lights flickered on as the descending sun lost its flair. Her heels scuffed the cement with each lengthy step. She swallowed a deep breath to steady the building tears. It didn't help. Her chest collapsed. Sharp, piercing throbs were followed by twisting cramps.

Sarah didn't want to cry. Not over John. Not for knowing about his weekend getaway with the bartender. Not because her life was falling apart so rapidly. But something inside her couldn't help it. Something inside had finally broken.

It wasn't until she entered the privacy of her class that the stifled weeping increased to outright cries. Sarah wiped her arm to each cheek. She didn't dare turn on the lights. No. Only the darkness was invited to enjoy her pain. Her weakness.

The leather chair provided comfort, as did the way she buried her face in her palms. "Why?" Her voice quivered. "Why is this happening?"

The door hinges squealed and settled. A shadow appeared from the dimly lit hall and took an apprehensive step inside.

"Mrs. Baker?"

She knew his voice. Far better than a teacher should have.

"I saw you walking through the quad," Shawn said. "I couldn't tell if you were sad or pissed."

"Both."

"You want to talk about it?" He moved closer to the

desk. His form, no longer a shadow, came into view. "If you can't tell by your morning lectures, I'm a fairly good listener."

She scoffed. Her cheeks, still wet with tears, pulled tight. "There's nothing to talk about, Shawn. Please, just go."

"Not until I know you're gonna be okay. Sign me up for detention. Tell Principal Randolph. I don't care." He leaned against her desk. The gray button-up tightened around his shoulders and biceps. "If it's because of Hannah, I—"

"That *girl* is the least of my problems."

He chewed on his lower lip. "Well, whatever you said got to her. She's probably still at the table where I left her."

The image of Hannah sitting alone, while satisfying, didn't help Sarah in the slightest. Elbows on the desk, she propped her face in her hands. "You wouldn't understand, Shawn."

"Why? Because I'm just a kid? Is that really how you see me?"

"Yes." *Of course not.* "You are my student. My personal affairs should not carry over to the classroom."

"Well, think of this place as a gray area. We're in a classroom, sure, but this isn't a class. There's no other students. No books. No papers to grade. It's way too dark to read anything." He smiled, and she hated him for it. "I won't say anything to anyone. Promise. It'll be our secret."

That word. *Secret.* She clenched her thighs together at the sound. The sensation it brought. The longing that accompanied. She lifted herself from her slouched, unattractive posture. The lily print dress, now hiked to her upper thighs, raised farther, and she didn't bother pulling it back down. She caught his smoldering gaze lingering over every inch. Invited or not, there was an underlying desire to lift the dress even higher.

"You can trust me."

*No, I can't. I can't trust anyone.*

When she didn't respond, he hung his head for a moment and stood upright. "Okay. I understand. I'm sorry I bothered you." Shawn sighed and turned for the door.

"He's fucking someone else," she blurted out before good conscience had a chance to object. The confession brought new, warm tears. She could no longer see him through the blur, but his presence was noticeable, nonetheless. "I pushed him away. It's my fault."

He wrapped his arms around her, and she buried her face in his abdomen. It wasn't as comfortable as she'd imagined. She rested her cheekbone in between one of six, if not eight, deep ridges. His shirt caught most of her weeping, and she was tempted to pull away when the fabric stuck to her face. She expected mascara to mark thick, black lines around the area as well, but was surprised to see only a few gray spots darker than the rest. He could've splashed water on himself while washing his hands. No one would know any different. They wouldn't know what really happened.

Shawn lowered his chin to her crown. "I wouldn't waste my time if I were you. He's an idiot if he doesn't see how beautiful you are."

She tilted her head, a newly formed smile replacing her sullen features.

He grinned back. "But … *I do.*"

What she would give to fold into every part of him. To forget the fear. The repercussions. The anxiety chipping away at her chest. All she wanted—no, needed in that moment was him. It could have been a lapse of judgment or maybe her own longing forcing itself through the walls she desperately created, but she hoisted her hands to both sides of his toned stomach, thumbs over his hip bones. His tie swayed between them like an apple ripe for the picking. To grab it and yank him down would be forceful. More incriminating than a happy accident. She resisted the urge despite the appeal.

He eased his arms to each of her shoulders. There they stayed, neither advancing forward. Her, the lead in this slow dance. Him, the student ready for instruction. Though not a single word was spoken, the conversation carried on in their embrace. He held the same confident yet unsure gaze she cursed him for displaying every first period. Something she could relate to. Confident in what she wanted. Unsure of the consequence.

Sarah, with a motion from Shawn to stand, peeled herself from the chair. She held her breath, and her chest rose to the occasion. Her hands still at his hips, she silently begged to inch them downward. One smooth pull was all it would take had her hands stopped trembling. No, it wouldn't be easy. It would take everything she had to forget how wrong, yet how right it all felt.

"Am I making you uncomfortable, Mrs. Baker?"

*Sarah. Say it. Say my name.*

"No, Shawn." Seven different scenarios played through her head on how to explain hugging a student in an empty classroom. It wasn't illegal. Immoral maybe, but not illegal. It would, however, raise questions. Questions that were impossible to answer. While Sarah struggled with these thoughts, Shawn leaned in and kissed her.

# CHAPTER THIRTY-FOUR

*Seven months missing*

SARAH WAS STIRRED awake the same way she had been for the past month. Soft flutters and kicks from her now protruding stomach. Sunlight piercing the fabric shades and settling on her face. Heartburn bile heaving up her throat, and depending on how she slept, careening up her nasal cavity. She could handle the baby's movements. Welcomed them even. The acid burning holes through her esophagus, however, was more torture than being shackled to the wall behind her. Michael was kind enough to leave a bucket next to her bed in case of nausea, but he was the only thing to sicken her as of late.

*Tonight*, she affirmed to herself and rubbed her fingers over the broken fork prong. They were leaving tonight.

She lifted her wounded leg in the air and bent her knee a few times before twisting it in every direction. A soreness still remained but was significantly less than the preceding attempts. *A fast healer*, Michael had said each morning while changing her bandages, until one day, she no longer needed them. The scars remained, as did the purple and black bruising covering most of her calf and ankle. The memory of this confinement was something she knew would never fully heal though.

"Michael?" she called. "Michael, I need to use the bathroom."

He didn't answer but his rustling around his room was response enough. Large feet hitting the cold wooden floor. A deep yawn and groan—presumably him stretching—echoing down the hallway. His toes cracking with each step. The sudden shift in the musty air. It had mirrored their mornings together. He was, as always, quick to rise at even the slightest noise, and Sarah became increasingly concerned her next escape attempt would fail to go unheard.

"I need to pee," she said when he approached.

He nodded and pulled the shackle key from his sweatpants pocket. Another yawn, and he unlocked the left wrist, followed by the right. The chains fell to her sides, rattling downward. They were cold, especially on the exposed skin of her thighs. When he left for the kitchen, Sarah grabbed the crutch near her bed and hobbled down the hall.

While her leg wasn't entirely ready to handle her full weight, limping was a bearable motion as she maneuvered herself to the toilet seat. Small traces of blood blotted the stagnant waters and slowly fused with her own urine. It wasn't alarming. Spotting during pregnancy was, according to the book Michael had given her, somewhat normal. It was being chained to a wall and tortured that wasn't mentioned anywhere.

She brushed the hair draping over her face and wiggled the faulty handle behind her. The murky waters swirled a few times before rushing down. Standing proved to be a more difficult task than sitting and required her to use the sink counter for support. Sarah lowered her raised foot to the linoleum. *Give me something. Anything.*

She shifted. The weight took to her feet pads first, and slowly traveled up her numb ankle. Like a beehive shaken loose from a branch, the tingling sensation buzzed in every corner from her heel to her toenails. The wound, slightly above the shin and just below her knee, ached and throbbed. *One.* She readied herself. *Two.* She winced, preparing for the impending agony. *Three.* She evened her full weight to both legs.

"Fuck!"

A gentle knock on the door silenced her.

"You okay in there, Sarah?"

"Fine," she groaned and stiffened her body to rid the sharp stabs piercing through her. "Just washing up."

"Lemme know if you need help."

Sarah clenched her teeth and balled her fists. "Fuck," she whispered. It had become painstakingly obvious her trip home wouldn't be as easy as she initially thought. Her wound was too far from healing to endure any actual weight. She wouldn't be able to walk down the mountainside. No, Sarah would have to crutch her way down.

She didn't bother washing her hands or face in the sink, certain whatever scum or disease floating around in the plumbing would manifest in some sort of rash or pink eye. Her body had enough problems, and she wasn't about to add dysentery to the list. Another minute fumbling the rickety door handle, and Sarah shuffled back to her bed.

Michael was pacing around the kitchen between a running faucet and lit burner, whistling to himself something familiar yet awful. Eventually, a hiss and sizzle overwhelmed the tune, followed by the screech of a metal spatula scraping an aluminum pan bottom.

"What are we having today?" she asked but knew it would be no different than the previous mornings. Eggs. Scrambled. No salt added for flavor. They were, for the most part, edible, although there was usually a considerable amount of runny yolk among the fluffy yellow portions. She assumed it to be the only breakfast dish he could manage, albeit poorly.

"Eggs," he raised his voice above the kitchen noise. "Well, what's left of 'em."

She rolled her eyes and tilted her head back to the propped pillow. "Can you at least give me some toast with it?"

"Didn't hear a please, Mrs. Baker." He began whistling again.

"Please," she said through gritted teeth and mouthed *ass-hole*.

The floorboards creaked when he entered the living room, a plate in each hand, and set the one with a larger portion to her lap. She lifted her arms, offering her wrists to be shackled, but he turned away for his armchair.

"No need for that yet. Jus' focus on eating."

Sarah poked at the stale bread heels cut into triangles.

"I know people usually toss those out, but they were the last of it. Figured best not let it go to waste." He took a bite and exhaled through his nose. "Toaster's busted, too. Gonna have to eat it as is."

She allowed a single crunchy mouthful. Crumbs flaked off the ends and into the runny egg water. Each chew had the stiffness of a crouton and a less than comparable taste. "May I have some water, *please*?"

The man across from her grinned. "Look at that. Didn't even have to remind ya."

"Who knew someone would have manners while a prisoner," she said snidely and smirked. "Maybe we can exchange Christmas cards."

He continued to the kitchen, shaking his large head along the way. "No need for that, Sarah. From the looks of you, we won't have the privilege of each other's company for much longer anyway." The faucet sputtered on and swished around whatever cup he was holding under it. "Baby will be here before you know it!"

"You still haven't told me what the hell your fascination with my baby is." She stabbed the fork into the biggest lump and grazed her teeth against the prongs. It was mushy. Tasteless. Not entirely unsatisfying though. "Why me, Michael? Why did you take me?"

He returned to the living room and handed her the brimful glass. "We've been over this before. I'm saving you. I'm saving this child." Michael plopped down to his chair and teetered into a comfy position.

"From what? What are you saving me from?"

"Not what. Who."

Sarah flinched. "*Whom.* And that doesn't answer my question."

"This baby doesn't get a choice. You have your hands on the wheel," he rasped and pointed at her stomach. "Whatever you do, that child does, unfortunately, and we both know you haven't been making the best choices lately, have you?"

"What the hell could you possibly know?" She wasn't sure whether he was bluffing or not, but if he had done some kind of research on her, she was curious enough to find out.

"Sarah Lynn Baker. Formerly Sarah Lynn Grant. Spouse of Jonathan Phillip Baker. Address: 1223 Shadow Ridge Way. Age twenty-eight. You have a missing cat named Mr. Biscuit. Graduated from Sacramento State with a bachelor's degree in English. Before that, attended East Nicolas High School in Yuba County, California. Your father, Eugene, was a contractor. Your mother, Susan, a homemaker. Father left when you were eight to pursue … other ventures, and your mother became a secretary for a small law firm until she passed away due to breast cancer in your early twenties. Need I recall your social as well?"

It wasn't only the information he possessed that unsettled her, but the way he had spit it out so concise and rapidly. She attempted to paint on a brave face, but her fingers began to tremble around her fork. "How—how do you know all this?"

"Know thy enemy. Army tactic. Not to say you are indeed my enemy, of course. I am just a proponent of getting the information necessary to complete any task."

She started to dig her nails into her exposed thigh. "Is that all you know?"

He raised his lengthy brow, and the beginnings of dimples his age hadn't gotten to emerged. "No. I know more about what happened at the homecoming dance than I'd care to admit, but I'd sooner step in a bear trap of my own than listen to more of your lies."

It was a gut punch missing the sting of knuckles. He

knew more than he cared to admit, and Sarah now scratched thick lines in her own flesh. Her legs whitened at each nail dug near the point of breaking skin.

"I have done my homework, Mrs. Baker. There is nothing you can say I don't already know."

She narrowed her gaze. How? How could he know all these things? If he wasn't in fact bluffing, why had he even bothered in the first place? "Why ask if you know whether I'm lying or not?"

"A confession of sin heals not only the victim but the perpetrator." Michael stood, plate in hand, and slowly marched toward her. "There's something else you want to ask, though, isn't there?" He lifted his free hand.

Just when she was certain he was going to backhand her, he grabbed the plate from her lap and ambled into the kitchen.

"Why do you know so much about me?"

"There's an old Irish proverb I'm pretty fond of," he said over his shoulder and placed the dishes in the sink. "Think it's a rather suiting answer. *The devil you know is better than the devil you don't.*"

# CHAPTER THIRTY-FIVE

*Eighteen days before Sarah went missing*

A KISS. SIMPLE. Slightly wet but dry enough to feel each ripple on his lips. Sarah tightened her grip on his waist in case she fell over—she thought she might. The desire to pull away withered. Every hair on her neck stood. Shawn caressed his hand over the dress and along the small of her back. Desire rolled in her stomach and teased her insides. She wouldn't settle until all of him was plunged to her depths. He pressed her against the whiteboard, interlocked their hands, and raised her arms high above her head. She welcomed the imprisonment. Relished in it.

The thin line between right and wrong cluttered until all that remained was pure, unadulterated lust. She freed herself from his clutches and stroked her hand downward. First his chest. Then his stomach. Finally, the bulge in his slacks. Sarah slid the zipper open. They kissed again, this time her tongue swirling over his. Reaching inside Shawn's pants, she wrapped fingers around him, rubbing from base to tip. Another kiss, and when that didn't cut it, she sank her teeth into the side of his neck.

Sarah unfastened his belt and pants. The buckle hit the floor first, followed closely by the slacks falling around his ankles. They pulled down his boxers in unison, and once he was fully exposed, she brought her lips to his. She could taste the tang of vodka when their tongues swiped together, undoubtedly from the bottle she'd nursed alone under the bleachers. Shawn paid it no mind, but was it off-putting to him? Maybe he never had alcohol before. He was, after all, only seventeen—

Sarah froze, and her body seized tight. *Seventeen.* She released him while he continued to invade her mouth, working through tightened lips. What was she doing? What was she thinking? The ache between her legs, though wet with longing, dissipated until good conscience finally broke free. She needed to stop this. She *had* to stop this.

The disgrace. The disgust. Handcuffs. Court sentencing. She in an orange jumpsuit, and Shawn, a witness sworn under oath. And just when Sarah thought she had the strength to pull away, he stuck his hand up her dress and rubbed the spot throbbing between her legs.

The repercussions dwindled. The fear disappeared. He no longer kissed against a forfeited opponent, but one that was there for a fight. And in that moment, Sarah was determined. Certain. Unequivocally positive she had to have every inch of him.

Her forearm to the desk, she swiped everything off. Papers shuffled and crinkled. Pens and pencils clanked off the tiles near her feet. She bent over the grainy wooden surface, hiked the dress to her breasts, and spread her legs wide. With her underwear dangling around her knees, she waited. Waited for that initial plunge. To dive face first into a life that wasn't Sarah Baker's.

Shawn stepped forward and held himself just outside of

her. "Mrs. Baker … are you sure?"

"Sarah," she said through ragged breaths. "Call me Sarah."

"But I don't have a—"

She couldn't wait any longer. Not for formalities. Not for pointless questions to ruin it for them both. No. She grabbed Shawn and guided him in slowly. Pain surged when she took all of him in, then—bliss. What was gentle and excruciating was now an upscale of pleasure like none she had felt. He slid back, hesitated for a moment, and filled her once more.

Shawn grabbed her waist. A firm, tight grip she couldn't break from if she tried. Not that Sarah would try. She was right where she wanted to be, where she needed to be, nails scratching thick lines on her desk and hair rustling over her face.

He rammed inside of her again, this time deeper. Her breath caught and the subtle moans emptying her throat were blanketed by the sound of his skin slapping into hers. Out. In. Out. In. She wailed without reserve. Each shove practically pushed her over the desk and closer toward ecstasy.

"Mrs. Baker …"

Sarah bumped back hard enough to send a shockwave through them both. She was close.

"Sarah," she cried. "Harder." She wasn't sure she could physically handle the request, but the way her life seemed to melt away in that moment gave reason to believe otherwise. She was there. Colorful spots took over her vision and intensified when she slammed her eyes shut.

"Sarah," he said, stuttering. "I'm … I'm …"

She bounced back into him again.

"I'm going to—"

Another slam.

"Harder!" The desk grated the floor as it was pushed forward with her and screeched from each impact.

"I'm almost—"

One final thrust was all her body could take; all it took, really. Sarah cried out until the remarkable sensation lost luster. Every muscle thumped in tune with her heartbeat, from Sarah's arms down to her toes. Warmth flooded within her, and when he slowly removed himself, a small dribble spilled down her leg.

"Sorry," he said, concern lacing his feeble voice. "I didn't mean to … And you wouldn't let me stop."

Sarah, still hunched over the desk, holding on for dear life, refused to move. She imagined herself in the open ocean, floating on nothing more than driftwood to protect her from the terrors beneath the surface. "It's fine, Shawn. It's fine," she said, winded.

Heels clicking outside the room hushed them both. The hallway echoed with the sound of a hasty retreat, and the only thing Sarah could see from the door's windowpane was blond hair fading away from view.

×

SARAH SHIMMIED HER underwear to its rightful position, and Shawn tightened the belt securing the trousers to his waist. He made it a habit to glance at her while fixing his pants, tucking in his button-up, and finally, adjusting his tie. It was far easier for her, however. Comb the dress down her knees and smooth her hair to her shoulders, ensuring no straggler was free from the bunch. Despite how gratifying their encounter was for her, if only for mere moments, only one thought coursed through her head.

*What have I done?*

Someone had been in the hallway. They could've been seen. Caught in the act. Lust was now replaced with regret.

"Was it"—he finally cut the silence—"was it good?"

She smirked in his direction. "Yes." The real answer, had she dared to utter it aloud, would've been *exhilarating.*

His dimples emerged in the room's encompassing darkness. "Good. Great. It was great. I really enjoyed it, too."

Sarah gave herself a once-over and leaned against the desk that, in her mind, she was still clutching. "This … This shouldn't have happened, Shawn."

"I know, Sarah. I didn't mean for it to." He tilted his head downward. "I'm sorry."

"Mrs. Baker," she corrected him, "and you have nothing to apologize for. What happened—well, happened. It can't happen again."

He nodded slowly, and his gaze was still fixed on the floor.

"Shawn," she snapped. "Look at me."

He didn't move his head but shifted his eyes to meet her more serious glare.

"I mean it. This will not happen again. We can't. I could go to prison if someone finds out. I could lose everything. Promise me." Her voice raised an octave, closer to the tone she might give one of her unruly students. "Promise me you won't tell anyone. That this will stay between us."

"Yes, ma'am. I promise. Could I at least ...?"

"What?"

He dragged his shoe on the tiles, nervously picking at his shirt. "Could I, maybe, just kiss you one last time?"

She released an uneasy breath, placed a hand on each of his cheeks, and pressed her lips to his. There they stayed for quite longer than she intended. Sarah relished their embrace. Missed it before it was gone. When they split, she gave him a final peck and stepped away, fearful she might just pull him back.

"Go," she said. "Go enjoy the rest of the dance. And remember"—Sarah put her index finger to her mouth in a shush motion but couldn't help her wide grin behind it—"our secret."

×

IT WAS APPARENT the dance was winding down when she sauntered in, her brave expression replacing that of a nervous wreck. *What have I done?* seemed to be the only thought she could muster. While she was cleaning herself in the bathroom. On the long walk to the gymnasium. Even now, Sarah Baker repeated the same four words in her head, each syllable cutting through her like a scalpel.

*What have I done?*

The students had lost their flair, and while most were sitting, a few still managed the energy to occupy the floor in some sweaty, half-assed motion. They were oblivious to her disappearance for the past twenty minutes. The only person who seemed to notice her absence was Coach Tanner, but even his attention was elsewhere.

"Long call?" he asked when she approached.

She stood closer to him than she ever would have. "Conversation with the husband. Fun enough to need a few cigarettes. Sorry I was gone so long. Thanks again."

Coach Tanner continued to bob his neck to the music. "No problem. You owe me one, though. Don't forget it."

Sarah gave her best impression of a sincere, flirty face, and even batted her lashes. "Oh, I won't."

Hannah was mysteriously absent, as was Sarah's biggest concern, Shawn. He couldn't be counted among any of the teenage boys in the room, not because he was mentally more mature than some adults, but that was the second thought to cross her mind. She assumed he left with Hannah, forcibly if she had to guess. Even though Sarah knew Coach Tanner would remember exactly when they left, she was too disgusted to find out how close he was watching Fulton High's head cheerleader.

"Last dance, Fulton High," the DJ announced and cut to a slower song. "Time to get that date on the floor and hold each other 'til the lights come on."

Most of the room partnered off and filled the space, save the wallflowers happier to observe from the sidelines. She debated careening throughout the gymnasium yelling her arm's length spiel but ultimately decided to save her breath.

"You, um, want to dance?" The coach offered his greasy palm in her direction.

"No thanks, Nathan. I actually need to leave if you don't

mind. I'm sure my husband's waiting for me at home." She applauded herself for how believable she came across. He wasn't at home. He was probably knee deep in that bartender, telling her everything she wanted to hear. No. The only person waiting at home was Mr. Biscuit, even though *home* seemed like a stretch as of late.

Coach Tanner waved his hands dismissively. "No worries. I'll have the JV players here help clean up. You go on and get home. But that makes two you owe me now." He held up two fingers for emphasis and winked.

She writhed in her skin and said, "Two for you," between her gritted teeth.

A string of cars waiting in the loading zone stretched down toward the football field fence line. Rows of parents sat patiently, some tapping their thumbs on the steering wheels, waiting to pick up their kids and get home before traffic clogged the streets. The heat from each running engine had overwhelmed the parking lot, creating a humid, almost summertime temperature in the near winter atmosphere.

Sarah neared her Dodge Neon at the back of the lot, loud music masking the sound of her own footsteps. She reached the driver's door, and before she could open it, a hooded figure reflected in the window, its face hidden by the darkness of the parking lot. The person didn't say a word, only extended a hand for her shoulder.

Sarah screamed and turned abruptly.

"I'm sorry! I'm sorry, Mrs. Baker. I didn't mean to scare you."

She narrowed her eyes. "Jessie? What in the hell are you doing?"

Jessie Jenkins lifted her hood and the blond hair cascaded out, leaving her fried blue ends at her chest. "I—I saw you leaving the dance." She lifted her arms defensively. "Hannah left me here. I wanted to see if you could give me a ride home?"

Sarah exhaled and required a few more breaths to still herself. "You can't just go sneaking up on people. What about your mom? She can't pick you up?"

The young girl swayed her head. "She isn't answering. I don't think she's awake. Opening shift tomorrow at Margery's. Will you take me, please? It's not far."

She exhaled again, this time from sheer annoyance. "Fine. Get in."

Jessie plopped down in the passenger side, fiddled with the seat belt, and brushed her fingers through her hair. Sarah started the engine after a few attempts and pulled out onto the main road leading to the center of town.

"Sunny Acres, right?" Sarah asked.

Jessie rocked her head back and forth as if she was still enjoying the music in the gymnasium. "Yes, ma'am."

There was alcohol mixing with the moldy odor of her car. It was strong. Eye-watering. Sarah first checked her own breath. Jessie leaned back and closed her eyes, the same method one might use to fight off the spins.

"Jessie? Have you been drinking?"

"On … only a little." She smiled at the ceiling.

"Fuck. Of course you have. What happened to your dress?"

"We, Hannah and me, were supposed to go to an after-party. I"—she paused and burped, mixing what she had eaten in the past few hours with the alcohol stench—"I brought a change of clothes." Jessie motioned to her hoodie and jeans but kept her eyes shut. "You like it?"

"Hannah and I," Sarah corrected her. "Yes. You look fine."

"Right … right. Hannah and I. I can't believe she ditched me!"

Sarah turned onto the road leading toward the highway. There was a small, dilapidated street that veered outward to a trailer park at the edge of town. She kept her high beams on even when the passing cars honked or flashed their brights at her. It wasn't getting pulled over she was worried about but getting pulled over with a drunk teenager in her passenger seat.

"I can't believe that skank ditched me!" she repeated. "Because of *Shawn*."

"What about Shawn?" Sarah asked with piqued interest. "What happened?"

Jessie rubbed her neck against the headrest. "He left her alone when she started crying about who fuckin' knows what. She told me to stop being a stupid bitch, so I went to go find him for her. Tell him to—to stop being an asshole."

"Well … did you?" Her heart rate spiked. Each throb pulsed through her forearms and fingertips.

"I didn't." She shifted to face Sarah, opened her dilated eyes, and grinned enough to display her uneven front teeth. "But you did."

## CHAPTER THIRTY-SIX

*Seven months missing*

ONCE HE FINISHED washing the two plates in the sink, Michael returned to his chair, a coffee mug in hand, and blew on the steam lifting from his morning roast. It was, at least for Sarah, a slap in her caffeine-deprived face. Even a sip could give her all the strength she'd need for the evening hike she had planned. A last-ditch effort to avoid finding out what the man across from her really wanted with the baby. She would sooner bleed out than hand it over willingly.

"You look nervous, Sarah," he said and took a steady gulp. "Something on your mind?"

She lifted her hand slowly to brush her hair to the side, forgetting she wasn't shackled. *Why keep your prisoner unchained?* Was he hoping for a casual conversation, one not disrupted by the constant chatter of chains? "You're the one with all the answers, Michael. You claim to know me. Why don't you tell me what I'm thinking?"

He smirked. "Just picking at your brain is all. Anyone in your situation would have more than a few questions on their mind."

Sarah narrowed her eyes and wished he was within reach so she could knock the hot coffee in his lap. She imagined him jumping up and down, and the idea—no matter how unrealistic—made her grin back. "You say you're honest. If I ask you something, will you tell me the truth?"

"Won't know 'til you ask."

She tilted her head to the side. "How did I get here?"

He sighed and visibly recollected. "I parked down the street from your house and let myself in. You should really lock your kitchen door more often. When you arrived in the afternoon, all it took was a few milligrams of Telazol, and we drove up here in that clunker you call a car. Barely made the climb, too."

"Is my car still here?" Her voice reached excitement. She sat up and carefully crossed her legs.

"No. Last thing I needed was some hunter passing by and noticing that bright red heap. It had to be disposed of. Some of it might be left, if that's any consolation."

"Someone would've noticed you driving around in my car, especially if people are looking for it."

He drew another gulp and smacked his lips. "Oh, sure. They were looking for a red Dodge Neon. Think there was an APB out on it and everything. What they weren't looking for, however, was a black Dodge Neon. Now, I'm no auto mechanic, make no mistake. But in the middle of the night, not one person would've noticed the poor job I did *redecorating*."

Sarah scoffed and said, "Smart" more sincerely than she wanted to. It was, after all, a genius way to move her car discreetly. Although she hated to admit it, he wasn't nearly as dimwitted as she hoped. Getting the better of him could be more difficult than she originally thought.

"Thank you. I thought so as well. Your busted headlight

had me a bit nervous if I'm being honest. I had to drive around with—"

"The brights on. Tell me about it."

Michael gave her a grin like none she had seen. It was different. Nothing compared to the man who had brought her bologna sandwiches in the dark with a slack face and stiff jaw. He was, at least for the small moment they shared, an actual person.

"That's gonna have to do for storytime, though," he said and finished the rest of the mug. "We are in need of some supplies if we'll make it to *his* grand entrance."

Sarah raised her brow. "Or *her* grand entrance."

"Oh no. This one's a boy. I know it." Michael went to the kitchen and placed the mug in the sink. When he returned to Sarah's side, he secured the chains. "I won't be gone long, and I expect you to behave, all right? Can't have you stepping in another bear trap."

"Okay," she said reluctantly.

"Is there anything you need while I'm out?"

"Chocolate? Cookies? At this point I'd take whatever sugar I can get."

He gave a throaty, chest-lifting chuckle. "I'll see what I can do." Michael turned for the door, pulled the keys from his pocket, and started to twirl them around his finger. He had one hand on the doorknob when Sarah spoke again.

"Michael? Are you really going to let me go?"

He stared at her for a while, almost taking in not only her question but everything about her. "Yes, Sarah. You'll be a free bird in no time." Michael closed the door behind him.

She was, for the time being, alone. This prison was now

more vacant than her classroom after the final bell on a Friday afternoon. Sarah imagined his trip would be like the two he had taken during the previous months when food was scarce. An hour, and if she was lucky, even longer. Truth was, she had no idea how far from town they were. It was too dark to see anything during her first escape attempt. Bits and pieces from that night manifested in a sightless and frantic blur. She could recall the sheer vacancy. The absence of anything besides dense, unkept wilderness and difficult, steep terrain.

"You doing okay up there?" Michael's thick voice was muffled and barely audible.

Sarah stalled her breathing to listen.

"Don't worry. The baby will be fine. Have a little more faith in me."

*He has his phone.*

Michael's boots shifted over the uneven ground, and eventually his voice started to circle the cabin. "Nah, she's still holding back. She'll talk when she's ready. Let us pray on that at least, and hope the baby isn't so damn stubborn." He chuckled.

Sarah followed the area his voice was coming from. *Who are you talking to?*

"No, no. I already told ya I wouldn't hurt her. A promise is a promise, remember?"

After his truck had powered on and the noise of loose gravel and dirt faded, Sarah began working off the chains. She had managed to get a few rounds of lock-picking practice in, but when winter arrived, Michael slept on the rocker in the living room to stay by the fireplace. The escape rehearsals had to stop after that. The fork prong, tucked securely in her sock, had been digging into her ankle like a well-placed thorn. She removed it, held it between her fingers, and prayed to the same God she'd cursed since her arrival for it to work.

She inserted the broken fork piece and carefully gripped the opposing end, fearful if she dropped it, the prong would scurry far from her reach. *Come on*, she pleaded. *Just a little more.* Sarah felt a soft click from the bolt. *Easy.* She began twisting gradually. Her thumb and finger pulsed around the prong. *Easy.* Despite how much pressure she added to the turn, it wouldn't give. She cranked it harder, wiggling back and forth while turning her wrist side to side. *Open, you son of a b—*

A loud crack was followed by the cuff falling from her arm to the mattress.

Excitement resonated first in her chest and then with the butterflies fluttering around the soggy eggs in her stomach. The next lock required less fumbling to open. *Voilà* came to mind, but she wasn't putting on some magic show for a group of kids. No. Sarah was taking a death-defying leap to get back home, no matter the cost.

Another fifteen minutes of locking and unlocking the shackles and she had become quite proficient at escaping with ease. While the chains rattled profusely, she was certain it sounded no different than when she adjusted in the bed throughout the night. If he hadn't come out to check on her whenever she changed to a comfortable position yet, it was unlikely he would do so tonight.

Sarah lifted herself from the bed, grabbed her crutch, and

stumbled down the hallway, set on the partially open door at the end. The hinges gave an eerie wail as she pushed the door open with the rubber tip of her crutch.

*Know thy enemy*, she thought back to Michael's words and entered the room carefully. A bed, no larger than a twin, was set against the farthest wall. The sheets and blankets were neatly tucked under the thin mattress. Next to the headboard was an oak dresser. Each of the five drawers were shut enough to create a uniform line from the top edge down to where the bottom met scraggly carpet.

"Who are you, Michael?" she asked and pulled open the first dresser drawer. Four pairs of socks were in tidy rolls. A few sets of underwear took up the space on the right, each with a stern crease and fold. She couldn't imagine why someone would take the time to be meticulous with undergarments, but maybe it was the military lifestyle he hadn't retired from.

The second drawer was as she expected. Shirts in an organized row, none of which with any logo or insignia. Jeans, maybe two or three pairs, filled the third drawer, and when she wrenched open the fourth, a camouflage uniform greeted her. Sarah lifted the fatigue top and inspected both the sleeves and chest. She rubbed her fingers over the empty Velcro where a nametag would normally be placed. The opposing area had a strip reading U.S. Army, and the gig line where the buttons could be fastened had a small patch with a golden symbol. *Rank*, she thought and outlined her finger on the oak leaf cluster.

She found it difficult to replace the uniform exactly as it was, especially when leaning against the crutch sure to be bruising her armpit. Once she was certain it appeared no different than when he had left it, she hunched over and grabbed the fifth and final drawer handle. It stuck in some places and required a bit of force, but she continued to tug it backward until it opened fully.

A picture. Michael and a young boy at the edge of a lake, inches from their shoes hitting the murky green shore. Cattails and reeds surrounded the clearing they were standing on, each with a fishing pole pointed to the center of the still, motionless water. The boy was facing away from the camera while Michael had turned toward it and gave a beaming grin. He was much younger. Age had yet to weather the skin around his eyes and forehead. His strong build was in tune with his appearance now but significantly less robust. Michael didn't have the same glare Sarah was accustomed to. He was, at some point in time … happy.

"You lied to me," she whispered and outlined the small boy in the backdrop. *I don't take honesty lightly*, he had said. She tossed the picture back to the wooden bottom. *No, I don't have any kids.*

"You lied to me." She dug her nails into her palms and pierced the first layer of skin. *Michael? Are you really going to let me go?* She remembered the way he glanced at her. The uncertainty in his eyes. *Yes, Sarah. You'll be a free bird in no time.*

"You. Fucking. Lied. To. Me."

# CHAPTER THIRTY-SEVEN

*Eighteen days before Sarah went missing*

SARAH CLENCHED BOTH hands around the steering wheel at the ten and two position. *The blond hair in the hallway. It was Jessie.* "How much ..." Sarah paused and swallowed the stomach acid rising in her throat. "How much did you see?"

Jessie giggled and poked her index finger into her closed fist. Sarah knew in this hand puppet show, she was the closed fist. Jessie's small giggles transformed into large snorts. "Everything."

Sarah's arms trembled. A deepening pit settled just below her rib cage, and like a black hole, began sucking the innards until only a terrible cramp remained. Pain lurched from her stomach upward and finally hit the dry spot in her throat. *Everything. She saw everything.* A few rapid blinks halted the heavy water rushing from her eyelids. Although the road in front of them was nothing more than a black and yellow blur, she continued forward.

"Can't say that I blame you, Mrs. Baker." Jessie nodded. "Hannah's been trying to fuck him for months."

"They"—she tapped her thumbs on the wheel—"they haven't?"

"Pffft! Course not. I mean, they've fooled around, sure.

Over-the-pants dance." Jessie began to sway to a beat that must've been in her head only. "Shawn told her he wasn't ready. That his first time had to be—"

"Enough," she cut her off. *First time? It was his first—* Vomit heaved up her esophagus and hit the back of her tongue. Sarah swayed unconsciously.

"I get it, Teach," Jessie said and fiddled with her hoodie strings. "You're not the only one who gives out extra credit." A wide grin formed. A cat's grin. "Since I know yours, I'll let you in on my secret. Me. Coach. Mm-hmm."

While it wasn't surprising, it was appalling, nonetheless. Sarah knew it was only a matter of time before he persuaded some naïve girl to stay after class. Maybe give them a ride home. Offer them booze, cigarettes, whatever else they couldn't get their adolescent hands on in exchange for sexual favors. A ploy no self-respecting adult would fall for. Jessie dropped right into the disgusting pig's trap.

Had Sarah baited a trap for Shawn as well? *I am nothing like him.* "Why didn't Coach take you home then?"

"Asshole said we couldn't be seen together anymore. That people were getting suspicious. I wonder how suspicious they'll be when I send out some of the pictures he texted."

Sympathizing for Coach Nathan Tanner was a difficult, damn-near impossible thing to do, but somehow, even Sarah found a small ounce of pity for him. Jessie was going to ruin his life and couldn't care less. There wouldn't be some grand plea bargain to avoid a prison sentence. Jessie had practically zipped up the orange jumpsuit for him.

*If she's going to do that to him, what is she going to do to me?*

"What do you want?" Sarah asked bluntly.

Jessie rolled her head and gazed at her from the passenger side. "I never said I wanted anything, Mrs. Baker."

Pinpricks skirted across her arms, leaving gooseflesh in its place. "So, this will stay between us? You won't say anything to anyone?" Sarah remained focused on the asphalt, and a green sign reading GREER AVE. came into view a few hundred yards ahead.

"Of course. Our little secret. But—"

Sarah gripped the wheel and dug her nails into the rubber.

"Since we're such good friends now, I will need you to pass me for the rest of the year."

"Done," she huffed out.

"Oh, and I'm getting sick of walking everywhere. It's exhausting."

Sarah tensed and scrunched her nose. "You expect me to drive you around?"

"Ha. No. Don't be silly. I want you to get me a car."

"A car?" Sarah spat. "I don't know if you've noticed, *Jessie*, but I'm a teacher. I can't afford to buy you a car. I can't even get myself a new one."

The young girl smirked and rubbed her palm along the dash, cleaning some of the dust. "That's okay. You can give me this one. It's a piece of shit but better than nothing."

She shook her head. "I don't fucking think so. You can't have my car."

Jessie pursed her lips to one side. "That's what Nathan said, too. He won't need it when his pictures go viral. You think you'll need yours when everyone knows about your late-night tutoring with Shawn?"

Sarah ground her molars. She tightened her knuckles until they cracked in sequence. "Why would anyone believe a thing you say? You have no proof. It will be your word against mine."

Jessie laughed something sinister. She then proudly displayed her phone and swiped through multiple photos and finally, a video. Shawn was behind her, hands on her hips, thrusting while they took turns groaning into the darkness of her classroom. Sarah's face, Shawn's face, both were unmistakable. Jessie shrugged and a shit-eating grin emerged. "Might take up photography as an elective next semester. I think I have a way of capturing the moment."

Greer Ave. was now fifty feet away on the left.

Sarah slammed on the gas pedal. The engine revved and redlined. A gentle rattle in the Neon's frame became rampant. One simple thought played in her head: *I can't let you tell anyone.* "Give me the phone."

Jessie displayed the same cheap grin and shook her head. "Not gonna happen."

"Give me the fucking phone."

"That's my stop," the young girl sneered and continued to dance in the passenger seat, her phone still clutched in her swaying hand. Sarah reached for the device, and despite Jessie's drunken state, she managed to pull away in the nick of time.

"Ah, ah, ah," Jessie said. "You'll get your phone back at the end of the day, Mrs. Baker."

Terror and frustration cramped Sarah's insides. She had

to get the phone and delete the pictures. She couldn't let the little sociopath ruin her life, too.

"Hello," Jessie said, and emphasized the O. "That's my stop!"

Sarah grated crumbs of rubber off the wheel with her hands. She lightened her foot from the pedal. "Are you going to give me the phone?"

"You'll never get it," she said in a singsong voice. "You'll never get it, but I'll get you!"

The Neon swerved as Sarah made another attempt to snatch Jessie's device, nearing the embankment before she corrected back to the road. The teenager cackled wildly, Sarah powered forward, and the sign for Greer Ave. became a blur in the rearview mirror.

"Where are you taking me?" Jessie's grin went slack, and she sat a bit straighter.

Sarah wasn't sure of that either. She couldn't take her home, not at least without deleting the pictures and video. Maybe she could scare her into giving up the phone? Make Jessie believe Sarah would harm her if she didn't. Kill her even. People did dumb things when their life hung in the balance, after all.

"Stop fuckin' around and take me home!"

"I can't let you tell anyone, Jessie," she whispered, and looked at the speedometer. Sixty-five miles per hour.

Confusion settled on Jessie's face. "So, what? You're gonna drag me up to the woods and kill me? Yeah right, Mrs. Baker. Ha-ha."

"Give me the phone." Seventy miles per hour.

"Oh, you want this?" Jessie dangled it between them and

giggled. "Well, take it. It's right here."

Sarah's body trembled. Eighty miles per hour. Jessie was toying with her. Taunting her. Laughing at the thought of her teacher caged in an eight-by-eight cell for the next five to ten years.

Ninety miles per hour. Sarah's cheeks felt hot. Her eyes stung with fresh tears. *Stop it. Stop it. Stop it,* she screamed in her head, and when Jessie continued, Sarah screamed out loud. "Stop it!"

Sarah locked her elbows, braced herself, and slammed on the brakes with both feet. The Neon screeched to an immediate halt, and Jessie's laughter shifted to a single, bloodcurdling shriek. They both lunged forward, and Sarah was able to keep from diving into the dash.

The seat belt caught Jessie's torso, effectively saving her from flying through the windshield. It did not, however, save her head from hurling face first into the glove box. Her nose and mouth smashed violently. A tremendous *thwack* silenced her. Jessie no doubt had a few missing teeth, possibly an entire row. Blood sprayed from her low-hanging jaw upon impact, leaving a red mist in the Neon's interior. Jessie's neck snapped back to the headrest, and the phone slipped from her fingers and under the seat.

At first, she was still. Motionless. Heavy breathing was all Sarah could hear, but she wasn't sure which of them it was coming from.

"I mean it, Jessie," Sarah said while panting. "Give me your phone."

Jessie Jenkins didn't respond. Didn't cry. She didn't even bother wiping away the blood trickling down her chin. She was limp. *Maybe the hit knocked her unconscious.*

*Or maybe she's …*

"Jessie? Jessie!" Sarah shook her shoulder, and the teenager's head bobbed back and forth until it eventually slumped downward. She looked like a churchgoer mid-prayer, but instead of her hands being tied together on her legs, Jessie's were limp and sprawled to the sides.

"No. No, no, no. Wake up, Jessie. Wake up!" Sarah tapped her cheek, noticing the red painting her fingertips. Jessie only slouched farther.

"Wake up, dammit!" Sarah said, and slapped her, leaving bloody streaks on Jessie's hair and face. Another slap. More blood, and some even splattered from her mouth to the passenger window. "Please wake up!"

Jessie didn't, and much to Sarah's horror, her chest didn't move either. She lifted her hand to Jessie's nose and waited. Waited for a small wisp of air to flee her nostrils. Listened for a cough, a wheeze, anything besides her own rapidly beating heart. When nothing happened, and her body remained limp, Sarah's head sank the same way Jessie's had.

*What have I done? What have I done?*

Another question bubbled up her throat like vomit.

"What do I do?"

Headlights shined in the rearview mirrors, tiny dots still a mile away, maybe farther. It was an accident. A horrible accident Sarah didn't mean to happen, but that didn't change the fact it did, and now, she had a choice to make before another car pulled up and found her with a dead Jessie Jenkins. There would be no lying her way out of this one.

No, the cops wouldn't buy some *deer jumped in front of me* story when they estimated how fast she was driving, *away* from Jessie's house no less. She glanced at Jessie again, taking in the blood drying to her sallow cheeks. The hair covering her battered face. The way the seat belt held her upright. And in that moment, all Sarah Baker could think was *I can't let anyone find out.*

They traveled up a winding road, Sarah and her silent passenger, leaving the faint glow of the Fulton main street behind them. After a few miles up rugged terrain, she parked at the Landing and left the engine to idle, fearful it might sputter and die, leaving her stranded with a dead teenager. A case no lawyer in their right mind would defend.

Dragging Jessie's limp body through the woods by her hoodie, Sarah put as much distance as she could muster from the dirt road. Her lily print dress wafted in the near morning breeze, as did Jessie's hair while dangling over her pale, freckled hands. When Sarah couldn't manage another step, she dropped the young girl with a *thwomp* in the dirt.

The bitter and expected cold started to form. Soon, the mildew-scented grass and leaves would have to endure an icy layer until daybreak. She wondered if the blood on Jessie's face would freeze over as well. If the tiny droplets still careening down each side of her mouth would eventually halt and break off like glass. She sat there for a moment, letting her heavy breaths escape in clouds like fog rolling inland. Then, she noticed something. Something she was equally hopeful and terrified of:

Sarah wasn't the only one breathing.

Small and irregular puffs escaped Jessie's red stained

mouth, and although her eyes were closed, her fingers and legs began to twitch.

"Jessie!" Sarah said and shook her, excitement leaving a trail of goose bumps along her arms. "Jessie, you're alive!"

She didn't say anything. Couldn't say anything it seemed. She might've been unconscious, but no matter how hard Sarah rustled her again and again, Jessie didn't stir, only drew simple breaths and twitched uncontrollably.

"You're going to be okay." Sarah started to scoop her up. "I'll take you to the hospital, and they'll—" She let go of her. *They'll ask questions. Want to know how she slammed into the dash hard enough to do this.* If she took her to the hospital, the next stop might as well be the state prison. She glanced at Jessie once more, tears filling her eyes.

"I can't let anyone find out," she said, an edge of panic in her voice. Everything inside of her pleaded—no, screamed at her—to think this through, but she already had. There was one way out of this, and rather than leave Jessie to die alone in the woods, Sarah searched around and finally settled on a stone near Jessie's head. The rock was dense, jagged, and larger than her palm.

"I'm sorry."

One. Two. Three violent smashes to her face.

Her nose caved from the first impact, followed by her brow. Each time she brought the rock down on her, Jessie's entire body convulsed. Blood spat in every direction, splotching not only the lilies on her dress but Sarah's neck. When the serrated end met her flesh, the bones beneath gave way to another meaty layer.

Sarah's tongue salivated and recoiled to the back of her

mouth. Vomit heaved up her throat and she swallowed it down sourly. Even after Jessie's last breath wisped from her partially open lips, Sarah thrust the makeshift bludgeon one last time.

She dropped the stone and armed her mouth to avoid puking on Jessie's lifeless body. Her fingertips dripped with her student's blood and brain matter. Sarah, like Jessie, couldn't move. Couldn't breathe. She glared at the unrecognizable corpse, held the girl's hand tightly, and cried. For herself, what she had to do, and most of all, for Jessie Jenkins.

When she finally regained her composure, Sarah went back to her car, still idling on the incline with its headlights shining into the surrounding wilderness. She opened the driver's side door, and before climbing inside, Sarah Baker doubled over and vomited everything she could.

# PART V

## The Child

## CHAPTER THIRTY-EIGHT

### Mills

*Seven months missing*

"Come on, Dog," Mills said begrudgingly and even patted his thigh to lure the beast from the backseat of his Bronco.

"Ya know, eventually you'll have to give her a name," Holloway said, exiting the passenger seat and walking around the front bumper. She was still wearing his sheriff's broad-brimmed hat. It was difficult to remember the last time she had taken it off.

Mills shook his head and spit thick brown saliva to the pavement. "She has a name. Dog."

"That's not a name. She'll never learn to respond to that."

He rolled his eyes and scratched at the widow's peak his felt hat would normally cover. "All right, Animal Whisperer. Watch this." He snapped his fingers, and Dog leaped from the Bronco, landing on all threes.

She was less mangled than when he and Holloway found her on the ridge. A helluva lot, to be exact. The once-matted black fur was trimmed, shiny, and easy enough for Mills to run his fingers through each night. Her ribs no longer resembled a bony xylophone, and her stomach—which had been inches from the poor girl's spine—now appeared healthy. Despite the amputation reaching just below her elbow, she was more mobile than he would've given her credit.

"Come here, Dog," Mills said, and she hobbled to him with her tail swaying. He rubbed her snout, neck, and finally scratched behind her ears. "That's a good *dog*." Both he and the black mutt smirked in Holloway's direction, although only one of them had excess spit rolling from their tongue.

"You're impossible."

"Hear that, Dog?" He knelt and let her lick the stubble on his cheek. "We're impossible. Yes, we are."

Holloway mounted the station steps, muttering incoherent nothings to herself while Mills trailed behind slowly. The pup skipped at his side but never gave up more than a single pace between them.

Simmons stood when they entered, and as he had countless times the past week, saluted Mills before promptly switching his attention over to Holloway. His shirt was adorned with wrinkles, and one side of his collar was folded down in place while the other was carelessly propped up. "Ma'am."

"Sheriff," she responded.

"No, ma'am. I'm your deputy. You're the sheriff."

Mills cupped his face and chuckled enough for stiff coughs and wheezing to take over.

Holloway pinched her brow. "You will address me as Sheriff, Deputy Simmons. Not Jenn. Not Holloway. Not *ma'am*. Sheriff."

He traced the ceiling with his puzzled gaze. "Yes, ma'am. Oh. Shit. Sorry, Sheriff."

Mills doubled over and cackled. The shepherd at his side wagged her tail like she was in on the joke as well.

"Are we done playin' grab ass here?" Holloway's cheeks were red and her glare stern. She flipped through the mess of pages on Simmons's desk and tossed them back down in the same disorganized clutter. "Have you found anything new? Anything helpful?"

"I called Richmond Supply and Lumber. Tried Fulton Repair and Smog. Shit, I even phoned some of the auto parts places out of town. No one has any transactions for this amount of black spray paint."

"I want you to check again. Check every store in town. Find out if they sell it, and if so, who had purchased a single can between fall and winter."

*Good girl. And don't forget—*

"And if they paid cash, get me a description," she said, right as the idea crossed Mills's mind. "The bastard that painted her car is involved somehow. We find who bought the paint, we find Sarah."

"Yes, Sheriff."

She started for her soon-to-be office and paused. "Oh, and Simmons? Fix your fucking collar. Appearance is everything. Can't have you on the beat lookin' like a goddamn goober."

Mills and Holloway excused themselves while Simmons fumbled the buttons on the phone. The shepherd began to follow as well, until she caught a whiff of the half-eaten club sandwich on Simmons's desk. Mills watched as she positioned herself near the table's edge. Her ears were perked, and her attention was focused solely on the pieces of white bread within view. Though she didn't lunge at the food, he imagined it wouldn't be long before Simmons had to make another lunch run.

After entering the office, he and Holloway both moved for the desk to which they staked claim. She grimaced, so he opted for the chair on the other end of the mahogany. It was far too stiff. Didn't support his upper back as much as the leather seat he had thrown himself to for years if not decades. He wasn't sure which made him more uncomfortable, the chair itself or having to settle into the backseat while she took the wheel. It was a bitter pill. One a quart of bourbon couldn't help him swallow.

Holloway paced in front of the board with different photographs, dates, and lines connecting them. It had the appearance of a roadmap missing a destination. An aimless drive through backroads without any direction to follow. This teacher, wherever she had been taken to, was the final stop. The missing puzzle piece. One last burden before their town—well, *Holloway's* town now—could return to normal. Sarah's portrait was tacked at the center, and no matter how far Jenn moved, the teacher seemed to shine her beaming grin in her direction, mocking her.

"Nothing, Jeff. We have absolutely nothing."

"I know, kid. Colder case than I've ever seen."

She stared at the photos, taking a small moment with each. "Where could she be? How can someone just up and disappear like this?"

Mills lifted his head and let the fluorescents rain down

on him. "Your guess is as good as mine. Lot of wilderness out there. Lots of places to make a shallow grave."

"Think she's still alive?"

"I think Sarah and whoever took her are the only ones that'd know for sure."

Holloway lifted the broad-brimmed hat from her crown and placed it on the desk. "Will you help me run through the timeline again?"

"Might as well. Couldn't hurt."

She grabbed the eraser, wiped away the red lines filling most of the board, and reached for the marker. "Okay. Tuesday, October thirtieth. The day she went missing."

"Final period lasted 'til around three P.M. She was spotted by students and faculty going to her car."

"Right." Holloway drew a line from Sarah's photo and scribbled the time. "From Fulton High to her residence is around ten minutes, give or take. Depending on whether she went straight home or not, of course. Let's say she arrived at 3:20 P.M. to be safe. Did she try to call or text him?"

Mills took the Baker file from the desk and flipped through one of many transcripts. "Last text was sent Monday the 29th. *We have a chance to fix this …* Maybe it had something to do with a baby brewing?"

"I'd bet my badge on it. Seems more suiting now that she could be expecting, too. Kid to solve the problems they couldn't fix themselves." Jenn placed the marker cap in her mouth and wrote in a barely readable cursive. "What time did John get home?"

Mills sifted through more pages. "Johnny boy said it was a bit after five. Couldn't give me an exact timeframe. He clocked out from the yard at 4:55 P.M., and the drive could be done in fifteen, depending on the driver. How much of a hurry he was in to get there."

"Around an hour and a half to an hour forty-five for her to manage a vanishing act until John supposedly arrived at 1223 Shadow Ridge Way."

"A lot can happen in that amount of time, kid. Shit, someone could travel damn near out of state."

Holloway loosened the top button collapsing on her thin neck. "I doubt it."

"Doubt what?"

"They took her somewhere else. Why would they bring the Neon back here and risk being caught? That'd be unnecessary. They'd want to distance themselves from any evidence, not drive up and down I-5 in a hot vehicle."

Mills swallowed the long cut saliva building in his mouth despite how difficult the heartburn would be later. "Valid point. The town's been on alert though. You know how these Jesus freaks love to gossip every time they plop down in a pew Sunday mornin'. Something would've come up by now if she was being kept in town, don't you think?"

"Maybe she isn't being kept in town. Kent's Salvage. Where the vehicle was found. It's on the outskirts. They could have killed her and hidden the body somewhere behind the beaters."

He gnawed at the skin flap in his cheek. "Nah. Known the Kents since I was a boy. Jerry wasn't the most pleasant person to be around, but he was always decent. Honest. No doubt he passed that onto Joseph. Even though I never talked to him more than to just shoot the shit, kid was a spittin' image of dear old Dad."

She turned back and narrowed her speculative gaze. "That doesn't exactly cross him off the list, Jeff. Her car was found on their property. It had been moved there and spray-painted by someone who knew what they were doing. Who better than someone that fixes up cars for a living?"

"Why would he call us first thing?" Mills said and shrugged. "With the equipment he owns, boy could've melted that Neon down to scrap metal. It's not the Kents. My old man trusted them, and hell, he'd roll in his grave if he knew I put their family's neck on the chopping block. You'll need to believe me on this if nothing else."

Holloway shook her head. "Okay. What other suspects do we have then? John? Her student?" She lifted the evidence bag housing Shawn's ID, displayed it, and set it down among the paperwork and files. "Shawn Watkins? I somehow doubt a seventeen-year-old could pull this off without a single slipup."

"You know how most of these cases turn out?"

"Husband did it."

"Exactly. It's obvious ol' Johnny has been knocking boots with Katie Bowman. There's your motive. He's an arrogant shit. Have you seen him shed a single tear? I sure as hell haven't. For all we know, he smothered her with a pillow after his late evening with Ms. Bowman, took her to the lumberyard before anyone got there, and chopped her up into tiny pieces. Maybe even scattered the body parts in the woods."

"It doesn't add up though. If he was the last person to see her alive, sure, I'd agree you have something. She was seen going to her car after school, remember? The station times show John phoning close to five thirty P.M. that Sarah was missing. He has an airtight alibi since he left work not forty-five minutes prior. Wouldn't give him much of a window to kill his wife, hide the body somewhere, and call us to report her disappearance."

"Much as I'd hate to admit it, you have a point. Not sure if it's the fact I can't trust the asshole as far as I can throw him, but he doesn't fit. Good work."

She smirked at Mills and drew a big red X over John's picture. "When something seems out of place …"

"It usually is. Unfortunately for us, that leads us back to square one with no suspects."

"Wouldn't exactly say no suspects." Holloway pointed at Shawn's ID. "Only real lead we have."

"You said it yourself. No way this kid pulled off a kidnapping without leaving an ounce of evidence." Mills grabbed the trash can and fingered the long cut from his lip into the bin. "Maybe Sarah found it on the ground, threw it in her backseat, and forgot to give it back."

Holloway held the bottom of the marker to her lips. "When was the last time he was seen around school?"

"Want me to call Janice to find out?"

Her eyes widened. "No, no. I've got it covered." She pulled out her phone and called the front office, standing rigid and tapping her foot into the desk. "Hi, Janice. It's Sheriff Holloway with the Fulton County Sheriff's Department. How are you?"

"Kiss ass," he said and crossed his arms.

She scowled in his direction but managed to keep her voice at a sweet tone. "I'm doing fine as well, thank you. I was wondering about one of your former students, Shawn

Watkins. When exactly was he unenrolled?"

Inaudible chirps from the other end filled the room, and Mills heavily debated sifting through the bottom drawer of his old desk for the bourbon he had left.

"I see. And when was the last day he was seen on campus?"

More chirping. A larger need to quench his thirst.

"Friday, October 26? So, he was absent both Monday the 29th and Tuesday the 30th as well?"

As always, Holloway asked the right questions, ones Mills himself hadn't even thought of. He attempted to appear unfazed by her keen ability but knew the attempt—at least to her—failed to go unnoticed.

She smiled nearly as wide as the photograph of Sarah Baker behind her. "Thank you, Mrs. Peterson. You, too. Buh-bye." Jenn pocketed the device. "Unenrolled a week after Sarah went missing. Hasn't been attending class since Friday, October 26. Seems a bit out of place to suddenly unenroll from school and move across the country with his mother to me. Especially right around the time his teacher goes missing. A teacher who had his personal effects in her vehicle."

Mills crossed his arms and glared once again at the fluorescents. "So, what's the theory here? Kid is smitten with his teacher. She refuses. Kid kills said teacher. Suddenly says he wants to live with Mama to avoid jail time?"

"Seems like the best option we have right now."

A few slight knocks on the doorframe and Simmons poked his head inside, showcasing his freckles and fiery-red hair. "Sheriff?"

"What do you have for me, Simmons?" Holloway said

with more authority in her voice than either of them had heard.

"Al's Market on Main Street. They sell spray paint." He entered clenching a notepad in his hand filled with scribbles. "Told me some of the black paint they had on special for Halloween was purchased. Two cans. Another four cans the day after. Paid in cash." Simmons slid the notepad across the desk and stared at the ID in the plastic bag. "The cashier couldn't remember his name, only what other people in line had called him. Watson."

"You get me a description at least?"

"This kid looks so damn familiar."

Holloway slapped her hand on the desk. "Focus, Blake. What did they tell you?"

"I know I've seen him somewhere before ..." He scratched at the back of his buzzed head. His curious, winced eyes shot open. "He was riding with—"

"Deputy," Mills chimed in. "You best answer her."

He straightened his posture, and his militant demeanor took over. "Permission to speak, Sheriff."

Mills and Holloway both rolled their eyes and said, "Granted" simultaneously.

"I pulled him over. Months ago. Well, he wasn't driving. Stopped them over on Fifth. Front headlight was out."

Holloway rubbed her reddened, sleepless eyes. "Who, Blake? Who was with Shawn Watkins?"

"Watkins ... That's the name the woman at Al's Market said. Watkins." The deputy glanced up at Holloway and peered at the board behind her. He pointed his pasty finger to the image tacked at the center. "Her. The teacher. She said she was driving him home."

# CHAPTER THIRTY-NINE

## Sarah

*Seven months missing*

I *NEED TO get out of here.* Sarah reached for the crutch propped against the bed. *I need to get out of here now.* Nightfall couldn't wait. There was, after all, no telling what Michael would do to her. He had lied the entire time. No. This was her only opportunity. Her only chance to survive.

Sarah hobbled back down the hallway, a newfound stride pushing her forward. Violent cramps twisted her insides. Her once-steady breaths were replaced with a choking wheeze. *In, in, out,* she coached herself and entered the living room, attempting to calm the panic surging through each limb.

Her abdomen wasn't the only victim enduring the assault but her back as well. Agony rippled what she assumed was every organ until the sharp stabbing sensation found her spine. Nerve endings ignited in sequence until scorching fires had been set through each appendage. *Get out.* She fought the crippling pain. *Get out.* Her usable leg, while shaking, began to comply. *GET OUT!*

Although the afternoon sun was dampened behind trees tall enough to touch the blue skies overhead, when she opened the door, blinding light eclipsed her face. The surroundings blurred. The vibrant colors dwindled and a white, heavenly haze remained in its place. She closed her eyes and blinked enough times to lose count.

"Where am I?" she asked herself and began to struggle down loose gravel and dirt. The cramps amplified. Each wave was more unbearable than the last, and the time in between felt instantaneous. Sarah hunched forward, hoping to relieve the tension tearing through her innards, and spotted something in the distance. Something that made her stand upright in an instant. The outlines of buildings.

She crutched down a steep incline, excitement leaving little regard for her footing. The thought of her bed. Her house. Hell, even John was appealing. Anything but the cabin at her back. Anything but the chains chafing her wrists. She needed to get down this hill. Roll down if necessary. Put as much distance from Michael as she could. To finally end this nightmare.

"Ahhh!" she screeched and whimpered. Her stomach throbbed as if knives had been thrust to her gut in sick, simultaneous fashion. She dropped to her knees, and the crutch bounced off the brush at her side. *In, in, out. In, in, out.* It didn't help. The pattern only induced labored breaths and excruciating torture. She hugged her stomach. Pleaded for it to end. To subside. Her prayers went unanswered as she continued to scream into the otherwise quiet wilderness.

A warmth trickled down her thigh slowly and soaked through the gray sweatpants. She was certain it was urine—given her distinct lack of bladder control as of late—and tried to rub the mess enough to dry it. When Sarah lifted her hand, her fingers were coated in dark red, almost brown stains. She peered down hesitantly. Needles pricked from her shins to her forearms. Dread took over in an instant.

"Help!"

The trees echoed her prayer and carried it down the steep landscape she herself couldn't trek. Her entire pant leg was drenched. The cottony fabric was now a crimson pool, soaking in new, brighter blood with each passing second.

"Someone help me!"

Once the reverberation had settled somewhere in the forgotten wilderness below, the peaceful silence returned. It was like the woods were laughing at her. Applauding how she was more alone than ever in a time when she needed someone most.

More blood oozed from her inner thigh, first passing her knee, and painting the yellow leaves beneath her red. Agony radiated from her belly and convulsed up her spine. She tried to count how long it took for each trembling spark to subside but easily lost track.

"Some—someone help … me," Sarah gasped, and then she fainted.

✕

"MRS. BAKER?"

She swayed her head side to side against the cushioned pillow caressing her neck.

"Mrs. Baker? Wake up," he said and patted her cheek gently.

She peered toward the voice, and in the blurry haze was a figure leaning over her. His face pieced together inch by familiar inch. It was him. Someone Sarah thought she'd never see again.

"Shawn?" She lifted her hand to graze his stiff jawline only to be refused by the chains restraining her. "Why—how are you here?"

He brushed the red locks from her eyes and forehead. "Easy now. The pethidine should help ease the pain."

"Shawn. What is going on? Why are you here? What is wrong with my baby?"

"I'm not sure. You were hemorrhaging when I found you. Lucky for me, you hadn't wandered far."

Her stomach throbbed like her heart had been sucked down to her gut. The pain was far less than before, but her own concern had tripled. "How are you here, Shawn?"

A long pause. "Sarah. That spill must've done a number on ya." He shook his head. "I warned you not to leave."

"Shawn—" She paused. It wasn't Shawn. This man's voice and appearance became strikingly clear. She thrust her nails for Michael's thick throat but was stopped by the restraints suddenly losing slack. "What the hell did you do to my baby?"

"I'm trying to save the child. Both you and the baby were put at risk the moment you decided to walk out that door." He pinched the broken fork prong between his thumb and index finger, displaying it for her. "Gotta admit. This was pretty ingenious. Never pegged you for a woman who could lock pick."

"You have no idea what I am capable of."

He pulled his shirt collar to the side, showcasing the scars on his chest. "I have an idea." He returned his collar to its rightful place and put his open palm at different parts of her bulging stomach. "I need to be honest with you, Sarah. I am concerned. That amount of blood when someone is expecting usually leads to ..." His scratchy voice trailed off. "Unfortunate circumstances."

"Then take me to a fucking hospital. If you really are concerned, take me to someone who can help me. Help the baby. Do you really want it to die up here?"

"You know that's not what I want, but that is also a risk I'm willing to take. You'll just have to trust me." Michael turned and retrieved something from the bag at his feet. When he faced Sarah once more, he was holding a very large, intimidating needle. The sharp point glinted off the sunlight peeking through the fabric window covers. "If the boy is going to survive, this is our only option. Please roll to your side."

She writhed against the mattress, and the chains clanked loudly on the wall behind her. "No. No! Get the fuck away from me!"

He shuttered his eyes. "I will hold you down if I have to, but there is a good chance I could damage your spine. We don't want that to happen. Please roll to your side."

Tears formed and spilled down her cheeks. "What are you going to do to us?"

"I'm going to save you both. Your side, Sarah. And you mustn't move. I will be as delicate as I can. Promise."

The tears reached her chin and continued down her bobbing throat. She knew despite everything inside her screaming the opposite, she had no other choice. Sarah had seen the amount of blood that crept down her legs on the ridge. She knew it could be a sign of miscarriage. If her baby was truly on the brink, Michael was her only hope to save it.

"Easy now," he said and assisted her to the side slowly. "This isn't going to be pleasant, but I will need you to be completely still."

She nodded through her uneasy sobs and took quite possibly the deepest breath she had ever taken. It began as a gentle pinch. Nothing unbearable but easily recognized. The pinch immediately increased to torture as it was buried another inch. She was certain the entire needle was piercing through her lower back and on its way out the other end. Then, a burning tingle radiated outward, adding a definitive amount of pressure up to her shoulder blades and as low as her rear.

"Good. Breathe. We're almost done."

Sarah grunted and exhaled softly, fighting the urge to shy away from the pain shooting through her.

"There we go," he said, removed the needle, and helped her to her back. "Should take a few minutes to kick in."

She wanted to believe he could help the baby. Needed to believe he could. Still, how was he so certain he could save the baby regardless of the warning signs pointing to one awful, two-syllable word?

"I will do everything I can, Sarah." He placed his hand on hers. "Believe me."

She pulled back from his touch. "I went in your room."

"I know."

"How?"

"Dresser drawers weren't lined up."

She peered with disbelief. "That's how you knew? A

drawer wasn't fully shut?"

He smirked. "Attention to detail. Not something you can unlearn. *Hooah.*"

Sarah winced. The pain in her stomach still lingered. "I saw your picture."

"Mm-hmm," he said and nodded in unison.

"Who was the kid you were fishing with?"

He drew a deep, grunt-like breath and exhaled through his nostrils. "That was my son."

Her face tensed. "You said you never had children."

"You asked if I *have* children. He is no longer with us. Physically at least."

"That's bullshit and you know it, Michael."

He returned to the bag at his feet and rustled around the contents. "Language, Mrs. Baker." Michael pulled a long metal tool from the bag and uncapped the top, revealing a sharp curved blade. "The anesthesia should have taken effect by now. It is vital that you hold still no matter what you see." Michael lowered her sweatpants until the bottom portion of her protruding stomach was exposed and leaned in with the scalpel firmly clasped in his fingertips. "Are you ready?"

# CHAPTER FORTY

## Mills

*Seven months missing*

"SIMMONS, WHAT THE fuck is wrong with you?" Holloway slammed her open palm on the large wooden desk.

He snapped to attention. "Sheriff?"

Mills wiped his hand over his lengthy forehead and down his face. "Listen up, dipshit. We've been after this teacher for months. In all of that time, you didn't find it crucial to mention you had interacted with her during a traffic stop before she went missing? A traffic stop where she was parading around town with a *student*?"

Simmons remained firm. Stiff. "I—couldn't remember, sir. And the kid, well, didn't look like a kid."

"Since I have worked for this department, you have told me in graphic detail every pair of boots you have knocked in town. Height. Hair color. Christ, even their fucking bra size." Holloway gnawed at her cheek. She then pointed her finger at Sarah's tacked picture. "You're telling me this woman didn't stand out in the slightest?"

He stood at ease and fidgeted. "I guess I'm not that interested in redheads."

They both eyed not only his pale, freckled complexion but his spiked and somewhat messy red hair as well. Laughter itched at Mills's hoarse throat, until, of course, he saw the sheer annoyance twitching Jenn's eyebrows. Best to keep quiet and avoid her wrath.

"You are fucking impossible," she spat. "Get me the date on the traffic stop."

"Yes, Sheriff."

He retreated to the bullpen, a small stagger in his step and head hung low the entire way. They watched him shuffle through the clutter on his desk for a moment and shared the same disconcerted glances at one another.

"Don't look at me. He's your problem now," Mills said.

Holloway huffed and grabbed the felt marker. She dashed a line right before the date Sarah had gone missing and added Shawn Watkins next to it. Patting the cap against her mouth, she turned to Mills. "You remember the Conrad case a few years back? Happened in North Carolina or New Hampshire. One of the two."

He fumbled a smoke from his breast pocket and lit it. "Doesn't ring a bell."

"There was a teacher. Heather Conrad. She had an affair with a student and convinced the kid that the only way for them to be together was for him to kill her husband. She left the back door unlocked and was out late into the evening with some of the faculty. They were her alibi. Anyways, the kid, fifteen I think he was, snuck inside with a .45 caliber pistol, went into the teacher's bedroom, and fired one shot straight through her husband's temple. Ultimately, the boy confessed to the killing and their relationship. She's serving life without parole now."

"I'm not really connecting the dots here, kid. It's the teacher that's missing, not her husband," Mills said.

She tapped her finger on the desk like a metronome, each loud click evenly spaced. "It goes to show how impressionable an adolescent's mind is. Especially when they truly believe they're in love. What lengths they'd go to keep the relationship."

Mills took another drag. "So, you think this student has something to do with her disappearance?"

"If she was giving him extra credit then suddenly came to her senses and cut it off, that'd be motivation enough to consider him a suspect. *If I can't have her* mentality. His ID wasn't just in her car, it was wedged between the seats. You said it was difficult to fish out. They could've been fooling around back there. Maybe it slipped out of his pocket during the act and fell between the folds."

"Could also be coincidence."

Her cheekbones tightened when she shook her head. "I don't think so."

Mills, intrigued in her theory, hoisted his boots to the desk and eased back into the firm and uncomfortable chair. "So, run me through it."

"Sarah found out her husband was a scumbag. Hurt her enough to make her do something stupid."

"Something stupidly illegal," he said and licked his dry lips.

"Could've been one time or a few. No way of knowing. She realized what she was doing and decided to call it off." Holloway lifted Shawn's ID. "He didn't like that idea. When you're offered a medium-rare steak, you don't just stop eating after a single bite. No. He was pissed. He took her. It would explain why he suddenly left town to live with his mother. Shawn killed the teacher, buried her in the sticks, and got a one-way ticket east."

"Not a bad play of events. Not bad at all. There's just one problem."

She placed her hands at her hips and pursed her mouth to one side. "He's long gone. No way to extradite him here without substantial evidence against him. Any suggestions?"

"Fly on the wall, remember? Use that noodle. Trust your instincts."

She stared at the teenager's ID and seemingly interrogated it. "Get a hold of the mother, ask to speak with Shawn regarding an ongoing investigation. Catch him in a lie, maybe about his relationship with Mrs. Baker or Simmons's traffic stop. Bring the evidence to the DA and pray to everything holy he's in a good mood."

Mills smirked and lifted himself from the chair. "It's a strong plan, no doubt. Might need a bit more *umph*, but I'm sure you'll find it. You've always had a knack for the detective work. It's a rare quality, *Sheriff*." The cigarette clasped between his lips was on the verge of dumping a mound of ash to the carpet. He removed the holster housing his father's revolver, held it in front of him for a moment and set it on the desk. The finely polished barrel gleamed off the lights shining down to the rich mahogany surface. He didn't expect to feel such a weight lifted, not by removing a few pounds' worth of a six shooter from his person. It was an odd sensation. A feeling of all burden suddenly floating away in the

Fulton winds.

"Jeff … I can't. I really appreciate it, but I can't."

He snuffed out his cigarette on the ashtray at the corner. "The hell you can."

"It's your—"

"It's yours," he cut her off. "Don't insult this old man, and take the damn thing."

Her dimples emerged along with a slight smile. "Yes, sir."

"I'll let Simmons know to get you a number for Watkins's mama on my way out." His boots shifted the uneven floorboards as he walked for the threshold. He imagined it to be the last time the station's gentle creaks would play in tune with his heavy-footed steps.

"Where are you going? We still have a lot to figure out."

He paused at the door. "You'll figure it out. I'd put my eggs in that basket. Me? Well, it's high time I enjoy a meal without a gun at my hip and walkie chirps in the background. Jus' a nice, quiet lunch." Mills winked at her and left.

# CHAPTER FORTY-ONE

## Holloway

*Seven months missing*

JENN WAITED PATIENTLY—WELL, as patiently as one could—for the cashier to return to the register. She was young. High school age, maybe. Intimidated enough by the badge on Holloway's chest glinting off the ceiling lights to the candy racks. She fled to the back room nearly five minutes ago, and something told Jenn it'd be another five before the manager came front and center.

"Michael," the clerk at the checkout in front of her said. "I didn't think I'd see you for at least another month. Back already?"

Holloway continued staring at the double doors leading to the back room, waiting for the manager to make their grand appearance. Out of the corner of her eye, however, was a large man unloading a small basket to the conveyor belt. She steadied her focus. *Not here to shoot the shit.* Mills's voice accompanied the words in her head.

The man chuckled. "Had to come back for some supplies, Deb. Can never be prepared enough."

"I know the feeling," she said and swiped item after item, each one creating beeps reminiscent of a heart rate monitor.

"Diapers? You find a baby up in Cedar's Pass?"

"Nah. Dropping them off at the clinic for the pups. We ran out a while ago. Figured was the least I could do with Aaron picking up my slack."

*Pups. Clinic. Aaron … Geyser.* Holloway snapped her attention to the register an aisle over. The man wouldn't make eye contact. No, he looked only at his items, the cashier, and the ceiling. It seemed he was purposefully looking anywhere but at Jenn.

"Well, that's nice of you. I'm sure he'll appreciate it."

The man smiled. "No one should seek their own good, but the good of others. Corinthians 10:24."

"Amen," the cashier said.

Holloway watched his every move. The way he pulled crumpled bills from his wallet. How he grabbed the bags. Finally, how he passed by her without so much as a nod or casual smile. The double glass doors slid open and out he went, not once glancing over his shoulder.

"Excuse me. Deb, is it?" Jenn asked the cashier posted across from her. "Who was that?"

The woman pointed at the exit. "Him?"

Jenn nodded.

"He's a local, Deputy. Runs the clinic off Main St. Good man."

"Sheriff," Holloway corrected and stiffened her posture. "What is his name?"

"Michael, ma'am."

Holloway's heart rate spiked. It was as if her uniform top had shrank two sizes, vacuum-sealing her body until the air escaped in one uncomfortable gasp. *It's him.* She tried to ignore the pain in her chest. The steady thumping increasing in rhythm by the second. *It's him. Shawn's dad.* "Michael—?"

"Watkins. Dr. Watkins."

Sheriff Jenn Holloway walked out the same double doors without another word. A blue pickup fled the parking lot as soon as she stepped outside. Michael was behind the wheel. She pulled the phone from her front pocket and hit call. The line trilled seven or eight times, but she lost count.

"You've reached Sheriff Jeffrey Mills with the Fulton County Sheriff's Department. I am currently unavailable. If this is an emergency, please hang up and call 9-1-1."

"Shit," she said through ragged breaths. A loud tone came through the line. "Jeff. I found Shawn's dad. He's leaving Al's Market right now. I'm not sure what I should do and could really use your input. Call me back."

Two voices warred in Holloway's head. One, softer, screamed for her to wait for a call back. To be patient. The other was rough and less forgiving. *Now help me finish strong, huh? Go out with another win?*

Jenn willed her body forward, dropped to the driver's seat of her Crown Vic, and turned over the engine. *Finish strong, Sheriff,* she said to herself. *Finish strong.*

# CHAPTER FORTY-TWO

## Mills

*Seven months missing*

*NINE OH SEVEN Third Street,* Simmons had said when Mills discreetly asked him for an address. Holloway was far too busy skimming through page after page on her desk to even notice the red-headed deputy typing on his computer. When Simmons asked if he wanted backup, Mills responded with a crook of his brow. It was answer enough for Simmons, but Mills assumed the poor bastard needed an excuse to get away as well. Unfortunately for the deputy, this was a job Mills had to do alone.

Mills stepped out of the Bronco—a sudden sense of nakedness without a badge, gun, hell, even a walkie—and stood on the vacant driveway for a moment. "Stay," he said through the open window to the large black pooch in his passenger seat. She tilted her head, mouth agape, and stared at him keenly.

"Stay. I'll be right back." She did as he told her without so much of a small whine. He peered calmly from one end of the street to the other. The surrounding houses all seemed just as empty as the one before him.

The Watkins's home itself was a narrow two story with

an odd brown exterior. He followed the path to the backyard, which slithered around overgrown grass and faux bark until stopping at the fence. Most of the boards were warped and had a distinct amount of rot, a side effect from the harsh snow seasons the town endured. Although it might've been easier to simply push the dilapidated fence over than vault the thing, Mills opted for a more subtle approach and yanked on the string connecting to the latch, hoping there wasn't a padlock blocking his quiet entrance.

The door swung open, albeit slowly while scratching against the cement, and revealed a long stretch of brown and yellow grass leading to the patio, he assumed. On his right was a door to the garage. He gave the handle a firm twist.

Nothing. The knob halted after barely a quarter turn. He'd have to get creative. Maybe pray for an unlocked window, or in a last-ditch effort, break one to get inside. The latter, while necessary, still gave him a certain amount of unease, badge or no badge.

He spent the next ten minutes trying to find a way inside to no avail. Each window was latched tight, and the patio door even had a makeshift stick wedged on the track to ensure no amount of thrusting could shake it open. His chances of an easy, almost silent entry were dwindling by the second, as were his chances of remaining out of the watchful eyes of could-be neighbors sticking their nose in the only lead to his unlawful investigation. Mills finally decided to do what he did best. Improvise.

*Thumpf!* The door leading into the garage exploded inward like a saloon panel and smacked into the wall behind it. There was a distinct print from sole to toe next the door handle, but in such a blue-collar town it would be difficult to pinpoint the culprit. Hell, even a trip to Al's on a Sunday evening could produce five to ten new suspects with an exact match.

Although he could see the fluorescents dangling at the middle above him, next to the garage pulley, the lights were off and from wall to wall was pure blackness. Nothing was distinguishable. His phone produced the only noise in the two-car space, vibrating relentlessly in his khaki pants pocket.

*Bzzt. Bzzt. Bzzt.* A long pause. *Bzzt. Bzzt. Bzzt.*

He didn't answer of course. Figured it was Simmons asking him to grab a bite on his way back to the station. The deputy's appetite for greasy shit was never satisfied, as was Mills's desire for a solid lead to drop in Holloway's lap. Eventually, his phone stopped pulsing at his upper thigh, and he continued searching in the dark for a switch of some sort.

There was a musty odor as well, much more than Mills would've guessed, as if the rains and quite possibly the snow had found a way to maneuver in through roof cracks and the shoddy foundation. It was apparent the garage hadn't been allowed to breathe for some time, and Mills, much like the carport, was struggling to inhale, too.

He swiped his arm along the wall, and following a subtle *click*, the lights flashed brightly from one tube to the next. After his eyes made a brief, squinted adjustment, the contents of the garage became quite clear.

Nothing. No blood. No pieces of flesh sewn together on some mannequin. No teacher's body contorted and twisted in the corner. Nothing. What exactly was he expecting to find? A dead body at least would spell an endgame. A closed case. But now all he could see were plastic tubs on each side stacked to the ceiling with unrecognizable contents. Maybe some clothes or seasonal decorations. Cardboard boxes were mixed in the bunch, housing what he only guessed the felt tip scribbles on the side suggested. *Clothes. Kitchenware. Toys. Clothes.* It would take hours to search through each one, and hours were something he didn't have while warrantless.

*Bzzt. Bzzt. Bzzt.*

"Christ, Simmons," he cursed at him absentmindedly. "If I didn't answer the first time." Mills thumbed the top button on his phone through his pants leg, effectively silencing the device.

His stiff eyes scanned over every inch he hadn't combed through previously. More boxes behind him. These appeared to have been tossed to their respective spots and forgotten, given the sheer amount of dust fleeing from the closed folds. Everything seemed to have sat there for some time. All except a can. A particularly curious can tilted on its side next to the largest pile of storage.

Thick black paint had hardened onto the label, running downward before the bottom edge. The cap was missing, as was the red tip one would press to expel the contents. It was off-brand, a bottom-shelf purchase at best. The color, however, was darker than a clouded sky before rainfall. The same color of the coat applied to Sarah Baker's Neon.

Mills ripped the phone from his pocket. *It was Shawn. I've got him. We've got him.* Before he could dial in to the station, a sequence of voicemail alerts prompted him first.

**Holloway** stood out in bold lettering.

*"Jeff. I found Shawn's dad. He's leaving Al's Market right now. I'm not sure what I should do and could really use your input. Call me back."*

In the next message, the wind was whistling, and the engine of a Crown Vic hummed in the background. *"Not sure why the hell you aren't answering your phone. Must be a good goddamn lunch. I'm following him. He's leaving town up toward …"* Static. *"No stone unturned, huh? Ha. I'll keep you updated. Call me back when you can."*

# CHAPTER FORTY-THREE

## Sarah

*Seven months missing*

ALTHOUGH SHE PROMISED him a few times to remain stiff as a board, as he had requested, Sarah still writhed against the uncomfortable mattress before and after the blade pierced through her. What her dulled nerve endings refused to pick up, her own ears were more than happy to oblige. Her stomach tissue, she assumed, was shredding in the exact tune of a piece of paper under the stress of a guillotine trimmer. A sick, unimaginable ripping.

Each time Michael lifted his white gloved hands above her protruding belly, there was a new coat of blood dripping from one of his five fingers. The scalpel, though still glinting off the unreliable and somewhat dim kitchen lights, even had fragments of flesh he hadn't wiped away on the towel beside him. Vibrations. Thick, steady vibrations rattled within her as he finished what she hoped was the only cut to her midsection.

Sarah didn't want to look. She couldn't. Her innards were a flap away from being visible to the world like a state championship trophy in the school's award case. The blankets and towels under her were damp with what she could only imagine were her own fluids. No, Sarah did as she had for the past fifteen minutes and stared at the ceiling, focusing solely on a small spiderweb crack that branched off in a few different directions. All she could do was wait. Sit as still as she could and wait for the soft cries of her newborn.

Michael set the blade aside and scooted closer to the opening. "I'm going to remove the baby now. Are you ready?"

"Do it. Just *fuckin'* do it."

He placed his palms together evenly in a praying shape and knifed his way into her lower abdomen. Despite the numbness, pressure filled her, filled her stomach, her head, her entirety. She had meant to scream out in agony but somehow settled for a horrible moan instead. Maybe it was the drugs or quite possibly the exhaustion refusing her throat such a sound. She wasn't sure. The only thing she knew for certain was that she was utterly terrified.

"Breathe. Nice deep breaths for me, Sarah."

She did as he asked once more, mimicking her strained breaths to the beat of her thumping chest. *In, in, out. In, in, out.* The organs inside her shifted and felt pushed aside. A gurgle. No. A flutter. A long, gut-wrenching flutter plagued her enough to stumble on the repetition of inward gasps. She closed her eyes and pictured the crying infant brought to her bare skin for the first time. Its tiny limbs wiggling free after months of confinement like its momma. How it would peer curiously at the world it had been brought into, and eventually, gaze up at the woman who had done what was necessary to achieve that moment.

"Almost there."

*Please be okay.* She gnawed at her lips, peeling back whatever loose skin she could. *Please. Be. Okay.*

When Michael removed his hands from her stomach, he immediately turned his large back to her. She caught the smallest of glimpses, and when the images pieced together slowly, the incision still leaking blood like an overflowing sink was the very least of her worries.

"What's wrong with my baby?" she asked hoarsely. "Why won't you let me see my baby?" She knew the answer based off the pure silence between the three of them. There were no cries for her. There was, in fact, no noise at all.

"Michael!"

"You did this." His voice cut off each syllable sharply. A finer edge than the scalpel he had opened Sarah up with. "You. Did. This." His forearm began shifting. Pulsing. He was prodding two fingers at the sternum of the baby dangling from his elbow to wrist. "You did this!" He raised his thick voice with each motion, repeating the same words in sync with his compressions. Crimson dripped from the limp extremities, which were, at this point, far too contorted to distinguish between arm and leg.

"You did this!"

Tears burst from her eyes in waves, as did her horrendous, spit-filled shrieks. Her midsection ripped open further from each heavy sob shaking not only the bed but the scratched wooden floors beneath them. Blood gushed from her open cavity in tremendous, currant spurts. She thrusted her wrists forward to grab her child only to have her arms halted by chains. Each attempt clanged the intertwined metal violently. "Give me my baby," she screamed and jerked forward again. "Give me my fuckin' baby!"

Three heavy knocks pounded the front door rhythmically. "Sheriff's office."

Michael and Sarah exchanged glances. *Scream.* His eyes were wider than they had ever been, large enough to showcase the horrible red lines filling in the whites. *Scream.* His face didn't drain of color nor did his limbs tremble. No. His features hardened. Knuckles cracked. He exhaled slowly. Calmly.

*Scream.*

It was what the military trained him to do after all, keep cool under pressure. What plan was keeping him from losing it completely?

*Scream!*

He tilted his head to Sarah once more and waited for her to make the first move. Begged her to do so even. It was as if he had been willing the thought in her head all along.

*Scream!*

"Help me!"

Michael rushed down the hallway as quickly as the words grazed her mouth. He disappeared into the darkness of his room, the baby still nestled in the crook of his arm.

"Please. Help me. Please."

*Thumpf!* The cabin door exploded inward. A woman, badge pinned to her chest and broad-brimmed hat creeping over her stern brow, took cautious steps inside. She trained her revolver muzzle first to the corners of the living room and finally to Sarah. Horror washed over her face, and Sarah knew it wasn't the chains but how her insides were practically spilling to the blankets and towels.

"Sarah Baker?" she managed.

Sarah could only nod in response.

"Don't worry, ma'am, you're safe now. Where is he?"

The chains rattled over her limp wrist when she pointed, or at least attempted to motion down the hallway.

The woman squeezed her shoulder walkie. "Simmons." A fuzzy squelch was followed by static. "Simmons, do you copy? I found her. I found Sarah." Another wave of static, and she cursed under her breath. Both hands on the engraved handle, she took cautious side steps to face the hallway opening. "This is Sheriff Holloway. Come out slowly with your hands up." She thumbed back the hammer and eased one finger to the trigger.

"Let's not do anything rash, *Sheriff*." The long barrel of his rifle emerged first, and the wooden floors strained when he joined them in the living room. The child was still cradled in one arm, motionless and silent. Its eyes and mouth were sealed shut, and its skin was on the verge of purple. In his other arm the rifle extended from the stock near his bicep to his hand clutching the grip. "I have no desire to hurt you. All I ask is that you walk away."

"You move and this bullet is going straight through your head."

"And risk hitting the baby? Wouldn't want that on your conscience, I'm sure."

The woman gnashed her front teeth together and held steady. "I have backup on the way. You're not getting out of this. Lower your weapon and put the child down. This is your final warning."

"You will not take him from me. *She* has already taken

enough. He's all I have left." Michael aimed the muzzle at the young woman's chest. "I'd rather die than let her take my grandson, too."

# CHAPTER FORTY-FOUR

## Sarah

*Seventeen days before she went missing*

SHE HAD SPENT the better part of Sunday afternoon scrubbing the Neon for any trace of Jessie Jenkins. A hair. A piece of clothing. Anything. Small traces of blood blotted the interior roof like it was flung from a paintbrush. First, she tried carpet cleaner, but the pin-sized dots only doubled in size. She then, after an exhaustive internet search, mixed a tablespoon of dish soap with two cups of cold water and rubbed the affected areas harshly with the only thing she could find having firm bristles. She silently thanked John and his toothbrush for their contribution to the cause.

The passenger seat and floorboards were vacuumed six times, each pass requiring a different angle for accuracy. Jessie had long hair, and it wouldn't be unheard of for a stray strand or two to cling to the fabric, especially with how she was rubbing against the seat like it was a dance partner. No, Sarah would clean the car until it was pristine. A finer condition than when she and John drove the thing off the lot, and although the afternoon sun beat down on her freckled arms and legs, she wiped away any evidence linking the murder of Jessie Jenkins to her front door.

Her pocket jolted violently and stopped just as quick. A text. One more to add to the thousand she had felt since she removed Jessie's phone from the floorboard. Hannah again. What started off as a simple "hey" evolved into a flurry of back-and-forth messages, most of which demanded Jessie stop babysitting—Sarah's idea—and go to the Richmond estate to quote unquote *chill.* Sarah was quite impressed with herself, especially while portraying an everyday, alive, Jessie Jenkins. She never used caps. She never spelled a single word correctly. All her responses were riddled with grammatical errors. They were, despite the lemon-sucking face Sarah made after hitting Send, perfect.

She did, however, come across something on the device she wasn't expecting. Something she wasn't sure she could simply scroll away from. A saved number in the contacts.

×

"THAT WAS THE last time," she managed between erratic, fulfilling breaths. Her smile was hidden behind the darkness overwhelming the otherwise abandoned parking lot of the school, save the bright yellow buses lined in a neat, meticulous row on the far end. The streetlights on the road stretched out enough to highlight the vacant fields opposite the school, but they somehow couldn't pierce through the thick, foggy layer on each window. It was 11:21 P.M. on a Sunday. She knew they wouldn't be interrupted, and after such a tremendous round of fucking, she thanked herself for being right.

Sarah lifted from him and threw herself to the empty

window seat while he remained idle. He couldn't be bothered to lift the gym shorts over his rapidly softening member. No. There he sat perfectly still like a possum, not quite dead but not quite sure the danger was over as well. He didn't say a word, but she assumed he only needed a moment to catch his breath, maybe to wipe the sweat from his brow and taut cheeks.

She smoothed the sunflower dress down to her knees, certain that his seed would continue to spill down her thighs until it eventually pooled on the seat beneath her. *Tablespoon of dish soap and two cups of cold water*, she thought. It was, after all, less visible to the naked eye than blood and should make for an easy enough cleanup.

"Was I …?" he finally said.

She leaned her head onto his large, bare shoulder. "Perfect. You were perfect."

"How did you get my number anyway?"

"Are you going to ask questions?" She ran her fingers down his chest and abdomen, enjoying the way they glided. "Or are you going to shut up and fuck me again?" *This is the last time*, she repeated in her head as they locked lips, and this kiss, despite every bit of her conscience begging her to stop, was more addicting than ever.

*The last time.*

×

*Fourteen days before she went missing*

"SHIT!" SARAH SCREECHED when she heard his tires grinding the rocky and uneven path leading to their house. He had come home straight from work, and the seventeen-year-old hovering above her, sucking on her neck no less, only created a brand-new gut-wrenching surge of panic. She pushed Shawn off her—threw him off actually—and while he stumbled onto the hard floor, she frantically searched for her clothes they had both taken turns removing. "My husband is home. Get dressed. Get out!"

His confused expression melted away and was replaced with terror. He scoured the hardwood on all fours, checking each corner of the room and even under the bed for his missing clothing.

The brakes made a horrendous *eeeee* sound as John slowed near the porch, stifling the noise they made recklessly tossing on whatever was in reach. Shawn had managed to pull up his boxers and throw on his shirt before Sarah started shoving him down the hallway. His pants were dangling around his ankles, and he hopped the entire narrow way to the kitchen. She wasn't anywhere close to dressed but figured explaining why she was uncovered in her own home was easier to justify than a partially nude student fleeing the scene.

John shifted on the front porch, his heavy boots creaking the steps. His swaying shadow could be seen through the shades covering the front window, a looming figure seconds from catching her in a lie she'd have no chance in hell of explaining.

"Go. Go, go, go," she whispered sternly, opened the kitchen door, and chucked his shoes into the backyard. Shawn stopped at the threshold and faced Sarah, his back to the unkept yard complete with mounds of orange and brown leaves every few feet. He leaned into her slowly. *A kiss for the road*, she knew he was thinking. The front doorknob rattled. Twisted. The hinges started to squeal.

"Go!" She rammed him off the back steps and turned around in time to watch the sunlight peek through the opening crack until it shined inside fully. *Fuck. Fuck, fuck. What do I do? What do I say?*

John stood there, not quite in or out but in between, staring at her with downright confusion. "Sarah? What the hell are you doing?"

Something came over her. Something wrong. Something revolting. Something … ingenious. She strutted forward like a runway model, flipping her flowing red hair excessively until she was sure the spot Shawn had been giving extra attention to on her neck was completely hidden. John continued to remain frozen. Fixed in place. His widening eyes was the only noticeable movement from the stupid bastard. That and possibly his mouth dropping. He hadn't even realized the door behind her was wide open and swaying in the wind. Sarah gazed seductively at him for the first time in months if not years. "I've been waiting for you," she said and gnawed at the bitter area the words left on her tongue. "Do you like what you see?"

There was ample dirt on his collared shirt and faded blue jeans. Stains under each arm. Streaks of dried sweat across his exhausted face. He had been through the trenches. Today was probably a rougher day than most, and even though she had practically shoved an apple in her mouth and rested over a sexual silver platter, something in her doubted his appetite would hunger for her. This was the same person he hadn't tried to touch for weeks. His last resort if the bar sluts saw through his bullshit. *No. He won't take the bait*, she thought and almost pleaded. *He won't want me.*

John continued to stare lustfully and nodded. "Yes," he said and closed the door behind him. "I *love* what I see."

For the next fifteen minutes, Sarah was his. She had to be. It was different. Unenjoyable. She could only close her eyes while laying across their mattress facedown, waiting for him to finish, and moaning as enthusiastically as possible. Each thrust had only cemented one idea. One terrible, awful, but intensely honest idea.

*I need it again. One last time.*

⨯

*Twelve days before she went missing*

MR. BISCUIT HAD been missing since Wednesday, and each time nightfall descended on Fulton, Sarah grew more worried that her tabby cat was the victim of a lurking predator in the surrounding woods. He had gotten out before but never stayed gone long. Never this long, in fact. She continued leaving his food bowl on the back porch and even filled it with a combination of dry food and the wet kind he loved.

Why the back door was left open while they were—well, while John was in the throes of passionate lovemaking was a secret, one she'd sooner cut out her own tongue than explain. After Sarah had cleaned up, she excused herself to the kitchen and knew immediately the door had been left open for far too long. Mr. Biscuit had disappeared.

She'd spent the last two days searching the backyard into the late evening hours, carrying only a small flashlight and with a heavy fog leaving her frost-bitten lips. She checked the local veterinary clinic for any found animals, but the receptionist said no such orange cat was brought in. Tears became her new friend. In her car before first period, at her house after another late-night search, even while with Shawn, the need arose to let out a few good cries for her missing feline.

John had been coming straight home from work every day like a dog wagging its tail before the food bowl was dropped in front of it. It was strange to her and even more bizarre to him when she refused his advances after such a provocative show. A sitcom where she played the ever-loving wife ready to satisfy his needs and desires. What he didn't know was how she snuck out that evening to finish the deed she and Shawn started earlier that day, or how she had taken it upon herself to teach him the art of cunnilingus in the backseat of her Neon.

This escape for her was simply that. An escape. One last time had become empty words rather than an actual remorseful thought. A mantra she'd repeat in her head to ease the idea that her shortcomings would eventually end. They didn't. While they had taken more precautions, even came up with code phrases to exchange during class, like *you're falling behind in your studies* (hers) or his less cryptic message he'd relay to the other students, *I think I might walk home today*, they both knew the other would be waiting behind the gas station off Fifth Street. They had become familiar both personally and intimately in every way imaginable, and Sarah wasn't so sure *one last time* would ever truly stick.

×

*Four days before she went missing*

SARAH HAD AWAKENED two hours before her alarm with sour bile pillaging up her throat. *It was a dream. It was just a dream.* This was the third time that week Jessie's rotting corpse made an appearance in her nightmares. The poor girl could only moan the way she did at the Landing. Tonight, Jessie spoke to her and pointed a finger while the mangled purple flesh of her face sagged off the bones. "They'll all know, Mrs. Baker," she had said. "They'll all know what you are."

Sarah managed to stop from spilling her insides over the comforter and rushed to the bathroom toilet. The toilet water splashed in her face when the chunky yellow mess exploded from her mouth. The sight of it was awful, the smell even more so. At one point, she clamped her legs around the porcelain and continued to heave until she was certain there was nothing left.

Shawn texted her an hour or so before first period. "*Have time to go over yesterday's assignment?*" She knew he meant a quickie in the Neon on one of the backroads, but she wasn't sure she was up for the task. "*Can't*" was her only response. Sure, she could have endured a round with a queasy stomach, but the ache coursing through each limb proved a different beast altogether. Her breasts were sore to the touch, sorer than they had ever been, and when she was putting on her bra, it was as if a fire had been lit in each cup simultaneously.

There was a freshly plucked rose waiting on her desk

when she arrived in her empty classroom, the fourth one this week. Its vibrant petals expelled a wondrous scent. The vase in her home was now overflowing with a sea of delicate red, and she wasn't quite sure it could handle another. Sarah tucked the small gift in her drawer anyway, if even to have something to marvel at between periods.

✕

*Three days before she went missing*

IT COULDN'T BE real. It had to be some sick joke played by the pharmacy clerk hoping to fool an unsuspecting customer. She wouldn't have thought twice to buy the damn thing, but after a second early morning round filled with puke and overwhelming nausea, Sarah had to be certain. And each time she scanned the stick again, the double pink bars remained fully intact and her seizing heart dropped to her stomach.

*Pregnant.*

Sarah sat firmly planted on the bathroom floor, too terrified to even remove herself from the tile she was sure to be coated in John's urine. No. Here she would stay for ten agonizing minutes with only her panicked shrieks bouncing off the four eggshell-colored walls closing in around her.

John hadn't come home the previous night. After a few days of rejected advances, she wasn't surprised. A Friday at the Streams followed by getting his needs satisfied with the bartender, she assumed. It was half past noon, and he had yet to make his grand entrance. Would John expect Sarah to be happy he was home? Excited? That she would think he was a good husband and not out shoving his cock wherever it'd fit? Sarah would give him no such satisfaction. In fact, something else came to mind. Something that could possibly ruin his time with *her*.

She pulled her phone from the sink top and snapped a picture of the test in her hand, sure to focus closely on the results. It was fuzzy but unmistakably readable. She attached the photo to a text bearing John's name at the top, and with it, three simple words.

*"Good morning, Daddy."*

For the first time since she had awoken and nearly vomited on her pillow, a small grin crept from cheek to cheek. Whether he was still sleeping off the sauce or knuckle deep in his mistress, she knew the gut punch would land exactly as expected. She debated even telling his mother, Barbara, first and letting him explain why he hadn't been home to share the moment with his wife. But the idea of an immediate phone call with Barbara squealing on the other end gave her pause. Not because Sarah wasn't sure she could handle the call while sobbing on a piss-covered floor, but for the simple fact the baby now swelling in her stomach hadn't come from John.

*"We need to talk"* she had texted someone else along with the same snapshot.

×

THE COLOR IN Shawn's face had visibly paled, and when she picked him up from the back of the gas station off Fifth Street, he seemed to stumble over himself while getting in.

Neither said a word when he plopped down to the passenger seat, and as she drove off toward one of their many rendezvous sites, they occasionally glanced at one another. He tapped nervously at his knees like a polygraph machine detecting a string of lies, and each loud thump distracted from the street noise of passing cars.

"I, um," he finally said and recoiled. Sarah, too, shared his embarrassment. "There's a place. Somewhere I used to go with my dad as a kid. Can we go there? It helps me think."

"Okay."

They drove past the Fulton main roads leading to one of many paths ascending the sky, it seemed. Shawn continued to give her hand signals, and at times said, "left here" or "right up there," depending on the direction. There was one ridge in particular, the largest formation on the opposite end of the highway, that stared down at them in intimidating fashion. Cedar Pass.

It was one of five different crests surrounding the city but by far the largest and fullest. Thickets of trees made land invisible to the eye, and it was as if the heavens had burst with snowfall on this mountain peak alone while the rest remained undressed for the winter season. Throughout her time in this miserable little town, she had never once scaled the unpaved roads of Cedar Pass. Never wanted to, anyway. Now, she was flooring her gas pedal to make it up the smallest incline before the actual climb began.

"There's a turnoff ahead on your left. Small embankment. You can park there, and we can hike the rest."

Sarah, ill-prepared for a ruck up stiff terrain, tilted her head with confusion. "Hike?"

"It's not far. Trust me. The sight alone is worth it."

She did as he said and parked the Neon on a small gravel embankment near a quarter of the way up the ridge. The bug-eyed headlights were shining brightly to the trees vacant an icy layer like the areas above. When they stepped outside, the crisp mountainous breeze had swept over them, a chill like none she had endured. What the grounds lacked in snow it more than made up for in freezing temperature.

"This way," he said and started up a small footpath between the brush. The sun, now setting over Parley's Canyon at their backs, took with it the visibility. Had Shawn not been wearing a bright red sweater, following his movements would've been a near-impossible task.

"Where are you taking me?"

"It's not much further, Mrs. Baker."

"Farther," she corrected him on impulse and tried to maneuver around thick branches without slipping. "Not much farther."

He turned to her and gave the exact smile he had every morning. A wide grin short of actual laughter. His eyes devilishly piercing. "Farther. Yes, ma'am. Not much farther."

Although wearied breaths sprang from their lips with each passing step, they pushed onward, nearly losing sight of the Neon and Fulton itself. They paused at the first flatland for miles, surrounded by a quartet of trees evenly spaced like enemies ready to attack from all sides.

"Right up here," Shawn said and waved her over. He moved beyond the bark-ridden assailants to a clearing, and Sarah hesitantly followed. Insurmountable questions simmered in her near-frozen throat, and each one shriveled her voice further.

*Where is he taking me?*

Her body seized when the spot he had led them to came to fruition. Hidden on the backside of Cedar Pass, far away from the dirt road winding up to the mountain peak, was a canyon overlooking the untouched valley stretching forever it seemed. The bright pink and blue skies descended to miles of Douglas fir treetops and elegant oaks still filled with vibrant orange and yellow leaves.

He grabbed her hand and interlocked their cold fingers. "Beautiful, isn't it?"

"Yes," was all she could manage.

"After my mom left, my dad used to take me out here to talk. Talk about her. Talk about why she left. Why he never would." Shawn paused and swallowed hard. "To talk about everything. We come up to Cedar Pass every winter; his cabin is a few miles north. It's been a while since I've come to this place though. Few times over the summer to sketch the landscape is all."

Sarah kept her gaze firmly on the view, taking in each change like a different sip from wine on the comfort of her couch. She clenched Shawn's hand more when she saw the cliff face two feet from her. "Why are we here, Shawn?"

He leaned into her and wrapped his large arms around her waist. She, too, joined in the embrace, whether for warmth or something else, and realized just how tiny she was in comparison. Even with an eleven-year difference in age, he towered over her the same way Cedar Pass had. A looming, dreadfully tall figure she had to stand on her tiptoes to fully appreciate.

"The baby—our baby. What are we going to do?"

Although that very question had plagued Sarah all day and she had given it considerable thought, now she stared blankly at him, waiting for something, anything, to arise.

"Are you going to keep it?" he asked with strained brows.

She closed her eyes, hoping an answer was written on the backside of her lids. "Yes ..."

"Are you going to keep me?"

This question was somehow more troubling than the previous. Images of orange jumpsuits and thick lead bars flashed in her head. A newborn ripped from her arms. Cameras flashing sporadically as a judge slammed their gavel, effectively snuffing out her lively flame as well. "Shawn ..."

"I won't walk away from my child, Sarah. I—I can't do that. You can't ask me to."

Despite the hurt telling her to let go of him, she remained fixed in his grasp. "I am married, Shawn. You are a minor. Do you know what would happen to me? Where I'd end up?"

"We can leave. Go somewhere. Anywhere."

Sarah finally pulled herself free while he stayed in place. "No. No I can't."

"Can't or won't?" he asked.

She drew an icy breath, her face pinching. "This child—my child will not be part of some media circus. I have already told John that I—that *we* are pregnant. I promise the baby will always be loved, Shawn. I will always take care of it to the best of my ability. The only thing I ask ..." She swallowed hard. "The only thing I beg of you is that you never speak of this. Of us. That you walk away and move on with your life."

"I don't know if you've realized this, Sarah, but *you're white*. Your husband *is white*. What do you think is going to happen when the baby is born and looks like me? That people won't ask questions? Your husband will just accept a brown baby as his own? Are you really that stupid?" Shawn moved toward her, and when she didn't look up at him, he grabbed her by both shoulders.

"Let go of me, Shawn," she said and tried to shake him off.

He released her but kept his pleading gaze on her. Tears streamed down his firm cheekbones to his jaw. "How can you possibly explain that?"

Her own eyes filled. "I don't have a choice. It's a gamble I'm willing to take. If the baby takes after you, well, cheating on my husband with some stranger I met online would be easier to explain than cheating on him with you. My student."

Shawn scoffed. "Is that what we are? Just a hookup from some dating app?"

"Stop it. You know this isn't what I want."

"Hear that, everyone?" Shawn yelled and turned away from her to the canyon. He held his arms out like a performer addressing an audience. "This isn't what the perfect Sarah Baker wants to happen."

"Stop it, Shawn," she said at his back as he continued.

"We were meaningless, and me being a part of my child's life is unimportant. I should just move on."

Sarah curled her fists and gnawed at the loose skin on her lips. "Stop it."

His voice only became louder and echoed down the landscape beneath him. "Sarah Baker is pregnant with my baby!"

"Stop it!" she shrieked.

Before he could face her, she bolted forward, arms extended, and shoved him with every ounce of force she possessed. He staggered closer and closer to the edge, waving his arms for balance but flailed helplessly over the cliff and nearly sixty feet downward. He glared at her while falling, eyes agape and certain disbelief and panic in his chiseled features. His long-lasting scream carried until the rocky bottom endured a horrible and bloody *thud.*

# CHAPTER FORTY-FIVE

*Two days before she went missing*

SHE HADN'T SLEPT more than a few hours at a time the night before. It wasn't due to John being surprisingly present and a foot away from her snoring into the early morning hours. It proved bothersome, yes, but nothing compared to her thoughts running rampant the same way a dog might chase their own tail.

Shawn. How he flapped his long arms like a bird without the knowledge of flight. His body free-falling closer and closer to impending death. The way his guts and brains painted the jagged rocks below red. It played in her head on repeat, and each time was accompanied by the awful guttural scream. Her elbows were still sore from the shove in which he met his end. Finding a comfortable position to lay was troubling. The images when she closed her eyes, however, had made sleep impossible.

John was there when she arrived home from Cedar Pass. He was sitting in the living room, his hands interlocked and pressing against his lips. He didn't greet her at the door, nor did he say a word until she sat at the plush green love seat across from him. It was obvious he had spent some time in that exact position, whether cursing the idea of a child with her or not, she couldn't be certain. And although the extra phone in her purse was buzzing nonstop, Sarah sat patiently and took small breaths between glances to the man on the other end.

"Is it mine?" His words had cut through her. The sheer doubt, from him no less, was enough to anger her instantly. The gall he had to accuse her after weeks of infidelity. After straying beyond the bounds of their marriage so effortlessly. No. She wouldn't grant him the satisfaction.

"I'm not the one fucking around, Johnny," she lied. A tactful lie at that. He would know she meant business spewing the nickname he loathed so much. He would also know she knew far more than he intended to admit outright. Her cards, her bluff rather, couldn't be bested.

He rubbed his palm from the length of his forehead down to his chin. Staring at the intricately woven rug in front of him, he simply asked, "Can we fix this?"

Her answer was equally as simple. "Yes."

They had spent the remainder of the night in solitary discussion, choosing names for either gender, planning to tell his parents, setting a date for a baby shower. It was all perfect. The exact way she had imagined it on so many occasions. He was, for the first time she had seen in months, genuinely happy, and for her to give him that sensation rivaled her own excitement. Between laughter, John had made it a point to shower her with the kisses she had been deprived of, and even though they paled to the ones she'd received as of late, she was sure they would grow on her.

This morning was different. It was as if a renewed vigor had been set in place of the gone-at-all-hours-of-the-night John. His entire day seemingly revolved around Sarah and her own comfort. He had asked her more than a dozen times if she was hungry. When she refused, he brought the guest pillows from the closet to the living room and padded her spot with more cushion than a psychiatric ward might've held. Foot rubs led to hand massages, and he even placed his fingers on her bare stomach, attempting to guess the sex, his voice mimicking an obnoxious gameshow host. "Behind curtain numba one!" She couldn't help but laugh, and soon, John joined her, too. She had caught him on a few instances texting when he thought her attention elsewhere. Small, fast replies from the look of it. And as soon as he had hit Send, he was right back to giving his full, undivided attention. Unbeknownst to him, Sarah was sending texts of her own when she found a solitary moment.

*"Hey, Mom. Staying at Hannah's again tonight. She has clothes for me. Love you, TTFN—"* Ta ta for now. Something she noticed Jessie had used regularly and thought it best to keep consistent. The responses to Hannah had been shorter and far less complex. Babysitting was starting to put a wedge between the teens if she had to guess, and Sarah assumed it would only be a matter of time before Hannah recruited another minion and forgot Jessie altogether. She hoped so at least.

She was quite impressed with herself for keeping Jessie alive in one form or another, juggling different messages with ease and giving no suspicion that she was by now the prize of keen-eyed vultures circling above in the horizon. They would eventually find the battered girl in the woods, what was left of her at least. For now, though, Sarah sought to conceal her whereabouts until the rains had washed away any remaining evidence linking it back to her.

Shawn was a different matter. A far easier circumstance. An accident at the spot he and his father were known to frequent. *He had lost his footing and plummeted to his death*, she imagined the reporters would say. His phone sure to be shattered on the very rocks his own insides spilled over, and with it, the texts they had sent each other destroyed as well.

*No one will know*, she thought as John continued sautéing fresh onions on the stovetop. She watched him affectionately, the towel slung over his shoulder, the way he swayed side to side like he was caught in a slow dance. She smirked at him, rubbing gently at her stomach.

*No one will know.*

×

*One day before she went missing*

IT HAD BEEN a routine morning, minus Shawn's ever-watchful eye during the first period ninety minutes, of course. None of the other classmates found it odd. A simple sick day wasn't uncommon, especially with the winter season on Fulton's heels. In a matter of months, each of her students would phone in sick at one point or another like a game of musical chairs, slowly emptying her classroom until only a few remained. Shawn's chair was the first one empty of the bunch. Little did they know he wasn't home nursing a cold but nearly unrecognizable at the bottom of a steep canyon, his decomposing flesh days away from melting into the ground altogether.

It wasn't until second period that an unexpected visitor

barged inside. His presence was off-putting for the students, even more so for Sarah. She glanced up from grading the weekend assignments and felt her blood pumping in her ears.

"Good mornin'," he said and waved two fingers to the room.

His broad-brimmed hat was covering most, if not all, of his face, but Sarah was able to recognize him instantly. The khaki button-up complete with uniform brown slacks. Polished boots glinting off the ceiling lights. The gold badge pinned to his left breast. The rough, leather-like skin pushing up one side of his face when he smirked. Her heartbeat seized, as did the large unswallowable lump in her throat. *It's him.* She remained silent, too horrified to say a word and accidentally spill something that might damn her later.

She expected the cuffs to be drawn. For him to meander over to the desk, help her to her feet, and tell her to place her hands behind her back. She imagined the gasps working from one side of the room to the other, and finally, when he spoke of the sins she committed outright, the utter shock on each student's face. How all the classrooms in D-wing would halt at the spectacle of Sarah Baker being dragged to his car. News vans in the parking lot waiting to take snapshots of the Fulton monster in her natural habitat.

"I need to speak with Deidra Barnes."

"Good morning, Sheriff," she blurted out on impulse. *Deidra. Deidra. I didn't kill Deidra.* She glanced around the room frantically, hoping the girl was indeed alive and settled in the same seat she had always taken. Anything to get him away, for another few minutes might've suffocated her completely. "Deidra Barnes?"

It wasn't until a hand raised near the back of the room that she allowed an uneasy inhale to pass through her sealed lips. Hushed whispers followed the commotion, and Sarah—knowing her name wasn't among the gossip—eased back in her chair.

"Will that be all … sir?" she asked, expecting him to point a wrinkled finger in her face and state firmly, "You're next."

"Yes, ma'am. Thank you." He held the door against his back and welcomed Dee into the hallway. "Hi there, Dee. We just have a few questions for ya."

Once the door came to a sudden close and the classroom chatter erupted, Sarah craned her sunken head over the desk, near the point of hyperventilating, and forced back the tears.

×

*The day she went missing*

AN ANNOUNCEMENT CAME over the intercom system, interrupting the monotony of second period English. "Hannah Richmond to the office. Hannah Richmond to the office." *Click.* The entire class—including Sarah—had paused and listened attentively, but once they realized it wasn't their name being called, they returned to the assigned passage.

"Hannah's talking to the cops!" one of the students in the back had shouted. Sarah scanned from one chair to the next until she spotted Colin Hodges, his face nearly pressed up against the windowpane, staring off somewhere in the distance. The rest of the class soon followed suit, each jumping from their seats for a better look. Sarah, too, stood from her desk and glanced down the vacant grassy area between C- and D-wing to the office in which all their gazes were fixed. He was right. Hannah, a crazed and inconsolable Hannah, appeared to be screaming at the sheriff, and his arms were raised defensively.

*They found her*, and Sarah remembered the phone left absently buzzing in her purse all morning. Dread fought her weak limbs attempting to stay upright, all the way down to the black heels on her feet. Her brow twitched first, then her eyes, nose, and mouth. *They'll find me.* Panic manifested in the heavy saliva building on her tongue, and she knew from recent experience that chunky yellow vomit was sure to follow.

"Class," she said and swallowed, if not choked down, whatever was hiking up her esophagus. "Please return to your desks. I need to—um—go make some copies of tonight's assignment. I'll be back shortly." As she grabbed a stack of papers—most of which were blank—from her desk, she also grabbed Jessie's phone from the bottom of her purse. There were missed calls and texts highlighting the screen, but she paid them no mind and simply held the phone under the rustled pages, effectively hiding it from view. She didn't give them any instructions. She simply left.

Her heartbeat surged with each step. Although the air outside of the D-wing corridor was at a colder temperature than recent memory, it hadn't helped ease the pooling sweat on her forehead.

She saw him standing outside the office alone while Hannah was mysteriously absent. He was scuffing his boots against the cement walkway, ridding a rock lodged in the sole if she had to guess. He hadn't noticed her, but she was certain with the loud stomping of her heels, the gaudy *clicks* deafening any surrounding noise, it would be mere seconds before he did.

She passed by him, at this point her gaze focused solely ahead and clutching the many papers in dire need of being stacked together neatly. She walked with purpose. A hurry too important to be stopped. She would keep moving whether his gun had been drawn or not. There was lingering doubt whether he had glanced up at her, recognized her even. Her peripherals wouldn't divulge such a secret. He didn't greet her, speak to her. He was—luckily enough—too preoccupied to utter a single word. And when she rounded the corner of the office and headed toward the locker rooms, Sarah's thinned mouth was ultimately replaced with a grin.

⨯

SHE TRIED TO scream. His large arm continued to collapse down on her throat until only shallow breathing was allowed to pass. She fought, of course. Writhed. Attempted to wiggle free from his grasp to no avail. He was simply overpowering her with brute strength, one her feeble body and now dangling legs couldn't combat.

A numbness started first at her shoulders until her finger-tips, too, felt the annoying buzz of bees under her flesh. She tried to scream once more. The word *help* played more so in her throbbing head than out loud. She kicked her legs forward, flailing like a beached fish, and caught the point of her heel on the lanky wooden entry table against the wall near the front door. The glass vase resting atop it teetered slowly. The frayed-stem roses splashed side to side and settled. She kicked it again. Harder.

The vase shattered into a thousand pieces on the floor, spilling water and decapitated rose petals as far as the block feet of the couch in the living room. Glass chunks spit and rebounded in every direction. The roses—Shawn's roses—lay lifelessly still, mirroring his body splayed at the rocky tomb where she'd left him to rot.

The man, this intruder, didn't speak. He never allowed more than a stern, almost forceful grunt leave his lips. More pressure was added to keep her still, and the scent of impending death hung over them both like flies. A sharp pinch pricked the skin just below her ears and jawline, and in that moment, Sarah felt the subtle twitch of her eyelids beginning to close.

# CHAPTER FORTY-SIX

*Seven months missing*

"I'D RATHER DIE than let her take my grandson, too."

The sheriff—with a firm grip on the brandished revolver—took a pause and visibly recounted his words. Despite the blood dripping from her exposed flesh and the light-headedness enveloping her, Sarah glared shakily at the man. Her captor.

Shawn's father.

He was tall. Taller than the average man. His shoulders were broad as if an impervious weight had always rested among them. A stiff, almost serrated jawline, his less defined but there, nonetheless. Finally, his eyes. Deep and callous. Hazel. While Shawn never looked through her as Michael had, the resemblance became more recognizable.

"Put the baby down, Mr. Watkins. I won't tell you again." The sheriff's voice was equally as stern as her posture.

"You don't believe me?" he shouted. "I have his phone in my truck out front. Check the glove box and see for yourself. The texts are all there. Pictures, too. She baited my son. Stole his innocence!" He waved the rifle barrel in Sarah's direction, almost using it as an accusatory finger.

*His phone.* Her consciousness faltered. *No. It's at the bottom of the canyon with Shawn.* She slipped into the overwhelming black like a satin dress only to return to the cabin less cognizant than before. What was happening around her—was it real or some drug-induced nightmare she would soon wake from? She blinked rapidly, tears now on the verge of drying against her red-rimmed eyes.

"She killed him, Sheriff. She killed my boy." Michael's voice had cracked, and his challenging glare started to glaze over. He stepped forward. "I had to bury him here just so I could talk to him. Have a simple conversation with my son. I couldn't let them take him away in some van. Have his picture plastered on every news station across the state. And I sure as hell couldn't let this *monster* taint his memory."

*He wasn't talking on the phone all those times.* She imagined a finely dug plot outside the cabin. A graveyard missing decorative flowers on a headstone, wrought-iron gates padlocked by nightfall, and the watchful eyes of those also paying their respects. No. This was his own private place to mourn. Sarah could only stare down at the blankets beneath her collecting every drip her shredded stomach had to offer. The word *monster* thumped in her ears in tune with the last hint of blood fleeing her veins.

"Don't you come any closer!" Sheriff Holloway rubbed her index finger against the revolver trigger, and Michael moved forward again.

A deafening crash exploded, and everything shook. Tremored. Dust quaked from the walls and ceiling. Fresh gunpowder intertwined with the musty, unkept cabin, and in an instant, everything went still.

# CHAPTER FORTY-SEVEN

## Mills

*Seven months missing*

"WHADDYA MEAN SHE hasn't been in contact?" Mills shouted into his phone, one hand at the ten o'clock position and the other frantically shifting gears while careening down the Fulton main roads. He floored the gas pedal. The shepherd in the passenger seat wavered side to side with each sharp corner. He didn't bother turning on the jackpot lights, for any miserable bastard stupid enough to get in his way would answer to him first, and then their god. "What ridge, Simmons? Which one did she follow him up?"

"Cedar Pass. She said he was going up Cedar Pass."

"Fuck!" Mills hurled his phone at the dash, shattering it into three, possibly four different pieces upon impact. Dog flinched closer to the window and a worried expression worked from her eyes down to her panting jowls. "Sorry," he said and gave her a stiff but gentle pat on the back. The Bronco's RPMs reeled when he shifted to fourth, and the speedometer skyrocketed like an overflowing pressure gauge.

He hadn't made many treks up Cedar Pass, figured it best to let his old girl coast peacefully into the scrapyard. Now he would push her to the limit traveling up the steepest hill in town on unforgiving terrain. Mills wasn't a betting man, but the odds were heavily stacked on Rose sputtering, stalling, hell, even flipping over before he made the climb. It was going to be—as cliché as it sounded in his head—an uphill battle he was damn determined to win.

The foggy outskirts welcomed him gravely, and the overgrown weeds and fiddleneck seemed to wave him onto the dirt road leading in no other direction than up. A sizable dip bucked the Bronco's frame when the asphalt met uneven dirt. His passenger bumped, maybe even came off the seat, and settled back to her comfortable position. Puddles splashed behind each tire, leaving no amount of the side panel untouched by brown streaks. Something nagged at him. Begged him to lighten the pedal and take an easy drive through Fulton's most intimidating peak. Something else bubbled above the acid of better judgment in his chest, however.

*Holloway.*

Mills peered intensely between the many distorted tree limbs and bushes, hoping for the stark white paint of her Crown Vic to come into view. It didn't, and yet another steep incline revved the Bronco's engine toward the breaking point. He powered on, even dropped a gear when necessary.

Sticks and debris hammered into his windshield, and out of impulse, he jerked his head from side to side to avoid it. He closed in on a hill up ahead. There were two options. Take it slow and risk the Bronco getting stuck. Option two, jump it. He stilled his breath. A small sense of doubt lingered in the background. It was coming closer. Thirty feet. He dug his boot through the pedal to the floor. Twenty feet.

"Hang on!" The worn tires slipped and caught. Ten feet. He clenched his jaw and charged forward.

The front end lifted vertically, flying through the air the same way a plane might miraculously take flight. It wasn't the jump that terrified him but the hang time seemingly lasting minutes if not longer. The large dog was launched toward the ceiling, all three legs waving frantically for firm ground. He clenched both hands on the steering wheel now, more for grip than steering. Should he in fact tumble downward, he assumed his body was less likely to be thrown under such circumstances. All eight cylinders fired simultaneously, and it was possible other parts under the hood were roaring with the block. Finally, the back end smashed into the dirt and the Bronco tilted down to its rightful position. He hesitated for the smallest of moments, if only to be certain they indeed survived, shifted into gear, and drove onward.

The cabin roof was the first thing he noticed, followed closely by the blinding-white car parked feet from the porch steps. Her patrol lights were on, waving blue and red to the areas of the forest dark enough to catch it. Although Mills jumped from the driver's seat, the Bronco in neutral, it continued to roll a few feet before stopping all together. "Stay," he said—yelled almost—and Dog remained firmly planted on the beige seat, watching carefully as he climbed the four rickety steps leading to the partially open door.

"Sheriff's office. Make yourself known!" He cursed himself for not having a spare weapon in the Bronco to use for such an occasion. If the situation called for it, his battered knuckles would have to do. He pushed the door, and a lengthy creak expelled from the hinges.

"Sheriff's office."

The door continued to sway in front of him, revealing only bits of the cabin interior at a time. Wooden floor. A brown suede recliner. A black bag resting on the floor next to a bed with—blood. More blood than he had ever seen. It was spilling to a puddle on the floor, and each loud *drip* tapped the way a leaky sink might.

The hospital white sheets had very little white left, and the blanket beneath her appeared to be a sponge well past the point of absorption. Even slight pressure would indeed ring out thick red, and he assumed the floor couldn't possibly handle more. An awful stench—filthy pennies and maybe stale flesh—weighed heavily on his watering eyes, and when her motionless body became visible, he shut them and let his nose endure the sense alone.

It was her. Sarah Baker. Her chained arms dangled forward, like she died reaching for something. Her hair was matted, free from any blood but filled with knots and malnourishment at first glance. The skin of her face and limbs was whiter than the sheets and blankets she was splayed over, but her freckles were strikingly recognizable. Her eyes were lifelessly staring at the ceiling and as glossy and vacant as a doll.

"Jeff?"

He shifted furtively. Holloway was propped up against the wall reaching for the broad-brimmed hat at her sprawled feet. Her hand was trembling around a phone from the look of it, and her shoulders could barely hoist the weight of her arm. Her hair was no longer in a neat bun but draped loosely in no way he had ever seen. Her eyes, one partially closed and the other half-open, focused on the man above her. "Jeff?"

He collapsed to his knees. "Kid?" he said, inspecting the fresh wound leaking from her badge to the khaki breast pocket. "No, no, no! Jenn. Stay with me. You're gonna be all right. You'll be jus' fine."

He applied pressure, two fingers to the sizable chunk missing from her chest. Blood squirted on his own uniform top like a water pistol. He tried to ignore it. Tried to imagine it was nothing more than a scrape on her elbow. Part of him knew though. He couldn't quite shake the size. How it had pierced through more than simple flesh. How her ragged heartbeat was pumping slower and slower through his fingertips. She coughed violently, and Mills could practically taste the copper on her breath.

"I found her," she gasped and aimed her finger to Sarah. A triumphant smile emerged on her face, dimples and all. "I promised I would. I found her." She leaned her small head against his shoulder and nestled into him.

"You found her, Sheriff. You sure did." His eyes glazed over, and he brought her in close. Closer than he had ever hugged another person, his own father included. He let these tears flow freely for once, down his weathered cheeks until they cut off at his chin. Her irregular heartbeat had slowed significantly. Dwindled. Suffocated like a fire enduring heavy rain. He brushed the hair from her brow and brought his lips to her forehead.

"I'm proud of you, kid."

# EPILOGUE

*Two months retired*

"WILL YOU STOP your whining, kid? We're almost there."

Jeffrey Mills drove down the coastal highway, a long stretch seemingly dropped amid the powdery sand and crystal blue sea extending for miles. The ocean wind fought its way in through the partially open windows, carrying the heavy scent of salt and the brisk watery air to its interior. He sang out loud to classic rock on the radio, belting his favorite lyrics into the vast and beautiful unknown. He took sips from the travel mug in his cupholder. A dark roast missing his usual creamer and bourbon, but he liked the taste just fine.

"We interrupt this broadcast for a special news bulletin," the radio announcer said. Mills twisted the knob until the volume was near max. "Police are still asking for any information leading to the capture of fugitive Michael Shawn Watkins. He is wanted for the murder of—"

"They're never gonna find him," Mills said above the announcement and shook his head.

"—and Sarah Baker. Recent reports have suggested another body has been uncovered from his cabin property in the Richmond hills. Sheriff Blake Simmons of Richmond

County couldn't be reached for comment. If you have any information leading to the capture of Michael Watkins, please contact—"

Mills silenced the radio. He wasn't surprised Simmons had yet to hold a press conference and even less surprised he now had the sheriff badge firmly pinned to his wrinkled uniform top. Once the town had learned of the horrors on Cedar Pass and Mills had officially stepped down, there was but one refutable option left for a panicking Mayor Richmond. Simmons. He was a dipshit. A great guy, but a remarkably ignorant dipshit. Mills recalled the pin-on ceremony in which he tacked the badge to his chest.

"This is your town now, Simmons," Mills had said while giving him a traditional punch on the badge, symbolizing that he would carry it on forever. Simmons accidentally forgot to clasp it all the way, and when Mills brought his knuckles to the shiny gold star, the sharp safety pin needle dug into his flesh.

Simmons had shrieked and frightened most of the room not two minutes before he was supposed to give his heralded speech. Mills had stayed for most of it but ultimately left the small group listening attentively behind to pack his things.

Holloway was right. She always was. Coach Nathan Tanner wasn't responsible for the death of Jessie Jenkins like Mills insisted. It was someone else. Sarah Baker. The teacher's fingerprints were all over Jessie's phone, not to mention the blood splatter Luther found when he searched the Dodge Neon. Simmons was able to retrieve some deleted pictures and videos from the device, and it became clear to the Fulton—now Richmond—County Sheriff's Department why a teacher might want her student dead under such circumstances. Coach Tanner still had to answer for the admitted statutory, which earned him a few years upstate. Mills doubted he'd ever go near another school again.

John Baker declined any interviews after his deceased wife's horrendous acts came to light. No, Johnny wanted to fade back into the unknown with an expecting Katie Bowman. Didn't even bother attending Sarah's funeral, not that Mills was surprised.

*I'm not sure. But I promise you, I will find out.* Jessie's mother was asleep when Mills knocked on her trailer that late July afternoon. When she finally opened the door, he gave her an affirming nod. She didn't wait for a name. She didn't wait for a reason. All she did in that moment was cry something fierce. There wasn't much else he could do for her or her boy, but Mills wouldn't leave them to grieve empty-handed.

"I think she'd want you to have this, Ms. Jenkins," he had said. The mother and toddler looked at pictures and watched videos on Jessie's phone as he left, and the cheers heard from the FHS bleachers every Friday night were remarkably clear.

Jennifer Elizabeth Holloway. Jenn to her friends. Acting Sheriff to the town of Fulton. Not a single pew was left empty at the First Baptist Church, and some of the townsfolk even wore blue ribbons on their chest as a show of support. Pastor Ryan delivered a long but respectable sermon, and when the floor was opened to anyone wanting to give parting words, Jeffrey Thomas Mills had taken the stage.

"I—um," he'd started and choked back whatever he could manage to swallow. "I didn't prepare a statement, but I think this letter will do jus' fine." Mills then unraveled the paper he'd typed in his study months before, noticing the wrinkles and tear stains from when she had read it.

"There comes a time in any sheriff's career, if you're lucky, that a deputy like Jenn Holloway walks through the front doors of your station. Anyone in this town could tell you how special she is after five minutes of talking to her." Most of the crowd had nodded. "Never in my tenure have I met a deputy with more heart and more drive to make Fulton a better place for its residents. I would like to take this time to acknowledge Jennifer Holloway as my successor. She is brilliant beyond her years, and there are none better suited for the role of Fulton County Sheriff. If voted to the position, she will bring pride to the town, the department, and to its citizens. She has my full confidence." Mills then used the long sleeves of his shirt to wipe under each eye. He walked down the steps to the open casket, placed a sheriff's badge on her chest, and said, "I love you, kid. I always will."

Mills parked the Bronco in the lot. It was, much to his liking, vacant, holding only a single car on the far end. The heat from the engine radiated above the hood like a barbeque mid-flame, and when he finally turned the ignition off, it rattled and thumped for a few minutes before silencing completely. Even in a gray tank top, cargo shorts, and flip-flops, he had to wipe the incomings of sweat from his brow. He glanced at the passenger seat for a moment and paused. "Come on, Jenn, we don't have all goddamn day."

She exited the Bronco slowly. Carefully. A certain ease in

her step until all three legs were firmly planted on the asphalt. From there, she bolted down the shore, kicking sand behind her with every skip. Eventually, her black fur was only a small dot where the waves made their final splash. Mills drew a deep, fulfilling breath and followed behind her closely.

Three Rocks Beach was a sight to marvel. The postcard hadn't done it justice in his mind. A picture couldn't give him the sand in his toes, the spectacular cliffsides overlooking the immersive ocean, and the cool, lively waters washing away a certain yesterday's regret. No. Each time that tide came inward, the stress his body had been carrying for longer than he could remember washed out to sea, leaving him forever without a single second thought.

And in that moment, Jeffrey Mills pulled his father's revolver from his pocket, ran his fingers over the engravings his dad was so proud of, and hurled it into the Pacific.

## The End

## Acknowledgments

The saying, “It takes a village,” comes to mind when I think of everyone I’d wish to thank for the journey this story has taken me on. My wife and daughter, for their patience and support whenever the need arose to get something on the page. To my brother and sister for always cheering me on through the highs and lows every author experiences. My mom for certainly passing on that creative spark, and my dad for his—sometimes—crude sense of humor.

To the entire Tule team and Jane Porter for the opportunity. Meghan Farrell for choosing my manuscript out of the hundreds if not thousands. Nikki Babri for guiding me through this process and answering all my emails even if they were, at times, okay… MOST of the time, all over the place. You’re a rockstar. My copy editor Nan Reinhardt, your attention to detail is unrivaled. Marlene Roberts-Vitale who proofread this manuscript and gave me so many great tools to utilize in later works. Last and certainly not least by any means, Julie Sturgeon. My developmental editor. Thank you for always being there to toss around different ideas, coaching me, and encouraging me along the way! I feel so honored and grateful to have worked with you and hope to do so again in the future.

Now the heroes that cannot go without recognition. My

beta-readers and critique partners. The ones spending endless nights going over my manuscript, sometimes twice, selflessly devoting their time to help me bring this story from a simple idea to a book.

Jessica Maldonado, my big sis. No matter what I send to you, you're always the first to read it without question as you have with all my writing endeavors. I know I can always count on you. Christie Curry. Your feedback was vital to a major issue in this story. You helped me save the plot hole I wasn't sure I could fix. Daphne Nugent and Rachel Blackie at *Spruce and Polish Editing*. You both provided wonderful feedback and added another notch to this story's belt. Jenn Mack. You put me in check more than a few times with my writing, and I am rather thankful for that. Harry Pearce. Your work ethic is enviable and something I strive for. Nadia Vanders. You kept me focused on my goal with this story. Cobie LaJeanne. You came across Sarah Baker in the early drafts and your input shaped what it eventually became. Ana Mae Wright. I came to you with a few scenes I was struggling with, and because of your notes, I knocked them out of the park. Rose Newton. Chava Kerzel. Shuli. Hagar. Tanya. Magda Johnson. Meg Hastings. Briana Newstead. Allison James. Jessica Kapp. You all helped me bring Sarah Baker to life, and I couldn't be more grateful.

## About the Author

Raised in a small California farming town, T.A. Cruz spent his childhood honing an imagination as vast as the wheat fields stretching around him for miles. With 6 years of military service and passport stamps from around the world, part of him will always be in that little town with a single stoplight and a population of 1500.

A lifelong lover of horror and things that go bump in the night, T.A. Cruz decided it was time to take that passion to the page and shock and terrify others for a change. When not diving face first into another project, Cruz enjoys spending time with his wife, daughter, two dogs, and axolotl.

Thank you for reading

## Have You Seen Sarah Baker?

If you enjoyed this book, you can find more from all our great authors at TulePublishing.com, or from your favorite online retailer.

Printed in the USA
CPSIA information can be obtained
at www.ICGtesting.com
LVHW091506010924
789859LV00008B/203